Italian Playboys: Innocence

LUCY GORDON

MELANIE MILBURNE

TRISH MOREY

MILLS & BOON

First Published in Great Britain 2021
by Mills & Boon, an imprint of HarperCollins*Publishers* Ltd,
1 London Bridge Street, London, SE1 9GF

www.harpercollins.co.uk

HarperCollins*Publishers*
1st Floor, Watermarque Building,
Ringsend Road, Dublin 4, Ireland

ISBN: 978-0-263-30272-1

MIX
Paper from responsible sources
FSC™ C007454
FSC
www.fsc.org

This book is produced from independently certified FSC™ paper to ensure responsible forest management.

For more information visit: www.harpercollins.co.uk/green

Printed and bound in Spain
by CPI, Barcelona

Lu ine journalism, interviewing ... the world's most interesting ... Moor ... met a ... been married ever since. Naturally this has affected her writing, where romantic Italian men tend to feature strongly. Two of her books have won a Romance Writers of America *RITA*® Award. You can visit her website at lucy-gordon.com

Melanie Milburne read her first Mills & Boon at age seventeen in between studying for her final exams. After completing a Masters Degree in Education she decided to write a novel and thus her career as a romance author was born. Melanie is an ambassador for the Australian Childhood Foundation and is a keen dog lover and trainer and enjoys long walks in the Tasmanian bush. In 2015 Melanie won the HOLT Medallion, a prestigous award honouring outstanding literary talent.

USA Today bestselling author, **Trish Morey**, just loves happy endings. Now that her four daughters are (mostly) grown and off her hands having left the nest, Trish is rapidly working out that a real happy ending is when you downsize, end up alone with the guy you married and realise you still love him. There's a happy ever after right there. Or a happy new beginning! Trish loves to hear from her readers - you can email her at trish@trishmorey.com

Italian Playboys

June 2021
Temptations

July 2021
Nights

August 2021
Tycoons

September 2021
Proposals

October 2021
Innocence

November 2021
Seduction

REUNITED WITH HER ITALIAN EX

LUCY GORDON

PROLOGUE

Venice, the most romantic city in the world.

That was what people said, and Natasha was becoming convinced that it was true. Where else could she have met the man of her dreams within hours of arriving, and known so soon that she was his and he simply must become hers?

Sitting in a café by a small canal, she looked out at the sun glittering on the water. Nearby she could see a gondola containing a young man and woman, wrapped in each other's arms.

Just like us, she thought, recalling her first gondola ride in the arms of the man who had changed the world in moments.

Mario Ferrone, young, handsome, with dancing eyes and a rich chuckle that seemed to encompass the world. She'd met Mario just after she'd arrived in Venice on a well-earned holiday. He'd insisted on showing her the city. As his brother owned the hotel where she was staying, she'd briefly thought this a professional service, but that idea soon changed. There was an instant attraction between them, and nothing had ever seemed more wonderful than the time they spent together.

Until then, there had been little in her life that could

be called romance. She was slim, pretty, humorous, with no difficulty attracting admirers. But where men were concerned she had an instinctive defensiveness.

It went back to her childhood, when her father had abandoned his wife and ten-year-old daughter for another woman. Until that moment Natasha's life had been happy. Her father had seemed to adore her as she adored him. But suddenly he was gone, never to get in touch again.

Never trust a man, her mother had told her. *They'll always let you down.*

She'd been content to heed the warning until Mario came into her life and everything turned upside down.

Her own reactions confused her. Her heart was drawn to Mario as never before to any other man. Sometimes her mother's voice echoed in her mind.

No man can be trusted, Natasha. Remember that.

But Natasha felt certain that Mario was different to all other men—more honest, more trustworthy, more faithfully loving.

Last night he'd kissed her with even greater fervour than before, murmuring, 'Tomorrow I want to…' Then he'd stopped, seeming confused.

'Yes?' she'd whispered. 'What do you want?'

'I can't tell you now…but tomorrow everything will be different. Goodnight, *mi amore*.'

Now here she was in the café where they often met, waiting for him to appear and transform her world yet again.

She almost ached with the yearning to know what he'd meant by 'everything will be different'. Was he going to propose marriage? Surely he must.

Oh, please hurry, she thought. How could Mario keep her on tenterhooks when it mattered so much?

Suddenly, she heard his voice call, 'Natasha!' Looking up, she saw him walking by the canal, waving to her from a distance.

'Sorry I'm late,' he said, joining her at the table. 'I got held up.'

She had a strange feeling that he was on edge.

'Is everything all right?' she asked.

'It will be, very soon,' he said.

His eyes never left her and every moment her conviction grew that tonight they were going to take the next step—whatever it might be.

He took her hand. 'There's something I've been trying to tell you for days but—'

'Trying? Is it so hard to tell me?'

'It could be.' His eyes met hers. 'Some things just aren't easy to say.'

Her heart was beating with anticipation and excitement. She knew what he was going to say, and she longed to hear it.

'That depends how much you want to say them,' she whispered, leaning close so that her breath brushed his face. 'Perhaps you don't really want to say this.'

'Oh, yes, you don't know how much it matters.'

But I do know, she thought happily. He was going to tell her how much she meant to him. In a moment her life would be transformed.

She took his hand in hers, sending him a silent message about her willingness to draw closer to him.

'Go on,' she whispered.

He hesitated and she regarded him, puzzled. Was it really so hard for him to reach out to her?

'Natasha—I want to tell you—'

'Yes—yes—tell me.'

'I'm not good at this—'

'You don't need to be good at it,' she urged, tightening her clasp on his hand. 'Just say it—'

'Well—'

'Traitor!'

The screamed word stunned them both. Natasha looked up to see a woman standing by the table, glaring at them. She was in her thirties, voluptuous, and would have been beautiful but for the look of livid hatred she cast on Mario.

'Traitor!' she screamed. *'Liar! Deceiver!'*

Mario's face was tense and pale as Natasha had never seen it before. He rose and confronted the woman, speaking angrily in Italian and pointing for her to leave. She screamed back at him in English. Then turned to Natasha.

'It's about time you knew what he is really like. One woman isn't enough for him.'

She raved on until Mario drew her into a corner, arguing with her vigorously. Natasha could no longer hear the words but there was no mistaking the intensity between them. The dark-haired woman's rage grew with every moment.

'He's a liar and a cheat,' she screamed in perfect English.

'Mario,' Natasha said, 'who is this woman? Do you really know her?'

'Oh, yes, he knows me,' the woman spat. 'You wouldn't believe how well he knows me.'

'Tania, that's enough,' Mario said, white-faced. 'I told you—'

'Oh, yes, you told me. Traitor! Traitor! *Traditore!*'

For a moment Natasha was tempted to thrust herself between them and tell Mario what she thought of him in no uncertain terms. But then her impetuous temper flared even higher, driving her to a course of action even more fierce and desperate. While they were still absorbed in their furious encounter, she fled.

She ran every step of the way to the hotel, then up to her room, pausing at the desk to demand her bill. Nothing mattered but to get away from here before Mario returned. It had all been a deception. She'd believed in him because she'd wanted to believe, and she should have known better. Now she was paying the price.

'You were right,' she muttered to her mother's ghost. 'They're all the same.'

The ghost was too tactful to say *I told you so*, but she was there in Natasha's consciousness as she finished packing, paid her bill and fled.

She took a boat taxi across the water to the mainland, and from there she switched to a motor taxi.

'Airport,' she told the driver tensely.

Oh, Mario, she thought as the car roared away. *Traitor. Traditore.*

CHAPTER ONE

Two years later...

'I'M SORRY, NATASHA, but the answer's no, and that's final. You just have to accept it.'

Natasha's face was distorted by anger as she clutched the phone.

'Don't tell me what I have to do,' she snapped into the receiver. 'You said you were eager for anything I wrote—'

'That was a long time ago. Things have changed. I can't buy any more of your work. Those are my orders.'

Natasha took a shuddering breath as yet another rejection slammed into her.

'But you're the editor,' she protested. 'Surely it's you who gives the orders.'

'The magazine's owner tells us what to do and that's final. You're out. Finished. Goodbye.'

The editor hung up, leaving Natasha staring at the phone in fury and anguish.

'Another one?' asked a female voice behind her. 'That's the sixth editor who's suddenly turned against you after buying your work for ages.'

Natasha turned to her friend Helen, who was also her flatmate.

'I can't believe it,' she groaned. 'It's like there's a spider at the centre of a web controlling them all, telling them to freeze me out.'

'But there is. Surely you know that. The spider's name is Elroy Jenson.'

It's true, Natasha thought reluctantly. Jenson owned a huge media empire that until recently had provided her with a good living. But he'd taken a fancy to her and pursued her relentlessly, ignoring her pleas to be left alone. Finally he'd gone too far, forcing her to slap his face hard enough to make him yell. One of his employees had seen them and spread the story.

'Everyone knows you made him look a fool,' Helen said sympathetically. 'So now he's your enemy. It's a pity about that quick temper of yours, Natasha. You had every right to be angry but…well…'

'But I should have paused before I clobbered him. I should have been calm and controlled and thought about the future. Hah!'

'Yes, I know it sounds ironic, but look at the price you've paid.'

'Yes,' Natasha said with a heavy sigh.

As a freelance journalist her success had been dazzling. Magazines and newspapers clamoured for her sassy, insightful articles.

Until now.

'How can one man have so much power?' she groaned.

'Perhaps you need to go abroad for a while,' Helen suggested. 'Until Jenson forgets all about you.'

'That would be difficult—'

'It needn't be. The agency found me a job in Italy, doing publicity. It would mean going out there for a while.

I was about to call them and say they'd have to find someone else, but why don't you go instead?'

'But I can't just… That's a mad idea.'

'Sometimes madness is the best way. It could be just what you need now.'

'But I don't speak Italian.'

'You don't have to. It's an international thing, promoting the city all over the world.'

'It's not Venice, is it?' Natasha asked, suddenly tense.

'No, don't worry. I know you wouldn't want to go to Venice. It's Verona, the city of *Romeo and Juliet*. Some of that story is real, and tourists love to see Juliet's balcony and other places where different scenes are set. So a group of luxury hotel owners have clubbed together to create some publicity for the place. Of course, I know you're not exactly a fan of romance—'

'It doesn't bother me,' Natasha said quickly. 'I'm not going into retreat just because one man— Well, anyway—'

'Fine. So why don't you take this job?'

'But how can I? It's yours.'

'I really wish you would. I accepted it impulsively because I'd had a row with my boyfriend. I thought we were finished, but we've made up and it would really suit me if you went instead of me.'

'But if they're expecting you—'

'I've been dealing with the agency. I'll put you in touch with them and sing your praises. Natasha, you can't let your life be ruled by a man you haven't seen for two years. Especially when he was a cheating rogue. Your words, not mine.'

'Yes,' she murmured. 'I said that. And I meant it.'

'Then go. Put Mario behind you and put Elroy behind you, too. Seize your chance for a fresh start.'

Natasha took a deep breath. 'All right,' she said. 'I'll do it.'

'Fine. Now, let's get started.'

Helen logged on to her computer and contacted the agency. Moments later, Natasha was reading an email, written in efficient English, offering her the assignment and giving her instructions:

You will be dealing with Giorgio Marcelli. The hotel owners employ him to handle publicity. He looks forward to welcoming you to Verona.

'You see, it's a no-brainer,' Helen said. 'I'll leave you to have a think.'

She departed.

Left alone, Natasha stared out of the window, trying to decide what to do. Despite what Helen said, it wasn't easy to make up her mind.

'Not Venice,' she had asserted and Helen had reassured her, because she knew that nothing would persuade Natasha ever to go back to that beautiful romantic city where her heart had been broken.

Natasha thought back to herself as a very young woman, haunted by her mother's warnings never to trust a man. She had pursued a successful career, devoting her time to her writing, avoiding emotional relationships. Of course she could flirt and enjoy male company. But never for very long. Eventually distrust would make her back away from any man who attracted her.

She'd been glad of it, sure that caution would protect her from suffering her mother's fate. On that she had been resolved.

Until she'd met Mario.

He had affected her as no other man ever had. Together they had walked the streets of Venice, drifting by the canals. In one tiny alley he'd drawn her into the shadows for their first kiss. Despite her attempts to obliterate the memory, it still lived in her now.

Her whole body had responded to him, coming alive in ways she had never dreamed of before. She could sense the same in him, although every instinct told her that he was an experienced lover. Wherever they went, women had thrown admiring glances at him and regarded Natasha with envy. She'd guessed they were thinking how lucky she was to be sharing his bed. That day had never come, although several times Natasha had been on the verge of giving in to temptation.

As the day of her departure neared, Mario had begged her to stay with him a little longer. Blissfully happy, she had agreed.

Even now, two years later, remembering that happiness was the most painful thing of all, despite her frantic attempts to banish it from her memory, her heart, her life.

She imagined his face when he'd returned to the table and found her gone.

Vanished into thin air, she thought. *As far as he's concerned I no longer exist, and he no longer exists to me.*

In fact, the man she'd believed him to be had never existed. That was what she had to face.

Bitterly, she replayed the scene. She'd been so sure that he was about to declare his feelings, but when he'd said, 'There's something I've been trying to tell you for days,' he'd actually been planning to dump her.

He'd probably spent the afternoon with Tania, perhaps in her bed.

She thought he was being unfaithful to her with me.

In fact he was being unfaithful to both of us. That's the kind of man he is.

After fleeing from Venice, Natasha had done everything she could to disappear for ever, changing her email address and phone number.

But one email from him had just managed to get through before the old address was cut off:

Where did you vanish to? What happened? Are you all right?

Yes, she thought defiantly. *I'm all right. I got rid of the only person who could hurt me. And nobody is ever going to do that to me again.*

She'd never replied to Mario, merely instructing the server to block his emails. Then she'd moved in with Helen. If he came to her old flat he would find the door locked against him as firmly as her heart was locked against him.

At night she would lie awake, dismayed by the violence of her response. He had touched her emotions with an intensity that warned her to escape while there was still time. That way lay the only safety.

Oh, Mario, she thought. *Traitor. Traditore.*

Since then she'd devoted herself to work, making such an impression that she came to the attention of Elroy Jenson. The media magnate had propositioned her, certain that a mere freelance journalist would never refuse him. When she did refuse he couldn't believe it, persisting until she was forced to slap his face and bring her successful career to a sudden end.

After that, her life had been on a downward spiral. Her

income had collapsed. Now she could barely afford the small rent she paid on the room she rented from Helen.

The time had come for firm action. And if that meant leaping into the unknown, she would do it. The unknown had its attractions, and suddenly she was ready for anything.

She exchanged brisk emails with Giorgio, the publicity manager. He informed her that she would be staying at the Dimitri Hotel and a driver would meet her at the airport. Two days later she embarked on the journey that might lead to a triumphant new life, or a disaster. Either way, she was venturing into the unknown.

During the flight to Verona she kept her mind firmly concentrated on work. *Romeo and Juliet* was a story that had long touched the world: two young people who fell in love despite the enmity of their families. In the end, they chose to die rather than live without each other.

Legend said that Shakespeare's play was based on real events. The lovers had really lived and died. It would be her job to immerse herself in the story and entice the world to join her.

The driver was at the airport, holding up a placard bearing the words 'Dimitri Hotel'. He greeted her with relief, and ushered her into the car for the three-mile journey to Verona.

'The hotel is in the centre of town,' he said. 'Right next to the river.'

Verona was an ancient, beautiful city. Delighted, she gazed out of the window, enchanted by the hints of another, mysterious age. At last they drew up outside a large elaborate building.

'Here we are. Dimitri Hotel,' the driver said.

As she entered the elegant lobby, a man came forward.

He was in his sixties, heavily built, with a plump, smiling face. He greeted her in English.

'The agency told me there had been a change of plan,' he said. 'Apparently the original candidate couldn't make it, but they say you have excellent credentials.'

'Thank you. I'm an experienced journalist. I hope I can live up to your expectations.'

'I'm sure you will. I'm very glad you're here. I promised the President the lady would be here for him tonight and it's never good to disappoint him.'

He gave a comical shudder which made Natasha ask, 'Is he a difficult man? Scary?'

'Sometimes. Mostly he's very determined. People don't cross him if they can help it. He only bought this hotel just under two years ago and set about changing everything practically the first day. There's been a massive redecoration, and the staff has been reorganised to suit him. Everything has to be done his way. Nobody argues.'

'You called him the President.'

'President of the *Comunità*. It was his idea that a group of hotel owners of Verona, the *Comunità*, should all work together. They thought it would be an easy-going organisation but he said it needed leadership. The others just did as he suggested and named him President.

'A while back one of the other owners thought of challenging him for the top job, but he was "persuaded" not to. Nobody knows how, but neither was anyone surprised.

'When he gives his orders we jump to attention, especially me, because he could fire me any time he likes. I'm only telling you so that you'll take care not to offend him.

'We'll dine with him tonight and tomorrow you will meet all the *Comunità* members. They're looking forward to having you spread the word about our lovely city.'

'But isn't the word already out? Surely *Romeo and Juliet* is the most famous love story in the world?'

'True, but we need to make people realise how they can become involved. Now, I'll show you to your room.'

On their way up they passed two men having a noisy argument. One was clearly in command, yelling, *'Capisci? Capisci?'* so fiercely that the other backed off.

'What does that word mean?' Natasha asked curiously. 'It really scared the other guy.'

'It means "Do you understand?"' Giorgio laughed. 'It's really just a way of saying "You'll do as I say. *Get it?*"'

'It sounds useful.'

'It can be, if you're trying to make it clear who's in charge.' He grinned. 'I've had it said to me a few times. Here's your room.'

Like the rest of the place, her room was elegant and luxurious. A huge window looked out over the river, where the sun shone on the water. The atmosphere seemed peaceful and she took a deep contented breath.

When she'd unpacked she took a shower and began work on her appearance. For this meeting she was going to look her best.

She was attractive so not too much effort was required. Her blue eyes were large and expressive. Her blonde hair had just a touch of red that showed in some lights but not in others.

Natasha pinned her hair high on her head, suggesting businesslike severity. Usually, she preferred to let it flow, curved and luscious about her shoulders in a more relaxed way.

But not tonight, she mused, studying herself in the mirror. *Tonight I'm a businesswoman, here to earn a living.*

She fixed her hair firmly away from her face until she felt it conveyed the serious message she intended. Giorgio had warned her that the owner was a man to be reckoned with, but she could deal with that. She'd meet him on his own ground, a woman to be reckoned with.

'I did the right thing in coming here,' she whispered. 'Everything's going to be fine.'

In Venice, a city where most of the roads were water, motor cars could only come as far as Piazzale Roma, the car park on the edge of town. In the glowing heat of a sunny day, Mario Ferrone went to collect his car, accompanied by his brother Damiano.

'It sounds like your hotel is doing really well,' Damiano said. 'You've got a great future ahead of you.'

'I think I just might have,' Mario said, grinning.

'No doubt,' Damiano said cheerfully. 'After all, look who taught you.'

This was a reference to Damiano's successful career as the owner of several hotels. Mario had learned thc trade working in many of them and had finally become ambitious for his own establishment.

'That's right, I learned from the best,' Mario said. 'And having a place in Verona is a help. Several of us hoteliers have got together to promote the *Romeo and Juliet* angle.'

'The city of lovers,' Damiano said wryly. 'That should suit you. You'd hardly believe some of the tales I've heard about you.'

'Not recently,' Mario said quickly.

'No, you've settled down these last couple of years, but before that I remember you gave a whole new meaning to the term "bad boy".'

'Most of us do before we find the right woman,' Mario pointed out.

'True. I wasn't a saint before I met Sally. But you haven't met your "Sally", so what made you suddenly become virtuous?'

'Virtuous? Me? No need to insult me.'

Damiano grinned. 'So is it just a smokescreen?'

'No. I really have changed, not necessarily for the better.'

'Don't say that. You're much improved—quieter, more serious, more grown-up…'

'More suspicious and demanding, nastier sometimes,' Mario said quietly.

'Hey, why do you put yourself down?'

'Perhaps because I know myself better than anyone else does. I'm not the nice guy I used to be—if I ever was.'

'So what made it happen?'

Mario clapped him on the shoulder. 'Don't ask me. It's a long story, and one that—well, that I don't care to think of too often. Let's leave it. I'd better be going. Giorgio has hired a journalist he says will be brilliant at promoting the *Romeo and Juliet* angle. I'm meeting her for dinner when I get back tonight.'

'Best of luck. Goodbye, brother.'

They embraced each other. Damiano stood back, waving as Mario turned out of the car park and across the causeway that led to the mainland.

From Venice to Verona was nearly seventy-five miles. During the journey Mario reflected wryly on his brother's words. Damiano didn't know that one of the turning points in Mario's life had been Damiano's marriage to Sally, four years earlier. Mario had been strongly attracted to Sally, something he'd had to fight. He'd fought it by working in Damiano's hotels in Rome, Florence, Milan, only rarely returning to Venice.

Until then his life had been free and easy. He was young, charming and handsome, with no trouble attracting women. He'd had many girlfriends. Too many, he now realised.

He'd returned to Venice for the birth of his brother's son and found, to his relief, that Sally no longer attracted him, except as a sister. He'd settled into a life of work and pleasure.

Then had come the other great turning point in his life, when he'd met the one woman who could make a difference, drive away the loneliness and give his existence meaning.

Fantasy dictated that she should feel the same and throw herself into his arms. The bitter reality was that she had walked out on him, slamming the door in his face, condemning him to a bleak isolation that was all the worse because he had glimpsed a glorious future, and come so close to embracing it.

Buying the hotel two years ago had been a lucky chance. The owner was eager to sell and accepted a discounted price, and now Mario felt that he was headed for success and independence. If he did nothing else in his life he would triumph in this, he vowed to himself. With that hope to guide him he could banish the pain and bleakness of the last two years.

At last he reached the hotel. Giorgio came to the entrance to greet him.

'It's all set up,' he said.

'Has the lady arrived?'

'Yes, an hour ago. She's not who I was expecting. The

agency made a last-minute change, but she seems serious and professional.'

'I can't wait to meet her.' As they walked across the elegant lobby, Mario looked around him at the place he was beginning to regard as his kingdom. 'You know, I have the best possible feeling about this,' he said. 'We're on the right road, and we're going to reach a great destination.'

'One where the money is,' Giorgio supplied with a grin.

'Of course, but that's not the only thing. Somehow, everything is beginning to feel right.'

'That's the spirit. Get settled in and then I'll introduce you to… Mario? Mario, is something wrong?'

But Mario didn't hear him. His attention had been drawn to the great staircase that led to the next floor. He was staring at it like a man stunned. A young woman was walking down the stairs. She moved slowly, pausing to look at the paintings on the wall, so that at first she didn't seem to notice Mario standing by the bottom step.

When her eyes came to rest on Mario she stopped suddenly, as if unable to believe her eyes.

A terrible stillness came over Natasha as she looked down the staircase, trying to understand what was happening. It was impossible that Mario should be standing there, staring up at her with a thunderstruck expression.

Impossible.

And yet it was true. He was there, looking like a man who'd seen a nightmare come to life.

She tried to move but the stillness enveloped her. Now he was climbing the stairs slowly, as though unwilling to approach her too quickly or come too close. When he spoke it was uneasily.

'I believe...we've met before.'

A dozen answers clamoured in her head, but at last she heard herself say, 'No, never.'

That took him off-guard, she could see. While he struggled for a reply, Giorgio's voice reached them from the bottom of the stairs.

'Aha! I see you two are getting acquainted.' Waving cheerfully, he climbed up to join them.

'Natasha, let me introduce Mario Ferrone, the owner of the hotel and President of the *Comunità*. Mario, this is Natasha Bates, the lady who's going to tell the world about Verona.'

Mario inclined his head formally. '*Buongiorno, signorina.* It's a pleasure to meet you.'

'How do you do?' she said, nodding towards him.

'Let's go and eat,' Giorgio said, 'and we can have a good talk.'

Downstairs, a table was laid for them in a private room overlooking the river. Giorgio led Natasha to the chair nearest the window and drew it out for her.

A waiter hurried in, eager to serve the hotel's owner. His manner was respectful and she was reminded of Giorgio's words:

'When he gives his orders we all jump to attention...'

She'd known him as a cheeky playboy, always ready to laugh and use his charm. It was hard to see the man he'd been then as the stern authoritarian that Giorgio described now. But his face had changed, growing slightly thinner, firmer, more intense. Even his smile had something reserved about it.

Turning her eyes to him briefly, she caught him glancing at her and realised that he was studying her too. What did he see? Had she also changed, becoming older, sterner, less relaxed? Probably. Perhaps she should be glad, for it would make her stronger. And she was going to need strength now.

Giorgio claimed her attention, filling her wine glass, smiling at her with an air of deferential admiration. He had probably been handsome in his youth, and still had the air of a practised flirt.

'How much were you told about this job?' he asked her.

'Only that some Verona hotel owners had got together to promote the city's connection with *Romeo and Juliet*,' Natasha said.

'That's right. It's already well promoted by the council, which works hard to bring tourists here. But the hotel owners wanted to enjoy a bit more of the spotlight, so they formed the Comunità di Verona Ospitalità so that they could make the most of being in the town that saw the greatest love story in the world.

'Shakespeare didn't invent *Romeo and Juliet*. There really were two families called Montague and Capulet, and they did have children who fell in love, and died. It happened in the early fourteenth century. In the next two hundred years the story was told and retold, until finally Shakespeare based his play on the legend. Tourists come here to see "Juliet's balcony" and imagine the balcony scene happening there.'

'Which it didn't,' Mario observed drily. 'The house belonged to a family called Capello, but the council added the balcony less than a hundred years ago.'

'But if everyone knows that—' Natasha mused.

'They know it but they ignore it,' Giorgio said cheerfully. 'People are often tempted to believe only what they want to.'

'How true,' Natasha murmured. 'That's why we're all so easily taken in.'

She didn't look directly at Mario as she said these words, but she had a sense that he was watching her with an air of tension that matched her own.

'And that's what we can make use of,' Giorgio said. 'Juliet's balcony, Juliet's tomb, where Romeo killed himself because he couldn't bear life without her, and where she killed herself for the same reason. Is it true? It is if we want it to be.'

'Oh, yes,' Natasha mused. 'True if we want it to be—until one day we have to face the fact that it isn't true, however much we want it.'

'But that's show business,' Giorgio said. 'Creating a fantasy that makes people happy.'

'And what more could we want than that?' Mario asked.

He raised his glass and drank from it, seemingly oblivious to her. But the next moment he said, 'Tell us something about yourself, *signorina*.'

She turned her head, meeting his eyes directly. 'What did you say?'

'I said I'd like to know about you. I'm sure there is much you could tell us. What are your family obligations? Are you free to live in Verona for several weeks, or is there someone at home who will be missing you?'

'I suppose there must be,' Giorgio said. He assumed a chivalrous air. 'This is a lovely lady. She must have crowds of men following her.'

'That doesn't mean that I let them catch up,' Natasha teased.

'Some women are very good at keeping out of sight,' Mario said.

'Of course,' Giorgio agreed. 'That's the secret. Let them chase after you, but don't let any of them get close enough to know what you're thinking and feeling.' He kissed her hand gallantly. '*Signorina*, I can see you're an expert in keeping your admirers wondering.'

'But just what are they wondering?' Mario asked. 'Will any of them arrive here to assert his "rights"?'

'What rights?' Giorgio demanded. 'She's not married.'

'That's irrelevant,' Mario observed. 'You have only to study *Romeo and Juliet* to see that men and women make that decision within a few moments of meeting. And nobody dares get in their way.'

'When people fear betrayal they can get violent,' Giorgio agreed.

Natasha nodded. 'And if they know for sure that they've been betrayed, there's no knowing how far they'll go to make someone sorry,' she mused, letting her glance rest on Mario.

She was glad to see that he understood the silent message. Before her eyes he flinched and averted his gaze. When he spoke again it was in a voice so defiantly businesslike that it told its own story.

'So we can expect a jealous lover to follow you out here?' he said curtly.

She faced him, reading the chilly hostility in his eyes, answering it with her own.

'On the contrary. You can be certain that nothing will make me leave before my work is finished,' she said calmly. 'Unlike some people, I'm honest about my intentions. I don't make promises and break them.'

'That's not exactly what I asked.'

No, she thought. *You asked whether I'd had the nerve to replace you with another man.*

She gave him her most confident smile, as though his questions merely amused her.

'Let me assure you that I am free,' she said. 'No man tells me what to do, and if anyone tried—' she leaned closer to him '—I would make him regret that he ever knew me.' She added significantly, 'I'm good at that.'

'I believe you,' he said.

Giorgio glanced at them curiously. 'Hey, do you two already know each other?'

'No,' Natasha said quickly, before Mario could speak.

'Really? I feel like I'm watching a fencing match.'

'It's more fun that way,' she said lightly. 'Go on telling me about Verona. Unless, of course, Signor Ferrone has decided he doesn't wish to employ me. In which case I'll just pack up and go. Shall I?'

She made as if to rise but Mario's hand detained her.

'No need for that,' he said harshly. 'Let's get on with the job.'

'Yes, that's the only thing that matters,' she said, falling back into the chair.

For a moment he kept his hand on her arm. 'So we are agreed? You will stay?'

'I will stay.'

CHAPTER TWO

MARIO RELEASED HER. 'As long as we understand each other.'

Natasha drew a tense breath as the bitter irony of those words swept over her. They had never understood each other. Nor could they ever, except on the lines of mutual defensiveness and mistrust.

She turned to Giorgio, assuming her most business-like tone.

'So it's time I consulted with the Publicity Manager. Tell me, what are my instructions?'

'We must go on a trip around Verona,' he said, 'studying all the significant places. Especially the balcony. These days you can even get married in Juliet's house. And afterwards the bride and groom always come out onto the balcony for the photographs.'

'Useful,' she said, taking out her notebook and beginning to write. 'The balcony scene is the most famous part of the story.'

'Yes, people love to imagine Juliet standing there, yearning for her lover, saying, "Romeo, Romeo, where art thou Romeo?"'

'She doesn't say "where",' Natasha objected. 'She says "Wherefore". It means "Why?" She's saying "Why did you have to be Romeo, a Montague, and my enemy?" In Shakespeare's time, if you wanted to know why someone had behaved in a certain way, you'd say—' she assumed a dramatic attitude '"—Wherefore did thou do this, varlet?"'

'Varlet?' Giorgio queried.

'It means rascal. You'd say it to someone who'd behaved disgustingly.'

Giorgio gave a crack of laughter. 'I must remember that. Rascal—*briccone*.'

'Or *traditore*,' Natasha observed lightly.

'Aha! So you know some Italian words?' Giorgio said eagerly.

'One or two,' she said with a fair assumption of indifference.

'I'd give a lot to know how you learned that particular one,' he said cheekily.

'You'll just have to wonder,' she chuckled.

Mario wasn't looking at her. He seemed completely occupied with his wine.

A man appeared in the doorway, signalling to Giorgio.

'I've got to leave you for a moment,' he said. 'But I'll be back.' He laid a hand on Natasha's shoulder. 'Don't go away. I have a very good feeling about this.'

'So have I,' she said. 'I'll be right here.'

When Giorgio had gone, Mario refilled her wine glass.

'Be cautious about Giorgio,' he said. 'He turns on the charm as part of his trade.'

'But of course,' she said cheerfully. 'It's a form of show business. No harm in that.'

'As long as you're not taken in.'

'I'm not. These days, nothing and nobody manages to deceive me.'

He raised his glass to her in an ironic salute.

'This is quite a coincidence,' he said. 'I wonder which of us is more shocked.'

'We'll never know.'

'Just now you were very determined to say we didn't know each other.'

'Would you have said differently?' she asked, watching him.

'No, but I doubt I'd have said it so fast or emphatically. You denied knowing me as though your life depended on it.'

'But we didn't know each other. Once we believed we did but we were both wrong. You thought I was easy to fool or you wouldn't have wasted your time on me. You never reckoned on Tania turning up and showing me what you were really like.'

'I admit I once had a relationship with Tania, but it was over.'

'Was it? I don't think she believed that. She still felt you were hers. That's why she felt so betrayed when she saw us. No, it was me you were planning to leave. That's why you kept hinting about something you wanted to tell me. You said it wasn't easy, but then it's never easy to dump someone, is it?'

He turned very pale. 'Isn't it? You dumped me without any trouble.'

'Dumping you was the easiest thing I'd ever done, but that's because you gave me cause.'

'But the way you did it—vanishing so that I could never find you. Can you imagine what I went through? It was like searching for a ghost. I nearly went mad because you denied me any chance to explain—'

'Explain what? That you were fooling around with

both of us? If you'd been the man I thought you— Well, let's leave it there. You weren't that man and you never could be. It's best if we remain strangers now.'

'Remain?' he echoed sharply. But then his voice changed to wry, slightly bitter acceptance. 'Yes, we always were strangers, weren't we?'

'Always were, always will be. That's a very good business arrangement.'

'And you're a businesswoman?'

'Exactly. It's what I choose to be. *Capisci?*'

He nodded. '*Capisco.* I understand.'

'From now on, it's all business. The past didn't happen. It was an illusion.'

'An illusion—yes. I guessed that when you vanished into thin air. And now you've reappeared just as suddenly.'

'Another illusion. I'm not really here.'

'So if I look away you'll vanish again?'

'Perhaps that's what I ought to do.'

'No,' he said with a hint of suppressed violence. '*No!* Not again. You could never understand how I— Don't even think of it. *Capisci?*'

'*Capisco.* I understand very well.'

'Promise me that you won't leave.'

'All right.'

'On your word of honour.'

'Look—'

'Say it. Let me know that I can trust you this time at least.'

'Trust me *this time*? As though I was the one who deceived— You've got a nerve.'

'He's coming back,' Mario said hurriedly, glancing to where Giorgio had appeared. 'Smile.'

She tried to look at ease but it was hard, and as soon as Giorgio reached the table she rose.

'I'm going to bed,' she said. 'It's been a long day for me, with the flight.'

'You're right; get some rest,' Mario said. 'We'll all meet here tomorrow morning at nine.'

They shook hands and she departed at once.

Giorgio watched her go, then eyed Mario wryly.

'What's going on with you two?' he queried. 'You're on edge with each other. For a moment I really thought there'd been something between you.'

'Not a thing,' Mario assured him. 'And there never could be.'

'Pity. Romeo and Juliet were "star-crossed lovers". It could have been interesting to have them promoted by another pair of star-crossed lovers. After all, if a couple is meant for each other but just can't get it together—well, it's not in their hands, is it? They just have to enjoy it while they can, but then accept that fate is against them.'

'Isn't that giving in too easily?'

'It's what Romeo and Juliet had to accept.'

'And then they died.'

'They died physically, but it doesn't usually happen that way. Sometimes people just die inside.'

'Yes,' Mario murmured. 'That's true.'

'I'll call the other members of the group and fix a meeting. They'll just love her. We've found the right person. Don't you agree?'

Mario nodded and spoke in an iron voice. 'The right person. Not a doubt of it. I must be going. My work has piled up while I've been away.'

He departed fast, urgently needing to get away from Giorgio's sharp eyes that saw too much for comfort.

Upstairs, he headed for his bedroom, but paused before entering. The room allocated to Natasha was just across the corridor and he went to stand outside, looking at her door, wondering what was happening behind it.

The evening had torn his nerves to shreds. The woman he'd met had been as unlike the sweet, charming girl he remembered as steel was unlike cream. His heart told him it was impossible that they should be the same person, but his brain groaned and said it was true.

This was the heartless creature who had vanished without giving him a chance to defend himself, leaving him to hunt frantically for weeks until he'd realised that it was hopeless. And her manner towards him had left no doubt that she was enjoying her triumph.

A sensible man would have sent her away at once. Instead, he'd prevented her leaving, driven by instincts he didn't understand, nor want to face.

From behind her door came only silence. He moved closer, raising his hand to knock, then dropping it again. This wasn't the right moment.

Instead of going into his room, he turned away again and went downstairs into the garden, hoping some time in the night air would clear the confusion in his mind. But also doubting that anything would ever be clear again.

Natasha paced her room restlessly. After such a day she should have been ready to collapse into sleep, but her nerves were tense and she feared to lie awake all night, thinking the very thoughts she wanted to avoid.

Mario had blamed her for disappearing without giving him a chance to defend himself, and in so doing he'd touched a nerve.

Perhaps I should have let him say something, she thought. *Why didn't I?*

Because I'm my mother's daughter, said another voice in her mind. *And I can't help living by the lessons she taught me. Never trust a man. Don't believe his explanation because it'll be lies and you'll only suffer more. In fact, don't let him explain at all. Never, never give him a second chance.*

She'd fled Mario because she feared to listen to what he might have to say. Thinking the worst of him felt safer. That was the sad truth.

But now, meeting him again and getting a sense of his torment, she felt uneasy about her own actions.

'No,' she said. 'No, I'm not going down that road. What's done is done. It's over.'

In the last year she'd often suffered from insomnia and had resorted to some herbal sleeping pills. She took them out now, considering.

'I'm not lying awake fretting over him. This is war.'

She swallowed two pills but, instead of going to bed, she went outside for a few minutes. The tall window opened onto a balcony where she could stand and look down on a narrow strip of garden. There were flowers, a few trees and beyond them the Adige River, glowing in the evening light. Now it was easy to slip into the balcony scene and become Juliet, yearning over the man who'd captured her heart before she knew who he was. When she'd realised that she'd fallen in love with an enemy, it was too late.

'Too late,' she murmured. 'The last thing I wanted was to meet him again. I came here to start a new life. *Mario, Mario, wherefore art thou, Mario?* But it had to be you, didn't it? When I'm looking forward to meeting new people, you have to pop up. *Wherefore did thou do this, varlet?*'

In her agitation she said the words aloud. Alarmed at herself, she retreated through the window, shutting it firmly.

Outside, all was quiet. Darkness was falling, and there was nobody to notice Mario standing, alone and silent, beneath the trees. He had come straight into the garden after leaving Natasha's door, wondering if some light from her room would reassure him. What he had seen stunned and confused him. Her whispered words seemed to float down, reaching him so softly that he couldn't be sure he'd actually heard them.

To believe what he longed to believe was something he refused to do. That way lay danger, disillusion—the things he'd promised himself to avoid in future. So he backed into the shadows, his eyes fixed on her window until the light went out and his world was full of darkness.

Promptly at nine o'clock the next morning Mario appeared at the breakfast table, frowning as he saw only Giorgio there.

'Where is she?' he demanded. 'I told her nine o'clock.'

'Have a heart,' Giorgio begged. 'It's only a few minutes after nine. She's not a machine, just a lovely lady.'

'She is an employee being paid a high salary, for which I expect punctuality and obedience to my wishes. Kindly call her room.'

'I've been calling it for half an hour,' Giorgio admitted. 'But there's no reply. Perhaps she doesn't want to talk to us.'

Or perhaps she can't, said a voice in Mario's mind.

He remembered the woman she had been the evening before, bright, completely at ease, ready to challenge him every moment.

Yet there had been something else, he realised. Beneath her confident manner he'd sensed something different—troubled, uneasy. Their meeting had taken them both by surprise. His own turmoil had startled and shaken him, making him struggle not to let her suspect his weakness, the more so because she had seemed free of any weakness.

But then he'd seen a new look in her eyes, a flash of vulnerability that matched his own. It had vanished at once, but for a brief moment he'd known that she was as alarmed as he was.

He remembered how he'd stood under her balcony last night, watching her, sensing again that she was haunted, but resisting the impulse to reach out to her. Her disappearance now hinted at new trouble. If he went to her room, what would he find? The confident Natasha, laughing at his discomfiture? Or the frail Natasha who couldn't cope?

Abruptly he took out his mobile phone, called her room and listened as the bell rang and rang, with no reply.

'If it was anyone else you'd think they'd vanished without paying the bill,' Giorgio observed. 'But we're not charging her for that room, so she's got no reason to vanish.'

'That's right,' Mario said grimly. 'No reason at all.'

'I'll go and knock on her door.'

'No, stay here. I'll see what's happened.'

Swiftly, he went to his office and opened a cupboard that contained the hotel's replacement keys. Trying to stay calm despite his growing worry, Mario took the one that belonged to Natasha's room and went upstairs. After only a moment's hesitation, he opened her door.

At once he saw her, lying in bed, so still and silent that alarm rose in him. He rushed towards the bed and leaned down to her, close enough to see that she was breathing.

His relief was so great that he grasped the chest of drawers to stop himself falling. Every instinct of self-preservation warned him to get out quickly, before he was discovered. But he couldn't make himself leave her. Instead he dropped onto one knee, gazing at her closely. She lay without moving, her lovely hair splayed out on the pillow, her face soft and almost smiling.

How he had once dreamed of this, of awakening to find her beside him, sleeping gently, full of happiness at the pleasure they had shared.

He leaned a little closer, until he could feel her breath on his face. He knew he was taking a mad risk. A wise man would leave now, but he wasn't a wise man. He was a man torn by conflicting desires.

Then she moved, turning so that the bedclothes slipped away from her, revealing that she was naked. Mario drew a sharp breath.

How often in the past had he longed to see her this way? He had planned and schemed to draw her tenderly closer! The night of their disaster had been meant to end like this, lying together in his bed, with him discovering her hidden beauty. But then a calamity had descended on him and wrecked his life. How bitter was the irony that he should see her lovely nakedness now.

She moved again, reaching out in his direction, so that he had to jerk away quickly. She began to whisper in her sleep, but he couldn't make out the words. Only escape would save him. He rose, backed off quickly and managed to make it to the door before her eyes opened. Once outside, he leaned against the wall, his chest heaving, his brain whirling.

At last he moved away, back to the real world, where he was a man in command. And that, he vowed, was where he would stay.

Giorgio looked up as Mario approached. 'No luck finding her?'

Mario shrugged. 'I didn't bother looking very far. Try calling her again.'

Giorgio dialled the number, listening with a resigned face.

'Looks like she still isn't—no, wait! Natasha, is that you? Thank goodness! Where have you been? *What?* Don't you know the time? All right, I'll tell Mario. But hurry.' He shut off the phone. 'She says she overslept.'

Mario shrugged. 'Perhaps the flight tired her yesterday.'

Giorgio gave a rich chuckle. 'My guess is that she was entertaining someone last night. I know she'd only just arrived, but a girl as lovely as that can entertain anyone whenever she wants. I saw men looking at her as she came down those stairs. Did you expect such a beauty?'

'I didn't know what to expect,' Mario said in a toneless voice.

'Nor me. I never hoped she'd be so young and lovely. Let's make the best of it. Juliet come to life. Oh, yes, finding her was a real stroke of luck.'

A stroke of luck. The words clamoured in Mario's brain, adding more bitterness to what he was already suffering. He didn't believe that a man had been in Natasha's room last night, but the sight of her naked had devastated him. He could almost believe she'd done it on purpose to taunt him, but the sweet, enchanting Natasha he'd known would never do that.

But was she that Natasha any more?

Had she ever been?

'I just know what she's doing right this minute,' Giorgio said with relish. 'She's turning to the man next to her in the bed, saying, "You've got to go quickly so that nobody finds you here." Perhaps we should have someone watch her door to see who comes out.'

'That's enough,' Mario growled.

'With a girl as stunning as that, nothing is ever enough. Don't pretend you don't know what I mean. You were fizzing from the moment you saw her.'

'Drop it,' Mario growled.

'All right, you don't want to admit she had that effect on you. After all, you're the boss. Don't let her guess she's got you where she wants you—even if she has.'

'I said drop it.'

'Steady there. Don't get mad at me. I was only thinking that if there's an attraction between you, we can make use of it.'

'And you're mistaken. There's no attraction between us.'

'Pity. That could have been fun.'

Slowly, Natasha felt life returning to her as she ended the call from Giorgio.

'Nine-fifteen!' she gasped in horror. 'I was supposed to be downstairs at nine. Oh, I should never have taken those sleeping pills.'

The pills had plunged her into a deep slumber, which she'd needed to silence her desperate thoughts of Mario.

But at the end he'd invaded her sleep, his face close to hers, regarding her with an almost fierce intensity. But he wasn't there. It had been a dream.

'I just can't get away from him,' she whispered. 'Will I ever?'

She showered in cold water, relishing the feeling of coming back to life. Dressing was a simple matter of putting on tailored trousers and a smart blazer and fixing her hair back tightly. Then she was ready to go.

She found Giorgio and Mario downstairs at the table.

'I'm so sorry,' she said. 'I didn't mean to be late but I was more tired than I realised.'

'That's understandable,' Giorgio said gallantly.

Mario threw him a cynical look but said nothing.

'Where's that waiter?' Giorgio asked, frowning. 'I'll find him and he can bring you breakfast.'

He vanished.

'I'm glad Giorgio's gone,' she said. 'It gives us a chance to talk honestly. Last night you stopped me getting out of my chair, and told me to stay. But is that really what you want? Wouldn't you be better off without me?'

'If I thought that I'd have said so,' he retorted.

'But think of it, day after day, trying not to get annoyed with each other, pretending to like each other. Surely you don't want that? I'm giving you the chance to get rid of me, Mario.'

'What about you? Do you want to make a run for it?'

'I can cope.'

'But you think I can't. Thanks for the vote of confidence. We're business professionals and on that basis it can work.'

'You're right,' she said. 'Shake.'

'Shake.' He took her extended hand. 'Perhaps I should

warn you that Giorgio has some rather fancy ideas about you. He thinks you had a lover in your room last night and that's why you overslept.'

'*What?* I'd taken some herbal pills to get to sleep after a strenuous day. A lover? I'd only been here five minutes.'

'Giorgio sees you as the kind of woman who can attract men as fast as that.'

'Cheek!'

'In his eyes it's a compliment.'

She scowled for a moment, then laughed. 'I guess I'll learn to put up with him.'

Giorgio reappeared with her breakfast.

'Eat up and we'll get to work,' he said. 'I'll get you a map of Verona.'

'I've got one,' she said, drawing it from her bag. 'I bought it at the airport so that I would be ready. The more you plan, the simpler life is.'

'True,' Mario murmured, 'but there are some things that can never be planned.'

'And you can't always anticipate what they might be,' she agreed. 'You can try, but—' She shrugged.

'But they always take you by surprise,' he murmured.

'Not always. Just sometimes. It's best to be ready.'

Giorgio looked from one to the other as if his alarm bells had sounded again.

'It's time we were making plans,' he said. 'I've called the others in the group, and they're dying to meet you. We're all invited to dinner tonight at the Albergo Splendido.' He beamed at Natasha. 'It'll be your big night.'

'Then I'd better prepare for it,' she said. 'I'll look around Verona today so that I can sound knowledgeable at the dinner. Otherwise they'll think I'm an amateur.'

'Good thinking,' Giorgio said. 'I'll escort you, and we'll have a great time.'

'Now, here—' Natasha pointed to a street on the map '—this is the Via Capello, where I can visit Juliet's house. I'd like to go there first, then the house where the Montagues lived. Finally, I'd like to see the tomb. Then I can work out my plans.'

'We'll leave as soon as you've finished breakfast,' Mario told her.

CHAPTER THREE

THE CHAUFFEUR-DRIVEN CAR was waiting for them, and soon they were on their way around the city.

Natasha already knew a good deal about Verona, having read about it on the plane. It was an old city, much of which went back to Roman times, two thousand years ago. Several places survived from that era, including a huge arena where gladiators had once slain their victims, but now was used for musical performances.

The streets were lined with historic buildings, many hinting at mystery and romance, all seeming to come from a more intriguing and beautiful age. She kept her eyes fixed on them as they drove through the town, trying to absorb its atmosphere.

'We're just turning into the Via Capello,' Mario said. 'We'll reach Juliet's house at any moment.'

A few minutes later the car dropped them at the entrance to a short tunnel. They joined the crowd walking through to the courtyard at the far end, where the balcony loomed overhead. Natasha regarded it with shining eyes.

'It's lovely,' she said. 'Of course I know it was put up less than a hundred years ago, but it looks right. It fits the house so perfectly that you can almost see Juliet standing there.'

'She's actually over there,' Giorgio said, pointing at a figure standing a little ahead, beneath and to the side of the balcony. It was a bronze statue of a young woman.

'Juliet,' she breathed.

As she watched, a woman walked up to the statue and brushed her hand against its breast. She was followed by another woman, and another, then a man.

'It's a tradition,' Mario explained. 'Everyone does it in the hope that it will bring them good luck. That's why that part of her is shining, because it's touched so often. People like to make contact with Juliet because they see her as a woman who knows more about love than anyone in the world.'

'Perhaps that's true,' Natasha murmured. 'But she knows tragedy as well as love.'

Intrigued, she went to stand before the statue. Juliet's head was turned slightly to the side, gazing into the distance as though only in another world could she find what she sought.

Natasha watched as a woman touched Juliet, closed her eyes and murmured something. At last her eyes opened and she stepped back with a smile, evidently feeling that she had received an answer.

If only it was that simple, Natasha thought. *If Juliet really could give me advice I'd ask her about the way my head is whirling, about how I'm feeling, and how I* ought *to be feeling. But she can't help me because she doesn't exist. She never really did, not the way people believe in her. That kind of love is just an illusion.*

She turned away to find Mario waiting. He moved closer, leaving Giorgio at a distance, and speaking quietly.

'Were you consulting Juliet?' he asked, raising an eyebrow.

'No,' she said. 'She's a fantasy. Nothing more.'

'How very prosaic.'

'I am prosaic, and I'm glad. It's useful.'

'But if you're going to promote the romantic fantasy, shouldn't you believe in it?'

She surveyed him with her head on one side and a faint ironic smile on her face.

'Not at all,' she said. 'It isn't necessary to believe something to persuade other people that it's true.'

'I wonder if you're right.'

A flash of anger made her say quickly, 'You know I'm right. We all know it at heart.'

'So—' he hesitated '—you're telling me that you've toughened up?'

'By a mile. So beware.'

'No need to tell me that.'

'So I've got you worried already? Good.'

For a wild moment he was tempted to tell her of the confused reactions that had rioted in him when he first saw her on the stairs. There had been an incredible moment of pleasure that the sight of her had always brought him, and which even now remained. But it had collided with a sense of alarm, as though a warning bell had sounded, letting him know that she would bring fear and darkness into his life.

But he suppressed the impulse to speak. How satisfied she would be to know that she could still throw him into confusion.

'Don't tell me I'm the only one who's toughened up,' she challenged him. 'Haven't you?'

'No doubt of it. It's called survival.'

She nodded. 'Right. As long as we both understand that, there's no problem.'

For them there would always be a problem. But there was no need of words.

'Now, I have a job to do,' she said briskly.

'Yes, let's look around further.'

Suddenly there was a cry from the far side of the courtyard.

'Buongiorno, amici!'

'Amadore!' Giorgio exclaimed, extending his hand in welcome.

The three men exchanged greetings in Italian, until Giorgio said, '*Signorina*, this is Amadore Finucci, a fellow member of the *Comunità*. Amadore, this is the Signorina Natasha Bates, who doesn't speak Italian.'

'Then it will be my pleasure to speak English,' Amadore said, seizing her hand.

She gave a polite response and he carried her hand to his mouth.

'Miss Bates,' he said.

'Please, call me Natasha.'

'Thank you—Natasha. When did you arrive?'

'Yesterday,' Giorgio said. 'Your father has invited us to dine at your hotel tonight.'

'Yes, he told me. I must leave now, but I look forward to seeing you this evening.'

He departed. Natasha eyed Mario curiously, puzzled to find him frowning.

'You're not pleased about this invitation?'

'That's because his hotel is one of the most luxurious in town,' Giorgio said. 'Mario's jealous.'

'I'm not jealous,' Mario said firmly. 'I admit I envy him having a bottomless pit of money to spend on the place.'

'His ballroom has to be seen to be believed,' Giorgio told her.

'Ballroom,' she echoed. 'Romeo and Juliet met in a ballroom.' She turned to Mario. 'Does your hotel have a ballroom?'

'No. None of the other hotels do.'

'Then that gives me an idea. Can we return to the hotel now? I need to get to work.'

'Aren't we going on to Romeo's house?' Giorgio asked.

'I'll do that tomorrow. Today, I have urgent things to do.

'Could you please provide me with a list of every member of the *Comunità*, and their hotels? Then I can check their locations and assess their requirements.'

'I'll see to it as soon as we arrive.'

As they walked back to the car, Giorgio murmured to Mario, 'A woman who knows her own mind. Perhaps we should beware.'

'There's no perhaps about it,' Mario replied grimly.

On the way back to the hotel Natasha took out her notebook and wrote in it swiftly and fiercely. Ideas were coming to her in cascades and she needed to capture them fast. This was the part of any project that she liked best. So absorbed did she become that she was unaware of the journey, and looked up suddenly when the car stopped.

'We're here,' Mario said. He'd been watching her silently.

'I need something to eat,' Giorgio declared. 'Suppose we meet downstairs in half an hour, for a feast?'

'Not me, thank you,' Natasha said. 'Perhaps you could send something up to my room?'

'But we could all celebrate together,' Giorgio protested.

'We can celebrate when I've made a success of this job. Let's hope that happens.'

'It'll happen,' Giorgio said. 'You're going to be just fantastic, isn't she, Mario?'

'No doubt of it,' he said bleakly.

'You're very kind, both of you. Now, excuse me, gentlemen.'

Giving them both a polite smile, she headed for the lift.

Upstairs, she plunged into work, making more notes about the morning before things went out of her head. She was so immersed in her work that at first she didn't hear the knock on the door. It had to be repeated louder to capture her attention.

'Sorry,' she said, pulling it open, 'I got so—' She checked herself at the sight of Mario standing there with a trolley of food.

'Your meal, *signorina*,' he said.

She stared at the sight of the food. Someone had taken a lot of trouble preparing this meal, which Mario laid out for her with care.

'Giorgio told the kitchen to produce their best, to make sure you stay with us,' he said. 'So you have chicory risotto, followed by tiramisù, with Prosecco.'

Her favourite wine. How many times had he ordered it for her in Venice? And he had remembered.

'It's delicious,' she said politely as she ate.

'I'll tell Giorgio you approve. And I brought you this,' he said, handing her a large file.

It was the information she'd requested about the *Comunità*—hotels, owners, background information.

'That man I met today seems to come from the biggest and best,' she said, flicking through it. 'The Albergo Splendido.'

'It was a palace once. You'll like it. You're making a considerable impression, you know.'

'Amadore certainly seemed to think so.'

'Just don't take him too seriously. He flirts with every woman on the planet.'

She gave a brief laugh. 'You warned me about Giorgio; now you're warning me about Amadore. But you don't need to. I can recognise when a man is role-playing. He puts on a performance as the "romantic Italian" because he thinks an Englishwoman is bound to be fooled. I don't mind. He's charming. But don't expect me to fall for it.'

'I suppose I should have known you'd say that,' Mario growled. 'I wonder if you ever fall for anything.'

'Not these days. Never again.'

'And you think that's admirable?'

'I think it's safe.'

'And safety matters more than anything else? Never mind who you hurt.'

She turned on him, her quick temper rising. 'Who *I* hurt? Did I really hear you say that? After what you did?'

'I didn't do what you thought I did, and I could have explained. But you vanished without giving me a chance to defend myself.'

'What was there to defend? I know what I saw.'

'Natasha, why won't you realise that you misunderstood what you saw? Yes, I'd been having an affair with Tania. I'm not a saint. I've never pretended to be. But it was only a casual relationship and I'd started to feel that it must end. Things had changed in my life. I'd met you and nothing looked the same. I had to face the fact that I wanted you, not her.

'So that day I met Tania and told her we couldn't be together any more. But I couldn't make her believe it. When I left her she followed me, and that was how she found us together.

'I went after her, trying to explain that I was sorry to hurt her, but she screamed at me and ran off. I came back to our table, hoping I could make you understand. But you were gone. I tried your phone but you'd turned it off. I went to the hotel but you'd left just a few minutes earlier. Over the next few days I tried your phone, your email, your apartment, but you'd shut off every way of contacting you. It was like you'd ceased to exist.'

'Exactly. I *had* ceased to exist. The girl I was then—naive, slightly stupid, ready to be fooled—vanished into nothing. But now there's another woman in her place—suspicious, awkward, ready to give as good as she gets. She exists. She's me. She's rather hard. You won't like her. Be wise. Get rid of her.'

His face was suddenly tense. 'I think not. I prefer to keep her around and make her face up to what she did.'

'Is that why you got me back here?'

'What do you mean by that?'

'I don't believe it's coincidence that we just happened to meet again.'

He paled. 'You think I manipulated this situation?'

'You could have.'

'And I'm telling you I didn't. How dare you? Perhaps I should accuse *you* of manipulation. Did you persuade your friend to let you take her place?'

'No way. I had no idea you'd be here until I saw you on the stairs.'

'Nor I. Let's get this clear, Natasha. I didn't trick you into coming here. I didn't want to see you again, not after the way you behaved.'

'The way *I*—?'

'You left me feeling as though I was hanging off the edge of a cliff.'

'I know that feeling,' she said softly, with anger in her voice.

'All right. For the moment we have to accept things as they are. We're enemies but we need to be allies as far as this job's concerned. Our fight is still on, but it's a fair fight.'

'Is it? I wonder if your idea of a fair fight is the same as mine.'

'I guess we'll find that out.'

A beep from her mobile phone interrupted him. Answering it, she found a text:

You didn't have to run away. We can sort this out.

There was no name, but there didn't need to be. This wasn't the first text that Elroy Jenson had sent her since he'd shut her out of his media empire. Clearly he'd expected her to cave in and come crawling back.

She had to make him stop doing this.

Swiftly, she texted back:

Forget me, as I've forgotten you.

His reply came at once:

If that were true you wouldn't have run away. Come home. I can do a lot for you.

She groaned, wondering how much more of this she could take. She'd thought that by coming to Italy she could put Jenson behind her.

'What's the matter?' Mario asked. 'Who has upset you?'

'It's nothing,' she said quickly. 'I'm fine.'

'I don't think so. Perhaps you should change your mobile number. Doing that works well because then the guy can't reach you. But of course you know that. Here—'

Before she could stop him he'd seized the phone from her hand and was reading the text.

'Just tell him to— What does he mean, run away?'

'I've been running away from him for months. He's Elroy Jenson, the man who owns a great media empire. It stretches all over the world—England, America, Europe—'

'Yes—' Mario broke in '—I've heard of him. Some of his papers are in this country. Not a man you'd want to antagonise.'

'I used to make a good living writing for his newspapers and magazines, but then he decided that he fancied me. I didn't fancy him but he wouldn't take no for an answer. He kept pestering me until I slapped his face. Unfortunately, some of his employees saw it and the word got out. Since then none of his editors will buy articles from me.'

'And he keeps sending you these messages? Why don't you just change your mobile phone number?'

'I have. Several times. But he always manages to get the new one. He's a powerful man and his tentacles stretch far.'

'Bastardo!'

'If that means what I think it does, then yes. Now I can't earn a living in England and he's coming after me.'

'Thinking you'll turn to him for the money? And he'd like that—knowing that you'd only given in to him out of need?'

'He'd enjoy it. He's that kind of man. But he's going

to be disappointed. I'll do anything rather than what he wants.'

'Anything? Including taking a job with a man you hate?'

'Even that. This job's a lucky break for me. It gets me out of England.'

'But you have to put up with me.'

'Stop being melodramatic. You're not so bad. I can manage. We've put the past behind us.'

He smiled wryly, trying to come to terms with her words. 'You're not so bad' implied a casual acceptance that should have been a relief but felt more like an insult.

'Yes, we've put it all behind us,' he agreed. 'And now we can concentrate on business, which is what we're here for. You need to make a living and I need to repay the bank loans I had to take out to buy this place.'

'That must be a heavy burden,' she said.

'It is. Damiano wanted to help me by lending me some money, and standing guarantor for the bank loan. But I wouldn't let him do either. This is my hotel, and mine alone.'

'I remember meeting Damiano in Venice. And his wife. They were very nice to me.'

'They both liked you a lot.'

In fact both Sally and Damiano had nudged him, saying, 'She's the one, Mario. Go on, make sure of her.'

And when things went wrong they had united again to call him 'The biggest idiot of all time'. It was a remark that still stung him.

'Why wouldn't you let him help you?' she asked.

'I just prefer to control my own life,' he said in a voice that was suddenly hard.

A tantalising memory flickered through her mind:

Mario, two years ago, young, carefree and easy-going. Somehow he had changed into this grimly self-sufficient man who mistrusted the world.

'I prefer it too,' she said. 'You feel safer, like wearing a suit of armour. But is that always a good thing to wear?'

'That depends on who challenges you,' he said.

His eyes, fixed on her, left her in no doubt of his message. Her presence was a challenge, one that he would fight off ruthlessly.

'But you wouldn't need a suit of armour against your older brother,' she said. 'Helping you is surely what older brothers are for?'

'Possibly, but I needed to stop being the younger brother, leaning on him. I told him I could do it alone, so I've got to prove that's true. I simply mustn't fail.'

'And I mustn't fail either,' she said, 'so in future we're going to concentrate on being practical. Please leave me now, and when I've finished my research I'll see you and Giorgio at supper.'

'Good luck with the work,' he said, and departed.

He went quickly to his office and went online. A few minutes' research told him all he needed to know about Elroy Jenson: his creation of a media empire, his money, his far-reaching power.

But it was the man's looks that amazed him. He'd expected a slobbering, middle-aged monster, a man no woman could want to be with unless she was after his money. But Jenson was well built, even handsome, with a riotous head of curly hair. A woman lucky enough to have captured his attention would have every reason to flaunt her triumph.

But not Natasha.

No man impresses her, he thought. *She decides what she wants, and woe betide him if he can't live up to it.*

He glanced at himself in the mirror.

'But could any man live up to it?' he murmured.

Researching the Albergo Splendido, Natasha could easily believe that it had started life as a palace. It was seven hundred years old and magnificently built.

To dine there meant dressing in style. Luckily she'd brought with her a black satin figure-hugging dress that managed to be both decorous and elegant.

Giorgio nodded approval. 'Lovely. You'll make their heads spin. Let's go.'

As they walked to the car Mario said, 'Aren't you making too much of her appearance? Surely it's her efficiency we need to promote?'

'Efficiency alone isn't enough. She's got that extra "something" special, and it's going to make all the difference.'

'I'll take your word for it,' Mario said coldly.

At the hotel Amadore was waiting for them. 'Everyone's here,' he said. 'They're longing to meet you.'

He led her into a room filled with tables at which sat crowds of men and women, who broke into applause at the sight of her.

There could be no doubt that she was the star of the evening. Amadore introduced her to each guest, one by one, giving the name of the person and of their hotel.

'Ah, yes,' she said to one elderly man. 'That's the place where—'

He listened, open-mouthed, as she revealed her in-depth research. She did the same thing with several of the other hotel owners and was rewarded by looks of admiration.

'You see what I mean?' Giorgio murmured to Mario. 'A brilliant lady, clever and hard-working. We've struck gold.'

Mario didn't reply.

When she'd met all the guests she sat down at the head table for the meal, which turned out to be a glorious banquet, adorned with the finest wines.

'Mmm, lovely,' she said, sipping from her glass.

'Everyone thinks of Verona as the site of the love story,' Giorgio told her. 'But it's also surrounded by vineyards. Most of the hotel owners have some sort of investment in vineyards.'

'The wine you're drinking now was produced in my own vineyard,' Amadore said.

'It's delicious,' she said, sipping again.

'Thank you, *signorina*.'

They clinked glasses.

Soon she saw that everyone was looking at her expectantly.

'They're waiting for your speech,' Mario murmured.

'But I can only speak English,' she protested. 'Will they understand?'

'Hotel owners tend to speak English because your country sends us many tourists.'

Mario got to his feet.

'My friends,' he said, 'it has been our pleasure tonight to meet the lady we've employed to promote us to the world. Now let us hear her plans.'

There was applause as Natasha rose. For a few moments she was nervous but the warm, friendly atmosphere enveloped her and she began to enjoy herself as she laid out the ideas that had been forming in her mind.

'Every hotel has something to connect it to the story,' she said. 'Some are near Juliet's house, some near Romeo's house, some are near the tomb.'

'Some of us aren't so lucky,' a man called. 'Our hotels aren't near anywhere significant.'

'Don't be so sure,' she said. 'Remember the scene where Romeo's friend Mercutio is stabbed to death by Juliet's kinsman? That happens outdoors in the street. But which street? Nobody knows for sure, but perhaps some of your hotels are nearby.'

Natasha looked out at her audience, smiling and nodding appreciatively as she spoke. She was fulfilling all their highest expectations. Applause rang in her ears.

CHAPTER FOUR

'NOW FOR THE next stage,' Natasha said. 'I'll want to talk to you all individually, and then I'm going to write my first piece explaining how "Romeo and Juliet" are still alive in Verona if people know how to find them. We'll invite them to come here, and stay in your hotels. By that time I'll have produced several more texts.'

'But who will publish these?' called a voice from the floor.

'Anyone she sends it to,' Giorgio called back. 'This lady is a very notable journalist with many connections. She gets published everywhere.'

More applause, but Natasha held up her hand for silence.

'We're not going to take chances,' she said. 'This "article" will actually be an advertisement. We buy a double-page spread and insert our own text and pictures. That way we can be sure of being read. What matters is to get things done the way we want. Of course it will be costly. Advertisements have to be paid for, and perhaps some of you won't want to accept that expense. Let's take a vote. Hands up anyone who's against the idea.'

Not a single hand was raised.

'We'll do it your way,' called a voice.

There were cheers and applause, which went on until they were interrupted by the sound of music.

'That's coming from the ballroom,' Amadore told her. 'Our guests like to dance in the evening.'

'A ballroom is wonderful,' she said. 'The Capulets gave a ball for Juliet and Paris, the man they wanted her to marry, which Romeo gatecrashed to see another girl that he was in love with. Instead he met Juliet and they fell in love within a few minutes. Without that ball it might never have happened.'

'Then come and have a look,' Amadore said eagerly.

Everyone crowded after them as he led her along a short corridor, throwing open a double door at the end, revealing a huge, beautiful room where couples were whirling.

'Perfect,' she murmured.

Amadore took her hand. 'Dance with me.'

Smiling, she let him draw her into his arms and guide her onto the floor. He was an excellent dancer and she responded gladly. When the music stopped another man stepped in to claim her, then another.

At last she found herself facing Mario.

'You've danced with everyone else,' he observed. 'Will it ever be my turn?'

'Not until you ask me.'

'No,' he said. 'I'm not going to ask you.'

But as he spoke his arm went around her waist in a grip too firm for her to resist, even if she had wanted to.

They had danced together once before. One night in Venice, when they had been having supper at an outdoor café in St Mark's Square, a band had started to play and before she knew it she was waltzing in his arms.

'Is this all right?' he'd whispered.

'I'll let you know later,' she had teased.

It had lasted only a few minutes, and she had promised herself that one day she would dance with him again. But the next day they had broken up, and it had never happened again. Until now.

It was unnerving to feel his arms around her, his hand on her waist, holding her close. Her heart was beating softly but fervently. She glanced at him, trying to know if he felt the same. Would he invite her to dance with him again?

But before he could speak they became aware of a middle-aged man on the edge of the crowd, trying to attract their attention.

'Ah, there's Francesco,' Mario said. 'I hoped he'd be here. He owns one of the biggest hotels, and I always like to have him on my side. Let's go and say hello.'

Francesco beamed, greeting Natasha with an embrace.

'It's a pleasure to meet you,' he said warmly. 'Now, let me introduce my daughter, Laura.'

The young woman with him was in her mid-twenties with a beautiful face and an air of confidence that came from being always in demand.

'How have you done?' she said carefully to Natasha.

'No,' her father interrupted her. 'Not like that, *cara*. The English say "How do you do?" not "How have you done?"'

'How do you do?' Laura echoed, smiling. 'Is that right?'

'That is perfect,' her father said.

He spoke proudly and Natasha knew a slight twinge of sadness as a memory came back to her from long ago. She had heard that pride before, in her own father's voice, in her childhood, before he'd abandoned her without a backward glance.

But this was no time to be brooding over the past. She thrust the memory aside, returning Laura's greeting with the appearance of warmth.

Then Laura turned her attention to Mario, saying, 'And how do you do?'

'There's no need for such formality,' Mario said, shaking her hand. 'We already know each other.'

'Indeed we do,' Laura said, glancing at Natasha as she spoke.

Natasha returned her look with interest. She had the feeling that Laura was sizing her up as possible competition.

Then Amadore appeared beside them. 'Do I get another dance?' he asked.

'Of course.' Natasha let the charming hotel owner enfold her in his arms and twirl her gently across the floor.

Out of the corner of her eye she could just see Mario gliding past with Laura, who seemed to be trying to dance as close to him as possible.

'There the women go again,' Amadore said, 'parading themselves to get his attention.'

'Do you mean Signor Ferrone?' Natasha asked.

'Oh, yes. He's a lucky man. Every female makes eyes at him, and the rumour is that he can have any woman he wants.'

So nothing had changed, she thought, remembering how women's eyes had followed Mario during their time together. How they had envied her, being with him. How little they had known how he could make a woman suffer.

'Look at that,' Amadore said, still regarding Mario with envy. 'The way she's pressed up against him is almost indecent.'

Natasha managed to chuckle. 'Oh, come on. A man's entitled to enjoy himself if he can.'

'That's very generous of you. Most women don't take such a relaxed view.'

'I can afford to be relaxed. My life is arranged just the way I want it.'

'You're luckier than most of us then.'

Mario, just a few feet away, glanced at them only briefly before swinging Laura away to the far side of the ballroom. There, he found more female attention to distract him from sights he didn't want to see and thoughts he didn't want to think.

But it lasted only a short time. When he next looked at Natasha she was sitting down scribbling in her notebook. Two men were sitting beside her, while another two looked over her shoulders. As the music came to an end he began to approach her, but Amadore detained him.

'Lovely lady,' he said. 'Every man is interested. Luckily she's not interested in them.'

'She told you that?'

'We were watching Laura making a play for you. I disapproved but she said you were entitled to enjoy yourself. I complimented her on her relaxed attitude and she said she could afford to be relaxed as her life was arranged the way she wanted it.'

'She probably just said that to shut you up.'

'Maybe. But it wouldn't surprise me if back home she has a trail of eager pursuers.'

'You could be right,' Mario growled.

He could see that Natasha had finished making notes, and was rising to move away. He got to her quickly.

'Still working?' he said.

'I've had an idea. I need to talk to everyone again.'

'Then let's return to the dining room.' He offered her his arm, saying, 'You've done well tonight. The contract will be ready soon.'

'Contract?'

'For you to sign. The whole *Comunità* is determined to secure your professional services. Are you willing to stay with us?'

'Yes,' she said softly. 'I'm willing.'

When they were gathered in the dining room again she addressed everyone. 'I think we should take some photographs of Romeo and Juliet. They say a picture's worth a thousand words, and we can send ours all over the world. We'll need to hire actors, then we'll photograph them on the balcony, in the tomb, anywhere that seems atmospheric.'

'We can't pose them on the official balcony,' Mario said. 'There are always tourists there. But this hotel has a balcony that will do.'

It was agreed that they would all meet again when the arrangements were made. Now all Mario wanted was to get away. Nothing had prepared him for being so close to her for hours, and he needed to be alone.

'Sleep well,' he told her as he escorted her to a chauffeur-driven car. 'You've worked hard today and there'll be more tomorrow.' He opened the car door. 'I'll see you tomorrow morning. Goodnight.'

He walked away.

Back in her room, Natasha undressed and went to bed. It had been a successful evening and she should have felt triumphant. Perhaps she would have done if Mario had returned with her, and been here to share her sense of achievement. But he had left her alone while he spent the night somewhere else.

Images of Laura danced through her mind, pursued by Amadore's voice saying '…he can have any woman he wants.'

She tried to shut the thoughts down. She and Mario were no longer part of each other's lives, and she cared nothing where he was now, or who he was with.

She lay down and managed to sleep. When she awoke she could hear a noise in the corridor outside, as though someone was turning a key in a lock. She rose and opened her door just in time to see Mario's door closing.

It was six in the morning.

She half expected him to be late for breakfast but he was there before her, calm, collected and ready for work.

'You were right about hiring actors,' he said. 'We'll have a file of pictures soon. In the meantime I've been making some notes of my own—'

But before she could look at them her phone beeped with another text.

'Is he hounding you again?' Mario demanded.

'No, it's not him,' she said, looking at the screen. Then she drew in her breath sharply. 'Oh, no—no! *Please, no!*'

'What is it?'

'Nothing,' she said sharply.

'Don't tell me it's nothing when it affects you like that. Let me see.'

Without asking her permission, he took the phone from her.

'What's this?' he demanded, reading, *'Sorry, your cheque bounced.'*

'How dare you?' she said furiously, snatching the phone back.

'Who's hounding you for money? Is it him?'

'No, it's my friend Helen, and she's not hounding me. She's been letting me stay in her flat and she got me this job. Before I left I gave her a cheque for my share of expenses. I owe her so much and I've repaid her like this. I didn't mean to. I thought there was just enough in the bank.'

'Right, we'd better get your contract sorted at once. Wait for me here.'

As he left she sat there, deep in gloom. Shame pervaded her and for a moment she wished she could do what Mario had accused her of, and vanish into thin air.

After a few minutes Giorgio appeared.

'The boss says I'm to give you the contract to sign,' he told her. 'Let's go into his office.'

In the office he laid out papers before her. 'Just sign at the bottom.'

She picked up the pen, then paused. 'Wait, are you sure this contract is right?'

'The boss says it is.'

'But I know what the agency offered me—the money was far less.'

'The fee has been changed. The boss says you're worth more.'

Her head was spinning. The new amount was much larger than the one she had been quoted before.

'You need to give me your bank details so that some money can be paid to you today,' Giorgio said.

Dazed, she gave him the necessary information and signed the contract at the bottom of the last page.

'And you must put your initials on the other pages,'

Giorgio told her. 'He wants to make very sure that you're ours and nobody else's. He knows good value when he sees it. Ah, here he is.'

Mario had come into the room, and stood watching as Natasha finished signing. Glancing over the papers, he nodded and handed them to Giorgio, who left the room.

'I hadn't expected so much,' she said. 'You didn't have to do that. But thank you.'

'You have nothing to thank me for, *signorina*,' he said firmly. 'You're vital to this project and I've taken the necessary steps to make sure the *Comunità* keeps your services.'

She nodded, replying in the same formal voice, 'You can be sure that I will remain loyal to the *Comunità, signore*.'

'Excellent,' he said. 'Then we understand each other.'

'I'm sure we do.'

Oh, yes, she thought. They understood each other perfectly, but in ways that could never be expressed in words. He'd moved swiftly to save her from disaster, but in such a way that there was no fear of them growing closer. They were *signore* and *signorina*, and nothing else.

Not long after, she accessed her bank account on the Internet and found that a large sum of money had already been deposited, enabling her to pay her debt to Helen. That was a relief and she was able to enjoy an hour wandering the streets, absorbing the feel of the city.

When she returned she found that the photographs had arrived. Giorgio and Mario were going through them, studying the pictures of young models, seeking one with the perfect combination of beauty and innocence. She joined in and after a while she discovered exactly what she wanted.

Finding Romeo was harder. He had to be handsome, with splendid legs, since Romeo would be wearing tights. At last she found what she wanted.

'Perfect,' Mario said, studying the picture. 'Good-looking and vulnerable.'

'Vulnerable?' Giorgio queried. 'He's one of literature's great heroes.'

'He also fell for everything that was said to him,' Mario observed wryly. 'Not one of the world's great minds.'

'That's what happens to people in love,' Natasha said. 'They set their minds aside and believe what they want to believe.'

'And soon learn their mistake. All right, let's hire these two.'

Giorgio got straight onto the phone, made the contact and arranged for the two young people to appear in a couple of days.

'Paolo and Lucia,' he said. 'They'll be here ready to start on Thursday morning.'

'That's fine,' Natasha said. 'It gives me some more time to work on my ideas.'

The next two days were abuzz with action. Some of the time was spent visiting Romeo's house, and twice Natasha was invited to dine with other members of the *Comunità*. Mario accompanied her on these trips, but did not sit next to her at the dinner table.

She thought she understood. Having tied her down with the contract, both legally and financially, Mario preferred to keep a certain distance between them.

But the money in her bank account was a big relief. There was no doubt that in Mario she'd made a good professional association. She must cling to that thought.

By day they were absorbed in preparing for the photo shoot. Giorgio hired a photographer experienced in taking dramatic pictures. He also found a theatrical costumier.

'She'll join us tomorrow with a big variety of costumes,' he told Natasha. 'Our models can try several until we find the right ones.'

'Juliet will need something exotic for the ballroom,' Natasha said. 'Then an elegant dress for the wedding scene, and a very simple one for the tomb. Right, I'm going to bed. It's going to be a busy day tomorrow.'

'Does anyone know where Mario is?' Giorgio enquired.

'He left an hour ago,' Natasha said. 'He must be busy.'

On the way upstairs she wondered if Mario was in his room, or had he gone to be with the same person he'd probably visited the other night?

Passing his door, she couldn't help pausing to hear if any sound was coming from inside. She blamed herself for yielding to the temptation, but she couldn't help it.

Then she heard his voice. He was on the telephone, speaking Italian in a warm, laughing tone.

'Non è importante. Non è importante.'

She didn't need to know the language to understand what he was saying: 'It's not important'. Mario was reassuring somebody that what was happening now didn't matter to him.

She hurried into her room and locked the door, wishing she'd resisted temptation and vowing to be stronger next time.

Next morning Lisa, the costumier, arrived early. She was a tall businesslike woman who spoke perfect English and went through Natasha's requirements with no trouble.

'Let's hope Romeo is handsome and has a good figure,' she said briskly.

'He looked good in the photo I saw, but I haven't met him yet,' Natasha admitted.

'That's a pity. To be suitable he must be sexy. We need the women to sigh over him and say, "I want some of that".'

'But he'll only be a picture,' Natasha protested. 'We're selling the town, not Romeo himself.'

Lisa chuckled. 'You think that, do you?'

Natasha gave a wry smile. 'Well, it's what I need to believe. But I guess you're right.'

'Share the joke, ladies,' Giorgio called from nearby, where he was talking with Mario.

'You wouldn't understand it,' Lisa told him. 'We're laughing at men, and men never realise how funny they are.'

'That's very true,' Natasha said. 'And if you try to explain they still don't understand.'

Mario gave her an odd glance which she returned with an air of teasing confidence. She felt a certain cheeky pleasure in having disconcerted him. The day had started well. Whatever happened now, she felt she could cope.

They all set out for the Splendido, where everyone was waiting, eager to begin. The next hour was spent going through a variety of garments.

'I like this one,' Natasha said, holding up a long white ballgown. It was simple and elegant, perfect for a girl making her debut in society. 'Juliet can wear this at the ball.'

Giorgio looked impatiently at his watch.

'They should be here by now. What's happened to them?'

He snatched up his phone and dialled. Almost as soon as he was through, an expression of outrage overtook him.

'Sì? Che cosa? Cosa vuol dire che non posso venire? Oh, dolore bene!'

He hung up.

'What's happened?' Mario demanded.

'They're not coming. There's been a mix-up with the dates. They thought the shoot was next week.'

'Oh, no, what are we going to do?' Natasha cried. 'It's all set up for today.'

'There's only one thing we can do,' Giorgio said. 'Find another Romeo and Juliet.'

'But we haven't got time to search,' she protested.

'We don't have to search. We've got the duo we need right here.' He threw out his arms towards her and Mario. 'Romeo and Juliet.'

She stared. 'You can't possibly be serious.'

'I'm perfectly serious. You're beautiful enough to be Juliet, and Mario can just about get by as Romeo.'

'It won't work,' Mario growled. 'As though I could—'

'It's got to work,' Giorgio said. 'You're the only two who can do it in the time available. We've got to start right now, otherwise all our plans are in a mess. Come along, you two. Be professional.'

'He's right,' Mario growled. 'We have no choice.'

'Go next door and get changed,' Amadore said. 'Natasha, a maid will come with you.'

She looked around wildly. Surely there must be some other way. But there was no other way. Only this could save her plans for the success she simply had to have.

The maid appeared and took her to the room assigned as Juliet's dressing room. The dress fitted perfectly onto her slender, delicate figure. But her hair didn't seem right, pulled tightly back.

'I think Juliet would wear it hung loose,' she said.

The maid nodded, and got skilfully to work. Natasha watched, only half believing, as the self she knew disappeared and naive, vulnerable Juliet took her place. The merest touch of make-up heightened the impression, and she was ready to go.

As she entered the ballroom heads turned. Giorgio made a clapping movement and Amadore whistled.

She noticed neither of them. Her attention had been seized by the man standing a little further off. Mario had transformed into Romeo, wearing a dark blue doublet and tights. It would need a fine figure to get away with such a revealing costume, but Mario was tall, splendidly built and handsome enough to steal the spotlight.

Suddenly a memory came flooding back to her. Two years ago, during their precious short time together in Venice, they had spent a day on the beach. Her first sight of him, half naked in swimming trunks, had had a stunning effect on her, making her intensely aware that her own swimwear was a bikini, leaving much of her body uncovered.

Oh, yes, she'd thought as she enjoyed the sight of his long, strong legs as he raced across the beach. *Oh, yes!*

After that everything had changed. They spent the day chasing each other, bathing in the sea or stretched out on the sand, and with every moment she wanted him more. She'd feasted her eyes on his smooth, muscular body, seizing every chance to lean closer to him, cherishing the brief moments when her flesh brushed against his.

It had been her first experience of fierce desire and it revealed her to herself in a new light. In the past she had flirted, laughed, teased, but never before had she wanted a man with such fervour. When their eyes met she believed she saw the same intensity in him, and promised herself that soon he would carry her to a new world.

That night they'd parted with only a kiss. She had told herself he was biding his time, waiting for her to be ready to move on.

Three days later they had parted for ever.

Shaking off the memory, she began to walk towards Mario, tense for the moment when she would see his reaction to her. Would the past return to haunt him too? What would she see in his eyes?

At last Mario looked up, saw her and nodded.

'Splendid,' he said. 'Giorgio chose Juliet well.'

His tone was polite but nothing more, and his eyes were blank.

'And you look fine as well, Signor Ferrone,' she said, striving to match him for blandness.

'Well, like Giorgio said, I'll "just about get by".'

'Everybody ready?' Amadore called. 'This way.'

He indicated an archway at the far end of the ballroom. Mario offered Natasha his arm and she took it, saying, 'Thank you, *signore*.'

He leaned closer to her, murmuring, 'Don't call me *signore*. My name is Mario. If you address me formally people will think something is wrong between us.'

'And we mustn't let them think that,' she agreed. 'Shall we go?'

CHAPTER FIVE

THERE WAS A cheer when they came into the ballroom. Lisa nodded, as though to say that Romeo's looks met her high standards.

The photographer studied them with approval and said he would start with portrait shots.

'First I'll take you separately, then together. Juliet, you first.'

'Juliet? I'm Natasha,' she said lightly.

'No, today you are Juliet.'

'He's right,' Giorgio said. 'You don't pretend to be Juliet. You *are* Juliet. You can go back to being Natasha tomorrow.'

'If I want to,' she said, entering into the spirit. 'Natasha might be too boring.'

'That's the spirit,' Giorgio said with a grin.

She turned this way and that, smiled, looked sad, smiled again.

'Now throw your arms out,' Giorgio said. 'Imagine you're looking at someone who's the great happiness of your life.'

She did so, reaching towards the camera with a yearning look.

Mario, watching from the sidelines, turned his head

to avoid seeing that expression on her face. He remembered it too well from the past, and couldn't bear to be reminded of it now that the past was over.

Then he too had to pose for portrait shots.

'This way, that way,' the photographer called. 'Turn your head a little. Good. Now the two of you together.'

The first shot was a formal pose, with Juliet standing just in front of Romeo, his hands on her shoulders.

'Now turn and look into each other's eyes. Keep hold of each other but lean back a little so that I can see both of your faces.'

They obeyed, studying each other seriously, then smiling according to instructions.

'I think Romeo should frown a little,' Lisa called. 'And he should try to look sexy so that we know why Juliet fell for him.'

Mario scowled, annoyed at the comment and even more exasperated by the fact that Natasha collapsed with laughter.

'Don't worry,' she called. 'I can pretend if I have to.'

'And perhaps Juliet had to,' Giorgio said cheerfully. 'Maybe she didn't really fancy Romeo at all. She was pursuing her own agenda. *That's it!* Romeo, that grim look is perfect. Keep it up.'

'Yes, keep it up,' she chuckled. 'Just think how I'm going to thump you later.'

'Juliet, that smile is wonderful,' the photographer called. 'It says a lot about the kind of marriage they would have had if they'd lived. One where he got worked up and she laughed at him. I'm beginning to think nobody ever really understands this pair.'

'No,' she murmured so that only Mario could hear. 'Nobody really understands.'

'He's talking nonsense,' Mario growled.

'He's grandstanding to make us play our parts,' she said. 'It's his job. So we have to do ours.'

'Juliet,' Giorgio called, 'reach up and brush his hair forward a little, around his face.' She did so, hearing the camera click madly.

'That's it—now again—and again—gently—Juliet's longing to caress his face, and this is her chance.'

Natasha told herself that she was merely obeying orders, but she couldn't hide the truth from herself. She wanted to do this—wanted to touch his face, his body, his heart. Even through the lightness of her caress she felt the tremor that went through Mario, despite his attempt to suppress it. She could sense his reaction because it mirrored her own.

But could he suspect the feelings that were going through her at being so close to him? Suddenly, his face had softened. The grim look she saw on it so often faded, leaving a faint echo of the young, gentle man she had loved. His eyes were fixed on her intently but that might be no more than playing his part. If only she could tell.

'Right, that's it,' came Giorgio's voice. 'Now for the balcony scene. Come this way.'

The balcony at the back of the Splendido was decorated much like the one at Juliet's house, and had the advantage of being several feet lower so that Romeo and Juliet could be closer to each other. Mario stood below, reaching up, while Natasha leaned down to touch his hand while the camera clicked away.

'Perfect,' Giorgio cried at last. 'You two are doing a great job. It's wonderful how well you work together.'

They said what was necessary and followed him back

to the ballroom, where another selection of garments was laid out for them.

'Romeo believes that Juliet is dead,' Giorgio said. 'So he comes to the crypt where her body lies. He finds her there, says his farewells and takes his own life. Then she wakes, finds him dead, and she too chooses death. We'll shoot this scene in the cellar.'

With the maid's help, Natasha donned a plain gown and they all went down to the hotel's cellar, where a stone bench had been prepared for her to lie on.

'Ow!' she said, stretching out on it. 'That stone's really hard.'

'Is it really painful?' Mario asked her quietly.

'No, I'll be all right.'

'Let me put something under your head.'

'No, that would spoil it. But thank you.'

He still looked worried but let it drop.

'Walk up to her body,' Giorgio said. 'Look into her face as though you can't believe it's true. Good. Just like that.'

Lying there with her eyes closed, Natasha yearned to open them and see Mario's expression, to meet his eyes. But she must resist temptation and be content with the feel of his breath on her face.

'Lay your head on her breast,' Giorgio instructed.

The next moment she felt him lying against her and gave a slight gasp.

'Now kiss her,' Giorgio said,

She braced herself for the moment his mouth touched hers. It was the faintest possible sensation but she told herself to endure it.

'Again,' Giorgio said. 'Remember, you've lost the only woman in life that you could ever care about.'

Mario kissed her again before laying his head once more on her breast. At last Giorgio called out that the scene was over.

'Now for the big one,' he said. 'The moment when they meet.'

In the ballroom Natasha donned the glamorous gown and watched while the maid worked on her hair. When everything was ready Giorgio guided 'Romeo and Juliet' into position.

'It's during the ball. Juliet is standing there, watching everyone, particularly Paris, the man her parents want her to marry. But then she sees Romeo watching her. Their eyes meet.'

Mario turned his head so that he gazed at Natasha. She gazed back.

'He advances towards her,' Giorgio continued. 'That's right, Mario, a little nearer. He takes her hand, and asks forgiveness for touching her because he says he isn't worthy. But she says he is.'

Now Natasha's hand was clasped in Mario's. He was close to her, watching her intently.

'And Romeo dares to steal a kiss,' Giorgio said triumphantly. 'Go on. Let's catch that on camera.'

Gently Mario dropped his head, laying his lips on hers.

'Good,' Giorgio said. 'But I wonder if we should do it again. Natasha, it might be more effective if you put your arm around him.'

'It's too soon for that,' she said quickly. 'She doesn't yet know how she feels.'

'Nor does he,' Mario said. 'How would Romeo kiss her at this point? Would it be like this?' He laid his lips briefly over Natasha's. 'He might do it respectfully because however much he desires her he fears to offend her.

Or is he a shameless character who simply takes what he wants, like this?'

His arm went around her waist, drawing her against him, while his mouth covered hers firmly and purposefully.

She was stunned. The brief, light kiss he'd given her a few moments ago hadn't prepared her for this. Instinctively, her hands moved to touch him, but she snatched them back, unsure whether she would embrace him or push him away. She understood nothing except the disturbing pleasure of his lips on hers, and the maddening instinct to slap his face.

For two years she'd wanted to be in his arms, dreamed of it while mentally rejecting it in her rage at his betrayal. Now the sweetness of holding him again struggled with fury at his assumption that he could do as he liked and she would have to accept it.

But she could not repulse him. Whatever common sense might dictate, she must appear to react to him blissfully and chance what the future might bring. She let herself press against him, eager to feel his response, and then—

'All right, Giorgio?' Mario cried, standing back. 'Is that what you want?'

Natasha froze, barely able to believe what had happened. It seemed that the feelings that had pervaded her had been hers alone. Had he felt anything beyond the need to get the photographs right? Fury simmered inside her.

'That's fine,' Giorgio said. 'Do it just like that, for the camera.'

Then Mario's hands were on her again, drawing her nearer so that he could lay his lips on hers and hold her against him, unmoving. She could feel the warmth of his mouth, of his whole body, and her own responded to the sensation whether she wanted it to or not. Her anger flared further.

Somewhere in the background she could hear the sound of a camera, clicking again and again until at last Giorgio called, 'All right, that's it. Well done, you two. Now let's think about the next scene.'

'I need a little fresh air first,' Natasha said, quickly slipping out of the nearest door into a corridor.

She ran until she reached a corner behind which she could hide. She must escape Mario lest he suspect that she'd just discovered the power he still had over her.

But when she looked around she found him facing her.

'Did you follow me?' she demanded.

'I thought that was what you meant me to do. Don't you have something you want to say to me?'

'Oh, yes, I have a thousand things,' she said furiously. 'You've got a nerve, doing what you did back there.'

'Kissing you, you mean? But you owed it to me. When we parted you never kissed me goodbye.'

'I never thumped the living daylights out of you either, which I was surely tempted to.'

He seemed to consider this. 'So you think I deserve to have you slap my face? Very well. Do your worst.'

'What are you saying?'

'Go ahead. Slap me if it will make you feel better.'

He jutted his chin out a little and stood waiting.

'Stop talking nonsense,' she snapped.

'I mean it. You can do what you like and I promise not to retaliate.'

'This is all a big joke to you, isn't it?'

He shook his head. 'My sense of humour died the

day you left. In the weeks I spent trying to find you I buried it deep underground. So what now? Aren't you going to hit me?'

'Certainly not. It would be unprofessional. I might leave marks on your face that would spoil the next photographs. The matter is closed.'

He saluted. 'Yes, ma'am. Whatever you say, ma'am.'

'Oh, stop it—stop it! Stop trying to make a fool of me, of yourself, of both of us.'

Suddenly, his manner changed. The wry irony died and a bleakness came into his eyes. 'You silly woman,' he said quietly. 'Don't you realise that we all have our own way of coping.'

'And that's your way? Well, this is my way.'

Without warning, the swift temper she'd vowed to control swept over her, driving her to do something she knew was madness. She seized his head in her hands, drew it down and covered his mouth with her own. At once she could feel his hands on her and sensed the same confusion as she had felt herself—to deny the kiss or indulge it joyfully?

But he was going to indulge it. That was her decision, and she would give him no choice. She slightly softened the pressure of her mouth so that the kiss could become a caress, her lips moving over his in a way she had once known delighted him. She sensed his response in his tension, the sudden tightening of his arms about her.

Now she was ready to taunt him further. The pressure of her mouth intensified, and his breath came faster as his excitement grew. His lips parted as he explored her more deeply. He was no longer merely receiving her kiss but returning it in full, seeking to take command but not succeeding. The command was hers, and she would keep it whether he liked it or not. Her spirit soared. She was winning.

He drew back a little. 'Natasha—'

'Take warning, Mario. Two can play this game. You won't defy me again. If you do I'll make you sorry.'

She felt him tense, saw his eyes full of disbelief as he understood her meaning. Then it was all over. 'You had to do that, didn't you?' he rasped. 'You had to tease me—make me think—but it wasn't a kiss. It was revenge.'

'Revenge can be very sweet,' she said, pushing him away. 'That's one of the things I learned from you. Did you think you were going to get away with what you did back there? You just had to show me that you were the boss, and how I felt didn't count.'

He shook his head. 'You won't believe this,' he said in a hard voice, 'but I kissed you because I wanted to. I'm ashamed of that now because it seems so stupid to imagine that you had any kindly feelings left. But, idiot that I was, I thought some part of you might still be the old Natasha, the sweet-natured girl I loved and wanted to be with.

'But you warned me about that, didn't you? You told me that Natasha was dead. I couldn't believe it, but I believe it now. You did this to get your own back by reminding me of what I've lost.'

'You lost it because you didn't want it,' she said.

'Keep telling yourself that,' he said quietly. 'In the end you may come to believe it. In those days I wanted you more than I've ever wanted any woman. And I could have told you that if you hadn't vanished when you did. You landed us in this desert, not me. You did it by losing your temper and acting without thinking anything through. We didn't have to end up here. We could have been married by now, and expecting our first child. Instead—well, look at us.'

'Stop it! *Stop it!*' she screamed, turning away from him with her hands over her ears.

'Yes, the truth can be very painful, can't it? I could have devoted my life to loving you. Instead, I've come so close to hating you that it scares me.'

'Well, at least that's getting the truth out into the open. You hate me.'

'I didn't say that. I said I came close to hating you. I've never been able to take the final step, but I have a feeling that will come soon.'

She made no reply. The unexpected glimpse he'd given her of his own feelings had set off an aching misery inside her. He didn't hate her, but he would if he could. She wanted to scream and bang her head against the wall.

She turned away but he pulled her around to face him.

'You won't let me tell you my side of it and I think I know why,' he raged. 'Because you're a coward, Natasha. You're afraid to know the truth. If you had to face the terrible thing you did, you couldn't bear it. Everything could have been so different for us if you hadn't condemned me so quickly.'

She didn't reply. Something inside her choked the words back before they could escape.

'If you knew how I planned that day,' Mario said. 'I'd told you that I had something important to say to you. I was going to ask you not to go home, to stay with me, become my love.

'My relationship with Tania was never serious. She was a very experienced woman who surrounded herself with various male "friends". I knew I wasn't the only man in her life but it didn't trouble me because I wasn't in love with her and she wasn't in love with me.

'But when I met you, things changed. Suddenly I no longer wanted "a bit of fun". I wanted something serious and I wanted it with you. Nobody else. Just you. So I met up with Tania and I told her that we couldn't see each other any more.

'She was angry, but I thought she understood. Then it happened. She descended on us; you disappeared. If you could have seen what I went through trying to find you, how deep in despair I was—well, I guess you'd have enjoyed it.'

'I wouldn't have believed it,' she retorted. 'You? In despair, when you played the field so easily?'

'I'd done with playing the field. That life was all over for me. And if I could have explained that—made you understand… But what's the use? You only believe what you want to believe.'

She stared at him, trying to take in his incredible words. It was as though she'd become two people—one recoiling from him, one reaching out, longing to know more.

'Are you two there?' Giorgio's voice came along the corridor.

'We're here,' Mario called back.

'Ah, good.' Giorgio appeared around the corner. 'Time to get changed back into normal clothes. No more photographs today, but we're going to see Romeo's house.'

Natasha escaped to the dressing room and rid herself of the costume. It was a relief to don modern clothes and become herself again. Juliet could be banished, at least for a while.

The longer the better, she thought, staring into the

mirror and brushing her hair fiercely so that it fell down over her shoulders. It looked like spun gold in the afternoon sunlight. Once Mario had made a joke about it; 'my dangerous blonde bombshell' he'd said in a teasing voice.

'I'm not dangerous,' she'd protested.

'You can be when you act on instinct. Some of your instincts could scare a man.'

'Do I scare you?' she'd teased.

'You could if I scared easily.'

Today he'd told her frankly that her headstrong temper had done much to part them.

Suppose I'd stayed to listen to his 'explanations', she thought. *Should I have done that? Should I have trusted him? No! No!'*

She scraped her hair back as tight as it would go. When she was satisfied with her appearance she went down to join them.

Romeo's house was just a few minutes away from Juliet's and could only be seen from the outside.

'It looks like a fortress,' she said, 'with those battlements.'

'A lot of buildings were created like that in those days,' Giorgio said. 'Half of the city was almost permanently at war with the other half, hence the fight between the Capulets and Montagues.'

'Buongiorno!'

A cry from a few feet away made them turn to see a man hailing them. He seemed to be in his forties, tall and strongly built, and Natasha recognised him as a member of the *Comunità* that she had met on the first evening.

'You should have told me you were coming,' he said, giving her a hug.

'I wasn't sure until the last minute,' Mario said.

'Come and have coffee with me. My hotel is just around the corner.'

As they walked there Giorgio dropped his voice to say to Natasha, 'Mario would have avoided this meeting if he could. That's Riccardo, the rival who tried to challenge him for the presidency of the *Comunità*. He's very wealthy, owns more vineyards than any of the others, and likes giving orders just as much as Mario does.'

'You said Mario got him to back off.'

'Yes. Not sure how, but the rumours say some of Riccardo's business dealings wouldn't bear inspection.'

'You mean Mario threatened him?'

'I doubt if it was a blatant threat. That isn't Mario's way. He'll just make a remark that only one man will understand—and fear. Riccardo dropped his challenge very suddenly. Mario isn't a man you tangle with, not if you've got any sense.'

Riccardo's premises were lavish and decorative, even more so than the Dimitri Hotel. Wherever Natasha looked she could see that money had been spent without restraint. It might well appear that Riccardo was a man who could challenge Mario, but after only a few minutes seeing them together Natasha sensed that this could never happen.

Riccardo was afraid of Mario. That was the incredible truth. And Mario was content to have it be so. The young man who had once enjoyed getting his own way by charm now used power to bend people to his will.

He had blamed her for disappearing, leaving him to search frantically until finally he had accepted despair. She had resisted the accusation, but now it troubled her more than she could face. This man scared other people, but admitted that she scared him.

She fell into earnest conversation with Riccardo.

'I want to see the rest of Verona,' she said. 'It's not just about *Romeo and Juliet*. There's more to life than romance.'

'No doubt about that,' Mario agreed.

They clinked glasses.

'Right,' Natasha said. 'I've done my preliminary work. Now I'm going to shut myself away for a while to get everything written. I'll see you in a few days, gentlemen.'

'So we're no longer needed?' Giorgio asked comically. 'You're dismissing us just like that? Ah, it's a hard world.'

'That's how it is,' Mario said, reflecting Giorgio's theatrical manner. 'A woman dismisses a man when she no longer needs him. We just have to accept it.'

They all laughed.

'If I'm not required for a while I'll go back to Venice for a few days,' Mario said. 'Sally, my sister-in-law, is about to give birth again. She had a hard time with her last baby so I think Damiano might appreciate having me around for a few days. I'll stay in touch—*signorina*, Giorgio will take care of you.'

'Thank you. If I have Giorgio, what more could I possibly want?'

Mario left that afternoon, bidding her a polite goodbye in front of everyone else, adding, 'Giorgio can contact me if need be. Goodbye, everyone.'

He fled.

CHAPTER SIX

IT WAS A relief for Natasha to spend the next few days without Mario. She needed time to come to terms with what he'd told her.

If you knew how I planned that day... I was going to ask you not to go home, to stay with me, become my love.

She tried to block out the memory, but it haunted her. Mario vowed he'd broken with Tania because he loved her and was preparing to tell her.

We didn't have to end up here. We could have been married by now, and expecting our first child. Instead—well, look at us.

She tried not to hear the terrible words echoing in her mind. Mario had accused her of believing only what she wanted to believe. And perhaps he was right. If he was telling the truth it meant that she had created the disaster almost single-handed.

To escape that unbearable thought, she submerged herself in work, studying not just Verona itself but its surroundings. It stood in the Veneto, the northern region of Italy that was best known for the city of Venice.

'That's why we speak Venetian here,' Giorgio told her.

'Venetian? Venice has its own language?'

'Certainly, and it's spoken throughout the Veneto. People speak Italian as well, and English is very common because of all the tourists. But you need to know about the Venetian language to really understand this area.'

'And that's what I want to do,' she said, scribbling furiously.

The next day the photographer delivered the pictures of 'Romeo and Juliet' and she studied them closely.

Mario's face fascinated her. When they had met a few days ago, she'd thought he looked older, harsher, more tense. But in these pictures he had changed again, becoming more like the young man she remembered. She thought she could see a softening in his expression as he looked at Juliet, a glow in his eyes which the camera had caught wonderfully.

She had seen that glow before, two years ago. *He must be a very good actor*, she thought. *But I suppose I knew that.*

She spent some time wandering Verona alone, drinking in the atmosphere with nobody to distract her. She found a street she thought might be the place where Juliet's cousin Tybalt killed Romeo's friend, Mercutio. Just a little further on was where Romeo could have caught up with Tybalt and stabbed him in revenge.

Nearby were two *Comunità* hotels, where she was welcomed eagerly. She looked them over, and jotted down notes in readiness for the next despatch.

There were a dozen places to visit, but she had no energy to explore further today. She had coped with the emotional strains of the last few days, but they had taken their toll. Now she was tired and her head ached a little, so she set off back to the Dimitri Hotel.

It was a relief to get back there, order a coffee and sit in the hotel café. She closed her eyes, unaware that a man was watching her a few yards away, taking in every detail about her: her air of despondency, her appearance of being apart from the world, her loneliness.

Suddenly she looked up and saw him.

'Mario!'

'Hello, Natasha.' He went to sit beside her.

'You're back from Venice then?'

'Yes, I arrived ten minutes ago.'

'Is everything all right with your family?'

'Yes, Sally came through it well and now I've got a niece.'

'Congratulations.'

'Thank you. How are things with you? You look very tired.'

'I've had a busy day, but a very satisfying one.'

'Did anyone go with you, to make sure you didn't get lost?'

'Hey, there's no need to insult me.'

'What?'

'I'm not some silly girl who gets lost every time she's in an unfamiliar street.'

'Sorry, ma'am.'

'I could have asked Giorgio to escort me, but I refused. I can manage.'

He had no doubt of her real meaning. She'd needed time alone, free of the tension that was always there between them. He understood because he felt the same.

'You work too hard,' he said. 'You always did. I remember once before, when we first met in Venice, you said you'd been working so hard that you were exhausted. I took you for a ride in a gondola, and you fell asleep.'

He said it with a smile but she recalled that he hadn't been amused at the time. He was used to taking girls for gondola rides, but not used to them nodding off in his company.

'You took me back to the hotel and said goodnight very firmly,' she recalled, smiling. 'You felt insulted at my behaviour. I always wondered what you did for the rest of the evening, but I expect you found someone else who managed to stay awake.'

'I can't remember,' he said firmly.

'Very tactful.'

They both laughed. He couldn't tell her that he'd spent the rest of that evening alone, brooding about her seeming indifference to his attentions. She had intrigued him, and he'd sought her out early next day.

'That was always the way with you,' he reflected now. 'There, yet not there, keeping me wondering.'

'I didn't do it on purpose,' she said. 'You thought I was being a deliberate tease, but I wasn't. I was wondering too.'

And that had been her attraction for him, he realised. Where other girls were often willing, sometimes too willing, Natasha had always been just out of reach. It had driven him crazy but it had kept him in pursuit of her. Until finally she had vanished, leaving him devastated.

How much had she really felt for him? To this day he didn't know, and he doubted he ever would.

But one thing was certain. She was no longer the tense, nervy creature of a few days ago. The woman who had forced a kiss on him as revenge for his kissing her had simply vanished. Now she was relaxed, in command, humorous, alluring.

'I hear that you've been working hard,' he said. 'You've been contacting the other hotel owners to get information, and showing them what you planned to write so that they could approve it. They're very impressed. My stock has risen considerably since I performed the brilliant act of securing your services.' He gave a theatrical flourish. 'Only a genius like myself could have discovered you.'

'But you didn't discover me. It was Giorgio.'

'Hush. We don't say that.' He grinned. 'And neither does Giorgio if he knows what's good for him.'

'I see. The boss gives his orders and we all jump to obey.'

'Some do. I doubt I'll ever see the day when you jump to obey.'

'But you pay my wages,' she reminded him. 'Surely I have no choice but to obey you?'

'All right, all right. You've had your joke.'

'It's not a joke. You're my employer. I know it's Giorgio who directs me, but you're the authority. If you told him to fire me, he'd have to do so.'

'There's no danger of that.'

'Actually, there's something I've been meaning to say to you.'

'What is it?' he asked with a sense of foreboding, for her tone implied a serious matter. 'Go on, tell me. How bad is it?'

'It's not bad at all. I want to say thank you.'

'Thank you? For what?' he asked, sounding nervous.

'For changing my contract so that I'm making more money. I couldn't believe it when Giorgio showed me the new one and said you'd told him to increase it.'

'But you've already thanked me,' he said. 'You did so a few minutes afterwards. I told you then that it was essential to secure your professional services.'

'Yes, you told me that, but you knew how bad my financial problems were. You could have secured me without raising the money. I think there may have been a little kindness involved too.'

He gave a slight smile. 'Kindness? Me? I'm a businessman. I don't do kindness.'

'I think you do. I can remember things in Venice—that little girl who lost her dog, and you found it for her.'

'I was only trying to impress you.'

'And you succeeded. You don't like people to know about your kind and caring streak but it's there.'

'That's practically an insult.'

'Then you'll have to put up with me insulting you,' she said.

'I think I can just about manage that.'

'The thing is—that quarrel we had the other day, when we'd finished having the pictures taken… It just flared up but I wish it hadn't.'

'So do I. I said things I didn't mean.'

'You said I was afraid to face the truth, that everything could have been different if I'd listened to you. I think you meant that and I don't blame you.'

'But do you believe what I told you—about Tania, how I'd already broken with her?'

'Please—please don't,' she gasped. 'It's in the past. It doesn't matter now.'

'Meaning that you still don't believe me.'

'I don't know,' she said in anguish. 'There are so many things battling each other in my mind—'

'I know the feeling,' he said wryly.

'But it doesn't matter.'

'Natasha, how can it not matter? You always prided yourself on being logical, but if you think what happened between us didn't matter you're talking nonsense.'

'I didn't mean that. It mattered then, but not now. The world has moved on. We've moved on.'

'Ah, yes,' he said quietly. 'We've moved on.'

'And I think we were never meant to be together. Something was always fated to go wrong.'

'Now you sound like Giorgio.'

'What do you mean?'

'Just before you arrived, he and I were talking about Romeo and Juliet being "star-crossed lovers". Sometimes a couple is meant for each other but just can't get it together. They just have to accept that fate is against them.'

'Yes,' she said thoughtfully. 'You could say that fate was against us. My problem was that you had more women in your life than you could count. Or that I could count.'

'And mine was that you don't trust any man. I've always wondered why. Was there some other guy who walked out and broke your heart?'

'In a way, yes, but it's not how you think. The man who walked out was my father.'

She fell silent until he said, 'Tell me about him.'

'I loved him, and he loved me, so I thought. And then he just vanished. I never heard from him again. We seemed to be so close but he just wiped me and my mother out of existence.'

As you did with me, Mario thought, but was too tactful to say.

'My mother was so bitter. She told me a million times that no man could ever be trusted, but she didn't need to say it. I felt it for myself.'

'So when we knew each other you were always reminding yourself that no man could be trusted—especially me.'

'No, not especially you. You mattered more than anyone else but—'

'But you instinctively thought I was no different from the rest of them. Except perhaps a bit worse.'

'No, no—it wasn't like that.'

'From where I'm sitting it was exactly like that.'

'And so you've come close to hating me,' she sighed. 'Perhaps I can't blame you.'

'Please, Natasha, forget I said that. I was in a temper. I wanted to hurt you because I resented the way you'd just shown your power over me. The way you kissed me made a point I didn't want to admit.'

'A point?' Her heart was beating fast.

'You showed me that I'm not the strong, independent fellow I like to believe I am. So I hit back with the worst thing I could think of. I didn't mean it and I'm not proud of it. Do you think you can forgive me?'

'That depends.'

'On what?' he asked cautiously.

'On whether *you* can forgive *me*.'

'There's nothing to forgive.'

'Really? What about the way you say I—?'

'Stop there,' he said quickly. 'Whatever I may have said, I take it back. It's over. It's done with. Let us be friends.'

She considered a moment before smiling and saying wistfully, 'That would be nice.'

'It's settled then.'

'Shake?' She held out her hand, but he fended her off.

'No. We shook hands the first night as professional associates. But now we're friends—and friends don't shake hands. They don't need to.' He leaned over and kissed her cheek. 'That's what friends do. And they buy each other coffee.'

'Good. Waiter!'

'No, I meant that I'd buy you a coffee.'

'Stop giving me orders. I'm buying and that's that.'

'Yes, ma'am. Anything you say, ma'am.'

'Mind you, you'll have to do the talking.'

He nodded, gave the waiter the order in Italian, then watched as she paid.

'Have you explored anywhere recently?' he asked.

'I've looked around a bit, but there's still one big place I've set my heart on visiting and that's Juliet's tomb.

'Now it's a museum,' she said. 'It seems to attract as many tourists as the balcony, so I must go there and plan the next article.'

'There's a *Comunità* hotel nearby,' Mario said. 'The Albergo Martinez. You met the owner the other night. We could dine there tonight and hear anything they have to say. Let me call him.'

He took out his phone, made a call and started talking in Italian. While she was waiting, her own mobile phone beeped. Her heart beat hard with horror when she read the text message.

After a few minutes Mario hung up, saying, 'He's expecting us in a couple of hours.'

He stopped suddenly, frowning as he saw her staring into space, full of tension.

'What is it?' he asked. 'What happened?'

'Nothing.'

'No, something's the matter. What is it?'

'No—no—I'm all right. I'd like to go to my room.'

She got up and walked quickly away. Frowning, he followed her, hurrying until he caught up and could take a firm hold of her hand. She didn't resist but neither did she respond, and he had a feeling that she had taken refuge in another world, from which he was excluded.

He accompanied her as far as her door, noting that she still looked pale and tense.

'I'll collect you in an hour,' he said.

'I'll be ready.'

Once inside, she undressed and got into the shower. There was a kind of relief in being doused with water, as though it could wash away the shock that had overtaken her.

The text on her mobile phone had been from Elroy Jenson:

You won't get away from me.

He's driving me crazy, she told herself. *And that's what he wants.*

She wondered why she hadn't told Mario what had troubled her. It should have been easy since she had already told him about Elroy, and he would have been a valuable ally. But something in her was reluctant to reveal more vulnerability. Especially to Mario.

When she had showered she put on a neat dark blue dress, suitable for a polite gathering. For several minutes she teased her hair, trying to decide whether to be seductive or businesslike. As so often with Mario, her mind was filled with conflicting thoughts.

Their conversation had been fraught with double meanings. He'd said, *I wanted to hurt you because I resented the way you'd just shown your power over me.*

But he'd implied the power of a bully, not of a woman. They had made a truce, but the battle was far from over.

When he'd pressed her to say that she believed him now she had been unable to say what he wanted to hear. She longed to believe him, but she couldn't quite make herself take the final step.

But why should it matter whether I believe him or not? she mused. *That's all over. What matters is that we can manage to be friends.*

Nico was watching for their arrival at the Albergo Martinez and came to meet them with hands outstretched. Natasha recognised him from their meeting the first night.

Over supper he described the tomb.

'Juliet was buried in the church of San Francesco al Corso, a monastery,' he explained.

'Yes, it was Friar Laurence, a monk, who married them,' Natasha recalled. 'On their wedding day they went to his cell and he took them to the church to marry them.'

'True. And when Juliet died—or at least she'd drunk the potion and seemed dead—she was taken to the monastery to be buried. These days the monastery has become a museum. You can go to the crypt and see the sarcophagus that legend says was hers.

'The museum also hosts weddings. Many people choose to become united for life in the place where Romeo and Juliet were united in eternity. Of course, if they are seeking a hotel not too far away—'

'They'll be glad to discover yours,' she said in her most professional manner. 'I shall make sure that they do.'

'*Eccellente!* Mario, you've made a fine discovery in this talented lady. Don't let her go, whatever you do.'

'Don't worry; I won't,' he said with a cheerful nod.

'Now, let us go in to supper.'

Supper was served at a large table where many people were already sitting. As they sat down Natasha became aware of something she had seen many times before. From every direction women were casting admiring glances at Mario. It had been there from the beginning, two years ago. It was still there.

And why not? she thought. *He's got the looks to make it happen. And it doesn't bother me any more.*

She soon discovered that the man sitting next to her was an ideal choice. His name was Tonio and he was an academic, specialising in English history. As history had always been one of her interests, she was soon deep in conversation with him, intrigued by his prejudiced arguments.

'You're all wrong about Richard III,' she told him. 'Shakespeare depicted him as a monster but he wasn't really—'

'You English!' he exclaimed. 'You can never believe that any of your monarchs were evil.'

'On the contrary, the evil ones are the most fun. But Richard's evil reputation is mostly a kind of show business.'

'I've studied the evidence and I tell you—'

Heads close together, they stayed absorbed in their argument, with the rest of the table regarding them with amused fascination. All except Mario, who was looking displeased, which surprised Natasha when she happened to glance up. The luscious beauty beside him was paying him fervent attention that a man might be expected to enjoy. But he seemed to be tolerating rather than encouraging her.

'I see Bianca's got her claws into a new man,' said Tonio, sounding amused.

'You speak as though it happens often.'

'With Bianca it does. She likes to cast her net wide.'

'It doesn't look as though he's fallen under her spell.'

'Not now, but give him a little time.'

Bianca was clearly a practised flirt, convinced that any man was hers for the asking. When she patted Mario's face, giggling, he smiled back politely before returning his gaze to Natasha.

'You need to look at it like this,' Tonio said, returning to their discussion. 'King Richard couldn't possibly—'

She plunged back into the argument, enjoying herself for the next half hour, until somebody put on some music and people began to dance. Suddenly Mario appeared by her chair.

'Dance with me,' he said.

'Wouldn't you rather dance with Bianca?'

'No.' He grasped her hand, drew her to her feet and onto the floor.

'I thought you were having a lovely time.' She laughed as they twirled.

'Did you really?' he demanded ironically.

'Being hunted down by a woman who'd gladly have given you anything you wanted.'

'Which would be fine if there was anything I did want from her. But I don't.'

'That wouldn't stop some men. They'd just take anything that's going.'

'I was like that once, when I was young and stupid. I grew up in the end, but by then it was too late.'

He said the last words with a wry look. The next moment the temptress glided past them. She was dancing with another man, but even so she gave Mario a glance that made him tighten his grasp on Natasha.

'Rescue me,' he growled.

'How?'

'Anyhow.'

'All right. Here goes. Aaaargh!'

With a theatrical sigh, she drooped against his chest.

'Oh, how my head aches,' she declared. 'I really must go home.'

'I'll take you,' he said.

Turning to their host, he explained that it was necessary to take Natasha away at once.

'She isn't feeling well,' he said. 'She must go to bed.'

From somewhere came the sound of choking laughter. Mario ignored it and picked Natasha up to carry her from the room. He didn't set her down until they reached the car.

'Thank you,' he said as they drove away.

'No problem. I'm really glad to leave because I need some sleep. Of course, if you want to go back and spend time with Bianca—'

'If that's your idea of a joke, it's not funny,' he said in an edgy voice.

'Sorry, I couldn't resist it.'

'Perhaps you should try to resist it. I'm just a sitting duck as far as you're concerned.'

'All right, I apologise.'

'It was getting very difficult in there.'

'You know what they're all thinking now, don't you?' she chuckled.

'Yes, they think that when we get home we're going to— Well, you can imagine.'

'Yes, I can imagine.'

'And I'm sorry. But that woman was getting embarrassing.'

'Don't tell me you're afraid of her. You? A man who's afraid of nothing.'

'You'd be surprised at some of the things I'm afraid of,' he said. 'Once you were one of them. Now you're beginning to feel like the best friend I have.'

'Good. Then we have nothing left to worry about...'

CHAPTER SEVEN

NEXT MORNING THEY drove to the monastery museum and went down into the crypt, where several other tourists had already gathered, looking at a large marble sarcophagus.

It was open at the top, revealing that it was empty now, but legend said that this was where Juliet had lain after taking the drug that made her appear lifeless. Here, Romeo had come to find her and, believing her dead, had taken his own life, minutes before she awoke. Finding him dead, she had taken her own life.

'I just don't understand it,' said an elderly man, staring into the sarcophagus. 'How could two people so young take their own lives?'

'Maybe they didn't,' said one of his companions. 'Maybe that's an invention of the story.'

'No,' Natasha said. 'It's part of the story because it was inevitable. It's what you do if life has lost all meaning.'

'And that can happen at any age,' Mario said at once.

'No,' the old man said. 'They could have got over each other and found other lovers.'

'But they didn't believe that,' Mario pointed out.

'Youngsters never do,' the man said loftily. 'But when they get older they find out that nothing ever really matters that much. Love comes and goes and comes again. It's ridiculous to believe anyone discovers the full meaning of their life as young as that.'

'No,' Mario said. 'It's ridiculous to believe that such a discovery happens to a timetable. It happens when it's ready to happen. Not before and not after.'

The old man looked at him with interest. 'You sound like an expert, sir.'

'I guess we're all experts, one way or another,' Mario said.

There were some murmurs of agreement from the little crowd as they turned away, following their tourist guide to another part of the museum.

Now that they were alone, Mario watched as Natasha looked into the sarcophagus.

'They married and had one sweet night together,' she murmured. 'But when they finally lay together it was here.'

'They lie together and they always will,' Mario said.

She turned a smiling face on him. 'You know what you've done, don't you?'

'What have I done?'

'Given me a wonderful idea that I can develop for the piece I'm writing. "They lie together and they always will." Thank you.'

He made an ironic gesture. 'Glad to be of use.'

'Would you mind leaving me alone here for a while? I just want to—' She looked around her, taking a deep breath, her arms extended.

She just wanted to absorb a romantic atmosphere without being troubled by his presence, he thought. A dreary inconvenience. That was how she saw him now.

True, she had kissed him, but in anger, not in love or

desire. And hell would freeze over before he let her suspect the depth of her triumph.

He stepped aside to a place in the shadows. From here he saw her stare down again into the tomb, reaching out into the empty space inside. What did she see in that space? Romeo, lying there, waiting for her to join him? Or Romeo and Juliet, sleeping eternally, clasped in each other's arms, held against each other's hearts?

Whatever it was, she had not invited him to be with her, because in her heart she was certain that he had left the dream behind long ago. If he had ever believed in it.

If only there was some magic spell that could enable her to look into his heart and see the truth he had carried there ever since their first meeting. Might she then look at him with eyes as fervent and glowing as she had done once, long, long ago?

He stayed watching her for a while, expecting that any moment she would move away. But she seemed transfixed, and at last he went to her.

'Are you all right?' he asked. 'You seem almost troubled.'

'No, I'm not troubled. It's just the atmosphere here, and what this tomb represents.'

'Surely it just represents death?'

'No, there's more. Finality, fulfilment, completion. They were young; they could have gone on and had lives that would have seemed satisfying. But each meant more to the other than life itself. You put it perfectly when you said people can discover what really matters while they're still young, and then they lie together for ever. This—' she looked around at the walls of the tomb '—this says everything.'

'I think we should go now,' he said. Her fascination with the place was making him uneasy.

'Yes, I've done all I need to do here. I'll spend this evening working on it. Then I'll do a new article and send it around the *Comunità*, so they can tell me what they think. I'm sure their suggestions will be useful.'

'I see you've got all the boxes ticked.'

'I hope so. That's what you're paying me for. Shall we go? We're finished here, aren't we?'

'Oh, yes,' he agreed. 'We're finished here.'

No more was said on the way back to the hotel.

Once there, Natasha hurried up to her room to get to work. She had supper served to her there and did not go downstairs all evening. She needed to be alone to think about the day. Mario's observations at the tomb had left her wondering. The old man had said he sounded like an expert about love. Mario had replied, *We're all experts, one way or another.*

One way or another. Love might be a joy or a betrayal. Which had he meant?

But I don't need to ask that, she thought. *He feels betrayed, just as I do. But how is that possible? Can we have both betrayed each other?*

He'd accused her of refusing to listen to him because she feared the truth, feared to confront her own part in their break-up. She had denied it, but could there possibly be a grain of truth in it?

Surely not, she thought. It couldn't have turned out any differently. Could it?

She had felt her own pain so intensely, but now she was confronted by his pain and it was a bewildering experience.

We'll never understand each other, she thought. *I mustn't hope for too much. Or do I mean fear too much?*

She gave herself a mental shake.

That's enough. I'm here to work and when I've finished my job I'll leave, whatever he says or does.

But the next day everything changed.

In the morning she went exploring again, wandering Verona on foot until, in the afternoon, she reached Juliet's house. There, she looked around the courtyard, meaning to go inside and see the museum.

But something drew her to Juliet's statue, still standing as it had been before, gazing into the distance.

If only, she thought, she could indulge the fantasy of asking Juliet's advice, and imagining an answer. It might help sort out the confusion in her head and her heart.

She didn't know how Mario felt, or how she herself felt. When he had kissed her she'd wanted him so much that it scared her. So she had punished him with a kiss designed to show him what he'd lost. But she too had been reminded of what she'd lost.

Into her mind came Mario's face, looking as he had at the start of the photo shoot. His expression had been—she struggled for the words—cautious, perhaps a little nervous.

She had blamed him for kissing her, thinking him too confident and self-satisfied. But did she blame him too much? Had he been uneasy, secretly wanting the kiss but unsure of himself?

I know how that feels, she brooded. *In my heart I wanted him to kiss me. Perhaps that's why I was so angry when he did.*

She sighed and turned away. Then she stopped, tense.

Mario was standing there, watching her.

'I happened to see you in the street,' he said, 'so I took the liberty of following you. Have you been inside the house?'

'No, I was about to go in.'

'Let's go in together.'

Inside, they looked briefly around the sixteenth-century furniture, absorbing the perfect atmosphere for the legend. Then they climbed the stairs and stepped out onto the balcony.

A young couple was already there, wrapped in each other's arms.

'Sorry,' the girl said, moving aside. 'We just had to come and see it again. We're getting married here next week and all the pictures will be taken out on the balcony.'

'How lovely,' Natasha said. 'The perfect place.'

'We thought so.' They kissed and slipped away into the building.

How lucky they were, she thought, to be so sure of each other, of life, of the future.

Now the light was fading, and there were few visitors. It was easy to imagine herself as Juliet, standing there looking into the night sky, unaware that Romeo was down below, watching her.

'I wonder what it was like for her,' she mused, 'to stand here, dreaming of him, then finally realising he was there, seeing him watching her, not knowing that their love was fated.'

Before he could answer, there was a shrill from her mobile phone. But she ignored it.

'Aren't you going to answer that?' Mario asked.

'No, it can wait,' she said in a tense voice. 'I didn't mean to bring it with me. I don't want to be distracted.'

The phone shrilled again.

'Answer it,' Mario said. 'Get rid of them.'

Reluctantly, she pulled out the phone and answered.

'At last,' said the voice she dreaded.

'You again,' she snapped. 'Stop pestering me.'

'Stop telling me what to do,' said Jenson's voice. 'If I want to call you I shall. Who do you think you are to give me orders?'

'Who do I think I am? I'm the woman who told you to go and jump in the lake. I'm the woman who wants nothing to do with a man as disgusting as you. You should have realised that by now.'

From the other end of the line came a crack of laughter.

'No, you're the one who should have woken up to reality, you stupid tart. You don't know what I could do to you—'

'I think I do. You've made it brutally clear.'

'That was just the start. You don't know how sorry I can make you, but you're going to find out. I know something about you, Natasha, and by the time I've finished you're going to wish you'd treated me with more respect.'

Before she could reply, the phone was wrenched from her hand by Mario.

'Jenson,' he snapped. 'Go to hell. Leave her alone or I'll make you sorry.'

A bellow of ugly laughter reached him down the line.

'Not as sorry as you'll be if you're involved with Natasha,' Jenson bawled. 'She's made herself my enemy, and if you side with her you'll be my enemy too. I have a way with enemies.'

With a swift movement Mario severed the connection. 'Jenson's still pestering you?'

'Yes, he won't stop.' She was shaking.

'All right, let's deal with this,' Mario said. He put his arms around her firmly, protectively. 'Come on, we're going back to the hotel.'

Still holding her, he led her back to his car. She almost collapsed into the seat beside him and sat with her head in her hands during the drive. To his relief, there was almost nobody in the hotel lobby and he was able to take her upstairs quickly. As soon as the door closed behind them he clasped her once more in his arms.

'It's all right,' he said fiercely. 'There's nothing to be scared of. You're safe here. Jenson is in the past.'

'No, he's not,' she groaned. 'As long as he can reach me he's not in the past. Changing my number is useless. He always finds out my new one. That's how powerful he is. I'm scared. He haunts me. When I get a text or a call from him it's as though he's actually there. He's already ruined my career, and I can't be rid of him.'

'You're wrong,' Mario said. 'He hasn't ruined your career, and he isn't going to because I'm not going to let him.'

She took some deep breaths, managing to calm down a little. Mario touched her chin, lifting it so that he could see her face. For a moment he was tempted to give her a gentle kiss, by way of comfort. But, instead, he took her to the bed, still holding her as she sat down, then drawing her head against him again.

'Thank goodness you were there,' she said. 'I couldn't have coped alone.'

'I know you couldn't,' he said morosely. 'That's why I grabbed your phone in a way you must have thought rather rude. If something threatens me I like to know how serious it is.'

'But he's not threatening you.'

'Anything that threatens you threatens me. I told you—I'll deal with it.'

'Thank you.' She clung to him. 'It's lucky it was only a phone call. If he'd turned up in person I think I'd have done something violent, perhaps strangled him.' She made a wry face. 'You're right in what you've always said about my nasty temper.'

'I've never said it was a nasty temper,' he disclaimed at once. 'It's a quick temper. Act first, think later.'

'By which time it's too late to think,' she sighed.

He didn't reply, merely tightened his arms about her.

'It's been a curse all my life,' she said. 'My mother used to say I'd come to a bad end. According to her, I got my temper from my father, and I never heard her say a good word about him.'

'You mentioned him the other day. Didn't they split up?'

'He left her when I was only ten. Just walked out and vanished. It broke my heart. Until then I'd had a wonderful relationship with my father. I was the apple of his eye. But he left my mother for another woman and I never heard from him again.'

'Never? Are you sure your mother didn't keep you apart?'

'No, he didn't write or call. I used to watch the mail arrive and there was never anything from him. I tried telephoning him but he'd changed his number.'

He didn't reply. She waited for him to remind her how she'd done the same thing, but he only hugged her closer.

'You should put all that behind you,' he murmured.

'The past is gone, but you must make sure it *is* the past. Don't let it haunt your life, or it will control you.'

'You sound as though you really know,' she said.

'In a way I do. At one time I owed so much to Damiano that the need to get free and grow up became the most important thing in my life.'

'Grow up?'

'I took a long time to get to that stage.'

That was true, she thought, remembering him two years ago. Now he was so much stronger and more serious that he was almost a different man.

'"Haunt your life",' she murmured. 'My mother never got over him abandoning us. She told me again and again that you could never trust a man.'

'And her words have stayed with you always,' he said softly.

'Not just her words. It was also the way he cut me out of his life, after I'd seemed to mean so much to him. I'd believed in his love, but it meant nothing.'

Mario uttered a soft curse. 'I wish I had him here so that I could sock him in the jaw,' he said. 'But don't let your father—or Elroy Jenson—destroy your life, Natasha. Banish them into the past, turn your back and become the person you really are.'

'Too late,' she sighed.

'It's never too late if it's what you really want.'

She would have given anything to see his face as he uttered those words, but her head was pressed against his shoulder.

'Never too late,' she echoed, resting against him. A feeling of sleepy contentment was overtaking her, and she could have happily stayed like this for ever.

Mario sensed the moment when she began to doze.

He tightened his arms about her, laying his lips against her hair, feeling an unfamiliar warmth go through him. He wanted to hold her close, but not in the hope of making love with her, only to keep her safe.

It was a feeling he'd never known before. When they had first met she had seemed strong, full of confidence, able to challenge the world and emerge victorious.

He found his mind drifting back to his own past. Since the day he'd first begun flirting with girlfriends he had never been attracted by commitment. His girlfriends had all been strong, independent, fancying him but not needing him.

Immature, he thought now wryly. *Boy, was I immature.*

Four years earlier he'd met Sally, the woman who had married his brother, Damiano. His feelings for her had grown so deep that he'd fled their home in Venice for safety's sake.

Later, he'd felt safe enough to return occasionally. His interest in the hotel business had grown. Damiano had been an excellent teacher and Mario's talent had flourished until he could manage to buy and run his own hotel. But he'd remained a playboy, dancing from girl to girl, never choosing anyone who might seriously need him.

Now he realised how much things had changed. Natasha's sadness had touched his heart. She was alone and vulnerable, and the knowledge affected him strongly. The torment he'd endured when she'd deserted him had begun to fade, overwhelmed by her need. She needed a friend to be strong for her, and something told him that he should be that person because without him she had nobody. He tightened his arms, trying to send her a silent message of reassurance. Her breathing was steady and, although he couldn't see her face, he guessed she was still dozing.

Probably just as well that they couldn't talk, he thought. Words could be a trap, especially for a man like himself, with little verbal skill. He preferred to be judged by his actions rather than his words.

Since the day she'd arrived he knew he'd been clumsy, confused. The feeling had been increased by the suspicion that she enjoyed confusing him. He'd fought back, making matters worse, he now realised. But now he knew that his own feelings didn't matter. He only wanted her to feel safe.

He eased her down onto the bed. Her head drooped to one side and her eyes were closed, as though she'd slipped away from him into another world. And yet she was still with him.

And she always would be, he resolved. He'd lost her once. He couldn't bear to lose her again. He knew he had to keep her, but for the moment he must be silent about his decision. They had far to travel before things could be said openly between them.

Moving carefully, he lay down beside her, still holding her so that her head rested against him. For a while she was still, but then her arm moved, drifting slowly across his chest as though seeking him, his help and comfort.

For a moment he thought that she might awaken and he could say some of the things in his heart. But then she grew still again, and he knew she'd slipped back into another world. One where he did not exist, he realised. Did he exist for her at all?

He looked closely into her face, hoping to read in it

some hint of an answer, but she was fast asleep. Their time would come, but for now he knew he must be patient. He closed his eyes.

In the early morning light Natasha opened her eyes to find herself in a strange world, one where her head rested against Mario and his arms enfolded her protectively.

At once she knew it was a dream. It could be nothing else.

'All right?' asked his gentle voice. 'Are you awake at last?'

'Am I—what—what am I—?'

Mario saw the dismay come into her eyes as she realised that she was lying in his arms.

'You've had a good night's sleep,' he said. 'So have I.'

'What happened? How did we—?'

'How did we end up lying together? You got a call from Jenson and it scared you. You were so upset that it seemed best not to leave you alone, so I came in here and stayed with you. But don't worry. I was just being a friend. I haven't done anything I shouldn't.'

She knew at once that it was true. Her flesh was calm and rested in a way that wouldn't have been true if he'd touched her sexually. He had merely held her gently, comfortingly in his arms, thinking only of her welfare.

'Truly,' he said. 'Stop worrying.'

'I'm not worried. I'm just glad you're here.'

'Glad?' he echoed. 'Really glad?'

'Of course. How could I not be? You said you'd keep me safe and you did. Oh, if I could only tell you how good that feels.'

'If that's what you want, that's all that matters,' he said.

Her eyes glowed and he became tense. Desire was

growing in him. He wanted to kiss her smiling mouth, caress her warm body, feel her come to new life in his arms. But he had just reassured her that he had no such temptations, and her reaction left no doubt that this was what she wanted to hear.

He wanted her, but she didn't want him in the same way. That was what he had to accept. It was all he could do for her.

She stirred in his arms and he loosened his hold, thinking she was trying to move away from him. But she turned more towards him, closing her eyes again, sliding an arm around his body and murmuring, *'Mmm!'* as though she had discovered blissful contentment.

And that was what he brought her, he reflected. It was a kind of happiness, and better than the anguish of their first encounter, days ago.

'But there could be more,' he whispered softly into her ear.

'Mmm?'

'If we're patient, there could be more between us, surely? We could take it slowly, and then—maybe—'

'Maybe what?' she murmured.

'I know we still have things to put behind us, and it won't be easy. You didn't treat me kindly, vanishing like that, but, after the way your father behaved, I guess you don't trust any of us. And I hurt you but I didn't mean to. If only you could bring yourself to believe me about that. But you will. One day I just know you will, and then everything will be wonderful.'

'Mmm.'

He gave a gentle laugh. 'I wonder what "Mmm" actually means.'

She met his eyes. 'If I knew—I'd tell you.'

'No, you wouldn't. You enjoy keeping me guessing. All right. I'll play your game because the prize we could win is worth everything.'

'Yes,' she whispered. 'But will we win it?'

'Who knows?' he said. 'We *will* know. We must. But not just yet. Something will happen. It will make everything clear—soon—soon.'

'I guess you understand more than I do. You'll tell me when the time comes—whenever that is.'

She smiled at him in a way that filled him with hope.

CHAPTER EIGHT

'I'LL LEAVE YOU now so you can get some more sleep,' Mario said. 'See you in the morning.'

He fled from the room, downstairs and out into the garden. It was just becoming light and he went to the river, where he could lean over the wall and stare into the water, brooding.

It felt wonderful to have achieved a brief emotional contact with her, but he wondered how completely she understood him. He'd spoken of his hopes for the future, but were they any more than fantasies? She had said that something would happen. But when? How long must they wait to be sure?

He looked back at the building, where he could identify her room from the faint light that still glowed inside. As he watched, the floor-length window opened and she came out onto the balcony.

He backed away into the shadows so that she wouldn't see him, but she didn't even look down. She stood motionless, her eyes turned up to the heavens as though she could find the answer to a mystery in that distant place.

Watching her on the balcony, he thought that this must have been how it was for Romeo, seeing his beloved standing there above him.

On the night she'd arrived he'd gone to stand beneath her window, looking up, longing to see her. And there she had been, reaching out into the night, her body full of anguish, speaking words he had strained to hear. Then she'd gone inside again, leaving him standing alone in the darkness, struggling to come to terms with his conflicting feelings.

Now, here he was again, watching Natasha from a distance, condemned perhaps to be always at a distance, unable to voice his emotions openly.

Romeo's words came into his head. *It is my lady, Oh, it is my love! Oh, that she knew she were!*

'Yes,' he murmured. 'It is my love. Oh, that she knew she were.'

She does know, argued a voice in his head. *You've made it very clear.*

But does she want to know? queried another voice. *Is she ready to accept?*

Her voice was still there in his mind, asking if they would win the prize. That alarmed him, as it meant she could envisage a future apart. The way ahead was still strewn with doubts and problems, and who knew what the answers would be? Or if there would be any answers?

Romeo had reached out from beneath Juliet's balcony, letting her know he was there, telling her of his feelings. But Mario knew that path wasn't open to him at this moment.

Slowly he backed away, retreating deep into the shadows, never taking his eyes off her.

For a while, she stayed looking up into the sky, but then she lowered her head and wrapped her arms about herself, leaning against the wall. Her demeanour suggested confusion, sadness. Mario drew in his breath sharply. He'd tried to ease those feelings in her, and had briefly thought he'd succeeded. But she was still lonely, still vulnerable, and the sight hurt him.

Once he could have reached out to console her openly, revealing everything in his heart, inviting her in, rejoicing in the unity they had seemed to share.

But that unity had been an illusion, with traps along the way, ready to bring them both down. She needed him. He felt this as he had never felt it before, and the longing to fulfil her need was taking him over, heart and soul. But her feelings for him, whatever they might be, were undermined by a caution that barred her from believing that she was his love.

'Oh, that she knew she were,' he whispered again. 'Oh, that I could convince her.'

He slipped quietly away for fear that she might see him.

Inside the hotel, he found Giorgio waiting for him in a state of agitation.

'You were right about her all along,' he said.

'Right about who?'

'Her. Natasha Bates. You suspected something troubling about her as soon as she arrived. You said you hadn't met her before but it was obvious you guessed what a suspicious character she was. And she knew that you sensed it. That's why she's so edgy when you're around.'

'What the devil are you talking about?' Mario snapped.

'We've received an email about Natasha that you must see. It's from Jenson Publications.'

'Show me.'

The email was blunt and vicious:

You should be warned about your employee, Natasha Bates. She's well known in the media business for her dishonesty and inefficiency. If you are wise you will dismiss her at once.

There was no name attached. The missive merely came from the Jenson Publications head office.

'He didn't dare put his name to it,' Mario growled. 'But this comes from Elroy Jenson, a miserable, scheming bastard who I'll strangle if I ever get my hands on him.'

'But suppose it's true,' Giorgio argued. 'You've always sensed that she was dodgy.'

'Don't you dare say that,' Mario raged. 'None of this is true and if I ever hear you say such a thing again I'll make you sorry.'

'All right, all right,' Giorgio said, hastily backing off, alarmed by the look in Mario's eyes. 'My lips are sealed.'

'Don't say it and don't even think it,' Mario snapped. 'Understand?'

'Understand,' Giorgio said. 'Sorry. It just hadn't occurred to me.'

'Yes, there are a lot of things that hadn't occurred to me either,' Mario sighed. 'But when they do occur—well, you just have to face them. This email is a pack of lies. Jenson came on to her, she rejected him and now he's out to destroy her out of spite.'

Giorgio nodded as comprehension came to him. 'So you're on her side?'

'Yes,' Mario said slowly. 'I'm on her side.'

In the past few days he'd felt a desire to care for Natasha, but those moments were nothing compared to the storm of protectiveness that invaded him now. If Jenson had been there in person he would have throttled him without compunction.

'Don't tell her about this,' he instructed Giorgio. 'He's trying to scare her and I won't have it.'

'But shouldn't we warn her? She should know she's got an enemy.'

'She already knows. But she also has us, and we're going to take care of her. Not a word. I don't want her upset.'

She had every reason to be upset, he realised. Elroy Jenson might not be following her physically, but he was after her in a far more dangerous way. Through stretching out his tentacles of power across the world, he thought he could still make her suffer for defying him.

But he was wrong, Mario thought angrily. Now Natasha had him to defend her and he would do so, whatever it cost him.

'She mustn't suspect anything,' he said to Giorgio.

'If you say so.' Giorgio sighed reluctantly. 'But can we fend this man off?'

'We can and we will. She's going to be safe.' His face became set. 'I've promised her that and I'm going to keep my word.'

Turning back into her room from the balcony, Natasha returned to the bed and lay down. She had a strange yet pleasant feeling that Mario was still with her, whispering reassurances in her mind, or merely tightening his arms protectively around her, so that she understood.

But was that what he'd meant, or was she just listening to her own hopes? She was still wondering as she fell asleep.

She awoke feeling refreshed, eager to get up and face the day.

As soon as she swung her legs out of bed she knew something was wrong. The carpet beneath her feet was wet. Looking further, she found that the water came from the bathroom and covered most of the floor.

'Oh, heavens, I must have left a tap on!' she exclaimed in dismay.

But when exploring the bathroom she discovered not a tap but a leaking pipe, spilling water directly onto the floor.

Hastily, she called Mario and explained that she'd need a plumber. He arrived a few minutes later and swore when he saw the extent of the damage.

'This must be fixed quickly before it sinks through the floor,' he said. 'Pack your things and get out of here fast. I'll arrange another room for you.'

She was packed and finished in half an hour, glad to escape and leave the room to the plumbers who'd arrived. She found Mario waiting for her downstairs with a table laid for breakfast.

'There's a bit of a problem,' he said. 'It's high season and every room in the place is taken.'

'So I'll find a room somewhere else.'

'Certainly not. I have an apartment upstairs that you can have. I don't sleep there so the bed is free. You can relax in peace.'

'And do some work,' she said, gathering up her laptop.

His apartment was mainly a place of storage, filled with shelves and filing cabinets. She arrived to find a maid making up the bed.

'It's all yours,' Mario said. 'I'll leave you to it. Goodbye for now.'

She worked contentedly, sending her material to a dozen different sources. Then she felt the need for a short break, and crossed the room to switch on the television. But on the way her heel tangled in the carpet and she pitched forward. Reaching out, she grabbed hold of some small shelves, which promptly disgorged their contents onto the floor. With an exclamation, she dropped down and began gathering them up.

Then she stopped suddenly, as though something had grabbed her in a vice. An envelope had opened, spilling out several sheets of pale blue notepaper. On one of them she saw what was written at the bottom: *Your loving Tania.*

Her whole being was consumed by a silent howl of anguish. Tania was still communicating with Mario. After all his promises, his assurances that he had broken with her, that she meant nothing to him, the truth was that he had been in contact with her.

When she thought of how close she had come to trusting him she wanted to bang her head against the wall.

'Fool!' she murmured. 'Fool! You were so wise in the beginning. You should have listened to your suspicions.'

Was he still in touch with her? Or was it an old letter? If so, why had he kept it so long?

Because he's still involved with her, she told herself. *He's been lying all this time.*

With frenzied hands she pulled the letter open and began to read it. As she read she grew still. When she got to the end she went back and read it again. And then again, trying to believe the incredible words Tania had written.

Don't keep me at a distance. I know you told me it was over because you wanted to be with that Eng-

lish girl, but look what she did when she found out about me. She wouldn't have vanished if she'd really loved you. I thought you'd realise that and come back to me. Why won't you take my calls or answer my emails?

Don't keep rejecting me, Mario. Natasha can't possibly mean that much to you.

Your loving Tania

She read it again, murmuring the words aloud, as though in this way she could manage to convince herself that they were real.

Everything Mario had told her was true. He had broken with Tania, as he'd vowed. She had refused to accept it and kept hounding him, but it seemed that nothing would make him take her back.

'I should have believed you,' she whispered. 'Oh, my love, I should have trusted you. But why didn't you show me this? Then I would have known the truth.'

She noticed that the letter was written in English, and remembered how Tania had spoken mostly in English with the odd Italian word thrown in. Doubtless, English was her native language, and perhaps her closeness to Mario had helped his mastery of English.

Which is lucky, she thought. *If Tania had written in Italian I couldn't have understood, and I wouldn't have missed this for the world.*

A noise outside warned her that Mario was coming. Swiftly she gathered up the papers and thrust them back onto the shelf, except for the Tania letter, which she thrust into her pocket. She would want to read that again, many times.

Natasha was back in front of the computer when he came in.

'Did you manage to sort the plumbing problem?' shc asked.

'Yes, it's all taken care of. It'll be a couple of days before you can move back in but, thanks to you, I was alerted in time to avoid total disaster. How are you getting on?'

'I've managed to do quite a lot of work. Now I feel like taking the evening off. I think I'll have a stroll by the river.'

'Am I allowed to come with you?'

'Why not?'

It was a joy to have his company now that she could see him in a new light. All the pain and tension of the past two years had vanished, leaving only happiness and hope.

The light was fading as they left the building and crossed the street to the river. IIc slipped his arm around her shoulders, and she stretched hers about his waist. Clinging together, they strolled along the bank until they reached a café by the water, and he indicated for her to sit down. Waving a waiter over, Mario spoke to him quickly in Italian and moments later the waiter returned with a bottle of wine.

'I have a reason for bringing you here,' Mario said. 'This place buys all its wine from a shop that stocks products from my vineyard.'

'The best, naturally,' she said.

'Naturally. Everyone knows about Verona's romantic reputation, but its fame as a great wine centre tends to get blocked out.'

'I've been reading a little about it recently,' she said.

'There are wine tours, aren't there? We might do a little publicity for them too.'

'Good idea. You can turn your talents on to Vinitaly. That's a wine festival that happens every year in spring.' He grinned. 'There's a lot more to Verona than you think.'

'I'm sure there is. I look forward to discovering all its secrets.'

He raised his glass to her, saying, *'Ti vol un altro goto de vin?'*

'Is that Venetian?'

'You know about Venetian?'

'Giorgio told me. The more I know, the better.'

'It means would you like some more wine?'

'Yes, please. It's delicious.'

She sipped the wine, enjoying its excellent taste and the feeling that things might be going well at last.

He watched her, wondering at the smile on her face, unwilling to ask about it. There might be more pleasure in wondering.

When at last they rose and walked on he put an arm around her shoulder, saying, 'Are you all right? Not too cold?'

'I'm all right,' she said, looking up. 'Not too cold, not too anything. Everything's perfect.'

He gave a soft chuckle. 'Does that mean I haven't offended you recently?'

She looked up at him teasingly. 'Not that I can think of.'

'You can usually think of something.'

They smiled and moved on.

She barely noticed where they were going. It was like being in a new world. Nothing was the same. His voice had a note of warmth that she had never noticed before, and his eyes held a gleam that promised much.

'It's lovely out here,' she sighed.

'Yes,' he murmured in her ear. 'It's lovely, and you're lovely.'

'You have to feel sorry for Romeo and Juliet, who could never take this kind of walk, just enjoying being together and letting the world drift by.'

'I guess we're luckier than they were.'

She turned to look up into his face. 'Yes,' she said. 'We're lucky. We were always lucky, if only we'd known it.'

His fingertips brushed her face gently. 'I always knew it,' he said. 'Now I know it even more since I had to endure life without you. I thought I'd never see you again, and the future was nothing but a terrible blank. But then you were there again and I had my life back. Suddenly, there was something to hope for.'

'Yes, for me too,' she said. 'But sometimes I can be afraid to hope.'

'Better not to hope at all, than hope and have it destroyed,' he said.

'No, I don't believe that. Wonderful things can happen when you least expect it. You have to be ready for the best as well as the worst, and then— Oh, Mario, Mario!'

She was silenced by his mouth over hers.

'Be mine,' he whispered. 'Tell me that you're mine.'

'I always was. I always will be.'

'Do you really mean that?'

'Yes—yes—'

'Say it again. Make me believe it.'

'I'm yours—all yours—yours—'

'For ever. I won't let you go. I warn you, I'm possessive.'

'You couldn't be too possessive for me,' she assured him.

His answer was another kiss which she returned with fervour.

A group of young people passed by, cheering and clapping at the sight of them.

'It's too public out here,' she said.

'Yes, let's go home.'

They slipped back into the hotel without being seen. She was glad. What was happening now was for them alone.

He came with her as far as the apartment, then stopped at the door, regarding her uncertainly.

'Don't go,' she said, holding him in a gentle but determined hug. 'Stay with me.'

'Natasha, do you mean that?'

'Yes, I mean it.'

'But don't you realise that—if I stay—no, you don't realise. I mustn't stay.'

'Yes, you must,' she whispered. 'I say you must, and I won't let you refuse me.'

It hurt her to see how tense and vulnerable he seemed. After all the hostility that had simmered between them he couldn't believe that she was really opening her arms to him; even perhaps opening her heart. It was what he wanted but something he couldn't dare believe too easily, and she longed to reach out from her heart and reassure him.

'Trust me,' she murmured. 'Things move on. Nothing stays the same for ever.'

'Are you telling me that something really has changed?' he asked.

'In a way. I've learned to be more understanding. I was always so sure I was right, but now—now I feel like a different person. I have so much still to learn.'

She took a step back through the door, holding out her hand.

'Come in,' she said. 'Come with me—stay with me.'

He still could not understand her, but he put his hand in hers and followed her in perfect trust.

'Yes,' he said. 'Take me with you. Let me stay.'

His mouth was on hers, making her rejoice with heart, mind and body equally. There was pleasure but there was also a fierce possessiveness. She wanted him and she was determined to have him. She had waited as long as she could endure and now she was determined to enjoy her conquest.

With the door safely closed against the outside world, Mario felt able to yield to his longing and take her in his arms. Yet doubts and confusion still whirled about him.

'I don't believe this is happening,' he whispered. 'I've dreamed of it so often, so hopelessly.'

'Not hopelessly,' she told him. 'I've dreamed too. Dreams can come true. Let us believe that.'

'Yes, while I have you in my arms I can believe it.'

She drew his head down, kissing him with fervour and passion, rejoicing in his response. Gradually he began to move towards the bed, easing her down onto it so that they lay together. When she felt him start to undo her clothes she was there before him, pulling open buttons, inviting him to explore her.

He accepted the invitation, tentatively at first, caressing her gently, almost uncertainly. But as his hands discovered the soft smoothness of her skin their touch became more fervent, more intense, sending tremors through her. She reached out to him, now working on his buttons so that his shirt fell open and she could explore him in her turn.

Once, long ago in Venice, she had dreamed of this. But fate had denied her dream, banishing her into a wilderness where there was no love, no hope, no Mario.

Now, at last, the moment had come and it was everything she'd wanted. His caress was tentative, almost as though he feared to touch her.

She understood. In the depths of her heart joy was warring with disbelief, scared that this might not really be true, that she would wake to find it a delusion. And it was the same with him. Instinct too deep for thought told her this was true. After so long their hearts and minds were as one, just as their bodies would soon unite.

He laid his face against her. She drew him closer, wanting this moment to last.

'Yes,' she murmured. 'Yes.'

'Yes,' he echoed. 'Natasha—are you sure?'

'I'm sure of everything—sure that I want you—'

He gave a faint smile. 'Are you sure I want you? Or shall I try to convince you?'

'I don't need convincing.' She returned his smile in full measure. 'But don't let me stop you.'

'Whatever you please, ma'am,' he murmured, intensifying his caresses.

Her pleasure rioted, but more than pleasure was the joy of knowing that they were close again. The man she had loved long ago had been stolen from her, but now she had him back. And she would never let him go again. The world might turn upside down. The heavens might fall, the seas overflow, but she would never release him from her arms and her heart. On that she was resolved.

He worked eagerly on her clothes until nothing was left. Then he removed his own garments and they were naked together. He took her into his arms, kissing her mouth, her face, her neck, then going lower to smother her breasts in kisses. She took long breaths of delight at the storm growing within her, longing for the moment when he would claim her completely. When it came, it was everything she'd hoped.

CHAPTER NINE

AS THE FIERCE excitement died they lay quietly, holding each other, coming to terms with the new world in which they found themselves. Gradually they fell into peaceful sleep, lying motionless together until the room grew lighter and the new day had come.

Mario was lying with his face hidden against her neck, but then he raised it and looked down at her.

She met his eyes, seeing in them a look of loving possessiveness that made her heart skip a beat.

'Natasha,' he murmured, almost as though trying to believe that it was really her. She knew how he felt, for she was feeling the same herself. She had told him they must believe that dreams could come true.

'I've wanted this from the first moment,' he whispered. 'But I'd given up hope. And then suddenly—beyond my wildest dreams—why?'

'The time was right,' she whispered. 'Couldn't you feel that?'

'I've often felt it, but I was always wrong before. Suddenly—everything became different between us.'

'Everything became as it should be,' she said. 'This is how it was always meant to be.'

'You really mean that? Natasha, I'm not deluding myself, am I? Things are really all right between us?'

'How can you ask me that? After the way we've spent the last night, don't you think everything is all right?'

'Oh, yes.' He gave a wry smile. 'But I didn't mean that. I meant the other things that have come between us and separated us in the past. You didn't believe what I told you about Tania, that I'd broken with her because I'd met you and you were the one I wanted. Please, please say that you believe me, that you trust me at last.'

'I trust you, my darling. I should have trusted you long ago, but I was blind. It was like being lost in a maze. Every time I thought I'd found a way out it just led to more confusion.'

She promised herself that one day soon she would tell him about Tania's letter, and the way it had confirmed everything he said. But she didn't want thoughts of Tania to intrude just now. She wanted only Mario, the warmth, beauty and contentment they could find together.

'You trust me,' he echoed as though trying to believe it. 'And you're mine.'

'I'm yours.'

'For always?'

'Always and for ever.'

'Then everything's perfect.'

'Not quite,' she said. 'Don't you have an "always and for ever" promise to make me?'

'Of course. I just didn't think you needed to hear it said. I'm so completely yours that—'

He was interrupted by the sound of his mobile phone. Sighing, he answered it, speaking in Italian. Natasha didn't understand the language, but she understood that the caller was Mario's brother, Damiano.

'Come stai, fratello?' Mario said cheerfully. *'Come è Sally e il bambino?'*

After listening a moment he gave Natasha a thumbs-up sign.

'They've set the christening for this weekend,' he told her. 'I'm going and they want me to take you.'

'They want me? But how—?'

'Yes or no?'

'Yes. Oh, yes.'

'Damiano—Natasha *dice di sì. Va bene!*' He hung up.

'I don't understand,' she said. 'How did they even think of inviting me?'

'You mean how did they know you were here, and we'd found each other again?' He became a little awkward. 'When I went there for the birth a while ago I may have mentioned you briefly.'

She gave him a glance of wicked humour. 'Yes, I can imagine what you said. "That pesky woman has turned up again, when I thought I'd got rid of her."'

'Something like that,' he said with a grin.

'I'd give a lot to have been a fly on the wall.'

'You'd probably have had a good laugh. I talked about you non-stop. When I told them how amazed I was when our publicist turned out to be you, Damiano roared with laughter. And Sally wanted to know everything. She thinks it's a great joke to see me conquered by a woman.'

'But I haven't tried to conquer you.'

'Of course. If you had tried I'd have fought back and we wouldn't be talking like this now. But you caught me unaware, and I was finished before I knew it.'

And before I knew it, she thought. His words struck a disturbing chord within her.

'I remember everything so vividly,' he said. 'Our first meeting—you were sitting in the restaurant of Damiano's hotel when I came in. You were so lovely I just stopped and stared at you. Suddenly you looked up and saw me. And you smiled. Such a lovely smile, as though I was the only person in the room—in the world.

'I didn't understand straight away what had happened to me. But I did know that suddenly the world was focused on you.'

'And you came and sat down at the table,' she remembered. 'You said that you worked in the hotel and were offering your services—'

'That was just an excuse to talk to you, find out all I could about you. Were you married, was a man coming to join you? I hung on your every answer as though my life depended on it. And now I realise that my life did depend on it. And then—'

'What is it?' she asked, for he suddenly seemed troubled.

'It all happened again, didn't it? When you came here I asked you the same questions the first evening.'

'You said would a man turn up to drag me home?' she remembered.

'Yes, it sounded like the practical questions of an employer, but in fact I had this terrible need to know if there was someone in your life, just like the first time. It shocked me. I couldn't believe it had happened again—'

'With a woman you hated,' she said gently.

'I didn't hate you. I told myself I did because I needed to believe it. That was my defence and I clung to it. But things change and—well—'

'I wonder how much things change,' she murmured. 'Or do they only seem to have changed because *we* have changed?'

'Maybe we've changed in some things but not in others.'

'I wonder which is which.'

'We might find that out in Venice.'

'Mmm. So Sally thinks we're a joke. Yes, it's like fate played a joke on us. Sometimes I almost fancy I can hear laughter echoing from the heavens at the way we fell for it.'

'We didn't fall for it,' he said, drawing her close. 'We won. Fate lost. When Sally sees us together she'll understand that we're having the last laugh.'

'You really want me to come to Venice with you?'

'I think it's important that we go back there together.'

She understood. By returning they would confront their memories and that would help to show them the way forward.

'Everything that happened there looks different now,' she said.

'Yes,' he agreed gladly. 'So different. So much happier. The sooner we go the better. Then we can have a few days before the christening.'

At once he called Venice again, to say they would be arriving that evening. Then he stopped, regarding Natasha uneasily.

'Sally says one room or two?' he said. 'What's your choice?'

She was suddenly struck by inspiration. 'I'd like the same room I had last time.'

'That's a single room.'

'Perhaps we should be a little discreet.'

He seemed about to protest, but then understanding dawned and he turned back to the phone. At last he hung up.

'She's fixing it.'

'Does she think I'm crazy?'

'No, she said it made a lot of sense to put the clock back. I don't need to ask what that means, do I?'

'I don't think you do.'

'Let's get packing.'

Not long after, they bid farewell to Giorgio and set off for the Verona railway station to catch the train. It was just over seventy miles, and an hour and a half passed before they found themselves on the causeway that led over the water from the mainland to Venice.

She remembered the last time she had made this journey, leaning out of the window to see the beautiful buildings grow closer. How excited she'd been during that journey, how thrilled at the thought of spending time in the magical city.

At Venice station Mario hailed a water taxi and soon they were on their way to the hotel on the Grand Canal.

'There it is,' he said, pointing forward. 'Remember?'

'Yes, I remember,' she breathed.

It was a magnificent building, a converted palace that seemed to sum up everything that was glamorous about Venice. As soon as they entered Damiano and Sally came to meet them. Damiano and Mario slapped each other on the shoulders in brotherly fashion, while Sally embraced Natasha.

'It's lovely to see you again,' she said. 'And Pietro has really looked forward to your return. He says when you were last here you used to talk to him about football.'

'That's right. And last night England played Italy.' Natasha chuckled. 'Luckily, Italy won.'

Pietro appeared. He was in his early teens, already looking strikingly like his father, and full of beans.

'Did you see the match?' he challenged at once, after which perfect communication was established between them.

'How's Toby?' she asked, meaning Pietro's spaniel, who had helped bring Damiano and Sally together.

'Here he is,' Pietro said eagerly, drawing his furry friend forward.

She greeted Toby, received his welcoming lick and looked up to find Mario watching them with a pleased smile, as though everything was working out as he'd hoped.

Then Sally took them to see the two children she'd borne her husband—little Franco, nearly three years old, whose birth had nearly cost her life, and Elena, the little girl she'd borne recently.

'Supper's in half an hour,' Sally said.

As promised, Natasha had the same room as before which, at first, gave her a slightly weird ghostly feeling. But it soon faded against the different, happier, reality of the present. Mario's room was just a few feet along the corridor, and soon he appeared to escort her downstairs to Damiano's private dining room.

It was clear to Natasha that she was being welcomed into the family. During the meal that followed she was toasted as an honoured guest.

'Wait till you see the church where we'll have the christening,' Pietro said. 'It's where Mamma and Papà got married.'

'That was quite a ceremony,' Mario recalled. 'Toby was there too, practically one of the witnesses.'

'I'm sure he performed his role perfectly,' Natasha said.

As she spoke she tickled Toby's head and was rewarded with a *woof!*

It was a happy evening. A sense of peace came over her as she realised yet again the true purpose of this trip: to put right the mistakes and misunderstandings of the past.

Only Sally's brother Charlie was missing, which Sally explained with sisterly frankness. 'Out making himself objectionable again.'

'What kind of objectionable?' Natasha asked, laughing.

'Women, gambling—you name it, he can do it. Mind you, he's not as bad as he was. Mario helped reform him a bit.'

'Me? Reform?' Mario squeaked. 'That's practically an insult.'

'Well, Damiano told me you had a "guardian angel" side, and you did keep Charlie on the straight and narrow—more or less. Time for bed, anyway.'

The party broke up. Mario announced that he and Natasha wanted to take a walk. The others nodded in perfect understanding and slipped away.

'A walk?' she queried.

'Maybe. Maybe not.'

'What was the idea—?'

'I wanted to be sure of being alone with you. Let's have a coffee. Not here—in the restaurant.'

It was almost closing time and most of the restaurant tables were empty. At once she knew why he'd brought her here. There in the corner was the table where she'd sat at their first meeting. He led her over, showed her to a seat and sat beside her. A waiter brought them coffee.

'You were just here by the window,' he said. 'I watched you for a few minutes, trying to believe my eyes, rather like that guy over there.'

He pointed to a young man standing just inside the door, his eyes fixed on another table just a few feet away from them, where sat a young woman in her twenties. She was beautiful, and she was alone.

'I can guess what he's thinking,' Mario said. 'He's working out a good excuse to approach her.'

'You can't know what he's thinking.'

'Oh, yes, I can. When I look at him I see myself. In fact, I see every guy trying to summon up the courage to approach a woman he knows is going to matter more than any other. Look, there he goes.'

As they watched, the young man approached the girl and gestured to ask if anyone was sitting with her. She shook her head and he took a seat.

'Does he work here?' Natasha asked.

'No, he'll have to think of another excuse. He doesn't seem to be doing too badly.'

Amused, they watched the couple for a few minutes. Then Mario said with a touch of unease, 'There's something I keep wanting to ask you.'

'What is it?'

He hesitated, then said, 'What happened to you after we parted? I know you worked hard and Jenson gave you a bad time, but was there—anything else?'

'You mean another man? But I've already told you about that.'

'You've told me you're not married, you haven't settled down with anyone, but that's not what I meant.'

She gave a gentle chuckle. 'You mean am I secretly yearning for someone? Take a guess.'

'No, I can't see you yearning for someone who didn't return the feeling. But surely in the last two years you must have had some sort of romantic interest.'

'No. Apart from the horrible Jenson I've been alone. Which is a kind of freedom,' she added wryly.

'I know exactly how that feels.'

'Don't tell me you've been alone,' she teased. 'Every woman who passes gives you yearning looks.'

'But what matters is to be wanted by the one you yourself want,' he said. 'The others don't count.'

'That's true,' she said softly.

'So you're telling me there was no other man?'

'Hmm!' She appeared to consider this before saying gently, 'I suppose I could always say that it's none of your business. How about that?'

'It's certainly one response.' He gave her a wry smile. 'I could go and bury myself under the bedclothes because I couldn't cope with you snubbing me. Or I could get blind drunk. Or I could say that your lovers definitely are my business. And always will be. So now what?'

His eyes met hers, gleaming with a mixture of humour and intensity that struck her to the heart.

'My lovers,' she mused. 'I wonder just what you've heard.'

'Not a thing. After you vanished I tried to hunt you down for a little while, but when you never made contact with me I thought—well—' He gave a slight shrug.

'You thought, "To hell with the silly English girl! If

she wants to play it like that let her go and jump in the lake."'

'Well, maybe once or twice, but I didn't mean it,' he said, colouring.

'Oddly enough, I did end up in a lake shortly afterwards. It was a pleasure trip and the boat collapsed.'

'*What?* Were you hurt?'

'No, I just I got wet. Hey, I wonder if you made that happen. Strange to think we were in touch all that time and didn't know it.'

'Possibly. You were never off my mind.'

'Nor you off mine. And I did some cursing of my own.'

'I'm not sure I want to know about that,' he said with a grin. 'It could give me nightmares.'

'If we're asking about each other's lovers—what about yours? You must have had plenty.'

'Not lovers,' he said. 'Girlfriends, perhaps. I won't deny that I've enjoyed the company of a certain kind of woman because that way I could briefly forget the way you threw me overboard. But there wasn't anyone that I loved, even for a moment. It was always you, even when I most desperately didn't want it to be you.'

'Couldn't get rid of me, huh?' she teased.

'No matter how hard I tried.' He gave a warm laugh. 'You're a pesky woman. I told you a hundred times to get out of my heart but you just said, "Nope. Here I am and here I'm staying."'

'That sounds like me.'

He looked up suddenly. Following his gaze, she saw the other couple rise from the table and depart, hand in hand.

'I guess he got lucky,' Mario mused.

'Or maybe she did.'

'I didn't get lucky. Damiano called me to look after another customer and when I returned you'd gone. If only you could have heard me cursing.' He drained his coffee. 'Let's go.'

Upstairs, he came with her as far as her door.

'Remember last time?' he asked.

'Yes, we said goodnight at this door. I went inside and you went away.'

'I didn't really go away. I stayed out here in the corridor for ages.'

She opened the door and stretched out a hand to him.

'No need for that this time,' she said.

He took her hand at once, eagerly letting her draw him inside, then going into her arms, which she opened to him. It was she who drew them to the bed, he who followed her lead, but slowly, as though aware that they were rewriting history. Once they had wanted each other without satisfaction. Now they embraced satisfaction eagerly, joyfully.

There was physical pleasure in their caresses, but more than that was the joy of rediscovering each other. To retread the road, each seeing the other with new eyes, exploring new diversions, making wonderful discoveries; these were things they had never dared to dream of.

Afterwards, as they lay together in each other's arms, Natasha gave a sudden soft chuckle.

'What is it?' he demanded. 'What did I do that makes you laugh?'

'Don't get defensive. You could make me laugh and still be "macho".'

She laughed again and he frowned, demanding, 'So what is it?'

'It's what Sally said about you having a "guardian

angel" side. That's the last thing I'd ever have suspected about you. A rebel, a pain in the butt, a pesky clown—any of them. But a guardian angel? Or any kind of angel. I doubt it.'

His annoyance faded and he kissed her forehead. 'Thanks. I see you really understand me.'

'You don't mind being called those things?'

'Not at all. I'd have minded being called an angel. That would have been insulting. But I think "pain in the butt" rather suits me.'

'Definitely,' she said, kissing him. 'Now, I'm going to sleep. You've exhausted me for the night. Goodnight, "guardian angel".'

She snuggled against him and in a few moments she was asleep.

Guardian angel, he thought. *That's almost funny, considering how I hated you only recently. But somehow things took a different turn.*

He rested his head against her and in a few minutes he too was asleep. After several hours he awoke to find her eyes still closed and her head on his shoulder. When he ventured to move slightly her arms tightened, as though even in sleep she needed to keep him close.

He clasped her back, offering her the embrace she needed for reassurance.

Romeo's words drifted through his mind again. *It is my lady...oh, it is my love. Oh, that she knew she were.*

But she does know, he mused. *If she knows anything by now, it's that I love her.*

He kissed her gently, murmuring, 'You are my lady. You are my love.'

She sighed and nestled closer, smiling as though she'd heard him and been reassured. He leaned against her, happy and willing to sleep again, but then a noise from his phone disturbed him.

'Curses,' he muttered. 'My mobile phone. Where is it?'

Undressing hastily, he hadn't noticed it fall to the floor. Now he eased himself gently away from Natasha and leaned down to pick up the phone. Connecting, he found a text from an unknown number:

You're taking a bigger risk than you know. She's mine. Get lost.

For a moment he was simply bewildered. Who could the message be from? But then the answer came to him like a clap of thunder.

Elroy Jenson. The man who'd vindictively destroyed Natasha's career because she'd dared to defy him. The man who'd spied on her from a distance, watching where she fled to escape him. The man who still had his claws in her, and would deepen them if he could.

He was swept by such rage that his head was dizzy and the whole world seemed to turn black.

'No,' he whispered. 'She's not yours. She's mine. She's *mine.* She always was. *And she always will be.*'

Behind him, Natasha stirred, murmuring, 'Is something the matter?'

'No,' he said. 'Go back to sleep. Nothing's the matter. Nothing at all. Your guardian angel will deal with it.'

CHAPTER TEN

'How are you enjoying Verona?' Sally asked Natasha at breakfast next morning.

'I love it.'

'And Verona loves her,' Mario said. 'She's doing a great job for our hotels.'

'Perhaps she can come here later and do something for Venice hotels,' Damiano said.

'What a lovely idea,' Natasha said. 'I'll take a stroll around Venice this morning.' She glanced at Mario before saying slowly, 'Just to remind myself what it's like.'

He nodded.

After breakfast they slipped out into the narrow alley that ran by the hotel.

'You walked this way alone the first time,' he reminded her. 'But I wasn't far behind you.'

'I know.'

'You know? You mean you knew it then?'

'Yes, I told the receptionist where I was going, and you were nearby. When I came out I heard your footsteps behind me.'

'So you always knew I was following you?'

'No, but I hoped you were. I went into a shop to give you a chance to catch up. But you didn't.'

'I was tempted. When you stopped I worked out a plan to go into the shop casually and just "happen" to meet you. But I lost my nerve, so I waited a bit.'

'Lost your nerve? You?'

'You have that effect on me.'

'I'll remember that. It could be useful.'

'Be honest. You already knew that you scared me stiff.'

Laughing, they went on their way.

At last they came to the Grand Canal, the great S-shaped stream of water that wound through the city. Boats of every kind filled it. Just coming up was a *vaporetto*, one of the great water buses that transported passengers all over the city. Small water taxis were everywhere, but also the boats that everyone came to Venice to see, gondolas. Natasha looked eagerly at the slim, elegant conveyances, propelled by a man with one oar.

'You were standing here when you saw your first gondola close up,' he remembered.

'And I couldn't think how a gondola could go straight when it was only being rowed on one side,' she said. 'You told me that that side bulged more than the other, so the water took longer to slide past. I didn't understand, so you said I should take a ride in it. You hailed the gondolier—like you're doing now.'

The boat was gliding to a halt beside them. Gently, he handed her in and they settled down together. It felt wonderful, just as it had the first time.

'Aaaaaah.' Sighing with pleasure, she stretched out, looking around her at the little canal and listening to the singing coming from around the corner. 'It's lovely, but this is where I fell asleep.'

'That's right. You couldn't have made it plainer what you thought of me, Natasha—Natasha?'

She was lying back with her eyes closed. *Just like last time*, he thought.

The gondolier regarded him sympathetically. 'Some men are just unlucky, *signore*,' he said, speaking in Venetian dialect.

'True,' Mario said wryly in the same language. 'But some men are also luckier than they know. The problem is finding out which you are.'

He watched Natasha carefully for a moment, then leaned forward and kissed her. When she didn't react he repeated the kiss more forcefully.

'Hello,' Natasha said, opening her eyes.

'Hello. Sorry if I disturbed you.'

'Tell me, when I fell asleep the first time, did you kiss me then?'

'Don't you remember?'

She smiled up at him in a way he guessed was meant to drive him mad. She was certainly succeeding. Did she know that? Did she enjoy it?

'I'm not sure,' she murmured.

'Then let me remind you.'

He laid his lips gently over hers again, leaving them there for several moments.

The gondolier grinned. His job exposed him to a lot of enjoyable sights.

Natasha relaxed and put her arms about him. Although she had been asleep for their first ride, two years ago, she was sure he hadn't kissed her then because she would have remembered. Now she gave herself up to pleasure.

Afterwards, they sat leaning against each other, watching the little canals drift past. She had a mysterious sense that the journey might go on for ever, and wished that it would. But all too soon they drew up outside the hotel. Once inside, they became involved in the preparations for the christening, and for the rest of the day she barely spent a moment alone with him.

Next morning everyone set out for the church where the christening would take place. It was only a short distance away, so they went on foot.

'It's a big family occasion,' Mario said as they walked through the alley that approached the church. 'Damiano's first wife died giving birth to Pietro. One reason he married Sally was to give that kid a mother.'

'You mean it was a marriage of convenience? They seem so devoted to each other.'

'They are. They thought it was a marriage of convenience, but in fact they were really in love. They just hadn't realised it.'

She looked into her wine glass, murmuring, 'That can happen when people don't understand their own feelings.'

'So I've heard. It must be quite a stunning discovery.'

'Yes,' she said. 'It is. There's no recovering from it, or from blaming yourself for how stupid you were.'

'Would you call yourself stupid?'

'Mad, imbecile,' she said. 'Even worse than that. But a lucky fate gave me the chance to put things right.'

He raised his glass. 'Here's to fate.'

They clinked glasses.

'So did they realise they were in love?' she asked.

'It dawned on them eventually. She had a bad time when Franco was born. She might not have come through it. I thought Damiano would go out of his mind with fear and grief. He wasn't keen on Sally having another baby, but she really wanted it and he gave in.'

He gave a brief laugh. 'Few people know the real Damiano. To the outside world he's a ruthless businessman. But once that front door shuts behind him, he's a willing slave to his wife.'

'Oh, really?' She gave him a cheeky look. 'Is that how you judge a good husband? If he's her willing slave?'

'Who knows? Perhaps you'll have the chance to find out.'

There were already plenty of friends and family in place, smiling when they appeared and made their way along the aisle. Sally walked with her new baby in her arms, Damiano carried their toddler, Charlie and Mario walked together, while Pietro accompanied Natasha, holding her hand. Again she had the happy feeling of being part of the family.

It grew even better at the party that evening. Mario introduced her to everyone in the crowd, most of whom seemed to have heard of her already.

'We've all looked forward to meeting you,' said one elderly man.

'Just be a little patient,' Mario told him. 'You'll hear something soon.'

'What did that mean?' she asked as he drew her away.

'Just that people think we're a couple. Do you mind that?'

'Not at all,' she assured him. 'But what is he going to hear soon?'

'Why don't we go and talk about that?'

He drew her slowly out of the room, waving farewell to the other guests, who cheered them in a way that left no doubt that they were expecting to hear about a wedding very soon. Somehow, Mario had given that impression.

Once inside her room he kissed her before saying, 'I may have said more than I should have done without asking you first. But we so clearly belong together that people accept it.'

'And if you could have asked me first?'

'I'd have asked you to set the date for our wedding.'

'Yes, you really should have mentioned it to me.'

'Are you mad at me?'

'I'll let you know that later.' She drew him to the bed. 'For the moment I have other things on my mind.'

'So have I.' He was already working on her clothes.

We did the right thing coming here, she thought. *It's made things better, as nothing else could have done. The past is over. It didn't happen. We are free.*

Free. The word seemed to echo, casting hope over the future. As they made love she kept her eyes on his face, finding that he too was watching her, sending a silent message that she understood and returned with all her heart.

And he too understood. She recognised that from the long sigh of happiness and fulfilment he gave as they lay in each other's arms afterwards.

'If only we could have known,' he whispered.

'It was too much to hope for,' she replied. 'Even now I daren't hope. It's too good to be true. Something will happen to make things go wrong.'

'Nothing will go wrong,' he said firmly. 'I won't let it.'

'Oh, you think it's all up to you, do you, big man?'

'Right this minute I feel powerful enough to dictate everything in the world. You hear that?' he yelled up at the ceiling. 'Nothing is ever going to go wrong between us again. I insist on it. I order it.'

'Who are you giving orders to?' she chuckled.

'The little green men who try to dictate to us. From now on, I'm in charge.'

'Oh, yeah?'

'Not of you,' he said hastily. 'Just of them.'

They collapsed with laughter, rocking back and forth with delight.

Afterwards, Natasha was to remember that moment, a triumphant assertion of joy and confidence before catastrophe descended on them once more.

Next morning Mario suggested a walk through Venice.

'It was a good idea to come back,' he said as they strolled. 'The people we were then don't exist any more, and this way we've got rid of them.'

'I'm not sure I want to get rid of them,' she observed. 'There were things about you I think I'll cling to. You've always been the best-looking man for miles around. I'm not changing that.'

'Thank you, ma'am.'

He began to draw her in another direction, but she resisted.

'Why can't we stay here?' she asked.

'Because of that place,' he said, indicating an outdoor café. It was the one where they had had their quarrel.

But it need not have happened, she thought.

So many times she'd wanted to tell Mario that she knew the truth after reading Tania's letter, but somehow the moment had never been right. But perhaps this was the right time and place.

'Why don't you buy me a coffee there?' she said.

'Don't you realise what that place is?' he demanded.

'Yes, it's where we made our huge mistake and lost each other. Perhaps it's time to put it right.'

'I thought we'd already put it right.'

'Yes, but there's a little more to do. Come with me.'

She led him to the café and found that by a strange chance the same table was available.

'This is where we sat,' she said as they sipped coffee.

'Until we were interrupted, but that won't happen this time,' he said firmly. 'That woman is out of our lives for good.' He became suddenly tense. 'What's the matter? Why are you smiling like that? Don't you believe me?'

'Yes, I believe you.'

'Do you really? You believe that I was telling you the truth? You trust me? I would never deceive you. Tell me that you believe that.'

'I do. I believe everything you've told me. I know you're an honest man and you always will be.'

'You mean that? You really mean that?'

'Every word.'

He took her face between his hands and spoke softly. 'If you could imagine what it means to me to know that we're close enough for you to have learned to trust me.'

'I only want to tell you—' She stopped, silenced by a nervous feeling that she did not understand.

'You only want to tell me what? That you love me. That's it, isn't it?'

'Oh, yes, that's it.'

'Then that's all I need to hear.'

'But, Mario—'

His lips on hers silenced her. He was kissing her fiercely, powerfully, yet devotedly, longingly. She surrendered to the pleasure, knowing that this, and only this, was the whole of life.

At last he released her. She could tell that he was shaking and his breath came unevenly.

'My darling,' he whispered. 'What is it that you needed to say?'

'Nothing. It doesn't matter.'

Nothing mattered enough to break the spell of this moment. She took hold of him again, returning the kiss fervently. Around them the other diners laughed and cheered, and the waiter cleared his throat. Without looking at him, Mario pulled some money from his pocket. The waiter seized it and vanished.

'Let's go,' Mario said. 'This isn't the place for what we have to do.'

'*Have* to do?' she murmured against his lips.

'We have urgent business to attend to,' he whispered. 'Can't you feel it?'

'Yes—oh, yes.'

Seizing her hand, he rose and hurried away. She followed him joyfully. The words she'd planned to say could wait. Nothing mattered now but to be with him, in his arms, his bed, his life.

Together they ran through the streets of Venice, down alleys, over bridges, eager to get to the hotel, where they could achieve the fulfilment that awaited them, that they longed for.

At last they reached the hotel, hurrying through the entrance and across to the lift.

Sally appeared, calling, 'Ah, Mario, can I talk to you—?'

'Not now,' Mario called back.

They vanished into the lift, clinging to each other as it carried them up.

'Nearly there,' he said hoarsely.

'Yes, nearly there.'

She knew he meant they were almost at his bedroom, but to her the words meant far more. The glorious destination that had waited for them since the moment they'd met—they were nearly there.

They had reached the room. He flung open the door, drew her inside and began to undress her at once. She responded instantly, wrenching off his jacket, pulling open his buttons, tearing off his shirt.

They fell onto the bed, still working on each other's clothes until they were both naked and ready for each other.

'You're mine,' he said huskily. 'Now and for ever.'

'Yes—yes—'

She was dizzy with passion and delight, wanting him more than she had ever wanted anything in her life. Their previous lovemaking had been wonderful, but this one was pervaded by an extra sense of triumph.

She reached for him, offered herself to him, claimed him, and sensed his delight not only through his movements but by the glow in his eyes. His lovemaking was tender, emotional, and at first this was enough. But soon she wanted more. She was his, heart and body, and with every movement she demanded that he accept the gift and return it. When he claimed her finally she cried out with joy.

Afterwards, lying contentedly in his arms, feeling the warmth of his flesh and the gentle power of his embrace, she knew that she had come to the place that was always meant for her, and where she could live happily for the rest of her life.

She had meant to tell him about the letter, but things

beyond her control had swept her up. Was that an omen? she wondered. Should she try to tell him now?

'My love,' she murmured.

'My love,' he echoed, 'if you knew how wonderful it is to hear you call me that. I am your love and you are mine.' He stroked her breast. 'I was afraid this would never happen,' he whispered.

'It's not the first time we've made love,' she reminded him.

'No, but it's the first time we've made love like this, with all doubts settled, all fears gone, everything open and clear between us. When you told me that you trusted me I felt as if I'd gone to heaven.'

'Yes,' she whispered. 'I feel like that too.'

'And we must keep it that way. We lost two years, but we mustn't lose any more time. We must marry as soon as possible.'

'Marry,' she said in wonder.

'I told you yesterday that we should set the date. You didn't give me an answer. Are you trying to put me off?'

She glanced down the bed at their naked entwined figures. 'Does it look as if I'm trying to put you off?'

'I just want to be sure of you. Say yes. Say yes.'

'Oh, yes. Yes, with all my heart.'

'Now we've found each other,' he whispered, 'nothing can ever come between us.'

He kissed her again before saying, 'I've just remembered—you had something you were trying to say to me.'

'Did I?'

'Yes, it sounded urgent but I kind of distracted you.' He grinned, recalling the way he'd grasped hold of her and made her run.

'I suppose you could call this a distraction,' she agreed, smiling.

'So what were you going to say?'

Natasha's head was whirling. This was the moment she'd planned to lay bare the secret, but suddenly everything seemed different. To speak of it now would be to let Tania intrude on them again, and she was determined never to let that happen.

'Natasha?' he murmured.

'Mmm?'

'Are you awake?'

'Er…no. I—must have dozed off again. Did you say something?'

'I asked you what you'd been planning to tell me.'

'I can't remember. It's gone out of my head now, so it can't have meant much.'

'It's just that you made it sound important.'

'No, it couldn't be.' She touched his face. 'Only one thing is important now.'

'And that's us,' he agreed. 'You're right. Nothing else matters. Come here.'

She did so, taking refuge in his arms and his love, so that the rest of the world ceased to exist.

The letter didn't matter, she decided. This was how it would always be.

She opened her eyes next morning to find Mario regarding her anxiously.

'You did mean it, didn't you?' he asked. 'You really will marry me?'

'No,' she teased. 'I was just making fun of you. Oh, don't look like that. Of course I meant it. Would I have said it otherwise?'

'I can't be sure with you. You always seem to have a surprise to spring on me. I get nervous waiting for the next one.'

'Oh, really?' She regarded him with wicked humour. 'Let's see now. I could always thump you.'

'But that wouldn't be a surprise. You've already thumped me so often in different ways.'

'So maybe it's time to find another way. How about that?' She delivered a light pat on his shoulder.

'Ouch!' he cried comically. 'Now I'm in agony.'

'Good. Then I'll know how to bully you in future.'

She patted him again and they both burst into laughter.

'I don't believe this is real,' he said against her neck. 'Nobody could be as happy as I am now. It's an illusion.'

'No, we're going to teach the world what happiness looks like.'

'Mmm, that sounds nice. Can I thump you back?'

'Permission granted.'

He rolled her onto her stomach and lightly patted her behind. 'You be careful,' he said, 'or I'll do it again.'

'Is that a promise?' she chuckled.

'It's whatever you want.'

He was right, she thought, nestling contentedly against him. Nobody was allowed to be as happy as this. It must be an illusion. And she would do everything in her power to make it last.

CHAPTER ELEVEN

ENTERING THE BREAKFAST room downstairs, they found Damiano, Sally and Pietro waiting for them. They all looked up, eager for news.

'Have you got something to tell us?' Damiano asked. 'Sally seemed to think you might have.'

'You mean after she tried to talk to me yesterday and we dashed upstairs?' Mario said. 'Sorry, Sally. It was urgent.'

'Well, I gathered that,' she chuckled. 'So come on, tell us.'

'We're going to be married,' he announced. 'Natasha has decided she can put up with me.'

Pietro cried, 'Yippee!'

Sally hugged Natasha, and Damiano declared cheerfully, 'Welcome to the family, Natasha. We're all delighted that you're going to take charge of Mario and turn him into a sensible man.'

'Thanks, brother,' Mario said, grinning.

'By the time you discover your mistake it'll be too late,' Mario added. 'He'll have put the ring on your finger.'

'And I'll never let her take it off,' Mario said.

'You must marry here in Venice,' Sally said. 'After all, it's where you met. It'll be such fun to arrange.'

'That's very nice of you,' Mario said, 'but I think there's another place that would be more right for us. In Verona, we can marry at Juliet's house.' He glanced at Natasha, who nodded, smiling.

'Romeo and Juliet,' Sally mused. 'But you two can't be Romeo and Juliet. You're having a happy ending. I suppose there's still time for something to go wrong, but it won't.'

'No, it won't,' Mario said. 'We're together, and now nothing is going to go wrong. She is my Juliet, and Verona is the right place for us.'

Sally insisted on having a party for them that evening. Her warmth was a special blessing to Natasha. Her life had been lonely, with no relatives but her bitter mother. Now, suddenly, she had a brother and sister, and a cheeky nephew in Pietro.

They laughed and danced their way through the party, spent the night nestled together, and set out for Verona the following morning.

When Giorgio heard the news he roared with delight. 'Romeo and Juliet made it at last! What a story.'

'It's not exactly a story,' Mario protested.

'It is to me. You hired me as your publicity manager, and I'm going to do my job. When you've fixed the date we'll get some pictures.'

'The date will be as soon as possible,' Mario said.

'It'll have to be a Monday morning,' Giorgio told him. 'All wedding ceremonies are held then because the house has to be closed to tourists while it's happening. Then we'll have the reception here in the afternoon, and everyone in the *Comunità* will come.'

Later that day they went to the City Hall to make the booking for two weeks' time, and learned what they could about the wedding procedure. The actual ceremony would take place inside the building, with photographs taken afterwards, on the balcony.

Giorgio was in his element, planning to broadcast the information as far and wide as possible.

'This isn't just a wedding,' he said gleefully. 'It's the biggest publicity opportunity the *Comunità* has ever had. You really must make the best of it.'

'That's fine,' Mario said. 'I'm happy for everyone to know that I've secured the best bride in the world.'

But Natasha drew him aside, feeling some concern. 'Jenson will get to hear of it,' she said.

'Good!' Mario declared at once. 'I want him to know that his bullying has achieved nothing. That should stop his nonsense.'

'But suppose it doesn't?'

'Then I'll make him sorry he was born. Don't tell me you're still afraid of him. You're going to be my wife. There's nothing more he can do.' He took her in his arms. 'Trust me, darling. You have nothing more to fear from him. I told you I'd scare the living daylights out of him, and I have.'

'You scared Jenson? But how?'

'By slashing his advertising revenue. There are several media outlets I've been able to persuade to drop their adverts. Some here, some owned by friends of mine elsewhere. It should be enough to put the wind up him.'

'You did that for me?' she breathed. 'Oh, thank you—thank you.'

Blazing with happiness, she threw her arms around his neck.

'I told you I wouldn't let you be hurt,' he said. 'And I won't.'

'So you really are my guardian angel?'

'Angel? Not me. But I can put the wind up people when I want to.'

Chuckling, they embraced each other.

'It's such a weight off my mind,' she said. 'To know that he won't trouble me again.'

Now her most urgent arrangement was choosing a wedding dress. At Giorgio's orders, several gowns were delivered to the hotel for her to try on. She chose one of white satin, cut simply and elegantly.

'Perfect,' Giorgio declared when he saw it. 'It'll look great in the pictures. We must get started on them quickly.'

It seemed strange to be taking wedding pictures before the wedding, but they were to be part of Giorgio's publicity campaign to promote Verona as a wedding venue.

'The photographer will be here tomorrow morning,' Giorgio said. 'He's the same one who took the pictures of you as Romeo and Juliet. We'll put the two sets of pictures out together. Romeo and Juliet became Mario and Natasha.' He grinned. 'Or perhaps they always were.'

'Forget it,' Mario said. 'This story isn't going to end in a tomb.'

He was looking so handsome, Natasha thought as they posed together. For one picture she stood just in front of him, his hands on her shoulders as they both faced the camera. For another shot they danced together.

'Don't look so stern,' Giorgio called. 'Gaze into each other's eyes. Look romantic.'

'But why?' Natasha teased. 'We're getting married. 'That's not romantic; it's deadly serious.'

'Stop that,' Mario said. 'I'm quite scared enough without you scaring me more.'

She began to laugh. He joined in and Giorgio yelled with delight at the picture it produced.

'That's perfect,' he said. 'That says it all.'

As he'd predicted, the two sets of pictures worked splendidly together. When circulated to the rest of the *Comunità*, they produced a flood of excited congratulations.

There was one reaction Mario vowed to keep to himself. The text from Jenson was as spiteful as he'd expected, and he was thankful that Natasha didn't see it.

I've warned you but you didn't take any notice. Now see how sorry I can make you.

He checked the phone number of Jenson's organisation and dialled it.

'I want to speak to Elroy Jenson,' he told the receptionist.

'I'm sorry. Mr Jenson isn't accepting calls today.'

'He'll accept mine. Tell him Mario Ferrone wants to talk to him.'

A pause, some clicks, then a harsh masculine voice came on the line. 'What do you mean by calling me?'

'Ah, Mr Jenson. Good.' Mario leaned back in his chair. 'You know exactly who I am. You don't like me, and you're going to like me even less when I've finished.'

'You're wasting your time,' Jenson's voice came down the line.

'I don't think so. I think you'll find that some of my recent actions have been very significant.'

'What recent actions?' Jenson's voice contained a sneer but Mario thought he also detected a hint of nervousness.

'You'll be hearing from your Italian publications, wondering why whole batches of advertising have been suddenly cancelled.'

'Don't think you can scare me,' Jenson snapped. 'A few hotels and vineyards—'

'It'll be rather more than that. I've got friends working on this, friends you know nothing about but whose tentacles stretch great distances abroad. You'll be losing advertisements left, right and centre. And when they want to know why—I wonder what you'll tell them.'

'That's no concern of yours!' Jenson raged.

'Everything that concerns my fiancée concerns me, as you'll find out if you don't stop your nasty ways. You wrecked her career out of spite because she wasn't interested in your cheap advances and too many people got to know about it. Well, now the whole world is going to know about it.'

'What do you mean?' Jenson snarled.

'The digital age is a wonderful thing. A few texts and emails and the world will know what a pest Elroy Jenson is: a man so conceited that he felt no woman had the right to reject him, and with so little self-respect that he could never leave her alone afterwards.'

'There are laws of libel,' Jenson snarled.

'There's no question of libel. Once those texts you've sent her are revealed there would be no question everyone will know the truth.'

'Texts? I don't know what you're talking about.'

'Don't waste time trying to deny it. I've got records of every word you sent, and where they came from. I can reveal every word and prove it. The world will rock with laughter at you. And if you resorted to law you'd just keep yourself in an unpleasant spotlight longer.'

'What are you after? Money?'

'No, I just want you to leave Natasha alone. One more text or call from you and you've had it. Do you understand me?'

'You're very good at making threats,' Jenson snapped with his best effort at a sneer.

Mario grinned, feeling that he could risk a little vulgarity.

'I'm good at a lot of things,' he said. 'Which is why she chose me over you.'

'Why, you—'

'Goodbye. Go to hell!'

Mario hung up. Then he stared at the phone, trying to come to terms with his own actions. He was neither a violent nor a cruel man, but the need to conquer Jenson had brought out a side of him he'd never needed to use before.

But it was for her, and for her he would do anything. That was the effect she had on him, and now he realised that part of him had known it from the first day.

From behind him he heard a sound that made him turn in amazement. Natasha stood there, applauding.

'Well done,' she said. 'Wonderful! You've really dealt with him.' She engulfed him in an embrace.

'It was easy—just threaten to expose him as an idiot,' he said, returning her hug. 'He's far more afraid of that than losing business.'

'But I don't understand what you said about his texts. Surely you don't really have records of them?'

'Only the one he sent today. I don't have the others, but he doesn't know that and he won't take the chance.'

'No, he won't,' she breathed.

'And he won't dare send you any more because now he knows the risk he runs.'

'You're so clever.' She sighed. 'I never thought anyone could put this business right.'

'But you've got me to protect you now. And that's all I want to do for the rest of my life.'

He enfolded her in a fierce embrace.

'Three days before we're married,' he said huskily. 'I don't know if I can bear to wait that long to make you mine.'

'But I'm already yours. I always have been and I always will be.'

'No doubt about that,' he said, smiling. 'I'll never let you go.'

'That suits me just fine.'

Now things were moving fast. Two days before the wedding, Damiano, Sally and Pietro arrived and took up residence in the hotel's best suite. That evening there was a party attended by them, by Giorgio and by several members of the *Comunità.* Toasts were made to the bride and groom. Then the bride alone was toasted, leaving no doubt that she was the heroine of the hour.

As the evening wore on, Sally announced that she would retire for the night.

'I've got a bit of a headache,' she confided to Natasha.

'Me too,' she said. 'And I think Mario might enjoy chatting if he didn't have to keep breaking off to translate for me.'

Together they bid everyone goodnight and went upstairs. A warm, friendly hug and they said goodnight.

Natasha was glad to be alone for a moment for she needed to think. She must decide what to do about Tania's letter.

There had been a time when she might have told Mario

about it but events had conspired to distract her and now she knew the moment had gone. Her best course now was to destroy it so that it would be out of their lives finally and for ever.

Going quickly into her room, she went to the place where she kept it hidden.

She found the small piece of blue paper and unfolded it.

She read it again, taking in the words that had meant so much, thanking a merciful fate that had given it to her. Now she reckoned she must burn it.

'What's that?' said Mario's voice.

Startled, she looked up and saw him there. He had come in quietly, without her hearing him. Now he was standing with his eyes fixed on the blue paper that she held. With dismay, she realised that he knew what she was holding.

'What's that?' he repeated.

'It's just—'

'Give it to me.'

He wrenched it from her hand before she could protest. As he read it he seemed to grow very still.

'How did you get this?' he asked in a toneless voice.

'By accident. I came across it while I was in your apartment, after my room flooded.'

'And you kept it.'

'I needed to read it again and again. It seemed too good to be true. She says there that you'd told her it was over because you wanted to be with me. So after that I knew—'

'You knew I'd been telling you the truth,' he said slowly.

'Yes. It was so wonderful. After everything that happened, who could have thought it would be Tania who would make things right for us?'

There was a silence.

When he spoke he didn't look at her. 'Did she make things right for us?' he asked in a strange voice.

'She added the missing piece. She told me what I needed to know. After that, everything was different.'

If only he would smile and share her pleasure at the way things had turned out, but instead he was silent, frowning. It was almost as though her words troubled him.

'Tell me something,' he said at last. 'That night we took a walk by the river and when we got home you invited me into your room—had you read Tania's letter then?'

'Yes. I was so happy. Suddenly everything was all right.'

'Why? Because Tania had confirmed I was telling the truth? You knew that because *she* told you? But not because *I* told you?'

'I didn't know you as well in those days. I couldn't be sure what the truth might be. Oh, Mario, why didn't you show me the letter yourself?'

'I meant to. But I was waiting for the right moment.'

'But surely any time would have been right to show me the proof?'

'The proof?'

'The proof that what you were telling me was true. That you really had broken with her.'

A strange, tense look came over his face. 'So you could have believed me when you saw proof. But not my word alone.'

'Mario, I'm sorry about that. I see now that I should

have believed you. But does it matter now that it's been finally settled?'

'Settled.' He repeated the word softly. 'If only I could make you understand—'

'Understand what, my darling?'

'Since you came to Verona I've clung to a happy fantasy, a dream world in which we understood each other. In that world we grew close, loving each other more and more until you finally believed what I told you because you knew me well enough to know that I was true to you.'

'But I do know—'

'Yes, because you've got the evidence in that letter. But in my fantasy you didn't need evidence. You believed me because you loved me enough to trust me completely. We were so close that no doubt could ever come between us.

'That night, when you opened your arms to me, I felt I'd reached heaven. I thought our great moment had arrived at last, the moment I'd been longing for since the day we met. If only you knew how I… Well, never mind. It doesn't matter now.'

'But it does,' she cried passionately. 'Mario, don't talk like this. You sound as though everything is hopeless between us, but it isn't. We've discovered our hope at last. It's taken too long but we've finally found each other. Can't you see that?'

'I want to. If you knew how desperately I long to believe that everything can be all right now, but there's something missing and perhaps it always will be.'

She stared at him, struggling to believe what he was saying.

'Then blame me,' she said. 'I got it wrong; I took too long to understand the truth. But I understand it now.'

'Yes, because someone else told you. Not me. The closeness I thought we'd achieved doesn't exist. It was an illusion I believed because I wanted to believe it.' He gave a grim laugh. 'I remember you saying people believed what they wanted to, and boy were you right! In you I saw what I wanted to see.

'And now? Will we ever have that closeness? I doubt it. You said things were "finally settled". But when is something settled? When you finally have peace of mind?'

And now he did not have peace of mind with her. He didn't say it—but he didn't need to say it. She had thought that all was well between them, but after this would their love ever be the same?

'Do you understand the bitter irony of this?' he asked. 'The next thing is our wedding. We'll stand side by side at a site that commemorates the greatest lovers of legend. We'll vow love, loyalty, trust. *Trust!* Can you imagine that?'

'I do trust you,' she cried passionately.

'Do you? Perhaps you do, perhaps you don't. I'll never really know, will I?'

'Can't you take my word for it?'

He gave a harsh laugh. 'Are you lecturing me about accepting your word? That's the cruellest joke you ever made. I was looking forward to our wedding. Now I'm dreading it. I'm not even sure that I—'

He broke off, almost choking. His eyes, fixed on her, were full of hostility. Suddenly he turned, pulled open the door and rushed out without a backward glance.

'Mario—don't. Come back, *please*.'

But either he didn't hear or he ignored her, heading for the stairs and running down them. At the bottom he turned towards the entrance. Dashing back into the room,

Natasha went to the window and looked down, where she could see him heading down the street until he vanished.

She almost screamed in her despair. The perfect love that offered a wonderful future had descended into chaos. Now a terrifying vista opened before her. Ahead stretched a road of misery, where every hope came to nothing and only emptiness remained.

CHAPTER TWELVE

WHAT FOLLOWED WAS the worst night of Natasha's life.

It was over. Everything was over. She had lost Mario and nothing could ever matter in her life again.

Why didn't I tell him earlier? her heart cried.

But she knew the answer. However he had learned about the letter, he would have hated the fact that she'd relied on it. In his heart he no longer believed that she loved him. And now everything might be over between them. He had even hinted that he might not be there for the wedding.

For a moment she thought of chasing after him, but he'd had time to disappear and she would never find him. Her best hope was to wait for him to return.

She lay down, trying to control her wild thoughts and believe that there might still be hope. For an hour she lay there, listening for some sign of his return, but all she heard was the party breaking up.

Then there was silence and darkness, leaving her with an aching heart and terrified thoughts.

Why didn't he return?

Would he ever return?

She slept for a while and awoke in the early hours. There was no sign of Mario, but perhaps he'd gone to his own room. She slipped out into the corridor and went to his door, where she stood listening for a moment. But there was no sound from within.

Tentatively, she opened the door and slipped inside. The bed was empty. He had not returned.

'Come back,' she whispered. 'Don't let it end like this. Come back to me.'

But another two hours passed with no sign of him.

A terrible sense of irony pervaded her. Suddenly it felt as though she was Juliet again, a star-crossed lover facing the final destruction of her joy.

There was nothing to prepare her for what happened next.

A shrill from her mobile phone made her look to find a text. Incredibly, it was from Jenson.

You think you're clever, setting your lover on me. Take a look at this.

Below it was the address of a website. Studying it, Natasha realised that it was an English provincial newspaper, doubtless belonging to Jenson.

He'd said he knew something about her, implying that he could smear her in print. But she couldn't think of anything she would be reluctant to have known.

She got to work on her laptop, typing in the web address. There on the screen was a printed page with a photograph. A cry broke from her as she recognised her father.

Forcing herself under control, she looked closely at the text. It was dated eight years ago and named the man as Charles Bates. It seemed to be part of a series about people who had been brought down by misfortune. Charles

Bates had turned to crime and gone to prison following a tragic crisis in his life.

He had given the interview two days after being released. As she read what he'd had to say, Natasha felt her blood run cold.

> *'I blame my wife. I loved her and the girl I thought was my daughter. But then I discovered she wasn't mine. It broke my heart. I ran away as fast as I could go.'*

So her mother had betrayed her husband and she, Natasha, was not his child. She struggled to deny it, but lurking in her memory was a quarrel she had overheard between them. Her father had shouted, 'Who was he? Tell me!' And he'd called her mother some terrible names. The next day he had gone.

Another memory returned—Jenson walking into the room as she was telling this story to a fellow employee. How sympathetic he had been, encouraging her to talk. How kind she had thought him, while all the time he was softening her up so that he could pounce on her, while storing the information in case it could be a useful weapon. That was his way. He liked to have weapons against everyone.

Checking back, he'd found that one little item and made a note of it. Mario's action over the advertisements had convinced him he had nothing left to gain, and still he'd lashed out to hurt her for revenge.

Now she saw that years of being warned not to trust men went back to this point. Her mistrust had made her wary of Mario, but it was based on a lie. And that lie threatened the love they shared.

Unless she could find a way to solve the problem.

Suddenly she found words whispering through her head. *I have a faint cold fear thrills through my veins, That almost freezes up the heat of life.*

Juliet had spoken those words, faced with the decision that would change everything. And now Natasha felt the cold fear running through her. She must do something to make Mario return. But what?

'*She* will know,' she said. 'I'll go and ask her.'

Hurriedly, she flung on some clothes and rushed out of the room and downstairs.

Damiano was just crossing the hall. 'Just on my way to breakfast,' he said. 'No Mario?'

'He'll…be a while,' she stammered.

Damiano chuckled. 'Ah, still asleep, is he? I guess you must have exhausted him.'

She managed a smile. 'Something like that. I have to hurry away for a while.'

She quickly went out, seeing the hotel driver just outside. She approached him.

'Please take me to the Via Capello.'

In a moment they were away. She didn't notice Giorgio standing in the doorway with a puzzled frown.

For the whole journey she sat tense, watching Verona glide past her, wondering what the city would mean to her in future. The place where she and her Romeo had achieved their happy ending? Or the place where the star-crossed lovers had been forced to accept that their love was never meant to be?

At last they drew up outside the Casa di Giulietta and she got out.

'Shall I wait for you?' the driver asked.

'No. I don't know how long I'll be. Thank you, but go back.'

He drove off, leaving her standing there. Then she went to the house, which had just opened for the day. A doorman greeted her, recognising her as a bride who was booked in a couple of days ahead.

'You'll find everything just as you're hoping for,' he called cheerfully.

'I'm sure I will,' she called back politely.

But would her wedding be as she was hoping for? Would anything in her life be right again?

As always, Juliet was standing in the courtyard. Natasha headed for the statue, glad that for the moment they were alone.

'I never asked your advice before,' she said. 'I believed you were just a fantasy. But now my whole world is upside down, and maybe you're the one person who can help me.

'What can I do? I made a silly mistake but I was confused. I didn't want to hurt Mario. I just couldn't understand what it would mean to him. Now he thinks I don't really love him, but I do. How can I make him believe that?'

Silence.

'Oh, please, you must help me. You know more about love than anyone. Tell me what I can do.'

She pressed her hand against her chest.

'You understand that, don't you?' she said to Juliet, who also had a hand on her breast. 'You know what it's like to press your hand over the pain, hoping to make it go away. But it doesn't go, and you become frantic trying to think of something that will help. I can't think of anything. What can I do?'

She took a step closer to Juliet, seeking to look her in the eye. She told herself not to be fanciful, otherwise she might have imagined Juliet's soft voice saying, *He's as troubled and unsure as you are.*

I know. He's suffering terribly and it's my fault. I thought the worst of every man because of my father, but now I realise that I shouldn't have done.

Discovering that you'd read the letter hurt him. He hasn't completely recovered.

Nor have I.

You're coping better than he is.

Truly? What can I do now?

Be kind to him. He is confused.

But what is it that confuses him?

You. You always have, although he would never admit it.

Does our love really have a future?

Who can tell? You can only hope.

And hope might come to nothing. That fact had to be faced. She would return to the hotel and find him not there because he no longer wanted her. It was over. He would never return.

Tears filled her eyes, blurring her vision so that the street around her seemed to become a swirling mass. She groped her way forward, missed the edge of the pavement and crashed to the ground. She was intensely aware of pain going through her head before she blacked out.

The first person Mario met on his return was Damiano.

'So there you are!' his brother exclaimed. 'I thought you were still upstairs, sleeping it off while Natasha was away.'

'Away?'

'She came downstairs a few hours ago. She went off somewhere in a hurry.'

'Went somewhere? You mean she's gone? Where?'

'She didn't say where she was going. Just walked out and didn't come back. You don't mean there's something wrong, surely? The two of you are getting married tomorrow. She's probably making last-minute preparations for the wedding.'

'Yes, of course,' Mario said in a voice that was deliberately blank to hide the storm of alarm that was rising within him.

'I expect she's preparing a special surprise for you.'

Yes, Mario thought desperately. Natasha was preparing a surprise for him, and he had a dreadful feeling that he knew what the surprise was.

'Oh, no!' he breathed. 'How could she do this to me?'

'What do you mean?' Damiano demanded.

'She's done it again.'

'Done what again?'

'What she did before—leaving without a goodbye, when I wasn't there to see. Disappearing into thin air like she'd never existed.'

'I'm sure you're wrong about that,' Damiano protested.

Mario tore his hair. 'You have no idea,' he raged. 'She vanished and I spent weeks looking for her before I realised that I'd never find her because she'd shut me out of her life.' His voice rose in anguish. *'Now she's done it again.'*

Nobody had noticed Giorgio entering the hall. He stood watching Mario with a puzzled frown.

'What's happened?' he asked at last.

'Have you seen Natasha today?' Mario demanded.

'Yes, I saw her get into the car with the chauffeur a few hours ago. He was only gone half an hour.'

'Fetch him,' Mario said.

Giorgio went out and returned with the chauffeur.

'Where did you take her?' Mario demanded.

'To the Via Capello.'

'And you brought her back?'

'No, she told me not to wait for her.'

'So she's gone,' Mario muttered. 'She's gone.'

He turned away so that they shouldn't see his face, which he knew must betray his pain, greater than any he'd known in his life before. He'd wanted so much to believe in her. Since their quarrel the night before he'd brooded over what lay before him. A life with her, always worried about the strength of her love? Or a life without her?

He'd paced the dark streets for hours, trying to understand his own heart. By the time he'd arrived home he knew that Natasha mattered more than anything in the world. However hard it was for him, he would do what he had to for their love to succeed; the thought of losing her was unbearable.

And he had arrived to find her gone.

He wanted to howl with rage, but even more with misery. She had betrayed his love, abandoned him, while knowing what it would do to him.

'Why don't you look in her room?' Damiano said. 'If she's really gone she'll have taken everything with her.'

'All right,' Mario said heavily.

What was the point? he thought. He would find her room deserted and the brutal truth underlined. Moving mechanically, he went up to her room and opened the door. Then he grew still.

The wardrobe was open, and inside it he could see her clothes. Pulling open drawers, he found more clothing.

'She hasn't gone for good,' Damiano said, coming in behind him. 'Or she would never have left all this behind.'

'But where did she go?' Mario asked hoarsely.

'The chauffeur said he took her to the Via Capello,' Giorgio said. 'Surely she went to Juliet's house.'

'Yes,' Mario said at once. 'I understand that now.'

Everything was becoming clear to him. Natasha had gone to consult Juliet, and now she would know how the two of them could put things right.

One thing was clear. He must join her as soon as possible. He headed for the front door.

'Hey, Mario,' Giorgio called. 'Where are you going?'

Mario paused and looked back at him. 'I'm going to find my lady,' he said.

As he drove himself to the Via Capello the words haunted him, as they had many times before. *It is my lady. Oh, it is my love.*

'"Oh, that she knew she were,"' he murmured.

At last Juliet's house came in sight. He parked and ran down the street to the alley that led to the courtyard. There was no sign of Natasha. All he could see was Juliet, staring ahead, coolly indifferent to her surroundings. He placed himself in front of her.

'Was she here?' he demanded. 'Did she come to you and ask your help? Did you help her?'

No response. Nor had he expected one. Nobody else could help them now.

He wandered through the house, seeking her without success. In one room he stood looking around him, reflecting that this was where their wedding was supposed to take place, and wondering what the future held.

Once more he returned to Juliet. A small group of tourists had gathered in front of her, pleading for her attention.

'It's very tempting to talk to her, isn't it?' a woman said to Mario. 'We came here earlier and there was a lovely young woman talking to her as if it really mattered. But I don't think she had any luck because as soon as she left she got hurt.'

'Hurt? How?'

'I'm not sure what happened. She just seemed to lose her balance. She went down hard and hit her head on the pavement. The last I saw, she was being taken to the hospital.'

Barely able to speak, he forced himself to say, 'You said she was a young woman. What did she look like?'

'Pretty, blue eyes, blonde hair.'

'And how did she seem?'

'Not sure, really. She wasn't moving. I suppose she might actually have been dead.'

He swallowed. 'Thank you for telling me,' he said hoarsely.

It took him ten minutes to get to the nearest hospital. There, he tore inside and up to the desk.

'A young woman was brought in this morning,' he gasped. 'She had a fall in the Via Capello. I must see her.'

The receptionist made a phone call and a nurse appeared.

He followed her into a small side ward and held his breath at the sight of Natasha lying on the bed. Her eyes were closed and it seemed to him that she was frighteningly still.

'Is this the person you are looking for?' the nurse asked.

'Yes, this is the person I was looking for.'

'Please tell me who she is.'

'Her name is Natasha Bates.'

'And who is her next of kin?'

'I am. I'm her husband. At least, I will be in a few days. If she lives.'

He had to force himself to say the last few words, but the fear was more than he could endure.

'We don't yet know how seriously she's hurt,' the nurse said. 'She's still unconscious, but hopefully she'll soon come round.'

He moved to the bed, looking down at Natasha lying there. She seemed different to the strong, determined young woman he remembered: smaller, more frail and vulnerable.

A sudden fearsome echo haunted him: Romeo coming to Juliet in the tomb, seeing her lying there, silent and motionless, believing her dead. He tried to fight the thought away but he had a terrified feeling that she would leave him unless he could prevent her.

'Natasha,' he said, taking a chair beside the bed. 'It's me, darling. Can you hear me?'

She neither moved nor spoke.

'Are you there?' he begged. 'Please tell me that you're there.'

His heart sank. Her breathing told him that she was still alive, but in another sense she wasn't there. She was living in another universe, one where she might be trapped for ever.

'You went away from me once,' he whispered. 'I thought I would go mad at your rejection, but you came back and we found each other. Then today I thought you'd abandoned me again, and losing you was even worse than before.

'What happened was my fault. I couldn't bear discovering that I'd been living in a fantasy, that you loved me less than I'd thought. But if that's true—' he hesitated '—if the love is mainly on my side, then…then I'll live with that as long as I can have you. Do you understand? I'll accept any conditions as long as I don't lose you again. Even if—' he shuddered '—even if you never really wake up, but stay like this always, I won't leave you. I'll care for you and love you for years and years, until the day we can be finally together for ever.'

He leaned closer to murmur into her ear, 'Don't leave me. I'm yours in every way and I always will be. Natasha? Can you hear me?'

'Yes,' she whispered.

'I followed you all the way to Juliet's house. You went to ask her help, didn't you?'

'Yes.' She whispered the word so softly that he wasn't sure he'd heard properly.

'What?' he asked eagerly, leaning closer.

'She was very kind to me.'

He was suddenly sure that they understood each other. He must seize this moment, lest there should never be another.

'I tried too,' he said. 'But she stayed silent. I reckon she was telling me to see the truth for myself.' Inspiration came to him. 'And the truth we have to understand is that we love each other more than we can say in mere words. We've always known that, but we've never managed to face it before. But now the time has come and if I do nothing else in the world I have to make sure that you know.'

He kissed her again softly before murmuring, 'You are my lady. You are my love. Oh, that you knew you are.'

'Am I?' she whispered. 'Am I truly?'

'You know you are. And you will always know that you are.'

'How can I believe it? It's too good to be true.'

'Then I'll have to spend my life convincing you. I was so afraid you wouldn't wake up.'

'I was in such a strange place. I couldn't tell which way to turn, but suddenly you were there, beckoning me.'

'I always will be. I'll never let you go.'

The nurse appeared. She checked Natasha's pulse, read the machines and smiled at the result.

'This is what we hoped for,' she said. 'It's not serious. A few days' rest and you'll be back on your feet.'

When she had left they hugged, looking deep into each other's eyes, reading the depths for the first time. But now no words were spoken. No words were needed. Soon Natasha's eyes closed and Mario held her while she slept, thinking blissfully of the years ahead when he would hold her many times in his arms and always in his heart.

The wedding had to be delayed for two weeks, but at last the time came when they entered Juliet's house and made the vows of lifelong love and fidelity. Once, many years before, another couple had vowed the same, only to see their happiness cut short. But Natasha and Mario had no fear.

After the ceremony they went out onto the balcony, where Giorgio had arranged for a photographer to be clicking his camera madly. But the bride and groom were barely aware of him. They saw only each other.

'Just us,' he said as they held each other later that night.

'Not quite just us,' she murmured. 'There were two other people there. Couldn't you sense them?'

'Yes, they were there, watching over us as they've always done. And perhaps they always will.'

'No need,' she said. 'From now on we'll watch over each other.'

'Do you really think we can?'

'Yes, we can.' She turned in the bed, taking him in a fervent embrace.

'Come here,' she said. 'Come here *now*.'

* * * * *

THE TEMPORARY MRS MARCHETTI

MELANIE MILBURNE

To Sarah Lewer. Thanks for the inspiration
for this novel and thanks also for being such a
wonderful beauty therapist and gorgeous person.
XXXX

CHAPTER ONE

THE FIRST THING Alice noticed when she came to work that morning was the letter on her desk. Something about the officious-looking envelope with its gold embossed insignia made her skin shrink against her skeleton. Letters from lawyers always made her feel a little uneasy. But then she looked closer at the name of the firm. Why would a firm of Italian lawyers be contacting her?

She picked the letter up and her breath came to a juddering halt when she saw it was postmarked Milan.

Cristiano Marchetti lived in Milan.

Alice's fingers shook as if she had some sort of movement disorder. Surely he hadn't…*died*? A sharp pain sliced through her, her breath coming in short, erratic bursts, making not just her fingers tremble but her whole body.

Oh, no. Oh, no. Oh, no.

How had she missed that in the press? Surely there would have been an announcement for someone with Cristiano's public profile? They reported every other thing he did. The glamorous women he dated. The fading hotels he bought and rebuilt into stunning boutique accommodation all over the Mediterranean. The charity events he attended. The parties. The nightclubs. Cristiano couldn't change his shirt or shoes or socks without someone reporting it in the press.

Alice peeled open the envelope, her eyes scanning the brief cover letter, but she couldn't make any sense of it…or maybe that was because her brain was scrambled with a host of unbidden memories. Memories she had locked away for the last seven years. Memories she refused to acknowledge—even in a weak moment—because that was the pathway to regret and that was one journey she was determined never to travel. Her legs were so unsteady she reached blindly for her chair and sat down, holding the document in front of her blurry gaze.

But wait…

It wasn't Cristiano who had died. It was his grandmother, Volante Marchetti, the woman who, along with his late grandfather Enzo, had raised him since he was orphaned at the age of eleven when his parents and older brother had been killed in an accident.

Alice frowned and cast her gaze over the thick document that had come with the cover letter that named her as a beneficiary of the old woman's will. But why had his grandmother mentioned *her* in her will? Why on earth would the old lady do that? Alice had only met Cristiano's grandmother a handful of times. Volante Marchetti had been a feisty old bird with black raisins for eyes and a sharp intellect and an even sharper sense of humour. She had instantly warmed to the old lady, thinking at the time of how lucky Cristiano was to have a grandmother so spritely and fun, and had often thought of her since.

Maybe his grandmother had left her a trinket or

two—a keepsake to mark their brief friendship. A piece of jewellery or one of the small watercolour paintings Alice remembered admiring at the old lady's villa in Stresa. She began to read through the legalese with her heart doing funny little skips. So many words… Why did lawyers have to sound as if they'd swallowed a dictionary?

'Someone here to see you, Alice,' Meghan, her junior beauty therapist, said from the door.

Alice glanced at the time on her computer screen next to her appointment diary and frowned. 'But my first client isn't until ten. Clara Overton cancelled her facial. One of her kids is sick.'

Meghan waggled her eyebrows meaningfully and, lowering her voice to a stage whisper, said, 'It's a man.'

Alice had several male clients who came to her for waxing and other treatments but something told her the man waiting to see her wasn't one of them. She could feel it in her body. In her bones. In her blood. In her heartbeat. The awareness of imminent danger making a prickling sensation pass all over her flesh, as if her nerves were radar picking up a faint but unmistakable signal. A signal she had forced herself to forget. To wipe from her memory in case it caused her to regret the decision she had made back then. She pushed back her chair and stood but then decided it was better to remain seated. She didn't trust her legs. Not if she was going to come face to face with Cristiano Marchetti after all this time. 'Tell him I'll be ten minutes.'

'You can tell me yourself.'

Alice looked up to see Cristiano framed in the door, his chocolate-brown eyes as hard as two black bolts. All she could think of was how different it was seeing him in the flesh instead of a photograph in a gossip magazine or newspaper. Shockingly different. Heart-stoppingly different. *I'm-not-sure-I-can-handle-this* different.

For a moment she couldn't locate her voice. With him standing there, with his towering frame and commanding air, her office seemed to shrink to the size of a tissue box. Shoulders so broad he looked as if he'd been bench-pressing bulldozers—two at a time. An abdomen so hard and toned you could tap dance on it wearing stilettos and not leave a dent. Jet-black hair, thick and currently brushed back from his forehead in loose finger-groomed waves.

'Hello, Cristiano, what brings you to Alice's Wonderland of Beauty? An eyebrow-shape? Back and leg wax? Personality makeover?'

Alice knew it was crazy of her to goad him but she did it anyway. It was her defence mechanism. Sarcasm instead of emotion. Better to be cutting and mocking than to show how much his brooding presence disturbed her. It more than disturbed her. It unbalanced her. Her neatly controlled world felt as if it had been picked up and rattled like a maraca held by a maniac. The walls of her office were closing in on her. The floor was shifting beneath her feet like a sailboat pitching in a wild squall. The air was pulsing with crackling electricity that made her aware of every inch of her skin and every hit-and-miss beat of her heart.

His bottomless eyes roved her face as if he was looking for something he had lost and never thought to find again. His brow was etched in a deep frown that gave him a much more intimidating air than the way he had looked at her in the past. Back then he had looked at her with tenderness, with gentleness. With love.

A love she had thrown back in his face.

'Did you put her up to it?' he asked with a searing look that made the backs of her knees fizz as if sand were being trickled through her veins.

Alice placed her hands on the tops of her thighs below her desk so he wouldn't see their traitorous shaking. 'I presume you're referring to your grandmother?'

Something flashed in his gaze. Bitterness. Anger. Something else she wasn't ready to acknowledge, but she felt it all the same. It breathed scorching hot fire all over her body, stirring up memories. Erotic memories that made the blood in her veins pick up speed. 'Have you been in contact with her over the last seven years?' he asked in that same terse *don't-mess-with-me* tone.

'No. Why would I?' Alice gave him a pointed look. 'I rejected your proposal, remember?'

His jaw tensed so hard she could see the white tips of his clenched muscles showing through his olive tan. 'Then why has she mentioned you in her will?'

So he hadn't known about the terms of his grandmother's will until recently? Had the old lady not told him of her plans? *Interesting.* 'No idea,' Alice said. 'I only met her a couple of times when we were…back then. I've had zero contact since.'

He glanced at the will lying in front of her on her desk. 'Have you read it?'

Alice gave him another speaking look. 'I was getting to that when you rudely barged into my office.'

His eyes nailed hers. Hard eyes. Eyes that could melt a month's supply of salon wax with a single glare. 'Let me summarise it for you. You stand to inherit a half share of my grandmother's villa in Stresa in Italy if you agree to be my wife and live with me for a minimum of six months. You will also receive a lump sum on the announcement of our engagement, which is to last no longer than one month.'

Shock hit Alice like a blow to the chest. *His...wife?*

She fumbled for the document, the sound of the pages rustling overly loud in the silence.

Engaged to him for a month? Married for six?

She cast her gaze over the words again, her breath coming in such short spark bursts it felt as if she were having an asthma attack. Her heart was beating so heavily it felt as if someone were punching it from behind. She hadn't seen any mention of marriage in her quick appraisal earlier. She'd barely had time to read any of it before he had gatecrashed into her day. Why hadn't she put on her make-up before work? Why hadn't she worn her brand-new uniform instead of this one with the eyebrow-tint stain on the right breast? Why hadn't she done her own eyebrows, for God's sake?

But there it was in black and white.

Alice was to co-inherit Volante Marchetti's summer retreat on the shores of Lake Maggiore if, and only if, she married and stayed married to Cristiano for six months. *Six months?* Six seconds would be too long. And there was the other clause. They must be engaged for no more than a month before the wedding. What sort of weird time frame was that? It shamed her that Cristiano saw the pages of the document shaking before she put it back down on the desk. But at least he couldn't see the tumult going on inside her stomach.

His wife?

Live with him?

She had been to his grandmother's villa one memorable weekend with Cristiano. Memorable because it was the first time he'd told her he loved her. Apart from her mother, no one had ever said that to her before. She hadn't said the words back because she hadn't trusted her feelings. But then, she had always been a step behind him in their relationship. She'd thought they were having a fling while she was on a brief working holiday in Europe. He'd decided it was a relationship. She'd thought it was temporary because she'd planned to go back to England and set up her own beauty spa, but he had wanted it to be permanent.

Permanent as in marriage and kids.

For as long as she could remember Alice had been against marriage—or at least for herself. After witnessing her mother go through three of them with exactly the same result: misery, subjugation, humiliation and financial ruin. She had told Cristiano a little about her background, not much, but more than she had told anyone, which made her all the more annoyed he had still gone ahead and asked her to marry him. In a crowded public place to boot, which had added a whole other layer of pressure she resented him for.

His arrogance made her furiously angry. Had he really thought she would fall upon him with a grateful squeal of *Yes!* just because he was super-rich and said he loved her and wanted to spend the rest of his life with her? How long would that love have lasted? They'd had a passionate if a little volatile relationship. How could she be sure his desire/love for her wouldn't burn out as fast as it had been ignited?

If he had truly loved her he would have accepted her no as final and settled for a less formal arrangement. People lived together for years and years without needing the formality of marriage. Why be so damn nineteen-fifties about it? A marriage certificate didn't make a relationship any more secure. In fact, it could do the very opposite, forcing women into a subservient role once kids came along from which they could never escape.

But Cristiano at heart was a traditionalist. For all of his modern male sophistication, deep down he wanted a wife and family to come home to while he built his empire. So he had given her an ultimatum. Tried to control her. Tried to manipulate her into doing what he wanted.

Marriage or nothing.

Alice had called his bluff and ended their relationship then and there, and flown back to England, never expecting to hear from him again. Well, maybe that wasn't quite true. She *had* expected to hear from him with a big apology and 'let's try again' but it hadn't happened. Showed how much he'd 'loved' her. Not enough to fight for her. Not enough to compromise.

Not that she had offered to compromise, but still.

Alice brought her gaze back up to his glittering one. 'You're surely not going to go through with this...are you?'

A smile that wasn't quite a smile courted with the edges of his mouth. 'But of course. It is what Nonna wanted. Who am I to disregard her last wishes?'

Alice frowned so hard she could have frightened off fifty units of Botox. 'What happens if I don't agree?'

'To me?' He gave a careless shrug. 'Nothing other than a few shares in the company which will pass to a relative if I don't comply with the terms of the will.'

Alice wondered how important those shares were

to him. Was his easy-come, easy-go shrug disguising deeper, far more urgent motivations? Enough to marry someone he now hated? What about the villa? It was his grandmother's home, the place where he had spent much of his childhood being raised by his grandparents. Wouldn't he want to contest such an outrageous will? Surely he wouldn't want to share it with anyone, much less her? Why would he agree to such unusual conditions? She sent her tongue out over lips so dry it felt as if she were licking talcum powder. 'So…why would you want to marry someone who clearly doesn't want to marry you?'

His dark as night gaze gleamed, making the floor of Alice's belly shudder. 'You know why.'

Alice arched one of her brows, trying to ignore the pulsing heat his words evoked deep in her feminine core. 'Revenge, Cristiano? I thought you were a civilised man.'

'I am prepared to be reasonable.'

Alice affected a laugh. That was not a word she readily associated with him. He saw the world in black and white. He didn't know the meaning of the word compromise. What he wanted he got and woe betide anyone who got in his way. Not that she could talk. Compromise wasn't her favourite word in the dictionary, either. 'Reasonable in what way?'

He held her look with one she couldn't read. 'The marriage won't be consummated.'

Not...? Alice hoped she wasn't showing any sign of the numb shock she was feeling. Not just shock. Hurt. Humiliation. Their affair had been so wildly passionate. She had never had a lover before or since who made her feel the things he had made her feel. She had all but given up dating because of it. His touch was indelibly branded on her body. No one else's touch made her flesh sing—the opposite, in fact. Her flesh crawled when someone else touched her. The last time she slept with a date, well over a year ago, she came home and showered for an hour.

'You speak as if this…this preposterous marriage is a fait accompli,' she said. 'I said it seven years ago and I'll say it again now. I am not going to marry you.'

'Six months is not a long time. At the end of it you get joint ownership of a luxury villa to do with as you please. You can sell your half or keep it. The choice is yours.'

The choice wasn't hers. How could it be? She was being forced into a marriage with a man who no longer loved her—if he ever had. What he had wanted to do back then was control her. It was what he wanted to do now. What better way to punish her for having the gall to say no to him than to chain her to him in a loveless union?

Alice wouldn't do it. *No. No. No.*

She wouldn't subject herself to the humiliation of being his trophy wife while he continued to sleep with whomever he liked. He knew…*he knew* how much she'd hated seeing her mother cheated on by each of her husbands. It had been one of the things that had impressed her about him. He believed in monogamy—or so he'd said.

But what about your business plan?

Alice had somehow become the go-to girl for wedding make-up. The girl who had sworn against marriage was preparing brides all over London for theirs. *Go figure.* Her appointment diary was booked out for months ahead for the wedding season. It was becoming the biggest source of her income, especially high-profile weddings. She had plans to buy another salon—a larger place so she could extend her business because her Chelsea salon was getting too small to handle the burgeoning wedding market.

It had been a dream of hers for months. Years, actually. The only thing holding her back was the thought of taking on a load of property debt. Debt was something that terrified her. The mere thought of it kept her awake at night. She remembered too well how it had felt as a child to have not enough money for food, for clothes, for electricity when her mother had been between relationships.

She knew she could always rent another property like this one in Chelsea, but that left her at the mercy of landlords, something she had seen too many times during her childhood. Rents could be put up and buildings suddenly sold. The business she had worked so hard to establish would be jeopardised if she didn't own the property herself.

You could sell the villa after six months and be debt-free for the rest of your life.

Alice allowed the thought a little traction. The business she had sacrificed so much for was her baby, her mission, her purpose in life. Seeing it grow and develop over the last few years had been enormously satisfying. She had built it up from just a handful of clients to now one of the busiest salons in the area. She had celebrities and minor royalty on her books. People came to her because of the standards of excellence she maintained. To achieve her dream of setting up a luxury wedding spa would finally prove she had made it.

Failing wasn't an option.

Not after using her career as the excuse for not wanting to marry Cristiano. The career she put before everything else. Relationships. Holidays. Fun. Even friendships. All of it had been sacrificed for work.

But she couldn't marry Cristiano to solve that problem for it would throw her in the middle of an even bigger one.

Alice rose from her chair with her spine steeled with resolve. 'I've made my choice. Now, if you've finished catching up on old times, I have a business to run.'

His eyes continued to tether hers as if he were waiting for her cool composure to crack. 'Are you involved with someone? Is that why you're saying no?'

Was he *still* so arrogant? *Yes.* Arrogance was hardwired into his DNA. A man in his privileged position had no concept of why a woman wouldn't want to thrust her hand out for him to put a ring on it. He had it all: the money, the looks, the luxury lifestyle, the fast cars and exotic holiday destinations. Alice wished she had a lover to fling in his face. She considered inventing one but knew it wouldn't take him long to call her out on her lie. He wouldn't have to hunt around too far to find her social life was practically non-existent. Her work was her social life.

'I know you find it hard to believe you're irresistible because of your wealth and other…erm…assets, but I am not going to prostitute myself for the sake of an inheritance I neither asked for nor need.'

His expression gave nothing away. 'I meant what I said, Alice. It will be a marriage in name only.'

No one said her name quite the way he did. His Italian accent gave it a completely different emphasis. *Aleece.* The sound of it was like an erotic caress. It made the base of her spine shiver as if he had touched her with a brush of his warm male hand. Thinking of his hands made her want to look at them.

Don't. Don't. Don't.

But in spite of her rational brain's pleas, she looked. Those broad-spanned hands had travelled over every inch of her flesh. Those long tanned fingers had coaxed her into her first proper orgasm. They had discovered all of her erogenous zones, tortured them with such intense pleasure it had shaken her to the core of her being. She could feel the echo of it even now, as if just being in the same room as him, breathing the same air as him, made her body recognise him as her only pleasure giver.

Alice dragged her gaze upwards and collided with his. He knew. Damn it, he knew how much sensual power he had over her. She could see it in the knowing glint in his pitch-black eyes. She felt it when he sent his gaze over her body as if he too were remembering what it had felt like to hold her in his arms as she splintered into a thousand pieces of shivering, quivering ecstasy.

He lifted a hand to his jacket pocket and took out a business card and placed it on the desk next to the copy of his grandmother's will. 'My contact details should you change your mind. I'll be in London for the next week while I sort out some business affairs.'

Alice wilfully ignored the card. 'I'm not going to change my mind, Cristiano.'

I'm not. I'm not. I'm not.

A cynical smile lifted one side of his mouth. 'We'll see.'

We'll see?

What did he mean, 'We'll see'? Alice didn't get the

chance to ask him for he turned and left her office, leaving her with the lingering fragrance of his aftershave, the lemon and lime with a base note of leather that made her nostrils tingle…not to mention the rest of her body.

Meghan was bug-eyed when she came back. 'Oh, my God! You didn't tell me you knew Cristiano Marchetti. I didn't recognise him at first. He's much more gorgeous in the flesh than he is in photographs in the press. I nearly fainted when he walked past me just then and smiled at me. What did he want? Is he going to come here for treatments? Please let me do him. Can I do him? Please, please, please?'

Alice wasn't going to explain her past relationship with her employee even if Meghan was turning out to be one of the best she'd ever had. And as for Meghan 'doing him', if anyone was going to 'do him' it was going to be her. She would like nothing better than to get a pot of hot wax and strip that supercilious smile off his too-handsome face. 'He's not a client. I met him a few years ago. He just dropped in to say hi.'

'Met him as in met him and dated him?'

Alice didn't respond other than to purse her mouth. Meghan blushed and bit her lower lip. 'Sorry. I shouldn't have asked that. I know you insist on absolute confidentiality with celebrity clients. It's just he's so handsome and you never seem to date anyone and I wondered if it was because—'

'Can you get my treatment room ready for my next client?' Alice said. 'I have some urgent paperwork to see to.'

Alice blew out a breath once Meghan scuttled away. For seven years she had told herself she'd made the right decision. She had chosen her career over commitment.

Freedom over having a family. She had stood firm on her decision, not once wavering on it. Now, within her grasp was a way to finally achieve the success and financial security she had thus far only dreamt about.

Six months of marriage.

In name only.

She glanced at his business card. It seemed to taunt her with its presence.

Do it. Do it. Do it.

Alice snatched it up and tore it into as many pieces as she could and tossed them in the bin. It was kind of weird how they floated down just like a handful of confetti.

She hoped to God it wasn't an omen.

Cristiano would have had a stiff drink if he'd been a drinking man, but the death of his parents and his older brother to a drunk driver when he was eleven made him wary of using alcohol other than in strict moderation. Seeing Alice Piper again was like having his guts slashed wide open. And stomped on. The mere sight of her reopened the wound of his bitterness until he wondered how he had stood there without showing it.

He'd felt it, though. God in heaven, how he'd felt it. The blood rush. The pulse race. The adrenalin surge. The kick and punch of lust.

He had stood there and drunk in her features like a dehydrated man standing in front of a long cool glass of water. Her indifferent poise, her cornflower-blue gaze that could freeze mercury, the way she looked down her aristocratic nose at him as if he had crept in from a primeval swamp with his knuckles dragging. Her body was as lissom and gorgeous as ever—perhaps even more so. Her unusual silver-blonde hair with her naturally dark eyebrows and the creamy, ageless perfection of her skin gave her a striking appearance that never failed to snatch his breath.

Her rejection of him stung and burned and churned even after all this time. He had thought what they'd had was for ever. A once in a lifetime love. Their passionate affair had been unlike anything he'd experienced before. He'd wanted to build a future with her. A family. He'd believed it to be like the love his parents had had for each other. Like the love his grandparents had before his grandfather died. The death of his grandfather a couple of months before he met Alice had made him acutely aware of how important family was. It had been all he had thought about—having a family to replace the one he had lost so young. He'd felt ready. More than ready. He'd been twenty-seven and well established in the hotel business he had inherited from his parents. He was ready for the next phase of his life.

But Alice hadn't loved him. She had never said the words but he'd fooled himself into thinking she'd been showing it instead. How gullible he had been. How stupid to be so naively romantic when all she'd wanted was a quick fling with a foreigner to boast about with her friends.

What had his *nonna* been thinking? She had only met Alice a couple of times. Why bequeath her a share in a property worth millions and with such odd conditions attached? Six months of marriage? What sort of nonsense was this?

He hoped to God it wasn't some sneaky matchmaking ploy from the grave. His grandmother knew he had changed his mind about settling down. He had laughed off the suggestion every time she asked him when he was going to provide her with a great-grandchild. Nonna had expressed her disapproval of his playboy lifestyle on numerous occasions but he had always dismissed her concerns because no one was going to tell him how to run his life.

No one.

His grandmother had been disappointed when his relationship with Alice broke down. Terribly disappointed. But he had refused to talk about it. He'd had enough trouble managing his own disappointment without having to handle his grandmother's. Over the years she had stopped mentioning Alice's name knowing it would get zero response from him. Why then had she done this? Forced him back into Alice's life when it was the last thing he wanted?

The way the will was written meant if he didn't convince Alice to marry him then he would lose valuable shares in the family company to a cousin he had no time for. He wasn't going to hand over those shares only to have his cousin Rocco sell them to another party when he ran a little low on cash after playing the tables in a casino. Cristiano would rather marry his worst enemy before seeing that day dawn. He blamed himself for not telling his grandmother of Rocco's disturbing spending habits of late. But he hadn't wanted to burden her in the last months of her terminal illness.

Now it was too late.

The will had been written and now he had to convince Alice Piper to marry him.

Not that Alice was an enemy in the true sense of the word. She was a mistake he had made. A failure he wasn't particularly fond of being reminded about. He had wiped her from his memory. Every time a thought of her would enter his mind he would ruthlessly erase it like someone cleaning a whiteboard. He had lived his life since as if she had never been a part of it. As if he had never had such amazing sex with her it had made his body tingle for hours afterwards. As if he had never kissed that sensually supple mouth. As if he had never felt that mouth around him while she blew the top of his head off.

Cristiano wasn't going to let Alice think he was anything but delighted with the way his grandmother had orchestrated things. It suited him to let Alice think he was eager to put that ring on her finger and tie her to him for six months. Besides, maybe avoidance wasn't the way to handle the lingering sting of her rejection. Maybe some immersion therapy would finally end his torment.

Alice might have given him that haughty look and said no as if it were her last word on it, but this time he wasn't taking no for an answer.

CHAPTER TWO

ALICE NEITHER HEARD nor saw anything of Cristiano for the next couple of days. She had been expecting him to show up at work again, knowing him to be implacably determined when he set his mind to something. She had received a call from the lawyer handling the execution of the will, who explained some of the finer points. There was a time limit on accepting the terms. If she didn't marry Cristiano by the end of a month-long engagement the villa would be sold outside thc Marchetti family. Alice wondered what Cristiano would think about that—his childhood home sold to strangers. Was that why he was pushing for this marriage? Or was it purely revenge?

On the third day without sight or sound of Cristiano, Alice got a call from her salon building's landlord, Ray Gormley. 'I know this will come as a bit of a surprise, Alice, but I've sold the building,' he said. 'The new owner is taking possession immediately. You have a few months left on your current three-year lease so it shouldn't disrupt—'

'Sold?' Alice gasped. 'I didn't even realise you had it on the market.'

'I didn't, but I got an offer I'd be a fool to refuse,'

he said. 'I'm consolidating some of my interests. This guy's bought the building next door as well. Says he's going to make them both into a luxury hotel.'

Suspicion made every hair on the back of Alice's neck stand up and fizz at the roots. 'A…a hotel?'

'Yes,' Ray said. 'You ever heard of Cristiano Marchetti? He has boutique hotels all over Europe.'

Alice's jaw was so tight she felt the tension in her neck as if someone had a noose around it—which they did. *Damn it.*

'So…let me get this straight… Marchetti approached you completely out of the blue?'

'Yes,' Ray said. 'He's been looking for suitable property in London. The UK is the only place he doesn't have a hotel. This is stage one of his British expansion.'

Alice was still trying to get her heart out of her mouth and back in her chest where it belonged. Cristiano was her new landlord? What did he plan to do? Hike up her rent so she had no choice but to marry him? She had three months left on her three-year lease. It had always worried her having such a short-term lease, which was one of the reasons she wanted to buy her own property. But Ray had always assured her he wasn't selling any time soon. His wife and three daughters were clients of hers. She had thought—stupidly thought—she was safe.

But what would happen once Cristiano took possession?

Alice ended the call and started pacing her office so hard she thought she'd go right through the floorboards to the subway below. This was absolutely outrageous. Cristiano was going to such devious lengths to bend her to his will. She wished now she hadn't torn up his card.

Not that she had forgotten his number—no matter how hard she tried to erase it, for some reason, it remained fixed in her brain. But he might well have changed it. After all, she had changed hers.

She sat back at her desk and dialled his number. She listened to it ringing and ringing, her courage just about deserting her when finally it was answered by a husky female voice. 'Hello?'

Alice's stomach dropped. 'Erm… I'm not sure if I have the right number—'

'Are you looking for Cristiano?' the young woman said.

'Erm…yes, but if he's busy I can—'

'He's right here beside me,' the woman said. 'Who will I say is calling?'

Right here beside her doing what?

Alice clenched her teeth so hard she could have bitten through a pair of tweezers. It was the middle of the day, for pity's sake. Why wasn't he at work instead of in bed with some gorgeous nymphet?

'It's Alice Piper.'

She heard the sound of the phone being handed over and couldn't stop an image forming of him lying amongst the rumpled bed linen of a hotel with a naked woman's body draped over his. 'I've been expecting you to call,' Cristiano said. 'Changed your mind yet?'

Alice gripped her phone so hard she thought her knuckles were going to burst through her skin. 'No, I have not.'

'That's a pity.' There was a note of casual amusement in his tone. 'I didn't want to have to play dirty but needs must.'

Alice's spine tightened as if someone were turning a

wrench on each and every vertebra. 'I know what you're trying to do but—'

'Come to my hotel and we'll discuss this over a drink.'

Alice wasn't going anywhere near his hotel. A hotel room was way too intimate. If she and Cristiano were alone together with a bed nearby, who knew what might happen? It wasn't him she didn't trust. It was her. Her body remembered him like a language she thought she'd long forgotten. Even now it was responding to the deep gravelly cadence of his voice, making her senses reel as if she had ingested some sort of mind-altering drug. 'I'd rather meet somewhere less…'

'Dangerous?'

The silky tone of his voice loosened the bolts on her vertebrae.

Alice pressed her lips together, trying to garner her defences. He wasn't the same man as seven years ago. He had changed. He was harder. More ruthless. More calculating and brutally tactical. She was going to have to be careful dealing with him. He wasn't in love with her now. He hated her. He wanted revenge. 'I'm not scared of you, Cristiano.'

'Perhaps not, but you're scared of how I make you feel. It's always been that way between us, has it not?'

'I felt lust for you back then. Nothing else.'

'You still feel it, don't you, *cara mia*?' His voice was a teasing feather stroking over the nerve-sensitive base of her spine.

'You're mistaken,' she said, injecting her voice with icy hauteur. 'I feel nothing for you but contempt.'

'That's a strong word for someone who once shared their body with me.'

'You know something? I didn't break your heart,' Alice said. 'I bruised your ego. That's what all this is about, isn't it? You hadn't had a woman say no to you before. You weren't in love with me. If you were you would have accepted and respected my decision not to get married.'

'That is an argument for another time,' he said with a thread of steel entering his tone. 'I want to see you tonight to discuss the rent on your salon going forward.'

Alice stiffened. It was all right for him with the millions he'd inherited when his parents were killed. She didn't have any rich relatives to hand her an empire or to give her a financial leg up when things turned ugly. Everything she had worked for had been out of her own blood, sweat and tears—and occasional tantrum. If he turned the financial screws on her now, everything she'd worked for could be compromised. Or—God forbid—even lost. 'Sometimes I wonder how you speak so fluently with all those silver spoons hanging out of your mouth.'

A pulsing silence passed.

Alice wondered if this was going to turn into one of their massive arguments. With hindsight she could see a large part of their relationship had been a power struggle. They had constantly bickered over things without anything being resolved other than in bed. Neither of them had wanted to compromise or back down from a stance. Making love had diffused the battle temporarily, but it hadn't solved the underlying issue.

He had wanted control of her and she wouldn't give it.

Cristiano released a long breath. 'I would give each and every one of those silver spoons back if I could have my parents and brother back for a day, let alone for the last twenty-three years.'

Alice suddenly felt ashamed of herself. He couldn't help his background any more than she could help hers. It was a cheap shot, similar to the ones she'd tossed at him in the past. Their verbal sparring had been a sort of foreplay. The battle of two strong wills, combined with a fierce lust for each other, had created some combustible arguments on occasion. Too many occasions. When had they ever sat down and had a discussion without one or both of them flying off in a temper? Had either of them actually listened to what the other said? Or were they too busy trying to think of a cutting comeback? 'I'm sorry. That was...unfair of me.'

'I have to go. Natalia is waiting for me.'

A dagger went to Alice's belly. She'd forgotten all about his gorgeous little bed buddy lying right beside him while he spoke to her on the phone. Jealousy rose in her like a beast that had been woken too abruptly. Giant paws of jealousy clawing at her insides, making her feel strangely hollow. Why was she feeling like this? She had no right to feel this way. She had ended their affair. She'd been the one to walk away, not him. She didn't have any rights over him now. He was a free agent to sleep with whomever he pleased. There should be no reason why the thought of him talking to her on the phone while a woman was in bed beside him should... *hurt* her so much.

'I'm sorry to force you to talk business in the middle of pleasure,' she said. 'Maybe next time turn your phone to silent so you don't get interrupted during one of your marathon sex sessions.'

There was another little silence.

Alice wished she hadn't spoken with such crisp venom. Every word she had spoken sounded as if it were painted bright green. What was wrong with her? It was crazy to give him ammunition he could use against her. If he thought for a picosecond she was jealous he would exploit it every opportunity he could.

'I'll pick you up for dinner at seven,' Cristiano said as if she hadn't spoken. 'What's your address?'

'I'm not having dinner with—'

'You will have dinner with me or I'll cancel your lease as of now.'

Alice's heart banged against her breastbone. 'You can't do that!'

'Can't I?'

She swallowed a rush of panic. She had to get control of her tongue. It wouldn't help her cause to challenge him all the time. It would only make him all the harder to manage. She could handle dinner. Sure she could. It would be a test for her. It would be proof she could spend an hour or two in his company without wanting to tear his clothes off his hot body.

Yikes. Do not even think about that body.

It was probably still naked and sweaty from bed-wrecking sex. 'Won't Natalia mind you taking out another woman for dinner?'

'No.'

Alice was frustrated by his one-word answer so went digging for more. 'She must have a very laid-back attitude to relationships to allow you to entertain other women while she's involved with you.'

'Natalia knows her place.'

'Are you going to marry her?'

'She's already married.'

Shock rendered Alice speechless for a moment. What had happened to Cristiano's conservative old-fashioned values? The Cristiano of the past would never have slept with a married woman. He'd had no time for men and women who betrayed their marital vows. He'd spoken at length about the commitment his parents had made and how he admired and respected them for staying true to it until their untimely deaths. Until death do us part had been something he had believed in to the letter.

What had changed him?

You changed him.

The thought was an uncomfortable weight in the pit of her stomach. Had she been the one to destroy his faith in relationships? But she hadn't been ready to settle down back then. Rejecting a proposal wasn't a crime, was it? Surely she'd had the right to decide whether she wanted to be married or not. It wasn't the Dark Ages, for God's sake. But the thought continued to niggle at her. Had she turned him into a casual-living playboy who had no time for commitment? These days he used women to suit his needs. He was in and out of relationships faster than a racing driver changed gears. Was he really no longer a man who longed for a wife and family of his own? And why should that make her feel so…so sad? 'Well then, I'd better get off the phone so you can get back to your grubby little affair, hadn't I?'

'I'll see you tonight,' he said and before she could think of a comeback, or tell him she wasn't going, he ended the call.

Alice dressed for dinner as if she were dressing for combat. Each layer of clothing was like putting on a suit of armour. The armour of sophistication she had been so sadly lacking seven years ago.

She sometimes wondered what Cristiano had seen in her back then. She had been twenty-one years old and newly qualified as a beauty therapist. It had been her first trip abroad without friends accompanying her. She had been on a shoestring budget while she backpacked around Europe but she'd only got as far as Italy when she'd met him in a crowded street in Milan when a sharp catch on her backpack had become caught on his clothing, as she'd brushed past.

They'd stood in the middle of the street, comically locked together by their clothes. He'd made a comment about it bringing a whole new meaning to 'hooking up with someone' and she'd laughed. Once he had untangled himself he'd insisted on buying her a coffee.

One coffee had turned into two coffees and then dinner. Instead of going back to the backpackers' centre she'd found herself accepting his offer of accommodation for the night or two she'd planned to spend in his home city. At no time had she felt any pressure to sleep with him. She was not unaware of his interest in her and she hadn't been all that good at hiding hers in him. But his respectful handling of her had impressed her. Not many healthy and virile young men of twenty-seven, as he was at that time, would have asked a woman back to his place and not expected something in return.

In the end it had been Alice who made the first move. She still remembered their first kiss. Sometimes when she closed her eyes she could still feel those firm lips moving with such urgency against hers, making every cell in her body vibrate. One kiss hadn't been enough.

Next minute she was tearing his clothes off him and all but throwing herself at him.

Her mind drifted… The drugging kisses. The phenomenal foreplay. The earth-rocking sex. The mind-bending orgasms. The electric tingling of her flesh for hours afterwards.

How had she gone so long without it?

Alice sighed and picked up her lipstick. She had never found anyone else who made her feel desire quite like that, as if she would literally die if she didn't have him. Which meant she would have to be super careful around him now. She didn't want to betray herself, to give him any hint she hadn't managed to move on with her life. Of course she had moved on with her life. She was a successful businesswoman with money in the bank…most of it borrowed, but still.

What else did she need?

The doorbell sounded and she put her lipstick in her purse and picked up her evening wrap and went to the door. Even though she was in four-inch heels Cristiano towered over her. 'You're late,' she said. 'I thought you said seven. It's half-past.'

He gave a shrug of one broad shoulder as if punctuality and common politeness were no longer of any interest to him. 'I knew you'd wait for me.'

The way he said it made it sound as if she had spent the last seven years doing exactly that. She raised her chin and sent him a look that would have soured long-life milk. 'How did you find out where I lived?'

'Your very helpful *previous* landlord.'

The slight emphasis on the word 'previous' made Alice's nerves jangle.

She wound her wrap around her shoulders, wishing she could wind it around Cristiano's neck instead. 'Where are we going to dinner?'

'Aren't you going to show me around your house first?'

Alice pinched her lips together. 'My home is hardly on a league with yours.'

He glanced around her foyer with an appraising eye. 'Nice. How long have you lived here?'

'Two years.'

'Alone?'

Alice forced herself to hold that piercing gaze even though it made every atom in her body protest. 'At the moment.'

He gave a slight nod as if her answer satisfied him on some level. 'Big place for a single girl. How many bedrooms?'

'Four.'

His ink-black brows lifted in an arc. 'Are you renting?'

Alice threw him a black look. 'Why? Are you thinking of buying it too, and jacking up the rent? Sorry to spoil your fun but I own it.' *Or at least the bank does.*

His mouth curved at one corner in a half-smile that should not have caused her heart to stumble. 'You could pay this mortgage off and have money to spare if you agree to the terms of my grandmother's will. You could expand your business as well.'

Alice's brows snapped together in a frown. How did he know she wanted to expand her business? Who on earth had he been talking to? He had an unnerving ability to gain information about her. And read her mind. Not to mention her body.

Oh, dear God, why wasn't her body ignoring him? Damn it.

Her body was a traitor. It remembered him too well. It only had to be within touching distance and it went haywire. It was as if the last seven years hadn't happened. All her nerves were screaming out for his touch like starstruck teenage fans at a boy-band concert. 'My business plans are absolutely no concern of yours. Nor indeed are my private ones.'

His eyes moved over her body in an assessing sweep that made her insides coil with lust. She knew that look. The look that said, *I want you and I know you want me. And I can prove it.*

'It must get a bit lonely at times, living in this big old house by yourself, *sì*?'

'I'm not one bit lonely.'

He released a small puff of air that had cynicism riding on its backdraft. 'Sure you're not.' He was suddenly standing closer than she'd realised. Had she been so mesmerised by his gaze she hadn't detected him closing the distance between them? He reached out and picked up a tendril of her hair and wound it around the length of his index finger. It was too late to step back.

Why the hell hadn't she stepped back?

Every nerve root on her scalp was tingling from the tether of his touch.

'Have you missed me, *cara*?' His voice was a deep, seductive burr of sound that sucker-punched her self-control.

Alice had to swallow three times to locate her voice. *Three times!* As it was she only just stopped herself from giving a betraying whimper. 'If you don't let go of me this instant I'll file my nails on your cheek. Got it?'

His mouth curved in an indolent smile and he wound

her hair a little tighter. 'I'd much rather you'd rake them down my back.'

His incendiary words sent a shockwave of lust through her body. She swore she could feel the echo of where he had been in the past—the thickened length of him driving into her until they both lost control. Her blood simmered in her veins, rushing through her system as if it were on fire.

Get control. Get control. Get control.

The words were sounding an alarm in her brain but her body was blatantly ignoring it. Her body swayed towards his…or maybe his moved closer. His muscle-packed thighs brushed hers, reminding her of all the times they had trapped hers beneath their sensual power and superior strength. Sex with Cristiano had always had an element of danger to it. The dark unknowable power of it. The uncontrollable force of it had thrilled and frightened her in equal measure. Her body felt things with him it had never felt before or since. Not even close. She was spoilt now for anyone else.

Another good reason to hate him.

Alice pushed back against his chest even though it tugged cruelly on her hair. 'In your dreams, buddy.'

Cristiano's gaze had a mocking glint to it. 'I could have you in a heartbeat and you damn well know it.'

'Ah, but you don't want me, remember?' Alice said with an arch look. 'A marriage in name only, wasn't it?'

A whip-quick flicker of tension moved across his mouth. He stepped back and held open the door. 'We'll lose the booking if we don't make a move. I had to pull strings to secure it.'

'You're good at that, aren't you, Cristiano? Pulling strings to get people to do what you want?' Alice gave him a sugar-sweet smile on her way past him in the doorway. 'What a pity you can't get *me* to toe the line.'

He captured her forearm in the steel bracelet of his long, strong fingers, tugging her around so his gaze clashed with hers. His eyes were onyx-dark and brooding with indomitable purpose. 'I haven't finished with you yet. But once I am, I swear to God you'll be on your knees begging me to marry you.'

Alice flashed him a look of pure defiance and wrenched out of his hold, rubbing her arm as if it had been scorched. Which it had. Why, oh, why was it so damn exciting sparring with him? She hadn't felt like this in years. Alive. Switched on after a long time on pause. Running at breathtaking speed instead of idling. It was nothing short of exhilarating. 'You think you can bully me into doing what you want? Try it and see what happens.'

His eyes dipped to her mouth, setting off a feverish chain of reaction in her body. Only he could do that. Make her hot for him by looking at her. 'You'd be a fool to throw away this chance to build your asset base,' he said. 'Don't let emotion get in the way of a good business deal.'

'Who are you to lecture me about emotion?' Alice said. 'You're the one who was in love with me, not me with you, and now you're punishing me because I'm about the only person on this planet who has the backbone to stand up to you and—'

'I wasn't in love with you.'

The words stung like a hail of rubber bullets. Alice blinked. Swallowed. Blinked again. *Not in love with her?* Not even a little bit? Why that should bother her she didn't want to examine too closely. 'Right, well then, that's good to know. At least I did you a favour then in rejecting your proposal. We would've been divorced by now otherwise and think how much that would've cost you.'

He opened the passenger door for her, jerking his head towards the vacant seat like a police officer taking in a suspect for interrogation. 'Get in.'

Alice straightened her shoulders, throwing him a glare that could have stripped ten years of graffiti off a council estate wall. 'Ask nicely.'

A muscle flicked in his jaw and his eyes smouldered like black coals. 'You know what will happen if you push me too far.' His tone was silk wrapped around a will of steel.

Alice did know and it was perverse of her to keep doing it. But she couldn't seem to help herself. It was an urge she couldn't control. She wanted to push him. She wanted to bait him. To break him. To reduce him to his most primal. A spurt of excitement lit like a wick inside her, sending a radiant heat coursing through her body. Her breasts tingled as if they were preparing themselves for the possessive cup of his hands. Her thighs trembled with the memory of his intimate invasion, her blood stirring into a frenzied whirlpool that made her aware of every feminine muscle contracting and releasing in her groin.

Oh, how she had missed this!

No one made her feel so…so energised. So vital. So…*aroused.*

She kept her gaze locked on his. The air was so charged with static she could hear it like a fizzing roar in her ears. 'What are you going to do, Cristiano? Lug me over your shoulder and carry me off like the caveman you really are underneath that smart Armani suit?'

Another ripple of tension passed over his rigidly set mouth, his eyes blazing as they tussled with hers. His hand left the top of his car door and snared one of hers before she could do anything to counter it—if she had wanted to, that was—ruthlessly tugging her towards him so there was barely a breath of air between their bodies. Alice could feel the slight protrusion of his belt buckle digging her in the stomach, a shockingly erotic reminder of the latent male power stirring just below it.

'Been a long time between drinks, has it, *cara*?' he asked in that dangerously smooth tone.

Alice huffed out a laugh but it didn't come out quite as convincing as she would have liked. It sounded breathless. Uncertain. Out of its depth. 'You don't get to hear about my love-life. It's none of your business.'

His fingers subtly tightened around her wrist, his touch a band of fire that sent lightning-fast currents of hot electricity straight to her core. 'It will become my business once we're married next month.'

Next month? Eek!

Alice elevated her chin, sending him a look of undiluted disdain. 'You seem to have a big problem understanding the concept of the word no. I'm. Not. Marrying. You.'

His top lip lifted in a sardonic curl. 'You want me so bad I can smell it.'

Alice disguised a quick swallow. She could smell it too. The musk and salt of arousal coming off both of them like a black magic potion. A swirling wicked spell. Its dangerous tentacles were wrapping around her body, coiling like a serpent, strangling her resolve until it was gasping for air.

Only he could do this to her. Make her so wild with need she forgot everything but the greedy hunger in her body clamouring for satiation.

His thighs were flush against hers, the swell of his erection so powerfully male—so blatantly, unashamedly male—it made every feminine cell in her body roll over and beg. Somehow—miraculously—she managed to conjure up a mocking smile. ‘That ego of yours is so big it deserves its own postcode. Or its own government.’

A spark of amusement lit his gaze and his fingers around her wrist loosened slightly, his thumb stroking in a fainéant movement over the hummingbird leap of her pulse. ‘Did you miss what we had together?’

Alice schooled her features into a mask of cool indifference. ‘Not a bit.’

His probing gaze kept hers captive. ‘So why haven’t you had a serious relationship since?’

How on God’s sweet earth did he know that?

Alice arched a brow. ‘None that *you* know about. Unlike you, I don’t live my life followed by paparazzi documenting every time I sneeze.’

‘When was your last relationship?’

She flicked her eyelids upwards. ‘Oh, for God’s sake, what is this? Twenty questions?’

His gaze didn’t waver. ‘A long time, then.’

Alice pursed her lips and then released them with a rush of air. ‘Are we having dinner or are we going to stand here and swap dating histories? I can get you a list of name and numbers if you’d like? I could even do a printout of some of their messages and emails if that gives you a hard-on.’

Cristiano put his hand back on top of the rim of the car door. 'That won't be necessary.'

Alice brushed past him to get in the car, shooting him a glare through the windscreen when he strode in front of the car to take his place behind the wheel. He started the engine with a powerful roar and entered the traffic with a quick glance over his shoulder, the G-force sending her back against the butter-soft leather seat.

Why did his driving always remind her of sex?

The thunderous growl of his engine, the thrusting of the gears, the press on the brakes and the push down on the throttle made her think of all the times he had taken her to bed—or other places—and driven them both to paradise.

Alice's gaze went to his hands holding the steering wheel with such indolent confidence, the long, tanned fingers with their dusting of dark hair doing all sorts of strange things to her insides. What was it about those hands that made her squirm with need? How was she to get through an evening with him? Sitting across the table with him at a restaurant, for God's sake?

How the hell had he got her to agree to dinner?

That was one of the scariest things about Cristiano Marchetti. He had an unnerving ability to get her to do things she had no intention of doing.

But...

That tricky little 'but' kept gnawing at the wainscoting of her mind. But what if she did agree to it? Six months was nothing. It would flash past. And at the end of it she would be set up financially. For life. She could build her wedding spa with money to spare. She could buy the best equipment, lavishly decorate the place without the limitations of a budget. She could take a holiday—something she hadn't done in years.

Alice chewed it over… He was expecting her to say no. But wait a minute… What if he didn't *want* her to say yes? What if he was only making all this fuss to make her think he was keen to get that ring on her finger?

She smiled a secret smile. She would string him along for a while longer and then she would call his bluff and expose his true motivations.

Married for six months to her mortal enemy?

Game on.

CHAPTER THREE

CRISTIANO OPENED AND closed the fingers of his right hand where they were gripping the steering wheel. He could still feel the hot tingle of Alice's skin against his fingertips. His lust for her was pounding like a jungle drum deep in his body. He ached with it. Burned with it. Vibrated with it. No one but her could reduce him to this. To stir in him such primitive, out of control longings. Longings he had never felt for anyone else. Longings that made a mockery of the sex he'd had before her and since.

Not that he hadn't had great sex over the years. He had. Many times. He'd made a point of it—using every sexual encounter to drive home the point to himself he could live without her.

It was just that in comparison to what he'd shared with Alice...well, it wasn't in the same league. Her body, her touch, her wildcat-on-heat response to him triggered something in him. Something indefinable. Something that made his flesh shudder in reaction when she came near. Something that, even now, with her sitting less than a half a metre away, he could feel moving through his body like the aftershocks of an earthquake.

He had to get her out of his system.

He had to.

He could no longer tolerate the rush of adrenalin every time he saw a silver-blonde head in the crowd and the savage drop of his gut afterwards when he realised it wasn't her. He had to prove to himself he was over her.

Was this why his *nonna* had set her will up this way? To help him move past the five-foot-six blonde roadblock in his life? To force him to confront the failure he would give anything to forget?

Cristiano had made a promise to himself not to sleep with Alice. *Look, but don't touch.* But how long was that going to last? He was barely keeping his hands off her now. All he had to do was reach over and stroke his hand down the slim flank of her thigh peeping out from above the knee-high hem of her little black dress.

His fingers twitched against the steering wheel. His groin growled when she crossed one long leg over the other, her racehorse-slim ankle moving up and down as if she were feeling the same restless agitation he was feeling.

Of course she was.

Cristiano allowed himself an internal smile. His ego had nothing to do with it. He could see the struggle she was having controlling her desire for him. He had felt it from the moment he'd stepped into her office and seen her sitting like a starchy schoolmistress behind that desk. She'd used the desk as a barrier. She hadn't trusted herself to get too close to him. She knew her body would betray her as his was doing to him. It was the way they were together. Match and tinder. Spark and flame. Trigger and explosion.

It was only a matter of time before he had her where he wanted her. Begging him. Clawing at him with those little wildcat claws. Gasping his name between panting breaths as he showed her what she'd been missing. What *he'd* been missing. Dear God, how he'd missed it! Missed her. The feistiness of her. The razor-sharp wit of her tongue. The flashpoint temper and the come-and-get-me teasing that had made him feel as if he were living on the edge of a vertiginous cliff.

The way her body felt around him when he drove in to the hilt.

Getting her to marry him was his goal, not sleeping with her…although if what he had seen from her so far was any indication, sleeping with her might happen sooner rather than later. A little financial blackmail was not his usual modus operandi, but he had to get her married to him otherwise his shares would be lost.

Not to mention the villa.

He couldn't lose that. It was the place where his father had grown up. It was where Cristiano had spent numerous happy family holidays before his parents' and brother's death. It was his home for the rest of his childhood and adolescence, the place where overnight he had grown from boy to man. Losing the villa would be like losing even more of his family than he had lost already.

Why had his grandmother done such an outrageous thing as to force him to share it with Alice?

He didn't need a conscience right now. Six months would pass before he knew it. He would insist on Alice living with him because he wasn't going to let the press get wind of there being anything amiss with his 'marriage'. No way was Alice Piper going to make a laughing stock out of him in the daily tabloids. He would enjoy making her act the role of devoted wife. It would be amusing to see her push against the boundaries he laid down.

'So, we'll have a nice dinner and discuss this situation we find ourselves in,' Cristiano said after a time.

'Discuss?' Alice's voice held a generous note of scorn. 'You don't discuss. You command.'

He sent her a smiling glance. 'And as my wife you will obey.'

Even from the other side of the car he could feel the heat coming off her livid blue glare. 'They have rewritten the marriage ceremony since the nineteen-fifties, you know. Women no longer have to obey their husbands. Not that you're going to be my hus—'

'We'll have a month-long engagement as the will specifies,' Cristiano said. 'You either marry me at the end of it or find yourself paying a rent you can ill afford.'

Her face was a picture of impotent outrage, almost puce instead of her natural creamy colour. 'You…you *bastard*.' Her hands curled into tight little balls as if she was tempted to fly at his face and was only just stopping herself. 'You scheming bastard.'

He gave a careless shrug. 'Sticks and stones.'

It was a while before she said anything. Cristiano wondered if she were thinking things over, running her mind over the figures, so to speak. She ran a good business, he had to give her that, but it would not survive a big hike in rent. And to get her to do what he wanted, he was prepared to go as high as it took.

Whatever it took.

'Why engaged for a month?' she said. 'If you're in such a hurry to get a ring on my finger then why not frogmarch me to a register office right away?'

'I'm not having anyone speculate on why we're not having a proper wedding, that's why,' Cristiano said, wondering if she was speaking figuratively or if she was changing her mind about marrying him.

'But you can't really mean to go to such lengths? I mean, a wedding is a big expense.'

'I can afford it.'

There was another silence.

'All right.' Her breath came out in a whoosh. 'You win. I'll marry you.'

Cristiano hadn't expected such a rapid capitulation. He'd thought she would have fought it a little longer and a little harder. But then he wondered if she had a counter plan. She was clever. Whip-smart and streetwise. What devious plan had she cooked up? Did she intend to make him suffer every minute they were engaged? Did she really think she could outmanoeuvre him? He smiled another private smile.

Who knew this could be so much fun?

'I'm glad you're starting to see the positive side of our circumstances. It's a win-win for both of us, *sì*?'

The look she gave him would have sent a swarm of wasps running for cover. 'Everyone's going to know this is a farce the moment we're seen out in public together.'

'Ah, but that's where you're wrong, *tesoro*,' Cristiano said. 'We're going to act like a happy and devoted couple at all times and in all public spaces.'

A spluttering noise came from her side of the car. 'Not on your life—'

'Apart from when we're alone,' he continued as if she hadn't spoken. 'Then the claws can come out. I'm quite looking forward to it, actually.' He gave her another goading smile. 'It will be like old times, yes?'

Her eyes were spitting chips of blue ice, her mouth set in such a tight line her lushly shaped lips all but disappeared. Her whole body seemed to be shaking with rage. He could feel the vibration of it from his side of the car.

'Why are you doing this? Why? Why? Why?'

Why was he?

Good question. It wasn't just the shares, although that was a big part of it. It was more the sense of wanting to rewrite the past. To be in control this time. To be in charge of his emotions and passions. To be the one who told her when it was over, not the other way around. He was not going to be that person ever again—the person left behind. He had been that person as a child of eleven.

Left behind by his family.

The shock of that loss had never left him. Sometimes he could still feel that claw of despair in his chest, dragging, tearing at his organs. That terrible day when his grandparents had delivered the devastating news of the death of his parents and brother, he had felt as if he were the only person left on the planet.

Alone.

Abandoned.

Isolated.

It was the same feeling he'd felt when Alice walked out on his proposal. He stood in the middle of that crowded restaurant feeling as if a wall of thick glass were separating him from everyone else. No one could reach him. He could not reach them. He was blocked. Imprisoned in a cage along with his frustrated hopes and shattered dreams.

'We have unfinished business, Alice.'

'No. We. Don't.' Her words came out like hard pellets. 'Our business is finished. Kaput. Over. Dead and buried.'

Cristiano parked the car before he swivelled in his seat to look at her. She was sitting with her arms stiffly folded, her legs crossed, and her ankle jerking up and down as if she had a tic. 'It's not though, is it, *cara*? It's not one little bit finished.'

Her eyes met his and her throat moved up and down over a swallow like a small creature moving under a rug. But then she lowered her gaze to a point just below the knot of his tie. He heard her take a breath that sounded more like a shudder than a breath. 'You always did play dirty.'

'I play to win,' he said. 'So do you. It's why we clash so much.'

Her eyes came back to his. Hard. Bright. Flashing with such palpable rage he could feel it throbbing in the air that separated them. 'I won't let you win this, Cristiano. You might be able to blackmail me into marrying you, but you can't make me fall in love with you. That's what you want, isn't it? You want me to fall in love with you and then throw it back in my face like I threw back yours.'

'On the contrary, falling in love with me would be most inadvisable,' Cristiano said. 'Falling into bed with me? Well, that may be worth considering.'

Her eyes went as wide as the steering wheel he was resting his arm across. 'But you said you don't—'

'A man can change his mind, can't he?'

Her mouth opened and shut a couple of times, two flags of pink riding high on her cheekbones. 'I'm not going to sleep with you. I don't care how much you blackmail me.'

'Fine. Probably better that way.' He opened his door and proceeded to get out. 'I can get my needs met elsewhere.'

She sprang out of the car before he could get round to her side. 'Oh, no, you don't,' she said, hands on hips. 'You don't get to cheat on me. No way. If you can have lovers then so can I.'

Cristiano slowly shook his head as if dealing with a small, wilfully disobedient child. 'No. I'm the one who makes the rules. You follow them.'

She came at him with a pointed finger, drilling him in the chest like a tiny outraged jackhammer. 'I'm not obeying any of your stupid rules. I'm going to do what I damn well like and you can't stop me.'

Cristiano captured her hand, every cell in his body aching to tug her flush against him and show her what she was doing to him. But he was biding his time, waiting for her to come to him, as he knew in his bones she would. Her fiery nature stirred the banked-down embers of his. The heat was rising in a wildfire of lust, thundering through him like a runaway train on a steep decline.

He wanted her.

Oh, how he *wanted* her.

It was a thirst he couldn't quench with anyone else. A hunger that refused to be satisfied with another's touch. She was in his blood. In his body. She was a fever that had lain dormant until he had walked into her beauty salon and seen her sitting there with that coolly indifferent look on her face.

She wasn't indifferent to him. Not one little bit. He could see it in her eyes, the way they kept darting to his mouth and the way her tongue swept over her lips as if recalling the taste and feel of his crushed to its softness.

Cristiano slid one hand up her warm, silky smooth thigh. 'If we weren't in a public place I would take you right here and now.'

She pushed back from him as if he had suddenly burst into scorching flames. 'Get away from me.'

'Careful, Alice,' he said. 'We're in public. It's time to behave yourself.'

Her eyes went to needle-thin slits, her body visibly quaking with fury. 'Just you wait until I get you alone.'

He smiled and gave a mock shiver of delight. 'I can hardly wait.'

Alice was so angry she could barely read the menu. A red mist was before her eyes at the way he had turned things around so deftly. So he *did* want to marry her. But why? What did he hope to achieve? A bunch of stupid old shares he probably didn't need? She didn't buy that for a second. He wanted to marry her to punish her. To humiliate her.

But the more she thought about the long-term benefits for the short-term pain, she realised she really didn't have a choice. If she wanted to reach the pinnacle of success she had always dreamed of then this was the way to do it, and far quicker than she could ever have imagined.

She remembered his grandmother's villa. That lakeside villa was not some modest little run-down holiday shack. That villa was a luxury resort complete with lush gardens and trickling fountains and marble statues and a swimming pool big enough to set an Olympic record. If she walked away from a gift like that she would be certifiable.

Besides, the old lady had liked her and Alice had

liked her. A lot. She didn't want any paranormal consequences if she didn't accept the bequest with good grace. It was the sensible, respectful thing to do.

The only trouble was Cristiano was part of the deal.

The man who could make her come on the spot by looking at her with those sinfully sexy eyes.

Alice shifted in her seat, painfully aware of the swollen excitement of her body. For a moment there she'd thought he was going to kiss her. His body had been so close to hers she'd felt his warmth, smelt his lemon and lime and hint of leather scent that wreaked such havoc on her senses. She had seen the way his eyes had dipped to her mouth, lingering there as if recalling the way her lips had responded to his in the past. The even more shocking thing was she'd wanted him to. So much her whole body had ached to feel that firm mouth come crashing down on hers. To take the choice away from her.

What was wrong with her?

But wasn't that what he wanted? To show how weak she was when it came to him? He knew her as a maestro knew a difficult instrument. He knew what chords to strike, what strings to pluck, what melodies to play.

Alice was annoyed for thinking she could outsmart him. When had calling his bluff ever worked? He wasn't the type of man to be manipulated. He enjoyed power too much to allow anyone else to control him.

The truth was she had been a little shocked when he'd let her go seven years ago. Shocked and hurt. She'd thought he'd wanted her too much to let her go without a fight. She'd thought he desired her so much he would have moved heaven and earth and planets and whole galaxies to get her back. She'd thought he would contact her within a day or two when he calmed down and apologise for pressuring her with that public proposal.

But he hadn't contacted her.

Not a single word. No phone call. No text or voicemail message. No flowers. No cards. Days, a week, two weeks went past and still she heard nothing from him. But then she saw a press photo of him in a nightclub in Milan with a bevy of beautiful women draped all over him. And a day later another photo with just the one woman—his new mistress. A gorgeous international model. It had driven a stake through her chest to see him getting on with his life as if she had never been the 'only woman in the world' for him. What nonsense. He hadn't loved her at all. He had wanted to own her. To control her.

As if that was ever going to happen.

He might be able to stir her hormones into a fizzing frenzy, but no way was Alice going to let him take over her life. She would marry him to get what she wanted.

You want him.

It was an inconvenient truth but she would deal with it. She had willpower, didn't she? A month-long engagement was the first hurdle. It wasn't a long period of time. Anyway, she would be at work most of the time. September was still a busy time. And he had his little thing on the side. *Grrr.* Alice wasn't going to show she was jealous about his nubile little Natalia. If he wanted to play around then why should she care? If she was going to be Cristiano's fiancée and then wife, then she would be the worst fiancée and wife in the world.

Alice smiled a *you-ain't-seen-nothing-yet* smile and picked up her wine glass and drained it in a couple of noisy swallows. She put it down on the starched white tablecloth with a distinctive thud. 'Nice drop. So, when do I get a big rock on my finger? Or have you got your old one stashed away in your pocket?'

His dark eyes pulsed like the shimmer off a heat-wave. 'I do, actually.' He reached inside his jacket and took out the ring he'd bought her seven years ago.

Alice took it from the centre of his outstretched palm and slipped it on. 'Slipped' being the operative word. It was loose and the heavy diamond slipped around her finger so it was facing downwards. Those few pounds she'd carried at twenty-one had thankfully been whittled off with diet and exercise. The ring hadn't suited her hand back then and it didn't now. Which was perfectly fine because she didn't want it to suit. It wasn't going to be there long enough for her to worry about it being clumsily big.

'Lovely. I'll be the envy of all my friends.' She looked up to see a furrowed frown between his eyes and gave him a guileless blink. 'Is something wrong?'

His frown relaxed but his mouth lost none of its tightness. 'There are some domestic things to discuss. Like where we'll live for the next four weeks before the wedding.'

Alice straightened her posture. 'I'm not living with you. I have my own house and—'

'It will seem odd for us not to cohabit. You can move in with me at my hotel or I can move in with you. Your choice.'

Her choice? What a joke. Alice raised her chin to a combative height. 'What if I say no?'

His unwavering gaze made something in her belly turn over. 'How about a compromise? A few nights at your place, a few nights at mine.'

Alice snorted. 'Compromise? You mean you actually *know* what that word means?'

He ignored her taunt. 'After we're married we'll have to live under the one roof, and since my base is in—'

'I'm not moving to Italy so you can squash that thought right now. I have work commitments. I'm solidly booked till Christmas.' Not solidly, but heavily. Not that she was going to tell him that. Why should she give up her career when he wasn't giving up his?

A muscle moved in his jaw. In. Out. In. Out. 'I want you with me. Six months, that's all the will requires. I won't accept any other arrangement.'

Alice gave a mock pout and leaned forward as if she were talking to a spoilt child. 'Oh, poor baby, did you want to have it all your own way?' She sat back with a resounding thump and folded her arms. 'Sorry. No can do.'

Cristiano's eyes hardened. 'Must you always be so damn obstinate?'

'Me, obstinate?' Alice laughed. 'You win the prize for that. A mule has nothing on you. Your heels are dug so deep in the ground you could drill for oil.'

He gave her a droll look. 'I've booked a flight to Italy this Friday. We'll stay the weekend in Stresa so you can get acquainted with your new property. Think of it as a trial honeymoon.'

Honeymoon?

Alice's stomach dropped like an anchor. 'I presume you mean for the sake of appearances?'

A ghost of a smile flirted with the edges of his mouth. 'That depends.'

She disguised a lumpy swallow. 'On what?'

'On whether you have the self-discipline to say no to me.'

Alice gave him a look that would have withered poison ivy. 'Not going to happen, Italian boy. You're getting your needs met elsewhere, remember?'

'Natalia is my personal assistant.'

Alice arched her brow. 'And what, pray tell, does she personally assist you with? Your sex life?'

A smile cocked one side of his mouth, making his eyes crinkle attractively at the corners. Too attractively. So attractively she was having trouble keeping her eyes off it and remembering how sexy it had once felt against her own. 'You're jealous.'

Alice gave a honk of a laugh. 'Yes, of course I am. I'm just so in love with you I can barely stand it. I've been waiting all these years for you to show up and take me back to chain me barefoot to the kitchen sink and make me pregnant.'

His smile disappeared to be replaced by a thin line of white. 'I would've given you a good life, Alice. Better than the one you've got now.'

Alice helped herself to more wine, not caring it was going to her head. 'I love my life. I have my own business. I have my own house. Money. Friends.'

'But you're not happy.'

She stabbed a finger in his direction. 'You know what that is you're doing right there? It's projection. What you're really saying is *you're* not happy.'

'I will be happy when this six months is over,' he said, through tight lips. 'My grandmother had no right to meddle in my affairs.'

Alice toyed with her glass, wondering why his grandmother had taken it upon herself to orchestrate things the way she had. Hadn't Volante Marchetti realised how pointless it would be locking her and Cristiano together? They hated each other. They fought like cage fighters. What good would it serve? They would only end up worse enemies than before.

She realised then, she hadn't yet expressed her condolences for his loss. She knew how much he adored his grandmother. It was another thing she had liked about him—how much he respected the elderly and saw them as gatekeepers of wisdom. 'You must miss her terribly.'

He released a long sigh that sounded rough around the edges. 'Yes.'

'Was she ill for long or was it a sudden—?'

'Pancreatic cancer,' he said. 'Four months from diagnosis to death.'

'It must have been an awful shock.'

'It was, but less so than my parents' and brother's death. She was eighty-five and frail. She was ready to go.'

Alice wondered if he was close to his extended family. He hadn't spoken much about his family back in the day. She knew there were an uncle and an aunt and a few cousins scattered about. But having lost every member of his immediate family must surely be extremely painful, even now. She wasn't that close to her mother, and, while she had some contact with her father since they reconnected a couple of years ago, her extended family were not the sort of people she associated with. But even so, Alice couldn't imagine being all alone in the world.

The waiter came to take their order, and once he left, Cristiano switched the subject as if he didn't want to linger on the subject of his grandmother's passing.

'There are some legal things to see to. I presume you won't object to a prenuptial agreement?'

'No, why should I?' Alice shot him a *don't-call-me-a-gold-digger* glare. 'I want to protect my own assets.'

'Fine. I'll have the papers drawn up and make an appointment for tomorrow.'

He was moving things along so quickly Alice wondered if he was worried she would back out at the last minute and was taking measures so she couldn't. 'How are you going to handle the press on this?' she asked. 'I mean, who is going to buy this is a genuine love match?'

His expression gave nothing away. 'We have a history which makes the lie all the more believable. Everyone loves a love-wins-out-in-the-end story.'

'Well, don't expect me to get all gussied up for the wedding,' Alice said. 'Me in one of those big meringue dresses? Not my thing at all.'

There was a moment or two of silence.

The air seemed to ring with her words as if testing their veracity. Just as well Cristiano didn't know about the stash of bridal magazines she had at home. Dozens of them. It was a silly little pastime but she rationalised it by insisting it helped her follow make-up trends for her clients. And it was a tax deduction.

'You might never get married again,' he said. 'Why not go to town on this one chance to be a princess for the day?'

'You're darn right I'm not getting married again,' Alice said. 'I'm going to be drinking champagne by the bucket once our marriage is over.'

Once our marriage is over.

It was strange to say those words when most people entered marriage thinking it was going to be for ever.

Weddings had never been Alice's fantasy. She hadn't dressed up as a bride as a child or pored over bridal magazines as a teenager. She'd always seen marriage as a trap to keep women enslaved to the patriarchy. A tool to maintain male privilege in society. Women lost financial traction once they married and had kids and few ever truly regained it. She had seen her mother lose self-esteem and money with every failed relationship. Alice had lived in near poverty too often as a child to ever think of getting married herself.

But lately, Alice had dealt with a lot of brides. Happy brides. Brides who were madly in love with their men and their men with them. The excitement of building a future with a man who loved you and wanted to spend his life with you had rubbed off on her even though she'd thought it never would. Every time she prepared a bride's make-up for her big day she wondered what it would be like to be a bride herself. To dress in a beautiful gown and have her hair and make-up done. To walk into a flower-filled church and say the vows that couples for centuries had been saying to each other.

A lot of the brides she had done still came into the salon as regular clients. It might be an isolated statistic, but so far not one of them had separated or divorced. On the contrary, they seemed happier and even more radiant. Several of them had babies and young children now.

It made Alice wonder if her bias was a little unjustified.

'What will you do with your share of the villa once we get an annulment?' he asked.

An annulment? Wait, he was actually *serious* about not sleeping with her? But why the hell not? Alice knew she wasn't going to be asked to strut down a catwalk any time soon but she hadn't had any mirrors explode when she'd walked past, either. 'Of course I'll sell my share. It's the money I want, not the property. I wouldn't be able to maintain a property that size—even a half share in it—not while working and living in London. Old places like that cost a fortune in upkeep.'

Cristiano gave a single nod as if that made perfect sense. But Alice couldn't help feeling he was disappointed in her answer. What did the villa mean to him? Would he want to buy her share back once their marriage came to an end? Her conscience began to prickle her. Why should he be made to pay for something that should rightfully be his?

'Were you expecting your grandmother to leave her villa entirely to you?' Alice asked after a moment.

'Yes and no.' His expression was masked. 'I have enough property of my own without hankering after that old place. But that doesn't mean I want to see it sold to strangers.'

'It must hold a lot of memories for you.'

'It does. Both good and bad.' He reached for his water glass but he didn't drink from it. Instead, his index finger scrawled a swirly clockwise pattern on the condensation on the side of the glass. 'It was a happy place before it became a sad place. Over time it became happy again, mostly due to my grandparents' commitment to making my childhood and adolescence as normal as they could under the circumstances.'

Alice chewed at her lip. When had she ever talked to him like this? *Really* talked? She had tried asking him about his childhood seven years ago but he had always brushed the topic aside. Told her he didn't like talking about it. She had respected that and left well alone. But now she wondered if that had been a mistake. 'It must have been devastating to lose your family like that…'

'And then some.' He let out a small breath and began drawing on his glass in an anti-clockwise fashion this time. 'I still remember the day my parents and brother were killed… I was staying overnight with my grandparents as I'd caught a stomach bug and couldn't go to the party they were attending.' His mouth came up on one side in a rueful slant and his finger left the glass. 'Lucky me. Saved by a rotavirus.'

Alice swallowed against a knot of emotion for the little boy he had been. How lonely and desperate he must have felt to have his family wiped out like that. Never to see them again. Never to have the opportunity to say the words he'd wanted to say. All the questions kids ask their parents about themselves—the funny anecdotes of infancy and childhood that only a parent can relay.

Why hadn't she asked more about how he'd felt when they'd dated? Why had she let him fob her off? Had he been riddled with survivor guilt? Wondering why he had been spared and not his brother? How could it not have an effect on him even now? He had grown up without the most important people by his side. Yes, his grandparents were marvellous substitutes, but they could only ever be his grandparents. He carried the wound of loss in every fibre of his being.

'I wish I'd asked you more about your childhood in the past… You always seemed so…so reluctant to talk about it and I didn't want to pry.'

'I hardly ever talked about it, even to my grandparents.' He continued to stare at his glass, his brow creased in a slight frown. 'I thought it was my family coming back when I heard the car. But it was a police vehicle. My grandfather broke the news to me…'

The trench of his frown deepened.

'It's weird, but I never really thought about that until a few years ago. How it would have been for him to hear his only son and daughter-in-law and eldest grandson had died and then have to break that news to me in a calm and controlled and caring manner. He was so… so unbelievably strong. For me. For Nonna. I never saw him cry but I sometimes heard him. Late at night, in his study, long after Nonna and I and the staff had gone to bed. It was a terrible sound.'

Alice reached across the table and placed her hand over his large warm tanned one where it was resting on the snowy-white tablecloth. He looked up when she touched him, his gaze shadowed by memories. By sadness. Bone-deep sadness. 'I'm so sorry…' she said.

He pulled his hand away and leaned back in his chair. 'It was a long time ago. I never lacked for anything. My grandparents made sure of that.'

Alice wondered if anyone—even grandparents as loving and stable as Cristiano's—could ever make up for the loss of one's parents and only brother. Children were known to be fairly resilient, but how hard it must have been for him to know he would never see his parents and brother again. He had all the money anyone could wish for and yet he couldn't bring back his loved ones. Was that why he was so controlling? So rigid and uncompromising? Was that why he had insisted on marrying her seven years ago and wouldn't take no for an answer? He had wanted stability because he had lost it in childhood.

But Alice hadn't been in love with him back then…*or*

had she? It was a question she always shied away from. She didn't like looking back. Regrets were for people who weren't confident in their ability to make choices.

She had made her choice.

She had chosen her career over marriage.

Not because she couldn't have combined them both, but more because Cristiano wouldn't have wanted her to. He'd wanted her to have babies and stay at home to rear them as his mother had done for him and his brother. He hadn't wanted any talk of nannies or child-care. In his opinion, there was only one way to bring up a family and that was to have a wife and full-time mother running the household.

They had argued about it constantly. For a while, Alice had naively thought he was only doing it to get a rise out of her. That he didn't really think so strongly about the issue but enjoyed the way she reacted when he expressed his opinion. But when he'd dropped that proposal on her, she'd realised he was deadly serious about it. For him there was no middle ground.

Marriage or nothing.

Alice had chosen nothing. Which had been fine when she was twenty-one with her whole life ahead of her. Now, at twenty-eight, with all her peers pairing up and marrying and starting families, and her own biological clock developing a recent and rather annoying and persistent ticking, she wondered if 'nothing' was going to keep her satisfied…if she had ever been so.

They finished their meal without much further conversation. Alice tried a couple of times to talk to him about his hotel plans for London, but he seemed disinclined to talk about anything but the arrangements to do with their marriage next month. His single-minded focus was a little unnerving to say the least. She wondered if he had pulled the drawbridge up on his personal life because she had got him to talk about his childhood in a way he had never done before.

When he led her out of the restaurant she half expected him to suggest they continue the evening by taking her somewhere else for a nightcap or coffee. But he simply drove her home and barely lingered long enough to walk her to the door.

Alice stood in the frame of her front door and watched the red glow of his taillights disappear into the distance. She flatly refused to admit she was disappointed. But when she went inside and closed the door, her beautiful house with its spacious rooms and gorgeous décor had never felt so empty.

CHAPTER FOUR

THE MEETING WITH the lawyer to deal with the prenuptial agreements was held the following day. Cristiano had organised to pick Alice up from the salon but she got held up with a client who had turned up late to her appointment, so when Alice came out to Reception she found Meghan talking to Cristiano, who had been kept waiting for nigh on twenty minutes.

Meghan turned around with a beaming smile. 'Congratulations! Oh, my God, it's so romantic. It's all over social media—everyone's tweeting about it. I knew there was something cooking between you two. I just knew it. You're engaged!'

Alice had never considered herself a consummate actor, but right then and there she thought she was worthy of an Oscar *and* an Emmy.

She moved closer to Cristiano and slipped an arm around his lean waist. 'Thanks. Yes, it is exciting. We're very happy.'

His arm came around hers, his hand coming to rest on the curve of her hip, the heat of his broad palm sending a red-hot current straight to her core. 'Aren't you going to kiss me hello?' he said, smiling down at her.

Alice smiled back through mentally gritted teeth.

'Not in front of my staff. You know how I am about public displays of affection.'

'Oh, I don't mind,' Meghan said, with her hands clasped in front of her as if waiting for the penultimate kiss scene in a romantic movie.

Alice eased out of Cristiano's hold to collect her bag from behind the counter. 'I'll be out for a couple of hours,' she said to Meghan. 'I've called in Suze to help with my Saturday clients while I'm away on the weekend.'

'I'm so happy for you both,' Meghan said. 'Can I do your wedding make-up? Please, please, please? Or are you going to do it yourself?'

'Erm…we're not having that sort of wedding,' Alice said. 'We're going to do things simply—'

'Not have a proper wedding?' Meghan's pretty young face fell as if all her facial muscles had been severed. 'But you *love* weddings. You put so much time and effort into getting your brides ready. You're the best at it in the business. Everyone says so. Why wouldn't you want to be a bride your—?'

'Because I just want to be married without all the fuss,' Alice said before her young employee let slip about the bridal magazines under the counter. Yes, she had two stashes of them—one for clients and one for herself. 'Besides, we're being married next month. There's no time to do anything extravagant. Cristiano's in a hurry, aren't you, darling?'

Cristiano's glinting black gaze left no room for doubt on the subject. 'I've been waiting seven long years to have you back where I want you. I don't want to waste a second more than I have to.'

'Show me your ring!' Meghan said.

Alice took it out of the pocket of her uniform and slipped it back on her finger. 'It's a little loose but—'

'Oh…' Meghan's expression failed to conceal her disappointment. 'It's very…erm…nice.'

'It's not the official one,' Cristiano said. 'That's being designed as we speak.'

'Oh, how wonderful.' Meghan's face brightened as if a dimmer switch had been turned to full beam. 'Alice loves a good engagement ring, don't you, Alice?'

Alice wanted to slip between the polished floorboards of her salon. Why hadn't she been a little more circumspect when examining her clients' engagement rings? She had oohed and aahed over so many beautiful rings. It was the classical settings she loved the most. Simple and elegant instead of big and flashy. She stretched her mouth into a smile. 'Sure do.'

After Meghan's next client came in, Cristiano put a hand beneath Alice's elbow and led her out of the salon. 'Nice kid.'

'Yes…'

And I'm going to make her drink boiling-hot wax when I get back.

'She's very enthusiastic.'

'I should probably warn you there will be paparazzi hanging—uh oh, too late.' His hand on her elbow shifted to go around her waist when a cluster of people with cameras and recording devices surged towards them. 'Let me handle it.'

Alice stood in the circle of his arm and listened to him give a brief interview about their whirlwind romance. He was scarily good at lying. No one would ever think he wasn't in love with her. What her mother was going to say about their engagement was something that was niggling at Alice's conscience. She hadn't yet called her to give her the heads up. She'd been delaying it because she had been so preachy about her mother's multiple marriages. She hadn't attended the last one on principle. How was her mother going to react to this news?

'We'd like to hear a comment from the blushing bride,' a female journalist said, pushing the recording device towards Alice. 'Your reputation as the go-to girl for wedding make-up is on the up and up. Does this mean you'll expand the business into Italy and beyond or will you be keen to start a family?'

Alice blithely ignored the slight pressure increase from Cristiano's fingers and painted on a bright smile. Why should she let him answer for her? She wasn't a ventriloquist's puppet. He might have cornered her in private, but in public, well, that was where she could win a few points back. 'We're going to get started on the baby-making right away, aren't we, darling?'

His eyes sent her a warning. 'I'd like a little bit of time with you all to myself first.'

After the press moved on, Cristiano took her firmly by the hand and led her down the street. 'What the hell were you playing at?'

Alice threw him a glance that could have cut through plate glass. 'Why do women get asked such ridiculous questions? Why didn't that journalist ask you if you were going to give up your career to start a family? Why are women always expected to give up everything they've worked so hard for?'

His mouth was pulled tight. 'I'm not asking you to have a child, for God's sake, Alice. All I'm asking is for six months of your time.'

'I can't believe women still have to put up with this crap,' Alice said. 'It's no one's business but mine if I want a baby.'

'Presumably it would also be your partner's business.'

Alice sent him a sideways glance but his expression gave little away. 'Do you plan on having a family with… with someone else after we're—?'

'No.'

'But you were so keen—'

'It's not something I envisage for myself now.'

Why? Because I ruined your dream of happy families?

Alice didn't like the feeling she'd been the one to change his mind. He would make a wonderful father. Why would he give up that dream of having a family of his own? He had so much to offer a child. Stability. Security. Love. She stopped walking and glanced at him again. 'Did I make you change your mind?'

His eyes met hers for a brief moment before he looked away and continued walking in long purposeful strides. 'We're going to be late for the lawyer if we don't step on it.'

Alice blew out a breath and trotted alongside him. 'I'm a career woman. So shoot me.'

A career woman with a vague sense of something missing…

Cristiano led her into the lawyer's office where they dealt with the business of signing the prenuptial agreements. It was all so cold and clinical it made Alice feel uncomfortable, as if she was breaking some sort of taboo. What about, *What's yours is mine and what's mine is yours*? It was contrary of her to be feeling so piqued because she had her own financial interests to protect, but still it made her wonder, if she had married Cristiano seven years ago, whether he would have insisted on drawing up such a clinical agreement.

The lawyer brought their meeting to a close with the news that a lump sum as promised in the will would be deposited in Alice's bank account now her engagement to Cristiano was official. The money did not have to be refunded if the engagement came to an end as in the marriage not taking place, which was a surprising footnote to Alice.

It was a large sum of money, enough to pay a decent deposit on new premises plus some, if not half, of the mortgage. She found it hard to understand why Volante Marchetti had stipulated that particular clause. Or had his grandmother known Alice would think twice about walking away with such a large amount of money without seeing the whole arrangement through?

When they were leaving the lawyer's office Alice got a call from her mother. She looked at the caller ID and grimaced. 'Hi, Mum, I was about to call you—'

'Tell me I'm dreaming,' her mother said loud enough for Cristiano to hear. Possibly the whole street. 'My daughter—the daughter who swore she would never ever get married—is now getting *married*?'

Alice turned away from Cristiano's satirical expression. 'Yes, it's all happened very quickly and—'

'See?' Her mother sounded smug. 'I told you love hits you out of the blue. When you meet the right one you just know. When's the wedding? I'll have to get something flash to wear. Will you be able to help me pay for something? I don't want to look frumpish. But for God's sake don't invite your father. You'll have to get someone else to walk you down the aisle. Not that he's been a proper father to you anyway, running off with that woman when you were barely out of nappies and carrying on about paying maintenance for all those years. Why you have to have a relationship with him now after all those years of no contact, I will never know. I won't go if he's there.'

'Mum, there's not going to be a big wedding,' Alice said, mentally rolling her eyes at her mother's usual tirade about her father. Twenty-six years was a long time to be bitter, especially as her dad hadn't had an easy time of it since, bringing up a disabled child with his most recent partner. 'We're having a low-key ceremony. We don't want a lot of guests. We just want to keep things simple to make it more…meaningful.'

'Oh, well, if you're too ashamed to have your own mother at your wedding then so be it,' her mother said in a wounded tone. 'I know I'm not posh like some of your precious clients, but I'm the one who brought you into the world and made every sacrifice I could to give you a decent childhood.'

A decent childhood?

Alice wanted to scream in frustration. Nothing about her childhood had been decent. Her mother was the type of woman who didn't feel complete without a man in her life. *Any* man. It didn't matter how bad he was, as long as he fulfilled the role of male partner. During her childhood Alice hadn't known who would be at their flat when she got home from school. There had been a revolving door on her mother's bedroom in her quest to find 'The One'.

There had been numerous partners over the years,

two of whom subsequently became husbands. The second husband after Alice's father had been a financial control freak and heavy drinker who used his fists and filthy tongue when he didn't get his own way. The third had made a pass at Alice the day her mother introduced her to him, and stolen money from her purse on two other occasions. Alice refused on principle to attend their wedding as a result. And since the wedding, her mother had been subjected to constant put-downs and fault-finding, and such financial hardship she regularly called on Alice for handouts. But if ever Alice said anything about her mother's partner she would defend him as if he were Husband of the Year.

'Mum, I really can't talk now,' she said. 'I'll call you when I get back from my…holiday.' She hung up and slipped her phone back in her bag.

Cristiano was looking at her with a thoughtful expression. 'You okay?'

Alice relaxed her stiff frown but she could see he wasn't fooled for a second. She blew out a breath. 'My mother and I don't agree on some things…lots of things, actually.'

'She didn't ask to meet me?'

Alice gave him a wry twist of her mouth. 'As long as you're male you tick the box as far as she is concerned.'

His frown formed a crevasse between his dark eyes. 'But you're her only child. Why wouldn't she insist on meeting the man who's going to be your husband?'

'She's not the overprotective type. Anyway, I'm an adult. I'm old enough to make my own decisions.'

'Did you tell her about us when you came back from Italy after we broke up?'

Alice thought back to that time, how angry she had

been, and how that anger, once she had cooled down, had turned to a deeper hurt. But her mother had been in the process of separating from her second husband who had found another partner—a woman only a year older than Alice.

Alice had spent hours and hours listening to her mother lament the loss of another marriage—how she was losing the love of her life and how she wouldn't be able to survive without him, *blah*, *blah*, *blah*. Alice had suppressed her feelings about her own breakup and channelled her energies into getting her mother through the divorce process, and then on starting up her own beauty business. There hadn't been time to examine too closely how she felt about Cristiano.

Maybe that had been a mistake...

'We don't have that sort of relationship,' Alice said. 'Not all mothers and daughters are best friends.'

'What about your father? Do you ever see him?'

'I didn't use to,' Alice said. 'But he tracked me down a couple of years ago. We meet up occasionally. Mostly when he needs money.'

Why did you tell him that?

His frown deepened. 'You don't give it to him, do you?'

Alice didn't want to go into the complex details of her relationship with her father. Charles *call-me-Chas* Piper was a happy-go-lucky charmer who, in spite of everything he had done and not done as a father, she couldn't help feeling a little sorry for. He was a hobby gambler and a regular drinker, but to his credit—after years of abandoning partners once he got bored—he had stayed with the young woman he'd married a few years ago. They had a son with severe autism and money was always tight on getting little Sam the support and care he needed.

Alice was a soft touch when it came to people with special needs. She told herself the money she gave to her father was for Sam, even though deep down she knew some of it would be spent on other things. But she figured her father and his partner Tania surely deserved something for themselves after everything they had been through. 'He's my father. He's not a bad person—just an unlucky one.'

'Unlucky in what way?'

Alice shook her hair back and readjusted the strap of her bag over her shoulder. 'Are we done? I have to get back to work. I have back-to-back clients this afternoon.'

Cristiano held her gaze for a long moment. 'I'll be around tonight. I'll bring dinner.'

Alice sent him a reproachful look. 'Here's a lesson in manners for you. What you say is: Would you be free this evening? I would like to bring you dinner. See? Not that hard, is it?'

He ran a lazy hand down the length of her arm. She was wearing a cashmere-blend cardigan over her uniform but still every nerve stood up and took notice, especially when he encountered her hand. His fingers closed around it and then he brought it up to his mouth. Alice watched in a state of mesmerisation when his lips brushed against the backs of her knuckles, his eyes holding hers in a lock that made something fall off a high shelf inside her stomach. The scrape of his stubble sent a shockwave of lust straight between her thighs. The clean sharp citrus scent of his aftershave teased her senses until she felt slightly drunk. She couldn't stop staring at his mouth—the shape of it was pure male perfection. Strong and firm, and yet with a sensual curve that could unravel her self-control in a hummingbird's heartbeat.

'Are you free this evening?' he said. 'I would like to bring you dinner.'

Alice could have done with a bit of that self-control right about now. She knew saying yes would be saying yes to other things besides dinner. How long would she be able to resist that mouth? Those hands? That body? So far he hadn't kissed her. So far. But how long before he did? 'Yes, I'm free.' *Sucker.*

A smile lifted the edges of his mouth and he released her hand. 'I'll look forward to it.'

Cristiano walked back to his hotel after he left Alice at her salon. His mind ran back over their conversation. In the past she had told him a bit about her background but he hadn't realised—or been astute enough back then—to read between the lines. He had been quietly envious of her having both parents still living so hadn't been able to see how complicated her relationship was with both of her parents. Her mother sounded like a petulant child, and her father asking Alice for money now he was back in her life after years of no contact was nothing short of scandalous.

But one thing he did know was that kids—no matter how difficult they were—loved their parents. It was a fact of nature. Bonds were created in childhood and it took a lot to destroy them.

Alice had been adamant about not marrying. She had voiced her opinions on the subject volubly. Heatedly. Stridently. He had—naively, perhaps—thought she was only saying it because she hadn't wanted to come across as a gold-digger. He was well aware of how his wealth made him an attractive prospect for a woman who was looking for security. That was another fact of nature. Women had good reason to want to connect with a man who could provide for her once it came time to have children.

But Alice insisted she didn't want children. That was another thing he didn't take all that seriously back then. What young woman of twenty-one wanted children at that stage of their lives? He'd been confident—too confident—she would change her mind once they were married.

Cristiano had been too proud to go after her when she'd rejected his proposal. Proud and angry. Bitterly, blindingly angry. He'd expected her to come crawling back. That was another thing he'd been far too confident about. He'd thought she'd go home and think about what she was throwing away and call him and say she'd changed her mind. But the only thing she'd changed was her phone number.

That was the nail that finally closed the lid on his hopes.

But now he wondered what was really behind Alice's adamant stance on marriage. Lots of kids of divorced parents went on to have successful marriages themselves. Was it because she was a staunchly independent career woman? Having a career didn't mean you had to give up everything else. Did she still hold those views or had she shifted some ground over the passage of time?

Her friendly little employee gave the impression Alice was a big fan of weddings. Word on the street was she was the go-to girl for bridal make-up. Did that mean she secretly dreamed of a white wedding with all the trimmings? But she hadn't dated anyone seriously in years. That was another thing he'd found out from her loquacious little workmate. Alice virtually lived and breathed work. She had no social life to speak of and always made excuses when friends tried to hook her up with potential dates.

He didn't want to admit how pleased he was about that. If he hadn't been happy for the last seven years then why the hell should she be? But then, she was a tetchy little thing. Not many men would put up with her quick temper and acid tongue. But behind that prickly exterior was a warm-hearted person. Some of the time.

Funny, but her sharp tongue had been one of the things he'd most admired about her back then. The fact she didn't kowtow to him because he was super rich. Losing his parents so young had made everyone—even his grandparents at times—tiptoe around him. No one ever said no to him or argued the point with him. He was so used to getting his own way he hadn't factored in anyone else's opinion on things until he'd met Alice. She never ran away from an argument or a difference of view. She didn't cave in to please him. She stood her ground and wouldn't budge if she believed she was in the right.

But what if she had changed? What if those rigidly held opinions on marriage and children had softened?

Too bad.

Cristiano wasn't going down that road again. Family life was for people who could handle the risk of losing it in the blink of an eye. He had already lost one family. He wasn't going to sign up for a second.

His grandmother's machinations meant he had no choice but to jump through the hoops like an obedient circus dog, but that was as far as it would go. He had considered a register office ceremony but decided if he was going to get married then it would be the old-fashioned way. Besides, his *nonna* would come back to haunt him if he didn't repeat those wedding vows in front of a priest.

But you don't love Alice now.

Cristiano ignored the prod of his conscience. God would have to forgive him for borrowing His house of worship as a means to an end. Over the years he had downgraded his feelings. Told himself he hadn't loved Alice at all. It was too confronting, too painful to admit he had loved her and lost her. Instead he filed it away as nothing but a lust fest. A mad, once-in-a-lifetime passion that had taken him over like a raging fever. Consuming rational thought. Sideswiping common sense.

He was no longer that idealistic young man blinded by lust. He was older, wiser, harder. He could control his passion. He could control his desire. He could control his emotions.

A quiet church wedding with limited guests was the only way to go. There would be no chance of Alice misreading his motivations if he kept things clean and simple. And less complicated when it came time to end it.

For end it he would.

CHAPTER FIVE

ALICE TOLD HERSELF there was no reason she should be cleaning her house like someone with a serious case of obsessive-compulsive disorder but she wasn't going to have Cristiano counting the dust bunnies hiding under the sofa. She had never been able to justify employing someone to clean because she was hardly at home to make much of a mess.

Once she'd sorted the house, she got working on herself. That saying about plumbers with leaky taps equally applied to beauticians. When was the last time she'd waxed her legs? And as for a bikini wax…? It was so overgrown her 'lady land' looked as if Sleeping Beauty had taken up residence.

Well, come to think of it, maybe she had.

It had been about a hundred years since there had been any activity down there.

Alice reached for her perfume and spritzed her wrists and neck. This was probably a good time to ask herself why she was going to all this trouble.

You are so going to sleep with him.

She slammed the door on the thought. No. Not going to happen. She could resist him. Sure she could. He wasn't that irresistible.

Yikes. Yes, he was.

As long as he didn't kiss her it would be okay. Kissing him would be dangerous. Dangerous because his mouth had the amazing power to make her senses spin out of control like bald tyres on an oil spill.

The doorbell sounded and Alice jumped up and smoothed her skinny jeans down her thighs. She'd figured tight jeans might work as a reminder to her self-control. Not so easy to slip out of sprayed-on denim.

Then why did you put on your best bra and knickers?

Alice was getting a little annoyed with her conscience. Nice underwear was standard. So what if she'd put on her most expensive set? Her girls deserved the best support, didn't they? She opened the front door and tried not to swoon when she saw Cristiano standing there dressed in dark blue denim jeans and a crisp white casual shirt that was rolled up over his tanned forearms. His hair was still damp as if he had not long showered and his jaw was cleanly shaven. 'At least you're on time,' she said.

His gaze travelled over her slowly, smoulderingly, until she wondered if her clothes were going to be singed right off her body and left in a smoking heap on the floor at his feet. 'You look beautiful.'

Alice looked at his empty hands and then around him for any sign of the dinner he'd promised to bring. 'I thought you said you were bringing dinner with you?'

'It will be here soon.'

She stepped back and held the door open, breathing in a delectable whiff of his aftershave when he walked past. She closed the door and linked her hands in front of her body, more to keep them away from the temptation of touching him. 'I got the money,' she said. 'I checked my bank account an hour ago.'

'Good to know the lawyer is doing what he's been paid to do.'

Alice unhooked her hands and used one to tuck a strand of her hair back behind her ear. 'Any idea why your grandmother stipulated that clause? I mean, I could end our engagement right now and still be way out in front financially.'

'You could. But you won't.'

She frowned. 'What makes you so sure?'

He was standing close. So close she could see every individual pinpoint of his recently shaven jaw. So close she could feel the magnetic draw of his body. 'Because you're not the sort of girl who'd take money from an old lady without fulfilling the rest of the wishes she expressed.'

'But I hardly knew your grandmother. I only met her a couple of times. We chatted and all that but hardly long enough for her to want to include me in her last will and testament, I would've thought.'

'Maybe, but she liked you and you liked her.' He waited a beat. 'She saw something in you. A quality she warmed to.'

'Stubbornness?'

He gave a soft laugh. 'That and…other things.'

What other things? Alice wanted to ask.

'Would you like a drink? I have wine and soft drinks or—'

'Later.' He slipped a hand into the inside pocket of his dark blue blazer and took out a ring box from a designer jeweller. 'For you.' He flipped the box open and inside was a gorgeous diamond in a classic setting.

Alice took out the ring and watched as the light above their heads brought out the diamond's brilliance. It was so simple and yet so elegant. She slipped it over her finger and it sat there as if it had been made for her. 'It's…'

'If you say "nice" I will not be answerable for the consequences.'

Alice smiled and kept gazing at the ring. 'Perfect. It's perfect, that's what it is. It's exactly what I would have chosen.'

When she glanced up at him he was frowning. 'Would you have preferred that?' he asked. 'To choose it yourself?'

Alice had never seen him look so uncertain before. 'I guess if this was a normal situation then maybe I would have. But it's fine since it's not. Anyway, I'll give this back once we're done.'

'I don't want it back.'

'But it's—'

'It's yours, Alice. You can do what you want with it when we're through.' He released a short breath. 'I'm sorry. I should have consulted you on what you'd like. I didn't think. The old one was so…so inappropriate. I'm annoyed I didn't see that before. It didn't suit your hand at all.'

Alice shifted her lips from side to side. This was a new thing—Cristiano admitting to getting something wrong. 'Just your luck to pick someone so independent she can't even let a guy choose a ring for her.'

'It wasn't just the ring I got wrong, though, was it?'

Alice couldn't hold the sudden intensity of his gaze. She looked at the new ring instead and angled her hand so the light caught the facets of the diamond. 'Thing is, my mother has three rings, all of them ghastly. She pretended to love them when her partners gave them to her. I always wondered why she did that.' She glanced at him again. 'Surely if you're going to marry someone and agree to spend the rest of your life with them you'd be honest with them from the get-go?'

His mouth lifted in a rueful smile. 'That was another quality my grandmother liked in you. Honesty. You didn't filter your opinions. You spoke your mind and to hell with anyone who didn't agree with you.'

Alice couldn't help a tiny cringe at how outspoken she had been back then. She had been very much 'my way or the highway' in her thinking. She'd held strong opinions on issues that, in hindsight, she had not researched well enough to warrant holding such strident views. How many people must she have offended, or even hurt, by expressing such unqualified and oftentimes ignorant opinions? Back then she had considered the notion of compromise or backing down as a weakness, a flaw. But now…now she wondered if being able to give and take, and listen rather than speak, was a more mature and balanced way to approach life.

'I'm surprised your grandmother even remembered me. You and I were only together six weeks. There must've been a lot of women in your life since. I don't suppose she's left each of them—?'

'No. Just you.'

Alice wanted to ask if he had fallen in love with any of them but knew it would make him think she was jealous. Which to her great annoyance she was. It didn't seem fair that he'd moved on with his life so quickly when she had supposedly been his soul mate. What if she had changed her mind in the weeks after their breakup? Too bad, because he'd already partnered up with someone else.

'I know what you're thinking,' Cristiano said. 'You're thinking I didn't take long to replace you, yes?'

Alice hadn't realised her expression was so transparent. Or maybe he really could read her mind. Scary thought. 'You made no secret of your love-life. It was splashed over every gossip magazine.'

His gaze was unwavering. 'And that bothered you?'

Alice frowned. 'Why wouldn't it bother me? You bought me a frightfully expensive ring and told me I was the only woman in the world for you, and yet within a week or two of me ending our relationship, you're off with someone else.'

'Did you change your mind?'

'No, of course not.' Alice knew she had answered too quickly by the way one of his brows rose in an arc. 'I was just annoyed you hadn't…'

'Hadn't what?'

She let out a gusty little breath. 'Missed me.'

He stepped closer and placed his hands on the tops of her shoulders. 'You think I didn't miss you?'

Alice couldn't shift her gaze from his mouth. It was drawn there by a desire she could not override with self-discipline or common sense. The warmth of his hands was burning through her clothes, setting her skin on fire. Making her aware of his male body standing close—so close she could sense the stirring of his blood in tune with her own. She placed her hands flat against his chest, touching him, feeling the heat and strength of him.

Wanting him.

The deep thud-pitty-thud of his heart beneath her

palm reverberated through her body, sounding an erotic echo deep in the centre of her being. She curled her fingers into the fabric of his shirt, not caring that it caused it to crumple and the tiny buttons to strain against the buttonholes. She closed the hair's breadth distance between their bodies, an electric frisson coursing through her at the intimate contact.

What did it matter if she was the one to cave in first? It was what she wanted. What they both wanted. She had missed touching him.

Being held.

Being wanted.

Alice stepped up on tiptoe and pressed a barely touching kiss to the side of his mouth, her lips tingling from the contact with his newly shaven skin. Cristiano's minty fresh breath mingled with hers but he didn't take over the kiss. Was he trying to prove how strong he was compared to her? That he could resist her even if she couldn't resist him? She smiled to herself. She knew just how to get him to weaken. She sent the tip of her tongue out and licked the surface of his bottom lip. A cat-like lick to remind him of how clever she was with her tongue. How she had made him collapse at the knees when she got to work on him.

His hands went from her shoulders to her hips, tugging her so close she could feel the hardened, pulsing ridge of him against her belly. 'Haven't you heard that saying about playing with fire?'

Alice shamelessly stoked the fire by rubbing her pelvis in a circular motion against his. 'You want me.'

'I didn't say I didn't.'

'But you said our marriage won't be—'

'So, that rankled, did it?' A teasing glint danced in his eyes. 'I thought it might.'

So he'd said that deliberately to get a rise out of her? Did he want her or not? Or was he just playing with her? Letting her dangle like a pathetic mouse being tortured by a mean-spirited cat. Alice pursed her lips and tried to pull back but his hands were clamped on her hips. 'Let me go.'

'Is that really what you want?'

'Yes.' She all but spat the word out. But inside her body was screaming. *No-o-o-o!*

'Fine.' He dropped his hands and stepped away, a knowing smile lifting the edges of his mouth. 'No harm done, *sì*? But if you change your mind, you know where to find me.'

Alice ground her teeth so hard she thought her molars were going to crack. The only harm done was to her pride. Why had she allowed him to get the upper hand? He'd fooled her into thinking he had changed. He had even expressed his regret—albeit in veiled terms—about the ring he'd bought in the past. But at the heart of it all he wanted to prove was he had moved on from her—that he hadn't got any lingering feelings where she was concerned. He hadn't missed her one little bit. He'd soon found someone else to scratch his itch. He might still desire her, but that was all he wanted from her now. Sex.

How different from what he had offered her in the past. Back then he'd promised her the world—his heart, his soul, his love. Now all he promised was mind-blowing, body-tingling sex. A trashy little affair to pass the time until they could end their relationship once they'd fulfilled the terms of his grandmother's will. How could she agree to something like that when it was so unlike what they'd had before?

Because you still want him, that's why.

Not that much.

Are you sure about that?

Alice wasn't so sure about a lot of things any more. The desire Cristiano stirred in her refused to bank down in spite of all her efforts to control her response to him. It was like simmering coals deep in her body, just waiting to erupt into leaping, quick-licking flames. Could she risk an affair with him and to hell with the consequences? She could keep her feelings separate. That was what men did without any bother. Why couldn't she?

'I'm not going to let you play games with me, Cristiano.'

'Games, *cara*?' His brow rose above one eye. 'Isn't that your specialty?'

Alice pressed her lips together. 'You won't win this. You think you can get me to beg? Think again. I don't want you anything like the way you want me.'

A satirical light entered his gaze. 'There's one simple way to test that little theory of yours. Would you like to try it?'

Alice stepped two more steps back and folded her arms across her body. 'If you come any closer I'll… I'll bite you.'

'Promise?' His sexy half-smile made something deep in her belly turn over.

The doorbell sounded and Cristiano reached past her to answer it. 'That will be our dinner.'

Cristiano carried the meal he'd organised to be delivered from a nearby restaurant through to where Alice had set up the dining table. She was angry with him for not acting on her invitation. He'd wanted to. So much his entire body throbbed with the need to crush his mouth to hers. Still throbbed. He wanted her but on his terms, not hers. What was she playing at anyway? A teasing kiss or two to prove he had no resistance when it came to her?

That he'd *missed* her?

He'd missed her all right. He'd missed her so damn much it had taken him months to sleep with another woman. The women he'd been seen in public with after their breakup were just casual dates, but he had not pursued them any further. A drink or two, a dance, a dinner or a show—that was all. He hadn't been able to stop himself comparing them to Alice. Finding fault with their looks, their clothes, their manners or their conversation—or lack of it. Even when he did start sleeping with partners, he'd felt something wasn't quite right. But he'd put that down to the fact of how different having a hook up or fling was from having a relationship where you truly got to know the person.

But had he known Alice? Truly known her? He hadn't even got her taste right in rings. Not that any ring would have been right given she looked upon marriage as a form of modern-day slavery.

Not that his views back then had helped. It had taken him a few more years than he was proud of to see where Alice had been coming from. His conservative views on marriage had undergone some significant changes. He no longer saw a woman's role in such black and white terms. He understood the need for women to have the opportunity to reach their potential career-wise in the way most men took for granted. Having both a career and a family was something as a young man he had never questioned, and yet for a woman it had so many more implications. Careers and children were hard to juggle if one wanted to do both things well. Even men these days were starting to question the high demands of corporate life and how it impacted on their relationships at home.

But while Cristiano might have changed some of his strong views, he wasn't so sure Alice had changed hers. She seemed even more committed to her career, with expansion plans on the horizon. She hardly ever dated, according to her helpful employee Meghan. Why was that? Alice was a normal healthy young woman in the prime of her life. Why wouldn't she be out there doing what every girl her age did? She didn't even have a housemate. She lived all alone in a gorgeous house that looked as if it could be in a beautiful homes magazine.

But was she happy?

Cristiano didn't think so…but then, maybe that was because he was annoyed she hadn't been as committed to him as he had been to her. Or was it more because she was seemingly happy and he wasn't? He hadn't been happy, not from the moment she'd told him they were over. How had he got it so screwed up? He'd thought she loved him. Her body had if not her heart. She had been his most giving lover, and without doubt the most exciting. He had blithely thought she would accept his proposal with unbounded enthusiasm.

Blithely or arrogantly?

He hadn't expected her to say no because back then he had been the one with the money and status. He was the Prize Catch as the press put it. He had chosen the restaurant that night in which to deliver his proposal, not out of design but eagerness. That was what annoyed him the most. He had been too impatient. He had picked the ring up on the way to meet her after work. That, too, had been more impulse than plan. He had walked past a high-end jeweller's and that had been it. Decision made. No thought had gone into it. It had simply *felt* like the right thing to do.

Which showed how much feelings weren't to be trusted. He had been so excited about his dreams for their future, so focussed on securing her commitment, that he hadn't picked up on her mood. He'd been like a goofy kid unable to contain himself. If he had waited until they got home to his villa in Milan would she have given him a different answer? If he had given her more time? A few days, weeks or even months? Would she have felt less pressured? Less cornered?

So what's changed?

Cristiano winced at the nudge of his conscience. He had cornered her again. Forced her to bend to his will. He had a goal to achieve. He was focussing on the big picture instead of examining the finer detail.

But he had to get those shares back before his cousin blew the lot. And he had to do whatever it took to keep the villa otherwise it would go to some stranger. He didn't have a choice any more than Alice did.

It was marry her or lose a third of his family's company and the villa he knew as home.

As if he were going to allow *that* to happen.

CHAPTER SIX

AFTER DINNER THAT night, Alice didn't see Cristiano again until Friday when he picked her up to take her to the airport for their flight to Italy. Being stressed from having to organise another beauty therapist to cover her for the weekend when her usual girl had to pull out at the last minute, as well as see her own clients and get away on time, hadn't done her mood any favours. She hadn't had time to refresh her make-up or send a brush through her hair. And God only knew what she'd thrown in her overnight bag this morning when she'd missed her alarm and had to pack in a frantic hurry. How dared Cristiano look so damn fresh and clean and smell so divine? Didn't he have to work and sweat like normal people?

Once they were seated on the plane in business class—*of course*—Alice leaned her head back against the headrest and closed her eyes. 'You would not believe the day I've had.'

Cristiano's hand came to rest on top of hers where it was lying on the armrest. 'Want to tell me about it?'

Alice looked at his hand on top of hers. His skin was so tanned and the sprinkle of dark hair so masculine compared to the smooth, pale skin of hers. His fingers curled around her hand, reminding her of the way his strong powerful body gathered her close in the past. His thumb began an idle stroking across the back of her hand, a mesmerising rhythm that stirred her blood. She disguised a little shiver…or at least hoped she did.

'First, I didn't hear my alarm. My phone was on silent last night because I— Well, anyway. Then I had a staffing issue, which is the bane of my life as a small business owner. Suze, the girl I'd organised to come in to do my Saturday clients, caught a stomach virus. To her credit, she was prepared to work but I can't expose my clients to illness. It wouldn't be fair to them if they caught it.'

Alice stopped to draw breath to find him looking at her with an unwavering gaze.

'Am I boring you?'

His lips curved upwards in a slow smile. 'Not a bit. Go on.'

Alice had trouble remembering what she'd been talking about. All she could think of was how delicious his mouth looked when he smiled. Not a mocking smile, but a smile that said: *You're fascinating to me.* His eyes too made her brain scramble. Intensely dark, fringed with thick black eyelashes her clients would have paid a fortune to graft on.

'Erm…so then I worked through my clients and two were late, which is a nightmare because it has a knock-on effect that makes me late for my next client and so on and so on. And then, my last client wanted to talk once I'd done her waxing. Her husband is unwell—he just got diagnosed with cancer. I could hardly rush her out the door, now could I?'

'Of course not.'

She let out a long exhausted-sounding breath. 'Beauty therapists are like hairdressers. No wonder we're called therapists. Half the time I'm more of a psychologist than I am anything else.'

His hand picked up hers and turned it over, his thumb stroking the inside of her palm in a slow circular pattern that made every rigid muscle in her back soften like honey in a heatwave. 'You enjoy your work, though, don't you?'

Alice didn't even have to think about her answer. 'I love it. I love being able to make women—and it's mostly women, but I have male clients too—feel good about themselves. I like the skin-care element too. I've been able to help numerous clients with troubled skin. Nothing lifts self-esteem more than feeling good about how you look.'

'So how did the wedding arm of your business come about?'

Alice couldn't remember talking to anyone this much about her work other than her employees and a couple of girlfriends. Her mother never showed much interest—she was always too worked up about her own issues and only required Alice to listen, not talk.

'Sort of by accident or serendipity. I did the make-up for a bride about five years ago, and then her bridesmaid chose me, and then she told her friends, and everything built up from there. Word of mouth still rules in spite of the digital age.'

Cristiano's thumb was on her pulse now, that same slow stroking motion on the underside of her wrist making her sink even further into the plush leather seat. 'So tell me about your expansion plans.'

'Well...my salon in Chelsea is getting too small

when I do weddings as well as normal clients,' Alice said. 'My regular clients aren't too happy if I book the salon out too many Saturdays in a row for weddings. I have a dream to set up a luxury wedding spa where brides and the wedding party can be the focus of attention. There will be an area for official photos or glamour shoots too. Of course I'll have to move between both salons at first, but ultimately I'd like to concentrate on the wedding side of things.'

'Because you have a thing about weddings?'

Alice gave him a beady look. 'The *money.* Weddings bring in the money, especially high-profile ones.'

His thumb stroked the fleshy pad of hers, making her legs feel as if someone had removed all the bones. 'You don't find it slightly…ironic?'

'Ironic I want to make money?'

He smiled a crooked smile. 'You know what I mean, Alice.'

Aleece.

Oh, dear Lord, how was she supposed to stay sanc when he said her name like that?

She gave a little shrug. 'Just because I do a lot of bridal make-up doesn't mean I want to be one myself. You own and operate hotels, does that mean you want to live in one?'

His eyes didn't once leave hers. 'Not all marriages are slave camps. When a good marriage works it can be a wonderful thing.'

Alice gave him a pointed look. 'If you think it's so wonderful then why aren't you married by now?'

His thumb traced over the diamond on her left hand, his eyes still locked on hers. 'If all goes to plan I soon will be.'

Alice concealed a little swallow. 'But it's not like ours is going to be a normal one.'

'It could be if that's what you want.'

She frowned. 'You mean…last for ever?'

'No.'

Did he have to sound so damned emphatic?

'I meant we could have our fun while it lasts.'

Not for ever? Just 'fun' for now. Alice shifted her lips from side to side. 'If I agreed to…to having fun with you, does that mean you'll be having fun with other people at the same time?'

His mouth tilted in another smile. 'From what I remember of the fun we had together, I don't think I'd have the energy for anyone else.'

Alice held his gaze for a long moment. Was this wise? Offering to have an affair with him for the short duration of their engagement and marriage? What kind of arrangement was that? And could she trust him to remain faithful?

Funny, but she felt she could. He might have changed in other ways but she couldn't see him cheating on a partner. He wasn't that sort of man. 'Thing is… I haven't had a lot of fun just lately so you might be disappointed in what I bring to the…erm…game.' It seemed the right choice of word, all things considered.

Cristiano brought her hand up to his mouth, pressing his lips to the tops of her fingers, all the while holding her gaze with the steadiness of his. 'I can bring you up to speed in one session.'

I can well believe it. Alice tried but failed to suppress a frisson-like shiver. 'So…when would you want to…to start having fun?'

He slid a warm hand around the nape of her neck

and drew her inexorably closer, only stopping once her mouth was within a breath of his. 'I'd do you now but I wouldn't want to disturb the other passengers with your screams of pleasure.'

Alice kept her eyes trained on his smiling mouth, her heart leaping in excitement, her whole body trembling with feverish anticipation. Only he could make her sob with pleasure. Sob and scream and shudder from head to foot. How had she resisted him this long? It was crazy to keep denying herself the sensual thrill of his touch. So what if it only lasted a few months? A few months were better than no months. She'd spent the last seven years missing the magic of his lovemaking. Why not enjoy it while it lasted? 'You're not thinking of using one of the bathrooms?'

'No. I'm going to make you wait until we get home.'

Cruel. Cruel. Cruel.

Alice stroked a fingertip over his top lip, following the contours of his vermilion border, his stubble catching on her skin like a thorn on silk. 'I could take things into my own hands…' she said with a suggestive glance.

His eyes glinted and his hand on the back of her neck slid under the curtain of her hair, the slight drag on the roots sending a bolt of fizzing electricity down her spine. 'Hold that thought.'

Alice closed the distance between their mouths, touching hers down on his as softly as a butterfly landing on a petal. She eased back but because his lips were dryer than hers they clung to her softer skin as if they didn't want to let her go. He made a rough sound deep in his throat and brought his lips back to hers in a slow, drugging kiss that made her insides coil and twist and tighten with longing. His tongue entered her mouth in a smooth, deep glide that had a deliciously erotic element to it. It called hers into a sensual dance that made her feminine core contract with need. The kiss went deeper and deeper, drawing from her a response she had never given to anyone else. Shivers coursed through her body—her skin prickling, tingling, and aching for the touch of his hands. Her breasts suddenly felt too small for her bra—they were straining against their lace barrier, desperate to feel the warm, firm possession of his hands. To feel the stroke of his tongue, the hungry suckle of his lips, the sexy scrape of his teeth.

He shifted position, tilting her head to one side as he explored every secret corner of her mouth, the dark shadow of stubble around his mouth and on his chin abrading her softer skin like a fine-grade rasp.

Somehow the thought they were on a crowded plane and couldn't take the kiss any further only heightened the intensity of it. She couldn't remember kissing him in the past without it ending with them making love. Their first kiss had ended in bed. Every kiss of their affair had been the same. It was as if their lips couldn't touch without their bodies being engulfed by raging desire. They hadn't kissed in public other than a quick brush of the lips because she hadn't been comfortable about public displays of affection. Still wasn't, which made it all the more surprising—if not a little shocking—that she was doing it now, within sight and hearing of three hundred fellow passengers.

But every pulse-racing moment of it tantalised her senses until she completely forgot where they were. She spread her fingers through his thick black hair, greedily succouring his mouth as if without it she would die. She made a mewling sound in her throat, her need of him escalating. No one had ever kissed her like this. No one had ever made her feel this way. This madness, this ferocious need that clawed at her core and made every inch of her flesh scream and beg and plead for release.

Cristiano finally pulled back, his hands still cradling her face, his eyes so dark it was impossible to identify his pupils from his irises. He pressed the pad of his thumb to her kiss-swollen lower lip and then to a spot on the middle of her chin. 'I've given you stubble rash.'

Alice traced a fingertip around his mouth, the floor of her stomach giving a kick like a miniature pony when his masculine roughness caught at her skin. 'I'm running an autumn special on lip and chin waxes if you're interested.'

His eyes glinted their amusement. 'Thanks, but I'll pass.'

She stroked a fingertip down the bridge of his nose and then the shallow trench of his philtrum ridge down to where it met his top lip. His lips twitched as if her touch tickled. Then he captured her finger and closed his lips over it, drawing on it while his tongue stroked its underside, his gaze holding hers in a sensual lock that made her insides shudder.

How could it be possible to want any man more than she wanted this one? Was that why she had bolted when he'd pressured her to marry him in the past? Because he was the one man who could make her forget about her promise never to become enslaved to a man. Never to lose her autonomy. Never to need someone so badly they had the power to destroy her. Cristiano had the power to destroy her self-control. He only had to look at her and her self-control folded like a house of cards in a gale-force wind.

Cristiano took one of her hands and threaded his fingers through hers. 'I've been thinking… I don't remember ever kissing you before without it ending in sex.'

Alice ran her tongue over her lips, tasting him. Wanting him. Aching for him. 'I was thinking the same. Freaky, huh?'

His gaze searched hers for a long moment. A small frown tugged at his brow, making a two-pleat fold between his eyes. 'I seem to remember we didn't do a lot of talking back then, either.'

Alice gave him a wry look. 'I don't know about that. I talked but you didn't listen.'

His crooked smile had a faint touch of regret about it. 'We didn't listen to each other.' He released a long sigh and looked at their entwined fingers, his thumb rhythmically stroking the length of hers. 'It was a long time ago, *sì*?'

Alice settled into the seat, resting her head against his shoulder. 'It sure was.'

So much so I feel like a different person now.

CHAPTER SEVEN

IT WAS CLOSE to midnight when they arrived at Cristiano's villa in Milan. Stepping over the threshold was like stepping back through time.

Alice swept her gaze around the stunning entry, taking in the marble floors and the grand staircase that led to the upper floors with its decorative black balustrading. There were priceless chandeliers and wall lights, the marble and bronze statues and artworks that would be the envy of any serious art collector. Some things were the same, and yet others were different. It had been redecorated and repainted but it was still Cristiano's home—the place where he had spent the first eleven years of his life until the tragic death of his family.

The villa had been rented out following his parents' and brother's deaths as Cristiano had lived in Stresa with his grandparents. But Alice knew how much this place meant to him. He had spent the happiest years of his life here.

She had spent the happiest six weeks of her life here.

Cristiano took her hand and drew her to his side. 'Having second thoughts?'

Alice turned in the circle of his arms and linked her arms around his neck. 'No. Why would I? It's just sex.'

His gaze held hers for a long beat. 'You're not worried about the boundaries blurring?'

Worried? Damn straight, I'm worried.

'No,' Alice said. 'But clearly you are. What are you worried about? That you might fall in love with me all over again?'

A steel shutter slammed down at the backs of his eyes. 'I told you before—I wasn't in love with you. I was in lust.' He dropped his hold and stepped away from her. 'I'll take the bags up. You go on ahead. I'll be up in a minute.'

Alice stood without moving. Did he have to make it sound so…so clinical? He was making her feel like someone he'd picked up in a bar and brought home for a quick tumble. Where was the man who had once carried her up those stairs like an old-time Hollywood-movie hero? Who had treated her like a princess instead of a prostitute?

'Are any of your household staff here?'

'No. I gave them the night off. I called them before we left London.'

Alice could sense he was annoyed with her. Every muscle in his face was pulled tight, especially around his mouth, leaving it flat and white-tipped.

'Why don't we go up together?' she said.

'You know where my bedroom is.'

Alice lifted her chin. 'Oh, I get it. You want to play I'm-the-John-and-you're-the-hooker? Fine—I can do that.'

She shrugged off her light coat and let it drop to the floor. Then she unzipped her dress and let it puddle at her feet before she stepped out of it, leaving her in bra and knickers and heels.

His eyes turned black, his mouth compressed until his lips disappeared. 'Don't.'

'Don't what?' Alice said, unhooking her bra and tossing it to the floor near his feet. 'I'm having fun, aren't you?'

He kicked her bra out of the way and came to her before she could remove anything else. He took her by the upper arms, his fingers gripping her so tightly she was sure they would leave marks. 'Why must you always fight me at every turn?' he said.

Alice glared back at him. 'I'll fight you until you start treating me as an equal.'

'Then start behaving like an adult instead of a child.'

She pushed her naked breasts against the hard wall of his chest. 'How's this for acting like a grown-up?' She slid her hand down between their bodies to touch his swollen length. 'And this?'

His mouth came crashing down on hers as if some formerly strong leash of self-control inside him had finally snapped. It wasn't a kiss of tenderness, of exploring and rediscovering, but a kiss of raw, rampant hunger.

Alice kissed him back with the same frantic need, their tongues duelling, fighting—a heated, potent combat that made her senses careen out of control. She tore at his clothes, tugging off his shirt with no concern for the buttons. She barely registered the *plink, plink, plink* of them hitting the marble floor. Next she unhooked his belt and slipped it from his trouser lugs, letting it drop to the floor at their feet.

His hands shoved her knickers down past her thighs, his fingers stroking her damp heat with devastating expertise. The pleasure came at her from nowhere, ambushing her, throwing her into a whirling tailspin that left her gasping.

But no way was she allowing this to be a one-way affair. She ripped his zipper down and freed him into her hands, massaging him as she fed off his mouth, using her tongue against his to remind him of the sensual assault she had in mind for him. He made a guttural sound—a sound so utterly primal it made her insides quiver in excitement.

He wrenched her hand away with a muttered curse, his mouth coming back down on hers with a fireball of passion. He walked her backwards to the nearest wall, part walk, part stumble, and roughly stepped out of his trousers and shoes.

Alice broke the kiss to peel her knickers the rest of the way down her legs and kick off her heels. Cristiano tugged her by the hips back against him, letting her feel the full force of his arousal. Her hand went to him again, while her eyes met his. She loved watching the waves of pleasure contort his handsome features. It was the only time she had ever seen him lose control.

'Wait,' he said, breathing hard. 'Condom call.'

Alice would have thrown caution to one side like her clothes, but knew it would be irresponsible given their circumstances. Not that she didn't allow herself a tiny moment, while he sourced a condom from his wallet, to wonder what it would be like to carry his child.

Cristiano came back to her, one hand going to the wall next to her head, his mouth pressing a hot kiss to the side of her neck, and then over her collarbone and then to her breasts. His tongue stroked each upper curve before circling the nipple, in ever tightening circles until he took the nipple into his mouth, drawing on it in a sensual suck that made the hairs on Alice's head stand on end as if pulled from above.

He kissed his way back up to her mouth, taking it in a deep, plundering kiss that left her clawing at his body for the release she craved. He moved between her legs, lifting one of her legs up and anchoring it on his hip before entering her with a sure, swift thrust that made her gasp out loud.

It had been so long!

He set a fast rhythm as if he knew the sweet and savage agony her body was going through. He drove into her moist heat with determined purpose, his breathing just as ragged as hers. Alice gripped him by the shoulders, her fingers digging into his muscled flesh as the wave broke over her. A smashing wave that tossed her into a spinning whirlpool that shook and shuddered through her body. And then another and another followed in its wake, leaving her boneless, spent and quivering all over with aftershocks.

He continued to rock against her until he came with a deep groan of release, his body shuddering as it emptied, his breath hot and rapid against the side of her neck.

Alice unlocked her fingers and slid her hands down his arms and back up again. 'You certainly haven't lost your touch. But I guess you've had plenty of practice.'

He pulled away from her and removed the condom. Then he bent to pick up his trousers and stepped back into them. 'I'm not going to apologise for having a life.'

Alice stepped past him and scooped up his shirt and slipped her arms through the sleeves, drawing it around her naked body, figuring it was quicker than fumbling around the floor for her clothes, which seemed to be strewn from one end of the foyer to the other. 'Are you suggesting I haven't got one?'

He gave her a levelling look. 'You haven't dated in over a year. Why?'

Alice pursed her lips, locking her arms even tighter around her body where she was trying to hold his shirt in place. 'I've been busy at work. I'm always too exhausted at the end of the day for trawling around the nightclubs or online for a sex buddy. Thanks to your extremely generous grandmother, I can now indulge myself for the next six months with you. Lucky me.'

A line of tension pulled at his mouth. 'Is that all you want from men? Sex?'

'Not all men,' Alice said. 'Only the ones I can bring myself to sleep with.' She stepped forwards and trailed a fingertip down his bare arm. 'You tick all the boxes. You're rich, good-looking and you know your way around a woman's body. Oh, and you always have a condom handy. That's always a bonus.'

His hand capturing her wrist, he searched her gaze for a long pulsing moment. 'You're twenty-eight years old. Don't you want more for your life now than work and no-strings sex?'

Alice closed her mind to the image it kept throwing up of a tiny dark-haired baby with raisin-black eyes. 'Nope. Do you?'

Cristiano's frown made a roadmap of lines on his forehead. His hand fell away from her arm. 'No.'

Alice bent down and picked up her bra and knickers and bundled them into a ball in her hand. 'Then we've got nothing to worry about, have we? We're both in this for what we can get. You want your company shares and your share of the villa and I want the financial security my share in your grandmother's villa will give me once we fulfil the terms of her will.' She slipped on her heels before adding, 'Although, I'm not sure why you're insisting on having a church wedding. It seems a little over the top given the circumstances.'

'I told you my reasons. I don't want people thinking this is anything but a genuine relationship.'

'All the same, it's going to look pretty bad when we divorce in six months,' Alice said. 'Aren't people going to speculate and wonder how genuine it was then?'

He gave her an unreadable look. 'Perhaps you won't want it to end in six months. You might be enjoying yourself too much.'

Alice laughed. 'Funny man. You're good in bed, but not *that* good.'

He sent a lazy fingertip over the back of her hand where it was holding his shirt in place. 'Speaking of bed… I hope I didn't rush you just then?'

'Did you hear me complaining?'

A small smile lifted one corner of his mouth. He sent the same fingertip down the slope of her cheek, stopping beneath her chin to lift it so her gaze was on a level with his. 'I want you like I've wanted no other woman.'

Alice gave up trying to hold his shirt together and linked her arms around his waist instead. 'I bet you say that to every woman you've brought back here.'

He made a twisted movement of his mouth. 'You might not believe this, but I've never brought anyone back here. For a drink or dinner, yes, but not to have sex. Not since you.'

Alice did find it hard to believe. But why hadn't he brought anyone back here? Did it mean he had loved her after all? That he couldn't bear to have anyone here where he had made such passionate love to her? But he was so adamant now he hadn't been in love with her back then. 'But why not?'

His eyes dipped to her mouth but whether it was because he was thinking of kissing her again or avoiding her gaze she couldn't be sure. 'Every room reminded me of you.' He waited a beat before returning his eyes to hers. 'It was…off-putting.'

'It must have cost you a fortune in hotels,' Alice said.

His crooked smile made her insides shift. 'The upside of owning hotels is I don't get to pay for accommodation.'

'Lucky you.'

His hands went to her hips, holding her against the stiffening of his body. The sensation of him swelling against her stirred her blood, making her aware of the tingling nerve endings deep in her core. His mouth came down and covered hers in a long, slow kiss that ramped up her desire to a new level.

Alice returned his kiss, her tongue tangling with his in a sexy tango that made him tug her harder against him as if he couldn't bear to have any distance between them. She moved her hands up and down his back and shoulders, delighting in the freedom to touch him, to stroke him, to feel his sculpted muscles tense and flex under her caressing touch.

She couldn't get it out of her mind—he hadn't brought anyone back here since her. Not one woman. No one had shared his bed with him but her.

Cristiano's hands went from her hips to scoop her up in his arms. 'Time for bed?'

Alice played with the ends of his hair that brushed

his neck. 'You don't have to carry me. I'm too heavy. You'll herniate a disc or something.'

He pressed a brief hard kiss to her lips. 'You're a lightweight. I lift weights that weigh more than you.'

He had the muscles to prove it. She could feel them bunching and tensing under her knees and her back where his arms were holding her, a heady reminder of how strong he was and how potently male.

He took her to his bedroom, which had been redecorated since she had last been there. Had he tried to remove every memory of his time with her? Tried and failed? It was now decorated in a soft mushroom grey on a feature wall behind the bedhead, with white walls and ceiling, and white linen on the king-sized bed with a matching grey throw placed neatly on the end. There was a grey velvet linen-box-like seat at the foot of the bed half the height of the mattress. The carpet was a soft cream that threatened to swallow her up to the knees when Cristiano placed her on her feet beside the bed.

Alice kept her arms linked around his neck, pushing her body against the warm, hard frame of his. 'You've redecorated since I was last in here.'

'Yes.' He nibbled at her earlobe, sending a frisson scooting down her spine. 'Not that it worked. I still couldn't bring myself to make love with anyone in here. I spent a veritable fortune for nothing. Like it?'

'It's gorgeous.'

'Like you.' He kept kissing her neck, nipping and licking at the sensitive flesh.

Alice couldn't help a thrill of pleasure at his compliment. She didn't see beauty when she looked in the mirror. What woman did? She only saw the things she wished she could change. But when Cristiano looked at her with his dark eyes glittering with desire, she felt beautiful and desirable in a way she never felt with anyone else.

His mouth came to hers in a searing kiss, his tongue delving between her lips in search of hers. She gave herself up to the kiss, a soft whimper escaping her lips when he peeled his shirt away from her body and took possession of one of her breasts in his hand. The warm expertise of his touch made her skin tingle and her nipples tighten into buds. He rolled his thumb over her nipple, his hand then slipping to the underside of her breast, pushing the globe of flesh upwards for the descent of his mouth. He suckled on her engorged nipples in turn, his tongue hot and moist as it moved over the curve of each breast until her body was trembling with need.

He knelt down in front of her, kissing his way from her breasts, down her sternum and to her belly button. He lingered over the tiny cave, dipping the tip of his tongue into its whorled pool before going lower. Alice sucked in a sharp breath as his tongue skated over her lower abdomen, his warm breath a tantalising caress on her most intimate flesh. He separated her folds with his fingers and then brought his mouth to her, making every swollen nerve ending vibrate with delight. The spiralling waves of sensation pulsed through her body with earth-rocking force.

She tried to hold onto her consciousness but it was impossible to do anything but feel. Aftershocks of pleasure rang through her flesh, like a bell reverberating long after it had been struck.

Cristiano got up and eased her down on the bed, only stopping long enough to dispense with his trousers and access another condom. Alice reached for him as he came down over her on the mattress, her hands running over his muscled biceps and then the back of his neck, lifting her head to meet the descent of his mouth.

His kiss was long and deep, thrumming with a building urgency she could feel in every cell of her flesh where it was touching his. His erection probed her entrance and she opened to him, shifting her hips to accommodate him. It was like resuming a dance choreographed just for them. The fit of their bodies in that intimate embrace felt so right, so fluid and sensual—as unconscious and natural as breathing.

Alice stroked his back from his neck to his lower spine, concentrating in the dip above his taut buttocks. She knew all his erogenous zones and it thrilled her to feel his earthy response to her touch. She cupped his buttocks, holding him, rocking with him as he set a rhythm that was in perfect tune with her needs. The feel of him moving inside her body sent her senses into a frenzy of excitement.

No one filled her the way he did. No one knew her body as he did. No one else understood how much she craved this magic of motion, the friction that ruthlessly teased her sensitive flesh until she thought she would explode.

He turned her over so she was on top, his hands cupping her breasts, his dark gaze consuming her as a starving man did a meal he had long waited for in frustrated agony. Alice bent forward over him, her hands placed either side of his head, her hair falling forward to tickle his chest and shoulders. She moved her body in time with his, finding the extra friction that sent her over the edge. The savage pleasure pulsed through her in ever expanding waves like a boulder dropped in a pond. Every part of her body felt the rippling flow of release, until finally a warm soothing tide of lassitude was left in its wake.

His release was close behind hers, the spasms so powerful she could feel them echoing against the walls of her intimate flesh. She could see, too, the contortion of ecstasy played out on his face, and hear his sexy, breathless grunts that made her skin lift in a shower of goose bumps.

Cristiano rolled her back under him, and, balancing his weight on his elbows, he brushed the damp tendrils of hair back off her forehead. 'You never fail to surprise me.'

Alice teased the curls at the back of his neck with her fingers. 'In what way?'

He outlined her mouth with a lazy fingertip, the top lip and then the bottom one until her lips were tingling, his eyes sexily hooded. 'You respond to me like no one else.'

Alice didn't want to be reminded of all the other women he had slept with since her. Even if he hadn't brought them back here, she knew he had slept with dozens of women elsewhere. All those hook-ups in his hotels. Night after night. Year after year. It was too painful to think about—especially while her body was still thrumming with the magic of his touch.

She knew it was inconsistent of her to be so petty about it since she'd been the one to end their relationship. But the thought of him making love to someone else with the same intensity was nothing short of torture. How many women? Had he looked at them the way he looked at her? Had he touched them the way he had touched her? Was he making comparisons? Finding her a disappointment now he'd revisited their intimacy?

She dropped her hands from his hair and began to push against his chest. 'You'd better take care of that condom before we end up with more than a six-month marriage.'

A frown brought his brows together, his eyes studying hers for a beat or two. But then he rolled away and got off the bed and dealt with the condom. He picked up a bathrobe from the hook behind the door and slipped his arms into it and loosely tied the ties. 'Are you on the pill?'

'Of course.'

He bent to pick up his trousers from the floor and hung them over the back of a chair near the window. His expression had gone back to neutral but Alice couldn't help feeling he was annoyed with her again. She could see it in the way he was restoring order to the room. It was his way of controlling his feelings. A battening down of the emotional hatches, so to speak. Funny, but she hadn't realised he did that until now.

She hugged her knees to her chest and rested her chin on top of them, watching him fold his shirt he'd taken from her body such a short time ago. 'You're angry.'

He tossed the shirt to one side as if it personally offended him, and frowned at her. 'What gives you that idea?'

Alice unlocked her arms from around her knees and got off the bed, taking the bed throw rug with her as a sarong. 'I'm going to take a shower while you play housemaid.'

His hand captured her arm on the way past and he turned her to face him. 'What do you mean by that?'

'You're cleaning up the room as if you want to forget what just happened.' Alice unpeeled his fingers one by one, shooting him a look. 'Of course I'm on the pill. Do you think I'd sleep with you if I wasn't?'

His eyes held hers in a lock. 'Even the pill isn't foolproof. You could miss a dose or have an absorption problem.'

'True, so that's why we have to be careful.'

Even though every time I think about a baby my ovaries start jumping up and down in excitement.

His gaze continued to bore its way into hers. 'So you're as adamant as ever over not having kids?'

Alice hoped he couldn't hear her eggs jostling and shoving each other and saying, *Let me go first!*

'My business is my baby. It takes all my energy and commitment. I don't have room in my life for a child. Anyway, what's with the inquisition? You're not thinking of making an heir and spare to inherit your millions, are you?'

The skin around his mouth tightened until it was more white than tan. 'No.'

'That's quite a change from the man seven years ago who couldn't wait to start a family.'

'I have different goals now.'

'What did your grandmother think about that?'

Cristiano's expression turned rueful. 'She wasn't happy about it. She only had my father and would've loved more children but it never happened. She had a stillbirth before my father and numerous miscarriages after.' He let out a long slow breath and continued. 'She adored my mother. She treated her as if she were her own daughter. There was none of that mother-in-law angst everyone talks about. My mother loved Nonna as much if not more than her own mother. Family was everything to Nonna.'

Alice had seen that love of family first hand when she'd met Volante Marchetti. Even though the old woman had not long ago lost her husband Enzo, she had been nothing but warm and loving and welcoming towards Alice. And when it came to Cristiano, well, Alice had felt slightly envious to see the depth of love the old woman had for him. There were parents who didn't love their children more than Volante had loved her grandson. 'Why do you think she wanted you to marry me? Surely she must've known it was the last thing either of us would want?'

'I'm not sure…' He dragged a hand down his face, the sound of his palm scraping against his stubbly jaw loud in the silence. 'No, that's not quite true. She was unhappy with how I was living my life. She was quite vocal about it towards the end. She wanted the best for me, and, in her mind, didn't think I was getting it.'

Alice gave a soft little snort. 'I hardly think I'm the best thing that's ever come into your life.'

Cristiano's gaze met hers for a long beat of silence. 'Nonna would disagree.'

'That's very kind of her, but I'm—'

'It's fine, Alice,' he said. 'I'm not going to hold you to our agreement longer than necessary. I'm only allowing it to go this far because I can't allow those shares to get into my cousin Rocco's hands. I'm not going to watch everything my parents worked so hard for go down the mouth of a poker machine or on a gaming table.'

Alice frowned. 'Didn't your grandmother know about his gambling tendencies?'

He shook his head, his look grim. 'I made the decision not to tell her. Stupid, I know now in hindsight. But she was so ill and frail and I didn't want to send her to her grave with that worry on top of everything else. She changed her will a week or two after her diagnosis.'

'Would you have tried to stop her if you'd known at the time what she planned to do?'

He seemed to consider it for a moment. 'I'm not sure… Yes, no, maybe. It was what she wanted so what right did I have to try and change her mind? She wasn't suffering from dementia or any mental impairment brought on by her illness. She had a right to compose a will that reflected her dying wishes, and yet… I wish I'd warned her about Rocco, but, to be honest, I'm not sure I would have even if I'd known what she planned to do. She adored him. He's her late sister's only child and her godson. It would have broken her heart to know he wasn't the golden boy she believed him to be.'

Alice shifted her mouth from side to side, thinking about Volante Marchetti with her razor-sharp mind and intelligent gaze. Not much would have escaped that wise old bird's eye. 'What if she did know?'

Cristiano looked at her blankly. 'Know what? About Rocco?'

'Yes. Maybe she knew you would do anything to save those shares from being frittered away,' Alice said. 'Anything, as in marrying your enemy.'

He gave her a sideways smile and glided a hand down the length of her bare arm, making her skin lift in a veil of goose bumps. 'Is that what we are? Enemies?'

Alice put her hand to his face, sliding it down the raspy skin of his cheek. 'Well, you could say we are, except now we're making love not war.'

He gathered her close, locking his hips against hers,

stirring her senses into overdrive with the heated probe of his body. 'I thought you were going to take a shower?'

She moved against him, her inner core leaping in excitement to find him hard as stone. 'I was. Want to join me?'

He unwrapped her from the throw, his eyes going to her breasts. He bent his head and covered one tightly budded nipple with his mouth, drawing on the puckered flesh until she was restless with clawing need. She worked on his trousers, unzipping them with more haste than finesse. His mouth came down on hers in a scorching kiss, his tongue tangling with hers in a tango of lust that made her blood all but sizzle in her veins. She could feel the swell of her most intimate flesh, the dragging sensation of need that was part pain, part pleasure. His hands gripped her by the hips, holding her to the pulsing heat of his body, his chest crushed against her breasts, the masculine hair tickling and teasing her sensitised skin.

Cristiano took her by the hand and led her to the en suite. He prepared himself with a condom while he waited for the shower to get to the right temperature, and then stepped in with her. The water cascaded over their bodies, heightening Alice's senses as his hands skimmed her wet, naked flesh. She pressed her lips to his chest, kissing her way down to his navel, circling her tongue and then bending down in front of him so she could take him in her mouth. She had never pleasured another partner this way. Had never wanted to. Had made excuses not to. The thought of doing it with someone else was almost repugnant. But with Cristiano it felt like a sacred act, one that was mutually pleasurable, for she loved feeling the potent strength of him against her lips and tongue. She loved hearing his groans, and witnessing his knees buckle when she drew on him. She loved feeling his hands gripping her head to anchor himself against the tumultuous throb of release.

But this time he wouldn't let her take him over the edge. He pulled away from her and brought her back to her feet. Then he bent down so he was between her parted thighs, his mouth working its magic on her feminine folds. He knew exactly what pressure and what speed to trigger the explosion. It rocked through her body like a torpedo, sending ripples of delight through every cell until her thighs tingled as if they were being trickled with fine sand.

Alice tugged him by the hair to get him to stand up, pressing her mouth to his and tasting her own essence on his lips and tongue. He moved from her mouth down to her neck, nudging and nuzzling her while he positioned himself. She guided him with her hand, lifting one leg so it was balanced on his hip, a gasp puffing out of her lips when he surged into her with his own raw groan.

The water falling over them added another sensory delight, the rocking speed of his thrusts ramping up her need until she was on the knife-edge, teetering there but unable to go any further. Cristiano pulled out and, with a sexy glint in his eyes, turned her so that her back was to him. Alice planted her hands on the marble wall of the shower, standing on tiptoes so he could gain the access he wanted.

There was something about this position that had an element of wickedness about it. A primitive wickedness that was as thrilling as it was slightly shocking. He moved between her buttocks, the hot glide of his engorged flesh tantalising her senses until she was breathing hard in excitement. He surged into her wetness, the different angle catching her right where she needed it, the fast-moving friction of his urgent thrusts triggering an orgasm so powerful she felt it move through her like a high-speed missile. The whirlpool of pleasure stole every conscious thought, leaving her spinning in a swirling black sea of magic.

Cristiano gave three more powerful thrusts, his legs quaking against hers, his breathing rough and uneven next to her ear. Alice waited for him to collect himself before she turned in his arms, locking her arms around his neck and pressing a lingering kiss to his mouth. His hands settled on her hips, his mouth moving against hers with slow, heart-tripping deliberation.

After a long moment, he lifted his head, his gaze dark, rich and gleaming with sexual satiation. 'Like old times, *sì*?'

Alice licked her tongue over his lower lip, leaning into the hard warmth of his body. 'Better.'

Way, way better.

CHAPTER EIGHT

CRISTIANO WOKE NOT long before dawn to find Alice nestled up against his chest soundly asleep. Her hair was tickling his chin but he didn't have the heart to disturb her. Or maybe it was more because lying here with her was like time travelling back to a time in his life when he'd felt he had ticked all the boxes. Felt complete and satisfied in a way he hadn't since. One of her hands was resting against his chest, right over his heart. Her silken legs were entwined with his in an intimate linkage that made his blood stir.

Would this hunger for her ever be satisfied? How many times had they made love last night? He had been like a randy teenager. He couldn't seem to get enough of her. Was it a case of making up for lost time or… something else?

He didn't want to think about the something else.

He wasn't sure why he'd told Alice about his reluctance to sleep with anyone else here since her. Why should he care if she thought he'd bedded anything in a skirt for the last seven years? But somehow what they'd shared under this roof had meant something to him even if it hadn't to her. He hadn't wanted to dilute those memories with a host of other bodies, other faces, other smiles, and other perfumes. Or maybe it was a form of self-flagellation. A perpetual punishment for being so foolish to believe she had been The One.

No. He was fine with things as they were. What could be better than to make the most of their 'forced' time together? Wasn't that what he'd wanted? A chance to get her out of his system so he could finally move on with his life?

It was a good plan.

An excellent plan.

Why had his *nonna* orchestrated it other than to force him to revisit his relationship with Alice? His grandmother knew his life hadn't been the same since Alice left. She knew he hadn't moved on. Not properly. But to leave half of the Stresa villa to her seemed a bit of an extreme measure. Not that he'd let on to Alice how much the place meant to him. He'd let her think the company shares were his focus. The lakeside villa—like this one in Milan—had been in the Marchetti family for a hundred and fifty years. To lose one pebble, let alone half of the property, to someone outside the family was unthinkable. Even if it was to Alice, with whom he'd had the most passionate affair of his life.

There was nothing to stop her selling her share out from under him when their marriage ended. There was no guarantee she would give him first option. She might not even want to sell her share, which would mean he would have to sell his, or deal with having to share the villa with her on an ongoing basis. He could think of nothing worse than having to negotiate times to visit so he didn't run into her new lover or house-party guests. His family home reduced to a time-share property? Unbearable.

Alice's breathing was soft and even, but every now and again she would release a little purring sigh of contentment and nestle even closer. How many times had he watched her like this in the past? Dreaming of their future together, the life they would live, the children they would have, the happiness they would create together to make up for the tragedy he'd experienced.

He had her back in his bed, but would it be enough?

It would have to be because there was no way he was going to offer her anything else. His days of wearing his heart on his sleeve—or anywhere on his person, for that matter—were well and truly over. His heart was in lockdown. In solitary confinement. No walks in the exercise yard. No day release. No bail. No parole.

This thing between him and Alice was about lust now, not love. A lust that would burn brightly for a while and then gradually fade away just like every other relationship he'd had.

Except with her.

Cristiano sidestepped the thought. He would not allow himself to think like that. This was for now, not for ever. He wasn't a 'for ever' guy now.

He was a 'for the moment' man.

Alice opened her eyes and blinked up at him like a baby owl. 'Is it time to get up?'

Cristiano was already 'up'. His body had been up ten minutes ago when her legs had wrapped around his and her hand had slipped to his abdomen. 'Not yet.' He brushed back her tousled hair. 'There's no hurry.'

She gave him a naughty-girl smile when her hand slid lower and found him fully erect. 'No hurry, huh?'

Cristiano sucked in a breath when her hand started working its wicked magic. She licked her lips and slithered down his body, breathing her sweet hot breath over his abdomen and groin. No one but Alice could reduce him to this—to a quaking wreck of a man without the strength of will to stop her. He barely had time to source a condom before she took him to the stratosphere.

He sank back against the pillows to regain his breath, his arm drawing her close to his side. 'Give me a couple of minutes and I'll be right with you.'

He felt her smile against his chest where her cheek was resting. Her fingers did a piano-playing exercise on his right pectoral muscle. 'Is sex this good with your other partners?' she asked after a moment.

Cristiano had already revealed a little too much in that department. No point giving her more ammunition. 'Fishing, *cara*?'

She made a pouting gesture and went to move away but he held her still. He turned so she was trapped beneath him. She refused to meet his gaze so he inched up her chin so she had no choice. Her blue eyes glittered with resentment but behind that he could see doubt and insecurity moving like shadows. 'I'm not a kiss-and-tell man,' he said. 'I consider it disrespectful.'

Her lashes came down to half-mast over her eyes. After a long moment she released a serrated-sounding breath. 'The last time I had sex I came home and showered for an hour.'

Cristiano's gut clenched as if a steel-studded fist had grabbed his intestines. 'You weren't…?' He couldn't even say the ugly word.

Her lips twisted in a rueful motion. 'No, it was completely consensual, it's just I hated every minute of it. Not that there were too many minutes of it, mind you. Three or four at the most.'

Cristiano brushed back some strands of her tousled hair from her forehead. He hated the thought of her making love with someone else. Hated, hated, *hated* it. For years he'd refused to think about it. He wouldn't allow his mind to torture him with the thought of another man touching her body the way he had touched her, holding her the way he held her. He knew it was arrogant, but he wanted to believe he was the only one who brought that passionate response out of her. *His* body. *His* touch. His need of her triggered the fire in her blood in the same way she triggered his.

'If the chemistry isn't there then the sex will always suffer.'

Her fingertip traced a slow line around his mouth. 'That's something we were never short of, isn't it?' Her words had a faint wistfulness about them.

He captured her finger and kissed the end of it. 'No, that's one thing we had in spades.' In spades and buckets and truck and trailer loads. Still had. He could feel it thrumming between them, the way their bodies meshed as if unable to keep their distance.

Alice linked her arms around his head, her fingers lifting and tugging and releasing the strands of his hair in a way that made every inch of his scalp tingle. 'I've never enjoyed sex with anyone else like I do with you.' Her lips gave a little sideways quirk. 'I should hate you for that. You've ruined my sex life.'

Cristiano gave her a look of mock reproach. 'You haven't done mine any favours, either, young lady.'

Her eyes studied his for a long moment. 'Are you saying it's...better with me?'

He pressed a soft kiss on her forehead. 'It's different.'

Two fine pleats appeared between her eyes. 'How?'

He smoothed away her frown with the pad of his index finger. 'We should get a move on. It will take an hour or so to get to Stresa.'

Her frown snapped back. 'Don't change the subject. Talk to me, Cristiano. Tell me what was different—'

'Look, it just was, okay?' Cristiano rolled away and swung his legs over the edge of the bed. What did she want him to say? That he'd missed her every goddam day since? That every time in the last seven years when he'd touched another woman he'd thought of her? And how much he wished it *were* her? That sex was just sex with anyone else but with her it was making love?

No way was he going to say that.

Even if it was regrettably true.

He heard her sit up on the bed, and then felt her silky hand travel the length of his rigid spine, from his neck to his tailbone, in a soothing caress that made every knob of his vertebrae quiver. She leant her head against his back, her arms going around his waist, the little rush of air from her sigh tickling the skin behind his shoulder blades like the wings of a moth.

'Don't be mad at me,' she said.

Cristiano let out his own sigh and swivelled round to gather her against his side. He dropped a kiss to the top of her head. 'I'm not mad at you, *tesoro*.'

I'm mad at myself.

For still wanting her when he should have been well and truly over her. He wasn't some creepy stalker guy who couldn't let go. There should be no reason he was stuck on her to the point where he couldn't bear to contemplate a future with anyone else. He could have anyone he wanted. He didn't have to fight for dates. If anything, he had to fight them off. But something about

Alice had stayed with him. Like a tune he couldn't get out of his head.

Alice snaked a hand up around his neck, gazing into his eyes with such intensity he wondered if she could sense how much he had missed her. That in spite of all his denials and dissembling she knew—her body knew—he only felt this body-stunning magic with her. Her eyes went to his mouth, her tongue sneaking out to moisten the soft swell of her lips.

'I don't want us to bicker and fight any more. A relationship shouldn't be a competition. It's so…so exhausting.'

Cristiano slid a hand under the curtain of her hair, his mouth coming down to within reach of hers. 'Then we'd better put that energy to much better use, *sì*?'

Her eyes shone with anticipation and she lifted her face for his kiss. 'Now you're talking.'

After a quick breakfast, Cristiano drove Alice the ninety-kilometre distance to his grandmother's villa in Stresa situated on the shores of Lake Maggiore. Alice hadn't forgotten how beautiful the lake was with the historic Isola Bella and Isola Superiore a short boat trip from the shore. But seeing it again on a gorgeous autumn morning with the leaves just starting to turn was nothing less than breathtaking.

Cristiano pulled into the driveway of the villa, which had remained empty since his grandmother's death. He'd explained on the journey there that Volante had insisted on dying at home even though he had offered to have her with him in Milan. He had visited as often as he could and Alice was not surprised to hear he had been with Volante when she'd drawn her last breath. But it made her wonder if coming back now his grandmother was gone was far more painful than he was letting on.

Cristiano opened the front door and led the way inside the quiet villa. It was built on a grand scale with dozens of rooms both formal and informal. It was so big it should not have felt like a family home and yet seven years ago it had.

Not now, however.

Now it was a place of ghosts. The furniture was draped in dustsheets and the long corridors and high windows with their curtains drawn were like eyelids closed over tired eyes. Silence crept from every corner. Achingly lonely silence.

Alice slid her hand into Cristiano's, her own eyes suddenly tearing up. 'It must be so hard to come here now. Have you been back since…?'

He squeezed her fingers and turned to look at her. 'No.' His brows came together and he blotted one of her tears with the pad of his thumb. 'She would not want you to cry, *cara*.'

Alice blinked a couple of times and forced a smile to her lips. Their newfound truce was doing strange things to her emotions. Emotions she normally had under the strictest control.

'Sorry. I'm not normally so emotional. I hardly knew her…except I can't help thinking how different this place is without her.' She swiped at her face with the back of her hand. 'I wish I'd written to her. How hard would it have been to send a Christmas card? I just wish I'd let her know I'd never forgotten her, you know?'

He tucked her hand in under his arm. 'You're here now, which is what she wanted.'

Alice still couldn't understand why Volante had left

her a joint share in this villa and with such strange conditions attached. Not only was the villa—even a half-share—worth millions, it was where Cristiano had spent his childhood and adolescence after his family were killed. Surely if anyone deserved the villa it was him? But he had given no indication of being upset about not inheriting it fully. His focus had always been on the shares he stood to lose control of if he didn't fulfil the terms of the will. Even if it meant marrying the woman who had rejected him seven years ago.

'If you'd inherited the villa completely what would you have done with it?' she asked.

He gave a one-shoulder shrug. 'Made it into a hotel.'

'Really? You wouldn't have wanted it as a private retreat?'

He gave her a wry look. 'It's a bit big for one person.'

'Yes, but you might not always be on your own,' Alice said, torturing herself with the thought of who he might spend the rest of his life with. 'You might want to have a family one day. You can become a father at any age so—'

'It's a good location for a hotel,' he said as if she hadn't spoken. 'The gardens too are perfect for weddings and other functions.'

Alice kept her gaze trained on his. 'But doesn't this place mean more to you than that? Don't you have memories you—?'

'What is a house without the people you love inside it?' he said, with a flash of irritation in his gaze. 'It's nothing, that's what it is. It's just bricks and mortar. An empty shell where every room reminds you of someone you've loved and lost.'

Alice swallowed, watching in silence as he tore off

a couple of dustsheets and dropped them to the floor in puddles of white like collapsed sails. She pictured him as a young boy going back to his family's villa after the accident, her heart cramping at the thought of what it had been like for him to walk into that sad vacuum of a place that had once been full of love and laughter.

'I'm so sorry…' Her voice came out little more than a cracked whisper of sound.

He raked a hand through his hair and let out a long rough sigh. 'No, I'm the one who's sorry. I shouldn't have spoken so harshly to you. Forgive me.'

Alice closed the distance between them and slipped her arms around his waist, looking up at his grimly set features. 'It's fine. This is really painful for you.'

After a moment his expression softened a fraction as if her presence calmed him. He gave her a twist of a smile, his hand brushing an imaginary hair away from her face.

'I should have been back here weeks ago. I just couldn't seem to do it. I didn't want to face this place without her in it. It reminded me too much of the trip home after my parents and brother were killed.'

Alice moved her arms from around his waist and took his hands in hers, gently stroking their strong backs with her thumbs. 'I can't imagine how that must have been for you.'

He looked down at their joined hands for a moment before returning his gaze to hers. 'My grandparents tried to spare me the trauma of going back home but I insisted. It was weird…surreal, really. Everything at home looked the same but it was different. It was like the villa was holding its breath or something.'

His gaze got a faraway look and shifted from hers.

'It was like my life had been jammed on pause. I stood there thinking if only I could turn back the clock. Maybe if I hadn't been sick they wouldn't have had to make the detour to my grandparents' place, then they wouldn't have been on that road at that particular time.'

Alice clutched at his hands. 'You mustn't blame yourself. You were a child. Kids get sick all the time. You can't possibly blame yourself for someone else's stupidity. It was that drunk driver's fault, not yours, that your family were killed.'

Cristiano's fingers shifted against hers, his eyes still shadowed.

'I was cautious about expressing my grief because it only made it harder on my grandparents. If I showed how devastated I was then they would have that to deal with along with everything else. They were so strong but it can't have been easy bringing up a child at their stage of life. They'd stepped back from the hotel business to enjoy a quieter life, but of course all that changed. My grandfather had to run things until I was of an age to take over.'

He slipped his hands out of hers and walked over to one of the windows that overlooked the lake.

Alice wanted to follow him but sensed he was gathering himself. She couldn't recall a time when he had spoken with such depth about his loss. He had never seemed to want to talk about it before. Why hadn't she taken the time to encourage him to unburden himself? She had been so immature back then she hadn't seen how the loss of his family was why he over-controlled everything. She had been mulish and opinionated instead of compassionate and understanding. If only she had been less focussed on her own opinions she might have realised how tragic his life had been and how it had coloured everything he did.

Her background had its issues, certainly, but nothing compared to what he'd been through. She looked at his tall frame standing there and pictured the child he had once been. Trying to be strong for his grandparents. Containing his grief to protect them. Hadn't she done the same with her mother? Tried to be strong, becoming the adult instead of the child in order to help her mother through every broken relationship. Ignoring her own needs until she could barely recognise them when they cropped up. 'Oh, Cristiano…'

He turned and looked at her with one of his smiles that wasn't quite a smile. 'You know what's ironic? My brother was the one with his heart set on taking over the business. I had other plans.'

Shock ran through Alice in an icy tide. Plans? What plans? How had she spent six weeks with this man and not once realised he'd had other plans for his life than the hotel business? He was so successful. He owned and operated some of the most luxurious boutique hotels in the Mediterranean. When you thought of boutique hotels you thought of Cristiano Marchetti. But what had *he* wanted to do with his life?

'You mean you didn't want to be in the hotel business? Not at all?'

He picked up a photograph of his grandparents as a young couple that was on the walnut table near the window, his fingers moving over the carved frame as if he were reading Braille.

'No. I wanted to be an architect. But it was impossible once my parents and brother died. I don't think I even mentioned it to my grandparents after that. I knew my fate. The responsibility was ultimately mine otherwise everything my parents and grandparents had worked for would be lost. I had to shelve my plans and immerse myself in the business. But don't feel too sorry for me, *cara*.'

He put the photograph back down and glanced at her.

'I have plenty of opportunity to express my creativity when I'm working on renovating an old building.' His mouth twisted in a self-deprecating manner. 'I make the architect's life hell for a few months but that's life.'

Alice was in a turmoil of regret over not realising any of this until now. She had made so many assumptions about him. She had even playfully mocked him about his wealth on occasion. And not so playfully recently, when she'd made that crack about all the silver spoons hanging out of his mouth.

All the clues were there now she stopped to reflect on their time together. He had been reluctant to talk about his past because he found it so painful. Not just because of the loss of his family but the loss of the life he had mapped out for himself. He had lost control of everything the day his parents and brother were killed.

She thought of all the times she had talked to him about her plans to build her own beauty spa. She had told him how she had wanted to do it since she was a little girl when she went with her mother to a beauty salon when her mother got her nails done for her second wedding. Alice had been captivated by all the lotions and potions and the sense of luxury so unfamiliar in her life back then. She'd made a decision right then and there to own and operate her own beauty salon where women could escape the humdrum of life and spoil themselves with some pampering. She had fought for her dream and achieved it in spite of the disadvantages of her background.

But Cristiano's background—the one she had envied so much—had been the cause of him *not* being able to live his dream.

Alice walked over to where he was standing and placed her hand on his forearm. 'I've always felt jealous of your wealth, that you could buy anything you want, travel anywhere you like, do anything you like. But it's been more of a burden than anything else, hasn't it?'

He placed his hand over hers, bringing it up to his chest. 'It's both a blessing and a burden but I would much rather have the security of wealth than not. Don't get me wrong. I enjoy my work. I didn't for a long time, but I do now.'

'But who will take over from you once you get to retirement age?' Alice asked. 'Your cousin?'

'God no,' he said with a roll of his eyes. 'Rocco has no head for business. His idea of a hotel makeover would be to install slot machines in every room. My parents and grandparents would spin in their graves.' He sighed and released her hand. 'No, I'll probably sell the business outright when the time is right.'

'But if you had a family, a son or daughter, they could take over and—'

'You seem a little hung up on this issue, Alice.' His tone was on the edge of being crisp. 'Does this mean you've changed your mind about having children?'

Alice forced herself to hold his gaze. 'We're not talking about me. We're talking about you. You have so much to offer a child. You have a strong sense of family. You've had great modelling in both your parents and grandparents. Why wouldn't you pass on that wonderful heritage to your own offspring?'

'Let's talk about you, then,' he said, his gaze unwavering. 'Who will you leave your goods and chattels to? A dog's home?'

Alice pursed her lips and then puffed out a sigh. If they were supposed to be working at a truce then why shouldn't she be honest with him?

She shook back her hair and raised her gaze back to his. 'Okay, I'll let you in on a secret. I have thought about having kids. I've thought about it a lot recently.'

'And?'

'And it's something I'd like to do one day. When I find the right man, of course.'

His expression became shuttered. 'What made you change your mind?'

Alice picked up another photo next to the one of his grandparents. It was a family shot of Cristiano with his parents and older brother. She had seen it before without really seeing it. Cristiano was a happy child in that photo, smiling with an open and engaging expression. Nothing like the serious and closed-off man of today. She put the photo back down and looked at him again.

'It was a gradual thing rather than an overnight change of heart,' she said.

Not unlike my feelings for you.

'I realised what I'd be missing out on when I saw my friends and my clients with their babies. It's such a special relationship—unique, really—the love between a mother and child.' She gave him a flutter of a smile. 'My mother drives me completely nuts but deep down I know she loves me more than anyone else on this planet. I want to feel that love. I want to experience that bond.'

His mouth turned up at one side in a rueful angle. 'What a pity my grandmother meddled with your life. You'll have to put your baby plans on hold for another six months.'

Alice shifted her gaze. 'Yes, well, I'm only twenty-eight. I don't have to panic just yet.'

There was an odd little silence.

Alice wondered if he was thinking of the irony of their situation. He had desperately wanted a family seven years ago while she had wanted her freedom. Now he wanted his freedom while she was peering into every pram that went past.

What if she didn't find a man she could love enough to father her children? But who else could she want but Cristiano? Her feelings for him had been on slow burn in her heart. Banked down out of bitterness because he hadn't fought for her in the past. But the more she thought about her future, she couldn't imagine sharing it with anyone other than him. She would rather be alone than be with someone else.

Maybe that was why she had panicked and pushed him away. She had seen him as the one man who could make her sacrifice the dream of owning her own business. It had been too confronting for her as a twenty-one-year-old on the threshold of her life. Too threatening in case he hadn't loved her enough to give her the freedom to pursue her own goals instead of subsuming her life into the powerful engine of his.

But now…now she had established her business. She knew who she was and what she wanted for her life. And that included the things he no longer wanted. Marriage. A family. To love and be loved.

But Cristiano no longer loved her, if he ever had.

The only reason he was with her now was because of the shares that hung in the balance. If it hadn't been for his grandmother's will she would never have heard from him again. She had to remember that. He was only marrying her to get what he wanted. He might still desire her but he was a full-blooded man with a healthy appetite for sex.

This thing they had going on was for now, not for ever.

CHAPTER NINE

CRISTIANO LED ALICE through the villa but his mind was preoccupied.

She wanted a family.

After all those heated arguments in the past over not wanting kids. It had been a sticking point in their relationship. He had thought her selfish for putting her career above having a family. Selfish and unnatural. But now he was the one who was career focussed. He had made himself so busy he couldn't find time for a steady relationship, let alone a family that would need nurturing day by day, week by week, year by year. He didn't want it because the thought of losing it was too terrifying. Too awful to even contemplate.

He knew all too well how it felt to have his world ripped out from under him. Once was enough. More than enough. Loving someone meant you could lose them. You could lose part of yourself and never get it back.

'May I see the garden now?' Alice said, breaking through his reverie.

'Sure.' Cristiano took her hand and led her to the French doors leading out to the terrace. 'This was one of my grandmother's favourite places. She would sit out here for hours watching the birdlife in the garden.'

'It's such a beautiful place.' Alice's voice had a reverent note to it. 'Around every corner is another surprise. It's like a story unfolding.'

Cristiano waited on the terrace while she wandered about the garden. She stopped to smell the roses his grandmother had planted as a young bride, her fingers softly touching the fragrant petals. The sun caught her hair and turned it into a skein of shining silver, and she brushed some strands away from her face that the light breeze had toyed with and tucked them back behind her ear. She caught him looking at her and gave him a smile that made something inside his chest ache.

'This would make a great wedding venue, don't you think?' she said. 'The wisteria walk would be a gorgeous place for the bride to walk towards the groom.'

'Would you like to get married here?' Cristiano asked.

A slight frown creased her smooth brow. 'But I thought you wanted a church wedding?'

He shrugged. 'As long as it's legal who cares where it's conducted?'

She pulled at her lower lip with her teeth and turned slightly to look at the angel fountain his grandmother had installed after the stillborn birth of her first child the year before Cristiano's father had been born. So much of his family's history was embedded in this place. There wasn't a shrub or tree or yew hedge that hadn't witnessed a Marchetti triumph or tragedy.

After a moment Alice turned to look at him. 'To be honest, I'd rather be married here than in a church. It would make it less…' She seemed to be searching for the right word and bit into her lip again.

'Binding?' Cristiano said.

Her mouth went into a flat line. 'Don't you feel the slightest bit uncomfortable about all this? Marriage is a big deal. As the words of the ceremony say: it's not to be entered into lightly.'

Was she having second thoughts? His guts churned. If she didn't marry him he would lose the shares and the villa. He couldn't allow that to happen.

'Look at it this way. We're fulfilling an old lady's dying wishes by getting married. It's not about us. It's about Nonna. And I think she would be thrilled if we had the ceremony here. I'll get working on it straight away.' He held his hand out for hers, drawing her against his side. 'Now, let's make the most of the day here in Stresa.'

It was a lovely day in spite of Alice's misgivings about where things were heading in their relationship. Cristiano organised a private tour of the islands and a gorgeous lunch at a restaurant by the lake. They drove back to Milan late in the afternoon and, after a quick shower and freshen up, he took her to one of the city's premier restaurants, where the maître d' welcomed Cristiano by name and showered them with effusive congratulations and a bottle of champagne on the house.

Alice sat opposite him sipping her champagne and wondered if he was thinking about that other restaurant only a few streets from here where he had proposed to her while the rest of the diners looked on. With the benefit of hindsight, she wished she'd handled it a little better than she had. But the shock of his sudden proposal after only a few weeks of dating had thrown her into a panic.

Surely she could have let him down without publicly humiliating him. Why had she been so crass and immature? How must he have felt to be left in that restaurant with everyone staring at him open-mouthed? The ring he'd chosen thrown onto the table as if it were a cheap fairground trinket. She hadn't even gone back to his villa, because her passport had been in her tote bag, and she'd caught a taxi straight to the airport and got on the first flight she could.

'More champagne?' Cristiano asked into the silence.

Alice put her hand over the top of her glass. 'Better not. I've had too much already.'

'You're not driving so if you want another I don't mind.'

She waited a couple of beats. 'Did you ever meet the person who—?'

'No.' The word was delivered with such finality it sounded like a gavel falling.

Alice moistened her lips. 'Did they express any remorse? Make any effort to contact you or your grandparents?'

His mouth was twisted in an embittered line. 'No. He was the sort of person who blamed everyone but himself for his wrongdoing. He didn't even get jail time. The judge overseeing the case had connections with his influential father. But karma got him in the end. He was killed in a bar fight. A drug deal gone sour.' He shifted his water glass half a centimetre and then did a slow tap of his fingers on the tablecloth. 'I thought it would help to know he'd got his comeuppance, but strangely it didn't.'

Alice reached across the table and grasped his hand. 'That's because you're not at heart a vengeful man.'

His half-smile was a little crooked. 'Am I not?' His fingers toyed with her engagement ring. 'You would not have liked what I was thinking when you stormed out of that restaurant seven years ago.'

She looked at their joined hands rather than meet his gaze. 'I'm sorry I reacted the way I did back then. It was so…so petulant and immature of me to behave like that.'

He gave her hand a quick squeeze before he released it to sit back in his chair. 'I shouldn't have put you under so much pressure. I was in too much of a rush after my grandfather died.' He did that slow tapping thing again next to his glass, his forehead creasing in a frown. 'Funerals can do that to you. Make you realise how fragile life is.'

Alice thought about him attending his family's funerals, the weight of grief he'd had to shoulder so bravely as a child, and then as an adult saying goodbye to each of his grandparents in turn. She had only been to one funeral—an elderly client who had passed away after a short illness. It had been sad but not tragic. Her family had celebrated her long life and sent her off with a party that had gone on until the early hours of the morning. What did Alice know of how it must feel to say that final goodbye to someone so beloved as a parent, grandparent or sibling?

'All the same, I wish I'd been a little kinder to you.' She let out a tiny sigh. 'I guess that's why you didn't contact me.'

Something flickered in his gaze. Surprise? Alarm? Regret? It was hard to distinguish which. 'Did you want me to?'

Alice wasn't sure it served any purpose to admit to how much she'd hoped he would. What was done was done. It was in the past and best left there. 'No. We were over as far as I was concerned.'

His eyes held hers for a long beat or two. 'How soon did you date someone else?'

She gave a little shrug. 'I don't know...six or so months maybe.' She flashed him a brittle glance before she could stop herself. 'Certainly longer than it took you.'

There was a small silence.

'I made sure I was seen with other women within days of us breaking up,' he said. 'But it was eight months before I could bring myself to sleep with anyone.'

Alice flickered her eyelids in shock. He'd waited *that* long? 'Eight months? Really?'

He gave a grim nod. 'It just didn't feel right rushing into another intense relationship.'

'It was pretty intense, wasn't it?'

He gave that sexy half-smile again and reached for her hand. 'It still is.'

The door was barely closed behind them when they returned to Cristiano's villa when he reached for her. The drive home from the restaurant had been a form of foreplay. His looks, his touch on her thigh when he changed the gears, the throb and roar of the engine that reminded Alice of the potent hormones surging through his body. His mouth came down on hers in a scorching kiss, his tongue tangling with hers in a provocative duel that made her tingle with anticipation.

She tore at his clothes with desperate hands, sliding her palms over the warm hard flesh of his chest and abdomen. He shrugged off his shirt and set to work on her dress, ripping down the zipper at the back and sliding his hand down the length of her spine, holding her against his pulsing heat. He brought his mouth to her neck and décolletage, his lips and tongue lighting spot fires beneath her skin. His hands cupped her breasts from below, pushing them upwards for the descent of his mouth.

She gasped out her pleasure when his mouth closed over one tightly budded nipple, his tongue swirling around the sensitive areola until she was sagging at the knees.

Alice sent her hands lower to free him from his trousers and underwear, taking him in her hand and stroking and squeezing him the way she knew he liked. He groaned his approval against her breast, creating a buzzing sensation that made the hairs on her scalp lift in a Mexican wave.

He lifted his mouth from her breast, his voice low and deep and gravelly with desire. *'Ti desidero.'*

'I want you too.'

He lifted her in one effortless swoop and carried her upstairs to his bedroom. He laid her on the mattress and, after dispensing with the rest of his clothes, dealt with the rest of hers. But somewhere along the way he slowed down the mad pace of his lovemaking and subjected her to an exquisite worship of her body from head to foot that made every cell throb and vibrate with need. His lips, his tongue, his hands, even his breath skating over her skin built her desire to fever pitch until she was all but begging for mercy.

'How much do you want me?' he said against her belly, his stubble grazing her skin.

'So much. Oh, please...*please...*' She writhed and twisted, aching for that final push.

He sheathed himself with a condom and entered her in a thick thrust that set off an explosion in her swollen flesh. She arched her spine to keep the contact where she needed it, the rioting sensations shooting through her like fireworks. She had barely recovered from that first orgasm when another one followed, a deeper one that rolled through her in tumultuous waves.

The contractions of her body must have triggered his own for he tensed all over and then surged deeper into her and shuddered and spilled.

Alice flung her head back against the pillows with a blissful sigh. 'Wow. Double wow.'

He propped himself up on his elbows and traced a fingertip down between her breasts. 'Not many women can orgasm like that without direct stimulation.'

She smiled and stroked a hand down his muscled arm. 'So I'm special, am I?'

His gaze intensified. 'You're the most responsive lover I've ever had.'

Alice tiptoed her fingers over his bicep. 'That's really saying something since you've had so many and all.'

He frowned at her tone and moved away to deal with the condom. 'You shouldn't believe everything you read in the press. If I'd bedded even half the women the press said I had, I wouldn't have had time to run my business.'

Alice sat up and reached for the throw on the end of the bed, wrapping it around her body. She was annoyed for broadcasting her jealousy again. How would she be able to walk away from their relationship with any dignity once it was time to go if she kept yammering on about his playboy lifestyle? He had a perfect right to have lovers. Numerous lovers.

No one had stopped her doing the same. No one but her, that was. She should be feeling happy he had at least refrained from bringing anyone back to his villa since her. That was huge. And the fact he had waited eight months surely should make her feel a little mollified, but sadly it didn't. He might not have moved on as quickly as the press had reported but neither had he come after her. He had kept his distance and seven long years had gone past. Seven years they could have had together…

She stood from the bed. 'I'm going to take off my make-up.'

He came to stand in front of her, his expression softening. 'I thought we agreed not to take cheap shots at each other.'

Alice rolled her lips together and then sighed. 'I'm sorry.'

He lifted her chin, brushing his thumb over her lower lip. 'I want us to be friends when this is over. It's what my grandmother would've wanted.'

'You don't think she wanted us to…to make a go of it?'

His hand fell away from her face. 'If she did then that's too bad because it's not going to happen.'

But it could if he wanted it to.

Alice tried to ignore the tight spasm of her heart. He was ruling out any possibility of them being a proper couple. Refusing to contemplate a future with her. A future with all the things she longed for now. What a cruel quirk of fate to have their roles reversed.

'Did I say I wanted it to? I'm just saying she probably had it in mind when she conjured up this scheme. At the very least she would've wanted us to settle our differences.'

Cristiano ran a hand through his hair. 'We've done that.'

'Have we?'

He let out a long breath and stepped close to her again, cupping her cheek in one broad hand, his dark chocolate eyes holding hers. 'You no longer hate me, do you, *cara*?'

I never hated you.

Alice gave him a wobbly smile. 'Do you still hate me?'

He brought his mouth down to within a millimetre of hers. 'Does this feel like hate to you?' And covered her mouth with his.

It felt like heaven.

When Alice got back to work on Monday it was like stepping into controlled chaos.

Meghan greeted her with a beaming smile from behind the reception counter. 'You would not believe the number of clients who want to see you. You're fully booked for months and months. Years probably. Your engagement to Cristiano Marchetti has opened doors. Big doors. Guess which Hollywood superstar wants you to do their make-up for their wedding in November? You'll never ever guess.'

She pulled out a chair and pushed it towards Alice. 'Here, you'd better sit down before I tell you.'

Alice ignored the chair. 'It's all right—I won't faint. Who is it?'

Meghan named a rising-star female actor who was the current toast of Hollywood.

'And that's not all,' she continued in a rush of excitement. 'She's going to fly you, all expenses paid, to the wedding location. It's top secret so as to keep the press away so you won't be told until the very last moment. You'll have to sign a confidentiality agreement.

I bet it's going to be in Bora Bora or maybe at Richard Branson's place, you know, Necker Island. Or maybe St Bart's. Oh, God, imagine if it was in St Bart's. You'll need an assistant, won't you?' She clasped her hands as if in prayer. 'Take me with you? Please, please, please?'

Alice laughed at the exuberant puppy-like look on her young employee's face. 'I'll have to see if the booking comes off first. No point getting too excited. You know what some of those Hollywood celebrities are like. Their weddings are cancelled at a moment's notice.'

Some of Meghan's enthusiasm sagged. 'True, but if it goes ahead things will never be the same around here. You'll be the wedding make-up artist to the stars.'

I have to get through my own 'wedding' first.

Alice's first client of the day a few days later was a bride-to-be who was booked in for a trial make-up session.

Jennifer Preston was the epitome of a woman radiantly in love. She had been coming to Alice for years as a client and somehow over the time their relationship had morphed into friendship. Jennifer had always bemoaned the fact she hadn't been able to find a suitable partner. But now she was happily engaged to a man she had met on a blind date set up by a friend and it truly was a match made in heaven.

Even a hardened cynic like Alice had to admit love at first sight could happen. Jennifer's fiancé, Marcus, dropped her off at her appointment, and the way he looked at Jennifer when he kissed her goodbye made Alice feel like an imposter. Not that Cristiano didn't look at her with affection and tenderness, but it wasn't as if he were truly in love with her as Marcus was with Jennifer and had been from the moment they'd met.

During Jennifer's trial make-up session, she told Alice about her wedding dress and the romantic honeymoon Marcus had planned. 'You know, Alice, a few months ago I was single and hating it,' Jennifer said. 'Now I'm getting married to a man I adore and he adores me. But you know what I'm talking about. That man of yours is a seriously fast worker. Have you chosen your dress?'

'Erm… Not yet, but I plan to duck out between clients this afternoon,' Alice said. 'So much to do, so little time.'

Jennifer rolled her eyes. 'Tell me about it.' She leaned forward to check her make-up. 'Gosh, you've done a brilliant job. I look almost beautiful.'

Alice put her hand on Jennifer's shoulder and gave it a squeeze. 'You *are* beautiful. You're positively glowing.'

Jennifer placed her hand over Alice's, her eyes shimmering with excitement. 'I haven't told anyone else but Marcus yet, but I'm pregnant. Six weeks. Will you be godmother when it's born?'

Alice blinked in surprise. 'Me?'

Jennifer swung the chair around so she was facing Alice instead of talking to her reflection in the mirror. She grasped Alice's hands in hers. 'Why not you? You and I have been banging on about the paucity of good men in London for the last seven years. Now we're both getting married within weeks of each other. And who knows? Maybe you'll get pregnant soon too.'

Alice stretched her mouth into a smile that felt as fake as her upcoming wedding. 'I'd be thrilled to be godmother. Truly honoured.'

Jennifer smiled. 'That's settled, then. Of course, you're bringing Cristiano to my wedding? I'll talk to the wedding planner about changing the seating arrangements. I've put you on a great table.'

'That's very kind,' Alice said. 'I'll have to check with him to see if he's free that weekend.'

'I'm sure he'd do anything for you,' Jennifer said, eyes sparkling. 'He's a man in love, right?'

CHAPTER TEN

ALICE RUSHED OUT between clients to check a couple of wedding boutiques in the area but couldn't see anything that captured her attention. Or maybe it was her mood that was the problem. She'd been fighting a tension headache all afternoon. It didn't feel right trying on dresses for a wedding that wasn't going to last. It wasn't just the expense of a dress, which was astronomical at the top end of town, but more the thought of play-acting at bride and groom when all she wanted was for it to be real.

How different would this shopping trip be if she were a bride like Jennifer Preston? Trying on beautiful gowns and veils, imagining Cristiano's face at the end of the aisle when she appeared at the church.

Maybe even carrying his baby...

Instead, Alice was going through the motions of bridal preparation knowing in her heart that her relationship with Cristiano was doomed for despair. If he'd wanted their relationship to be for ever then surely he would have said something by now?

She had spent every night with him since they'd come back from Italy. Their relationship had settled into a less combative one but was no less exciting. Every time he looked at her, she felt the rush of attraction course through her flesh. The dark glint in his eyes was enough to make her shudder with excitement.

Like this morning, for instance. He had given her that look and she had put aside her breakfast and made mad passionate love with him up against the kitchen bench. His touch was as magical as ever, in some ways even more intensely satisfying than in the past. Or maybe that was because Alice knew his touching of her was only temporary, that within a few months they would part and go their separate ways. The thought of it was heart-wrenching. How had it taken her this long to realise she loved him?

Or had she always loved him?

Was that why his proposal had been so threatening? She hadn't been ready to admit to how she felt about him. She'd needed more time. More time to question the opinions she'd formed out of fear, not facts. Loving someone back then had felt like giving up a part of herself and never getting it back. But true love shouldn't be like that, surely?

True love was supposed to build up, not destroy.

To heal and create harmony, not hurt and dissension.

'Can I help you with anything?' a shop assistant asked in the last bridal boutique Alice wandered into. 'Oh, my goodness! You're Alice Piper, the wedding make-up celebrity. You did my friend's wedding make-up last year. Congratulations, by the way. Gosh, what an honour, you coming in here for your wedding dress. Let me show you around. Did you have a budget in mind?'

'Erm… I'm just looking at the moment,' Alice said, wondering how she could back out of the shop before the woman gave the paparazzi a heads up to boost her business. She wasn't the best shopper under pressure as it was. She needed time to think. Time to reflect. The last thing she needed right now was the press showing up and flashing cameras and microphones in her face.

The woman frowned. 'But aren't you getting married, like, in a couple of weeks?'

Don't remind me how close it is!

'October first,' Alice said, trying to ignore her thumping heartbeat and the beads of perspiration breaking out on her upper lip.

Cristiano had confirmed the details a few days ago. Their flights were booked, the staff notified at his grandmother's villa to get the place ready for a small wedding party. It was all happening so quickly and yet she felt on the perimeter of it all, like an observer on the sidelines.

'We can still get something made in time.' The woman gave Alice an obsequious smile. 'Especially for someone of *your* status. Nothing off the rack for Cristiano Marchetti's bride, hey? How about we look at some designs?' She whipped out a bridal magazine and fanned the pages open. 'White? Cream? Lace? Satin? Organza?'

Alice swallowed a ropey knot of panic. So many dresses… Who knew there were so many shades of white and cream? So many designs. So many decisions to make. So little time. How did brides do this without having a meltdown? No wonder so many of them got the Bridezilla tag.

The boutique was suddenly too hot, too stuffy, as if someone had sucked all the oxygen out of the room. Her head was in a vice, the pressure mounting until it felt as if her brain were going to explode through her skull.

She swayed on her feet, her vision blurring. The walls were buckling, closing in on her. Nausea churned in her stomach and then climbed up her throat on sticky claws.

'Are you all right?' The shop assistant grasped Alice by the arm. 'Here, sit down and put your head between your knees.'

Alice sank to the velvet-covered chair and lowered her head to her lap. She was vaguely aware of the shop assistant talking to someone on the phone and then a glass of water being handed to her. She sat up to take a few sips but the room was still spinning.

The woman took the glass from her. 'I've called an ambulance. They should be here soon.'

Alice looked up at her in alarm, her heart hammering like a drummer on crack. 'I don't need an ambulance.'

There was the sound of a siren screaming outside. It echoed the silent scream inside Alice's head. *No-o-o-o-o!*

'Too late,' the woman said. 'Here, give me your phone. I'll call your fiancé for you.'

Alice clutched her bag against her body as if it contained the Crown Jewels. 'It's all right—I'll call him. I don't want him to panic over nothing.'

The woman tottered away to greet the paramedics coming through the door. 'She's over there. She nearly fainted. She was talking to me as good as anything and then she went as white as that dress in the window. I reckon she's pregnant. I was exactly the same when I had my daughters.'

Shoot me now.

Cristiano had finished with his meeting with the architectural firm he'd employed to do the designs for the makeover of his Chelsea building so decided to call in at Alice's salon to see if she was finished for the day. He could have called or texted her, but he knew she kept her phone on silent when at work and sometimes forgot to unmute it. Besides, he liked seeing her in her work environment. She was always so professional but he got a kick out of knowing that behind that cool and composed façade and that neat little uniform was a feisty and passionate woman who came apart in his arms.

But when he walked into the salon Meghan, her assistant, was in a flustered state.

'Why are you here?' she said. 'Shouldn't you be at the hospital?'

Cristiano's stomach dropped like an anvil hitting concrete. 'Hospital?'

Meghan was wide-eyed with strain. 'Yes, Alice fainted in a shop. I got a call from the owner a few minutes ago. She said Alice has been taken to hospital for observation. I've been in such a state trying to cancel all her clients as well as do my own. Is she all right? What's wrong with her? They wouldn't let me speak to her.'

Cristiano's heart was giving a very good impression of needing urgent medical attention itself.

Alice sick? Taken to hospital?

Panic pounded like thunder in his blood.

No. No. No. Not again.

What if he couldn't get there in time? Things happened in hospitals. Bad things. People went in and didn't always come out. Or they did, but in body bags just like his family. 'Which hospital?'

Meghan told him and then added as he rushed out of the door, 'Oh, my God. You didn't know?'

'My phone's been off all afternoon.' He took it out of his jacket pocket and almost dropped it in his haste. But there were no missed calls from Alice and no text messages, either. What did that mean? She couldn't call because she was too ill? Unconscious? In a coma?

His heart flapped like a blown tyre. His pulse hammered. He was so consumed with dread it felt as if a pineapple were jammed halfway down his throat.

'Tell her I've got everything under control here,' Meghan called after him. 'Well, sort of...'

Cristiano hailed the nearest cab and then spent the entire journey wishing he'd dragged the cabby out of the driver's seat and driven the thing himself. By the time he got to the hospital he was so worked up he could barely speak. He had to draw in a couple of deep breaths when he walked through the door.

The clean antiseptic smell hit him like a slap, instantly transporting him to that dreadful day. After his parents and brother were killed he had gone with his grandparents to the hospital where they had been taken. He still remembered those long corridors with the sound of his trainers squeaking as he walked that agonising walk to where his family were lying lifeless. He remembered the looks from the doctors and nurses—a mixture of compassion, I'm-glad-it's-not-my-loved-ones-lying-in-there, and business-as-usual indifference. He remembered the shock of seeing his mother's and father's and brother's bodies draped in shroud-like sheets. Not being able to grasp the thought of them never coming home, of life never being the same.

It had felt as if he had stepped into a parallel universe—it hadn't been him standing there looking at his family but some other kid. Someone who *could* deal with it. Someone who wouldn't carry the wound of loss around for the rest of his life.

Cristiano found the emergency department and asked a nurse for Alice's whereabouts in a voice that sounded nothing like his own. He was led to a cubicle where Alice was lying with her eyes closed and hooked up to a saline drip. He saw the rise and fall of her chest and a giant wave of relief swept through him. He opened his mouth to say her name but nothing came out. He reached for her hand not attached to the drip and she opened her eyes and gave him a tremulous smile. 'Hi.'

He sank to the chair beside the bed because he was sure his legs were going to fold beneath him.

'What happened? What's wrong, *cara*? Are you unwell? I was so worried I thought you might be…' He swallowed back the word. 'You scared the hell out of me. Are you all right?'

'I'm perfectly fine. I just got a bit dehydrated and almost passed out. I didn't want all this fuss but the lady in the shop I was in was so pushy and—'

'It was a good thing she was,' Cristiano said. 'Why haven't you been drinking enough? Are you not feeling well? You should have said—'

'I was busy, that's all.' She gave him a weary smile. 'Since we got back from Italy I've been run off my feet. I didn't get lunch and I hadn't had anything to drink since breakfast and that was only a sip or two of tea.'

He cradled her hand in both of his. Guilt slammed through him. It was his fault she hadn't had a proper breakfast. He had distracted her with a passionate kiss that had ended with them making love up against the kitchen bench. He couldn't resist her when she was all dressed up for work in that crisp smart uniform. He couldn't resist her, period. He brought her hand up to his mouth and gently pressed a kiss to it.

'How soon before I can take you home or do they want to keep you in overnight?'

She lifted her arm connected to the cannula. 'Just until this runs through.'

Cristiano stroked her fingers. 'You almost gave me a heart attack, young lady.'

She gave him a rueful movement of her lips. 'Sorry.'

'What shop were you in?'

Her gaze fell away from his. 'A bridal boutique.'

Cristiano made a 'that figures' sound. 'Yeah, well, I felt like passing out when I came in here. Bridal boutiques aren't your favourite haunts and hospitals aren't mine.'

Her gaze came back to his, her brow wrinkled in concern. 'I'm so sorry for making you panic. I didn't want anyone to call you. I knew I'd be all right once I got some fluids on board.'

Why hadn't she got someone to call him? Didn't she realise how that made him feel? Didn't she have an inkling of what he'd gone through just then? 'But you should have called me or had someone do it for you.'

Her frown deepened. 'Why should I?'

He gave her a speaking look. 'Come on, Alice, we're engaged to be married, for God's sake. I'm the first person you or someone taking care of you should call when something like this happens.'

Her gaze slipped out of reach of his. 'We're not exactly like a normal couple, though, are we?'

Cristiano tightened his hold on her hand. 'This isn't the time or place to have this conversation. You're not well and I'm in no state to be rational.'

There was a long silence.

'Aren't you going to ask?' Alice said.

'Ask what?'

She turned her head to meet his gaze. 'Whether I'm pregnant.'

Cristiano's heart juddered to a stop and then started again with a sickening jolt. 'Are you?'

'No.'

He was glad…*wasn't he*? Of course he was. A baby was the last thing he wanted. A baby would change everything. He didn't want anything changed. Their marriage was two weeks away and that was all he wanted to think about right now. Get the job done. Mission accomplished. Move on.

'That's good.' He gave her hand a reassuring squeeze. 'I bet you're relieved about that.'

Another weary smile flickered across her mouth. 'Sure am.' She shifted on the bed as if the mattress was uncomfortable. 'I've been asked to be godmother to a client-stroke-friend's baby. I'm going to her wedding after I do her make-up next weekend. She's invited you since we're…you know, supposed to be engaged.'

'Would you like me to go with you?'

Her teeth sank into the pillow of her lip for a moment. 'I guess it'll be a good practice run, huh? See how it's done and all.'

'You've been to a wedding before, surely? Or has your aversion to them stretched that far?'

'I was flower girl at my mother's second marriage,' Alice said. 'I tripped going up the aisle and my stepfather told me off for it afterwards in front of all the guests. I was so mortified I wet my pants.'

Cristiano frowned. 'How old were you?'

'Six. He carried on about it for years and my mother never did anything to stop him.' She gave a little sigh. 'I was glad when he left her for another woman. But for a while after Mum blamed me for jinxing their wedding day.'

'Does she still blame you?'

'No, not now.' Another sigh wafted past her lips. 'But I didn't go to her third wedding on principle.'

'In case you tripped up the aisle?'

She gave him a worldly look. 'No, because her third husband has wandering hands and is a thief.'

Cristiano could see now why she had a thing about marriage. 'What about your father? Did he ever marry again?'

'Yes, and surprisingly it's working,' she said. 'He and Tania haven't had it easy, though. They have a little boy with severe autism. That's why I give Dad money from time to time, to pay for Sam's therapy.'

'That's kind of you.'

She gave a little movement of her lips that could have loosely passed for a smile. 'My dad isn't as bad as my mother always makes out. He just wasn't ready for marriage way back then. He's grown up now. He's taking responsibility for his wife and family. I know he wasn't an angel by any means when he was married to my mother, but he wasn't in love with her. Not the way he is with Tania.'

Her fingers plucked at the hem of the sheet.

'I guess that's what makes or breaks a marriage. Whether the love is strong enough to cope with what life dishes up.'

The nurse came in at that point and Cristiano moved aside so she could detach the drip from Alice's arm. He couldn't help thinking of how little he had known of Alice's background in the past. Why hadn't he asked her more about her childhood? Why hadn't he told her more about his?

They had been two people madly in lust with each other, sharing their bodies but not sharing their hearts and minds. Not communicating other than on a physical level. He had found out more about her in this hospital cubicle than he had in the whole time he had dated her in the past. Would it have made a difference if he'd talked to her? Really talked to her?

'You're good to go,' the nurse said once the drip was out and the paperwork dealt with. 'Take care of yourself, Alice. Keep those fluids up and get plenty of rest, okay?'

'I'll make sure she does,' Cristiano said.

Alice walked out of the hospital with Cristiano's arm around her waist. Her headache had eased and her stomach had stopped its churning. He had looked so undone by her being sick. She had never seen him look so distressed. Did that mean he cared more about her than he let on? Surely it wasn't an act for the sake of appearances?

But then there was a lot hanging in the balance. If she didn't fulfil the terms of the will then he would lose those shares and the home he had grown up in after his family were killed.

Or was that why he had been so rattled? Because hospitals reminded him of the accident that had taken his family from him?

Cristiano hailed a cab and within a short while they were home at her house and she was tucked up in bed with a long cool glass of water with a slice of lemon and ice cubes in it. He sat on the edge of the bed beside her, his hand taking one of hers in a gentle hold. 'How are you feeling?'

'Tired and a bit embarrassed about all the fuss I've caused.'

His fingers stroked the back of her hand. 'Yeah, well, you certainly gave me a bad half an hour or so.' His thumb did a slow brush over each of her tendons as if he were committing them to memory. He looked at her with a strained gaze. 'I thought I was going to lose you a second time.'

Alice squeezed his hand, her heart giving a little flutter at the depth of caring in his eyes. 'I wish I hadn't left the way I did back then. I ended up hurting myself more than you.'

'We hurt each other, *cara*,' he said. 'I can't believe I was so damn stubborn about it. I could've called you in a day or two. I *should've* called you. But I was too proud. Proud and angry. All those years went by. Not a day passed without me thinking of what could have been.'

His fingers tightened on her hand.

'I thought losing my family was bad, but losing you seven years ago was like a lid slamming down on all of my hopes. I decided it was better to be alone than to invite such rejection again. I've kept every relationship since as shallow and temporary as I could. Until now.'

Until now.

What did that mean? Did it mean he wanted their relationship to continue past the six months laid down in his grandmother's will? Alice reached up to stroke his face.

'We've been such stubborn fools—me in particular. I was so determined not to love anyone in case they took control of me, but I think I fell in love with you that first day when you made me laugh about my backpack catching your clothing. I spent the next six weeks denying it, blocking it. Sabotaging it.'

He pressed his lips against her bent fingers. 'We have a second chance to work at our relationship. Nonna has given us that. But let's talk about that when you're not feeling so out of whack.' He leaned forward to drop a kiss to her forehead. 'I'll sleep in one of the spare rooms so you get a good night's sleep.'

Alice hung onto his hand when he rose from the bed. 'No, don't go.'

'Alice, I—'

'Just hold me, okay?'

He gave a sigh and gathered her close, his chin resting on top of her head. 'As long as you need me I'll be here.'

How about for ever?

CHAPTER ELEVEN

ALICE WOKE THE next morning to find Cristiano lying beside her on top of the bedcovers with his legs crossed at the ankles. He was still fully dressed, although his tie was askew and the first three buttons of his shirt undone and his sleeves rolled up his forearms. His hair was rumpled as if he'd raked his fingers through it and his face looked tired and drawn.

She rolled to her side and tiptoed a fingertip down the bridge of his nose. His face gave a twitch or two and then his eyes opened and he sat bolt upright.

'What?' He sucked in a harsh-sounding breath. 'Oh, sorry, *cara*. You okay? Did you say something?'

'No, I was just watching you sleep.'

He dragged a hand down his face. 'Is that what you call it? I feel like I've been awake for a month.' He narrowed his gaze and lifted his arm to peer at his watch. Dropping it back to the bed with a dead arm flop. 'God. Five a.m.'

Alice stroked her fingers down the raspy slope of his cheek. 'Do you realise that's the first night we've spent together without making love?'

He cranked open one eye. 'Why do you think I'm on the outside of these sheets?'

She nestled closer, leaning over him so her breasts were crushed against his chest. 'I'm not sick now. In fact, I'm fighting fit.'

The other darkly glinting eye opened. 'I thought we weren't supposed to be fighting any more?'

Alice slipped a hand down to where he was as hard as stone. 'Feels to me you're already armed and dangerous.'

He gave her a sexy grin and flipped her so she was lying beneath him, his hand cupping her breast. 'If I were a good man I'd insist you have something to eat and drink before I ravish you.'

She trailed a fingertip across his lower lip. 'I'm only hungry and thirsty for you.'

He took her mouth in a long slow kiss that stirred her senses into overdrive. But just when she thought he'd reach for a condom and take things further, he pulled back and got off the bed. Something about his expression alerted her to a change of mood.

'Sorry, *cara*. I must be a better man than I thought.' He leaned down to brush her forehead with a light-as-air kiss, so light it was just shy of being impersonal. 'Stay right where you are. I'm going to give you breakfast in bed.'

Alice lay back against the pillows while she waited. Maybe they'd talk about their future over breakfast. Surely he hadn't forgotten what he'd said last night?

They'd been given a second chance to work at their relationship.

He was being so kind, so solicitous. He was acting exactly like a man in love...wasn't he? Last night he had looked so distraught at the hospital and again when they'd come home, fussing over her and holding her in his arms all night without getting a wink of sleep himself. Didn't that mean he loved her?

Then why hadn't he said something?

She'd told him last night she loved him…or at least that she had fallen in love with him the first moment they'd met. Why hadn't he said it back? Or hadn't he said it because he didn't feel that way now? Had his tenderness last night just been a reaction to the shock of finding her in hospital?

Alice couldn't stop the panic rising. What if she'd misread their conversation last night? What if he'd just said those words to settle her for the night after her health scare? Was it her imagination or was he withdrawing from her? When had he ever pulled away from a kiss? Was he backing away from a longer relationship?

Had her confession of love made him rethink their involvement?

In two weeks they would be married, but on what terms? Temporary. No future stretching out in front of them. No plans for making a family together and raising them with love and commitment. Their relationship, although it would be formalised with a certificate of marriage, would be nothing more than a transient affair—as he'd stated time and time again he wanted it to be.

How could she agree to that when she wanted the opposite?

Yesterday, when the doctor asked Alice if there was any possibility she could be pregnant, a balloon of hope had risen in her chest. But then she'd realised the futility of harbouring such a hope. Cristiano didn't want a family. He didn't want what she wanted.

The sad irony of their reversed wishes made her realise again how devastated he must have felt when she'd walked out on him that day in that restaurant. When the pregnancy test came back negative she was both relieved and disappointed. She didn't want to force him to stay with her. She wanted him to love her and commit to her, not because of a baby, not because of his well-meaning grandmother's machinations, but because he loved her more than anything else in the world. More than his stupid old shares, more than a luxury villa.

She thought of her friend Jennifer. She and Cristiano and Jennifer and Marcus would be married within a week of each other and yet you couldn't find two different couples. Jennifer and Marcus were deeply in love. They planned to do all the things young couples on the threshold of a life together planned.

What did Alice and Cristiano have? A six-month time limit. He wanted his shares and his family villa and the only way to get them was to marry her. Without his grandmother's will their affair would not have resumed. She would be fooling herself to think otherwise. He'd had seven years to do something about their 'unfinished business' and he had done nothing.

Cristiano came back with a tray with muesli and toast and juice and tea. One bowl. One plate. One cup. 'Here we go.' He balanced the tray on her knees. 'Breakfast in bed.'

Alice picked up the cup of steaming tea. 'Aren't you going to join me?'

'I have a couple of emails to see to. Stuff to do with the wedding and so on. Do you need a hand choosing a dress? I've got some time today if you're—'

'Don't you know it's bad luck for the groom to see the bride's dress before the wedding?'

Something about his slanted smile made her heart

shrivel like a dried-up leaf. 'It's not like we have to worry about that, do we?'

Alice searched his face for a moment, her teeth worrying her bottom lip. He didn't seem at all fazed by the fact their marriage was going to be temporary. Surely if he cared about her he would say something?

Why wasn't he saying something?

Didn't he have a conscience? Marriage was sacred. No one should enter into it without proper commitment and consent. It was a travesty to do otherwise. Didn't he feel the slightest bit conflicted about what they were doing? There was her answer right there. No. He didn't. All he wanted was the terms of the will ticked off. Goal achieved. Problem solved.

She put her cup back down and lifted the tray off her knees.

'What's wrong?' Cristiano took the tray off her, frowning. 'Why are you getting out of bed?'

Alice got to her feet and pushed her hair back behind her shoulders. 'I'm not sure I can do this.'

'It's just breakfast in bed,' he said. 'No one's insisting you take the day off work, although maybe I should. You push yourself way too hard. Meghan told me you never take a holiday.'

She turned and faced him. 'I thought we were going to talk. So let's talk.'

'About what?'

Alice wrapped her arms around her body as if to contain the emotions threatening to burst out of her. What was with his blank expression? Didn't he remember anything about last night? 'About us. About the fact I love you and want to have a future with you. A family.'

His expression locked down, every muscle on his

face freezing as if turned to marble. 'I don't think now's the right time to talk about—'

'When *is* the right time?' Alice said. 'We have two weeks until we get married. You told me last night we would discuss the fact we've been given a second chance at our relationship via your grandmother. So let's discuss it. I'm not unwell now.'

He moved to the other side of the room, straightening objects on her dressing table that didn't need straightening. His back was turned to her but she could see part of his reflection in the mirror. He was shutting her out. Withdrawing from her.

'Can we talk about this some other time? I have a lot on my mind right now.'

Alice wasn't going to be fobbed off. 'If we don't discuss it now, then I'm afraid I can't marry you. It wouldn't be right for me or for you.'

He turned from the dressing table, a flash of irritation firing off at the back of his gaze and a muscle leaping in his jaw. 'What are you talking about? You stand to inherit millions out of this.'

She let out a frustrated breath. 'Life isn't just about money, Cristiano. It's about much more than that. I don't care about the money. Do you really think if I were motivated by money I would've rejected your proposal seven years ago?'

'We're not talking about back then, Alice.' His voice was deep and steady but that muscle near his mouth was speeding up. 'We're talking about now. I've told you what I'm prepared to commit to and having a family is not even on the whiteboard.'

'I want more than a temporary marriage,' Alice said. 'I want a proper one. I want a family. Last night when the doctor told me I wasn't pregnant I realised how much I wished I were having a baby. But you don't want a baby. You don't want what I want at all.'

His eyes were obsidian black, the tension around his mouth making his lips appear white at the corners. 'We agreed on the terms. You're the one who's been on a soapbox for years about how marriage is a domestic prison for women, and now you want the white picket fence and the double pram?'

Alice held his gaze with a resolve she hadn't thought possible even minutes earlier. But she couldn't back down now. *Wouldn't* back down. He'd had plenty of opportunity to tell her he loved her but he hadn't. Even if he said it now, how could she believe it wasn't a ploy to make her agree to the terms of the will?

'I want the fairy tale and I don't want to settle for anything less than absolute commitment,' she said. 'I want my marriage to be for ever, not for six months.'

He stalked to the other side of the bedroom, his hand rubbing at the back of his neck as if something were burning him there. He swung back to face her, his expression going back to cold, hard marble. 'I'm not going to parrot the words you think you want to hear. Why are you doing this—?'

'I wouldn't believe you if you said you loved me now,' Alice said. 'You're completely focussed on getting those shares and keeping your grandmother's villa in your family's hand. That's all you care about. You don't care about me. I don't think you ever did. You care about what *you* want—what I would do for you by being your wife. Our relationship has always been more about you than us as a unit, and if you were honest with yourself you'd admit it.'

'Alice, listen to me.' His voice softened but she got the sense his anger was not far away. 'You're still not well. You're not thinking straight. You have too much to lose to throw this now. Just hop back into bed and I'll—'

'And you'll what?' Alice cast him a frosty glare. 'Seduce me into seeing things your way? That's what you always tried to do in the past. You never listened to me when we had a difference of opinion. You tried to solve everything with sex. But sex won't solve this. I want more from you than great sex. Much, much more.'

He drew in a deep breath and released it in a whoosh. 'So that's it? Marriage or nothing?'

Alice gave him a wry look. 'Your words, not mine, but they'll do.' She took off her engagement ring and handed it to him. 'I think it's best if we don't see each other again.'

He ignored her outstretched palm, his mouth curling up at one corner. 'Keep it. You can pawn it so you can set up your spa or throw it away for all I care.'

Alice closed her hand around the ring, not one bit surprised when it cut into her palm as sharply as his words had into her heart. 'You won't ever be happy, Cristiano, because deep down you don't think you deserve to be. You refuse to love someone in case they withdraw that love or fate takes it away from you.'

He snatched up his jacket from the back of the dressing-table chair. 'Leave your psychoanalysis for someone who gives a damn. You don't know me as well as you think.'

'I know,' Alice said. 'That's why we were doomed from the start. You don't want anyone to get close to you. I can't be in a relationship like that. I want emotional honesty.' *I want you to love me.*

'Oh, and you're the big expert on emotional honesty, aren't you, Alice?' His eyes blazed with bitterness. 'You think I'm going to believe you're suddenly madly in love with me? A few days ago you wanted to gouge my eyes out. What you're doing is manipulating. Trying to get your future sorted by issuing me with an ultimatum. How about a bit of intellectual honesty, hey? Let's try that instead. I can't give you what you want. Simple as that. Take it or leave it.'

'I don't hate you. I never hated you.'

He gave a snort. 'Yeah, well, guess what? I don't give a damn either way.'

Alice winced when the bedroom door snapped shut on his exit. She listened to the tread of his footsteps as he left her house, her breath stalling in the hope he would stop and turn back. Come back up the stairs and swing open her bedroom door and say he was sorry. That he would sweep her into his arms and say of course he loved her and wanted to spend the rest of his life with her.

But the only thing she got was silence.

Cristiano had never felt so flooded with such confusing emotions. Anger. Disappointment. Bitterness. Anger again. A hot cauldron of bubbling feelings was threatening to explode out of his chest. He had to stop to lean over and place his hands on his knees to get control of his breath. In. Out. In. Out. How could she do this to him? Now?

Two weeks.

Two miserable weeks and his shares and the villa would have been secure.

Why? Why? Why?

He'd thought they were fine. He'd thought everything was ticking along just as he'd wanted it. But just like seven years ago she had blindsided him. His guard had been down. He was so thrown by her being taken to hospital he hadn't seen what was right in front of him. That sexy little crawl over his chest to make him feel secure and then *wham*! She wanted to control him. Manipulate him into doing things her way.

No way was he going to be her puppet. He'd told her the terms. He'd been honest about what he was prepared to give. She was the one shifting the goalposts.

Just like you did in the past, dropping that proposal on her.

Cristiano swatted away the thought as if it were an annoying fly. *So?* He'd shifted them right on back. A short-term marriage was all he was prepared to have. And even that was a stretch. He didn't want the responsibility of maintaining a long-term relationship. He didn't want the *emotional honesty* such a relationship demanded.

If he opened up the vault of his heart then that would undo all the work he'd put in since he was that boy of eleven hearing his parents and brother were never coming back. He could not allow himself to be that vulnerable. Not again. Look at what last night had done to him. Rushing into that hospital to see Alice had thrown him into a chest-seizing panic. He'd lain awake most of the night with residual dread still chugging through his veins like jagged cubes of ice. He hadn't trusted her confession of love last night. If she'd loved him way back then, why had she walked out and never looked back?

You did the same to her.

Cristiano didn't want to be reminded of how badly he'd handled things in the past. It was better this way. He couldn't give her what she wanted. He wasn't that person any more. Maybe he'd never been that person. He was too damaged by the loss of his family. He kept people at a distance. He controlled them because it was the only way he could harness the fear. The fear that clawed at him. The fear that reminded him with sharp little jabs of how easily he could lose the ones he dared to love. It was easier not to love. To not even think about the word. To pretend his feelings were something else. Lust, attraction, mild affection.

Anything but love.

By the time Alice got to work she had another headache. But the pain in her head was nothing to the pain in her heart. Cristiano had summed up his feelings about her. He didn't give a damn either way. He could take her or leave her. He had chosen to leave her.

'Hey, where's your engagement ring?' Meghan asked when she came in for the day. 'My first client wants to see it. She read about you and Cristiano on…' She frowned. 'Is something wrong?'

Alice blinked away the moisture in her eyes. 'Cristiano and I are not getting married after all. We've broken—'

'Not getting married?' Meghan gasped. 'Why the hell not? You two are the most in love couple I've ever seen. The air crackles like a power station when you guys are in the same room.'

Alice pressed her lips together to stop them from trembling. 'He doesn't love me. He's…oh, it's too complicated to explain.'

'What do you mean he doesn't love you?' Meghan's eyes were slit-thin with incredulity. 'You should've seen him when he came here yesterday and found out you were in hospital. I thought he was going to pass out on the spot. He was as white as our deluxe collagen face mask.'

Alice wished it were true. Wished he loved her. But if he loved her he wouldn't be baulking at commitment. That was what love was all about. Commitment. Trust. A future, not a time line.

'He doesn't want what I want. He doesn't want kids.'

Meghan's face fell. 'Oh...well then, that's a deal-breaker.' But then she brightened again. 'But maybe he'll change his mind. Lots of men do. They come round to it eventually, when they—'

'He won't,' Alice said. 'He's stubborn like that.'

Meghan waggled her eyebrows. 'Mmm, like someone else I know.'

Alice frowned. 'Don't you have work to do?'

Meghan gave her a 'kicked puppy' look. 'I'm really sorry about you breaking up with Cristiano. But he's had a lot going on in his life—his gran dying and this big new development. Maybe he needs a bit of time to think things over.'

'Like another seven years?'

Meghan bit her lip. 'He really is stubborn, isn't he?'

Alice gave her a grim look. 'He could open a mentoring academy for mules.'

CHAPTER TWELVE

CRISTIANO WAS PRESSING on with his London development on principle. He wasn't the sort of man to walk away from a business deal because of personal issues. He kept work and his private life separate. Mostly. Although having to visit the Chelsea site with Alice's beauty salon on the ground floor of the building he'd bought was like having molars pulled with bolt cutters. Confronting failure was something he assiduously avoided. Returning to the scene of the crime, so to speak, was anathema to him. He would prefer to be on the other side of the globe right now. Siberia. Outer Mongolia.

Anywhere but here.

Somehow the press had heard the engagement was off. He had refused to comment and apparently so had Alice as the articles were evidently from 'reliable sources close to the couple' whatever the hell that meant. But after a week of being chased to and from his hotel by the paparazzi, things had settled down.

Seven days of living without Alice. Not seeing her. Not touching her. Not making love to her.

Nothing.

A big yawning cavern of emptiness stretched out ahead of him. Just like the last time, only this time it was harder. Much harder. How had he done this before and for seven years? He'd convinced himself he'd done the right thing. Let her be free to live the life he couldn't give her. But the thought of her getting on with her life without him was eating away at him. Gnawing on his nerves until he was all but twitching with restlessness.

Cristiano had to meet with the architect on site to discuss some of the plans he had for the refit of the building. But the whole time he was in the meeting his eyes kept drifting to the window in the hope of seeing Alice coming in or out of her salon.

He was surprised the architect didn't notice, or maybe he did and was too polite to say anything. He'd noticed a wedding ring on the architect's finger and noticed too the screensaver on the guy's phone when he answered a call. It was a photo of his wife and young toddler and newborn baby. All the things Cristiano had convinced himself he didn't want.

But he *did* want them.

The realisation was like a light being switched on, shining on all the dark lonely places in his heart. Illuminating the hopes and dreams he had stashed and hidden away out of fear.

Cristiano finished the meeting and was about to turn left away from Alice's salon when he stopped mid-stride. This was ridiculous. What was he doing? Walking away a second time? Turning his back on the best thing that had ever happened to him? Who was he fooling?

He wasn't in lust with Alice. He was in love. He had always been in love with her. That was why he was so damn terrified. That was why he'd rushed the proposal seven years ago. He'd been so worried he might lose her so he'd made her an offer he'd thought she wouldn't be able to refuse.

But he'd got it all wrong. So horribly wrong.

He'd thought losing the shares and his *nonna*'s villa was the worst thing that could happen to him. But losing Alice was far worse. He couldn't lose her. Not again.

He had to talk to her. He couldn't let another day—another minute—pass without telling her he loved her and wanted the same things she wanted. Why had he left it a week? Seven days of miserable hell. No way was he leaving it a second longer.

He spun on his heel and went back the other way but he'd only taken two strides when he saw Meghan from Alice's beauty salon trotting towards him.

'Hi, Cristiano,' she said. 'Bad news about your breakup with Alice. But don't worry. I've got it all sorted. I've found her a new man. I'm setting up a blind date for her. He's a friend of a friend and he's so keen on having kids he's already got cupboards full of toys. Isn't that sweet?'

Cristiano felt as if he'd been slammed across the head with a plank. 'A blind date?'

'Yup.' Meghan's eyes twinkled. 'It worked a treat for one of our clients. They're getting married this weekend. Jennifer and Marcus. Alice is doing Jennifer's make-up for it.'

Cristiano had trouble speaking past the knot of despair stuck in his throat. 'She can't do that.'

'What?' Meghan's expression was guileless as a child. 'Do Jennifer's make-up? Don't be silly. That's her specialty!'

What Alice's specialty was to make him as mad as a wasp-stung bull. How could she date another man so quickly? What the hell was she doing going on a blind date? What if the guy was a freak? Some stranger who would— He couldn't bear to think about it. Jealousy rose in him like bile. He was choking on it. He could feel it bubbling up his windpipe like an overflowing drain. 'Where is she?' he asked.

Meghan pointed to the salon. 'She's in her office working on accounts. But she doesn't want to be—'

'You can cancel your friend of a friend, okay?' Cristiano said. 'If she's going on a date with anyone it's going to be with me.'

Alice couldn't concentrate on the rows of numbers on her computer screen. Normally seeing all those healthy figures would have made her do a happy dance. But she had never felt more miserable. A week had gone past and no word from Cristiano. Not even a text message. Nothing. A big fat nothing. The press had done their thing for a few days but she'd refused to speak to them. She'd even resorted to using disguises to avoid them when walking to and from her house or the salon.

Her mother had been 'too upset' to talk to her, which was typical. As if it was Alice's fault the marriage wasn't going ahead. Well, it was, but that was beside the point. But how could she go ahead with a marriage that was the opposite of what a marriage should be? What she wanted *her* marriage to be?

Meghan had been a stalwart support, making numerous cups of tea and bringing in a steady supply of cinnamon-covered doughnuts—Alice's weakness when dealing with stress. Sugar and fat were the only pleasures she had in her life now.

There was the sound of bell tinkling as the salon door

opened…although tinkling wasn't the right word. Firm footsteps came striding through the salon and Alice barely had time to get to her feet when her office door slammed back against the wall and Cristiano appeared. 'What the hell do you think you're doing?'

Alice kept her expression cool and composed even though her heart rate was doing its hummingbird impersonation. 'Accounts. It's been a good week for me. One of my best, actually.'

His expression was thunderous, all stormy clouds and dark shadows and lightning flashes in his eyes. 'Meghan tells me you're dating someone else.'

Alice frowned. 'What?'

His mouth was pressed into a chalk-white line. 'Don't do it, Alice.' He released a tight breath. 'Please.'

Alice was starting to join some dots and it was creating an interesting picture indeed. 'When were you speaking to Meghan?'

'Just now, outside.' He jerked his head towards the street. 'She said she was setting you up on a blind date with some friend of a friend who wants kids.'

'I don't know anything about a blind date,' Alice said. 'And you've got a hide storming in here telling me what to do with my private life when it's no concern of yours and nor will it ever—'

'If you want to have kids so badly then you can damn well have them with me.'

Alice opened her mouth to fling back another round of fire but stopped and gaped at him instead. Had she heard him correctly? Kids? He wanted kids? But then she realised what was going on. Jealousy. Not love. The big green-eyed monster was behind his change of heart.

She narrowed her gaze. 'So, let me get this straight.

You're offering to be a sperm donor and a cardboard cut-out husband because you're...*jealous*?' She said the word as if it were some sort of contagion.

Cristiano came around to her side of the desk and grasped her by the upper arms.

'Damn straight I am. Alice, I love you. I've been a stubborn fool all this time refusing to acknowledge it. I can handle the loss of the shares. I can handle the loss of the villa. What I can't handle is the loss of you. I've already lost you once. I don't want to lose you again. I was already coming here when I ran into Meghan. Please believe me, *cara*. Don't let anything else keep us apart. Will you marry me? Not because of Nonna's will, not because I'm jealous but because I love you and want to spend the rest of my life with you.'

Alice looked at him with watering eyes. 'Do you mean it? You're not just saying it because of the deadline?'

His hold tightened as if he were terrified she was going to slip out of his grasp. 'I don't care about the deadline other than I want to do what Nonna wanted. She knew I hadn't got over you. She knew I was too stubborn to see you again so she orchestrated it so I had no choice.'

Alice smiled. 'Like Meghan.'

He frowned. 'Meghan?'

Alice laced her arms around his neck. 'I'm not going on a blind date. Why would I do that when I only have eyes for you?'

Relief washed over his features and he smiled. 'The little meddling minx. She and Nonna must be kindred spirits.' He gathered her tight against his body. 'She saw what Nonna saw, what I refused to see. I love you, *tesoro mio.* I love you desperately. Please say you'll marry me.'

Alice looked into his handsome features so full of love and adoration for her. The softness in his dark brown eyes, the way he looked at her as if she were the most precious thing he could ever hold in his arms—made her feel so happy she could barely speak.

'I will marry you, darling. I can't think of anything I would rather do than be your wife and the mother of your children.'

He crushed her mouth beneath his in a kiss that spoke of the depth of his feelings. He drew back to smile at her, his own eyes suspiciously moist.

'I've spent so much of my life avoiding getting close to people in case I lost them. But I got to thinking I might as well have jumped in my family's coffins with them if I don't live a full and authentic life. I owe it to them to make the most of the time that was snatched away from them.'

Alice touched the track of dampness leaking from his eyes. 'I wish I'd been able to meet them. I'm sure they were wonderful people who loved you so much. They would be thrilled you're embracing life at last. I'm sure of it.'

Cristiano brushed her hair back with his hand. 'I've been thinking about what we can do together. You could have your wedding spa as a feature of my hotel. Here in London but also in Italy and France and Greece. You could have your own franchise. It will be something to build together.'

Alice held his face in her hands and kissed him. 'You are making all my dreams come true. I would love that.

It would be so wonderful to do it together just like your grandparents and parents did.'

He kissed her soundly, only breaking away to gaze down at her with a look of such devotion it made Alice's eyes tear up again.

'We've only got a week to pull off this wedding,' he said. 'Do you think we can do it?'

She stroked his lean jaw, and looked lovingly into his eyes. 'Together we can do anything.'

One year later...

Alice smiled at Cristiano as he came in from bringing in their bags from the car. They were spending their first wedding anniversary at his grandmother's villa where they came every few months to relax and recharge. Yes, *relax*. That word she used not to have in her vocabulary.

Her beauty spa at Cristiano's Chelsea hotel had finally opened a few weeks ago to great fanfare and she had recently appointed Meghan as her business manager and it was working a treat. It meant Alice could have the occasional week off without worrying about her clients not receiving the attention she prided herself on giving them.

And because she intended to take even more time off in a few months' time.

Alice took Cristiano by the hand and led him to the walnut table in the sitting room where the family photos were arranged. Whenever they came back to the villa they stood there and quietly acknowledged his family. Their wedding photo was next to his parents' and grandparents' wedding photos, creating a sense of continuity she knew gave him great comfort. It gave her great comfort too to see him so happy and settled after so much heartache. She hadn't told him yet, but soon there would be photos of the next generation of the Marchetti family.

'I have something to tell you, darling,' Alice said, squeezing his hand in excitement. 'I wanted to wait until we got here so the rest of the family could hear it as well.'

Cristiano's dark brown eyes misted. 'You're... *pregnant*?'

'I did a test this morning. I've been bursting to tell you but then I thought how lovely it would be for you to hear about it here amongst those who loved you so deeply.'

He gathered her close, kissing her tenderly and then holding her with such gentleness she had trouble keeping her own tears in check.

'How far along?' he said. 'Are you okay? Not sick? Feeling faint? Shouldn't you be resting? What about work—?'

Alice put a fingertip to his mouth to stall his speech. 'Meghan is going to cover me while I take maternity leave. And I feel fantastic…well, apart from a tiny bit of squeamishness. I'm six weeks pregnant according to my calculations. It must have been the weekend of the opening of your hotel and my spa.' She gave him a twinkling look. 'I seem to remember we had a lot of fun together that weekend.'

Cristiano cupped her face in his hands, his own eyes gleaming. 'I didn't know the meaning of the word until I met you. You've made me so happy, *cara*.'

Alice smiled and drew his head back down so her lips were within reach of his. 'We make each other happy, which is what your *nonna* recognised right from the start. I can't imagine how miserable I would be now if it hadn't been for her meddling.'

Cristiano grinned. 'Wise woman, my *nonna*. She knew there was only one woman in the world for me.'

He brushed her mouth with his. Once. Twice. Three times.

'You.'

* * * * *

BARTERING HER INNOCENCE

TRISH MOREY

To Jacqui, Steph, Ellen and Claire

Four gorgeous girls who have grown up amidst the mess and chaos and deadline-mania of a writer's life, and who somehow still managed to turn out all right.

I am so proud of the beautiful, talented, warm and wonderful young women you have become.

I am so looking forward to seeing all that you can be.

juv nun

xxx

CHAPTER ONE

THE last time Tina Henderson saw Luca Barbarigo, he was naked. Gloriously, unashamedly, heart-stoppingly naked. A specimen of virile masculine perfection—if you discounted the violent slash of red across his rigid jaw.

As for what had come afterwards…

Oh God. It was bad enough to remember the last time she'd seen him. She didn't want to remember *anything* that came after that. She must have misheard. Her mother could not mean *that man.* Life could not be that cruel. She clenched a slippery hand harder around the receiver, trying to get a better grip on what her mother was asking.

'Who…who did you say again?'

'Are you listening to me, Valentina? I need you to talk to Luca Barbarigo. I need you to make him see reason.'

Impossible. She'd told herself she'd never see him again. More than that. She'd *promised* herself.

'Valentina! You have to come. I need you here. Now!'

Tina pinched the bridge of her nose between her fingers trying to block the conflicting memories—the images that were seared on her brain from the most amazing night of her life, the sight of him naked as he'd risen from the bed, all long powerful legs, a back that could have been sculpted in marble, right down to the twin dimples at the base of his spine—and then the mix master of emotions, the anger and turmoil—the anguish and despair—for what had come afterwards.

She pinched harder, seeking to blot out the dull ache in her womb, trying to direct her shocked emotions into anger. And she was angry, and not just about what had happened in the past. Because how typical was it that the first time her mother actually called her in more than a year, it wasn't to wish her a belated happy birthday, as she'd foolishly imagined, but because Lily needed something.

When did Lily not need something, whether it was attention, or money or adulation from a long and seemingly endless line of husbands and lovers?

And now she foolishly imagined Tina would drop everything and take off for Venice to reason with the likes of Luca Barbarigo?

Not a chance.

Besides, it was impossible. Venice was half a world away from the family farm in Australia where she was also needed right now. No, whatever disagreement her mother had with Luca Barbarigo, she was just going to have to sort it out for herself.

'I'm sorry,' she began, casting a reassuring glance towards her father across the room to signal everything was under control. A call from Lily put everyone on edge. 'But there's no way I can—'

'But you have to do something!' her mother shrieked down the telephone line, so loud that she had to hold the receiver away from her ear. 'He's threatening to throw me out of my home! Don't you understand?' she insisted. 'You have to come!' before following it with a torrent of French, despite the fact that Lily D'Areincourt Beauchamp was English born and bred. The language switch came as no surprise—her mother often employed that tactic when she wanted to sound more impassioned. Neither was the melodrama. As long as she had known Lily, there was always melodrama.

Tina rolled her eyes as the tirade continued, not bothering to keep up and tired of whatever game her mother was playing, suddenly bone weary. A long day helping her father bring in the sheep in preparation for shearing wasn't about to end any time soon. There was still a stack of washing up waiting for her in the kitchen sink and that was before she could make a start on the piles of accounts that had to be settled before her trip to town tomorrow to see the bank manager. She rubbed her brow where the start of a headache niggled. She always hated meetings with their bank manager. She hated the power imbalance, the feeling that she was at a disadvantage from the get go.

Though right now the bank manager was the least of her problems…

Across the room Tina's father put down his stock journal on the arm of his chair where he'd been pretending to read and threw her a sympathetic smile before disappearing into the large country kitchen, no real help at all. But then, he'd broken ties with Lily almost twenty-five years ago now. It might not have been a long marriage but, knowing her mother, he'd more than served his time.

She was aware of the banging of the old water pipes as her father turned on the tap, followed by the thump of the kettle on the gas cooker and still her mother wasn't through with pleading her case. 'Okay, Lily,' she managed while her mother drew breath. 'So what makes you think Luca Barbarigo is trying to throw you out of the palazzo? He's Eduardo's nephew after all. Why would he threaten such a thing? And in English, please, if you don't mind. You know my French is rusty.'

'I *told* you that you need to spend more time on the Continent,' her mother berated, switching grievances as seamlessly as she switched languages, 'instead of burying yourself out there in the Australian outback.'

'Junee is hardly outback,' she argued of the mid-sized New South Wales town that was less than two hours from the semi-bright lights of Canberra. Besides, she hadn't exactly *buried* herself out here, more like she'd made a tactical withdrawal from a world she wanted no further part in. And then, because she was still feeling winded by her mother's demands, she added, 'It's quite civilised actually. There's even talk of a new bowling alley.'

Silence greeted that announcement and Tina imagined her mother's pursed lips and pinched expression at her daughter's inability to comprehend that in order to be considered civilised, a city needed at least half a dozen opera theatres, preferably centuries old, at a bare minimum.

'Anyway, you still haven't explained what's going on. Why is Luca Barbarigo threatening to throw you out? What kind of hold could he possibly have over you? Eduardo left you the palazzo, didn't he?'

Her mother fell unusually quiet. Tina heard the clock on the mantel ticking; heard the back door creak open and bang shut as her father went outside, probably so he didn't have to hear whatever mess Lily was involved in now. 'Well,' she said finally, her tone more subdued, 'I may have borrowed some money from him.'

'You what?' Tina squeezed her eyes shut. Luca Barbarigo had a reputation as a financier of last resort. By all accounts he'd built a fortune on it, rebuilding the coffers of his family's past fortune. She swallowed. Of all the people her mother could borrow from, of all the contacts she must have, and she had to choose *him*! 'But why?'

'I had no choice!' her mother asserted. 'I had to get the money from somewhere and I assumed that being family he'd take care of me. He promised he'd take care of me.'

He'd taken care of her all right. And taken advantage into the deal. 'You had to get money for what?'

'To live, of course. You know Eduardo left me with a fraction of the fortune he made out that he had.'

And you've never forgiven him for it. 'So you borrowed money from Luca Barbarigo and now he wants it back.'

'He said if I couldn't pay him, he'd take the palazzo.'

'How much money are we talking about?' Tina asked, pressure building in her temples. The centuries-old palazzo might be just off the Grand Canal, but it would still be worth millions. What kind of hold did he have over her? 'How much do you owe him?'

'Good God, what do you take me for? Why do you even have to ask?'

Tina rubbed her forehead. 'Okay. Then how can he possibly throw you out?'

'That's why I need you here! You can make him understand how unreasonable he is being.'

'You don't need me to do that. I'm sure you know plenty of people right there who can help.'

'But he's *your* friend!'

Ice snaked down Tina's spine. *Hardly friends.* In the kitchen the kettle started to whistle, a thin and shrill note and perfectly in tune with her fractured nerves and painful memories. She'd met Luca just three times in her life. The first in Venice at her mother's wedding, where she'd heard his charming words and felt the attraction as he'd taken her hand and she'd decided in an instant that he was exactly the kind of charming, good-looking rich man that her mother would bend over backwards to snare and that she wanted no part of. And when he'd asked her to spend the night with him, she'd told him she wasn't interested. After all, Lily might be her mother, but no way was Tina her mother's daughter.

The second time had been at Eduardo's seventieth birthday, a lavish affair where they'd barely done more than exchange pleasantries. Sure, she'd felt his eyes burn into her flesh and set her skin to tingling as they'd followed her progress around the room, but he'd kept his distance and she'd celebrated that fact, even if he hadn't given her the satisfaction of turning him down again. But clearly her message had struck home.

The third had been at a party in Klosters where she'd been celebrating a friend's birthday. She'd had one too many glasses of champagne and her guard was down and Luca had appeared out of the crowd and suddenly his charm was infectious and he was warm and amusing and he'd taken her aside and kissed her and every shred of self-preservation she'd had had melted away in that one molten kiss.

One night they'd spent together—one night that had ended in disaster and anguish and that could never be blotted from her mind—one night that she'd never shared with her mother. 'Who said we were friends?'

'He did, of course. He asked after you.'

Bastard! As if he cared. He had never cared. 'He lied,' she said, the screaming kettle as her choir. 'We were never friends.'

Never were.

Never could be.

'Well,' her mother said, 'maybe that's preferable under the circumstances. Then you'll have nothing to risk by intervening on my behalf.'

She put a hand to her forehead, certain the screaming must be coming from somewhere inside her skull. 'Look, Lily, I don't know what good I can do. There is no way my being there will help your cause. Besides, I can't get away.

We're about to start shearing and Dad really needs me here right now. Maybe you'd be better off engaging a lawyer.'

'And just how do you think I'll be able to afford to pay for a lawyer?'

She heard the back screen door slam and her father's muttered curse before the screaming abruptly tapered off. She shook her head. 'I really don't know.' And right now she didn't care. Except to ensure she didn't have to go. 'Maybe...maybe you could sell one or two of those chandeliers you have.' God knew, from the last time she'd visited, it seemed her mother had enough of them to fill a dozen palazzos. Surely if she owed a bit of money she could afford to dispense with one or two?

'Sell my Murano glass? You must be mad! It's irreplaceable! Every piece is individual.'

'Fine, Lily,' she said, 'it was just a suggestion. But under the circumstances I really don't know what else I can suggest. I'm sorry you're having money troubles, but I'm sure I'd be no help at all. And I really am needed here. The shearers arrive tomorrow, it's going to be full-on.'

'But you have to come, Valentina! You must!'

Tina put the phone down and leaned on the receiver a while, the stabbing pain behind her eyes developing into a dull persistent throb. Why now? Why him? It was likely her mother was exaggerating the seriousness of her money problems—she usually managed to blow any problem right out of proportion—but what if this time she wasn't? What if she was in serious financial trouble? And what could she do about it? It wasn't likely that Luca Barbarigo was going to listen to her.

Old friends? What was he playing at? Ships that crashed in the night would be closer to the mark.

'I take it your mother wasn't calling to wish you a happy

birthday, love?' Her father was standing in the kitchen doorframe, a mug of coffee wrapped in each of his big paw-like hands.

She smiled, in spite of the heaviness of her heart and the sick feeling in her gut. 'You got that impression, huh?'

He held up one of the mugs in answer. 'Fancy a coffee? Or maybe you'd like something stronger?'

'Thanks, Dad,' she said, accepting a mug. 'Right now I'd kill for a coffee.'

He took a sip. Followed it with a deep breath. 'So what's the latest in Circus Lily then? The sky is falling? Canals all run dry?'

She screwed up her face. 'Something like that. Apparently someone's trying to throw her out of the palazzo. It seems she borrowed money from Eduardo's nephew and, strangely enough, he wants it back. Lily seems to think I can reason with him—maybe work out some more favourable terms.'

'And you don't?'

She shrugged her shoulders, wishing she could just as easily shrug off memories of a man who looked better naked than any man had a right to, especially when he was a man as cold and heartless as he'd turned out to be. Wishing she could forget the aftermath… 'Let's just say I've met the man.' *And please don't ask me how or when.* 'I told her she'd be better off engaging a lawyer.'

Her dad nodded then and contemplated his coffee and Tina figured she'd put a full stop on the conversation and remembered the dishes still soaking and the accounts still to be paid. She was halfway to the sink when her father said behind her, 'So when do you leave?'

'I'm not going,' she said, her feet coming to a halt. I don't want to go. *I can't go.* Even though she'd told her mother she'd think about it, and that she'd call her back, when she'd never had any intention of going. She'd promised herself she'd never have to see him again and that was a promise she couldn't afford to break. Just thinking about what he'd cost her last time… 'I can't go and leave you, Dad, not now, not with the shearing about to start.'

'I'll manage, if you have to go.'

'How? The shearers start arriving tomorrow. Who's going to cook for a dozen men? You can't.'

He shrugged as the corners of his mouth turned up. 'So I'll go to town and find someone who can cook. You never know, I hear Deidre Turner makes a mean roast. And she might jump at the chance to show off her pumpkin scones to an appreciative audience.' His smile slipped away, his piercing amber eyes turning serious. 'I'm a big boy, Tina, I'll manage.'

Normally Tina would have jumped at her father's mention of another woman, whatever the reason—she'd been telling him for years he should remarry—but right now she had more important things on her mind—like listing all the reasons she couldn't go.

'You shouldn't have to manage by yourself! Why waste the money on flights—and on paying someone to cook—when we're already begging favours from the bank manager as it is? And you know what Lily's like—look at how she made such a drama about turning fifty! Anyone would have thought her life was coming to an end and I bet this is exactly the same. I bet it's all some massively overblown drama, as per usual.'

Her father nodded as if he understood, and she felt a surge of encouragement. Because of course her father would understand. Hadn't he been married to the woman? He, more than anyone, knew the drama queen stunts she was capable of pulling to get her way.

Encouragement had almost turned to relief, and she

was more than certain he would agree. Until he opened his mouth.

'Tina,' he said, rubbing the stubble of his shadowed jawline, 'how long is it since you've seen your mum? Two years? Or is it three? And now she needs you, for whatever reason. Maybe you should go.'

'Dad, I just explained—'

'No, you just made an excuse.'

She stiffened her shoulders, raising her chin. Maybe it was an excuse, and if her father knew the truth, surely he would understand, surely he would be sympathetic and not insist she go. But how could she tell him when she had kept it secret for so long? Her shameful secret. How could she admit to being as foolish and irresponsible as the woman she'd always told herself she was nothing like? It would kill him. It would kill her to tell him.

And when defence wasn't an option, there was always attack…

'So why are you so keen to ship me off to the other side of the world to help Lily? It's not like she ever did you any favours.'

He wrapped an arm around her shoulders and hauled her close, holding her just long enough for her to breathe in his familiar earthy farm scent. 'Who says I'm keen? But she's still your mum, love, and whatever happened between the two of us, you can't walk away from that. Now,' he said, putting his mug down to pick up a tea towel, 'what's this about a new bowling alley in town? I hadn't heard that.'

She screwed up her nose and snatched the tea towel out of his hands, not because she couldn't do with the help or his company, but because she knew he had his own endless list of chores to finish before he could collapse into bed, and partly too because she feared that if he lingered, if he asked her more about her mother's predicament and how she knew the man Lily owed money to, she wouldn't know how to answer him honestly. 'How about that?' she said much too brightly as she pushed him towards the door. 'Neither had I.'

He laughed in that deep rumbling way he had and that told her he knew exactly what she'd been doing. 'Your mum's not going to know what hit her.'

'I'm not going, Dad.'

'Yes, you are. We can check about flights when we go into town tomorrow.' And he came back and hugged her, planting a kiss on her strawberry-blonde hair the same way he'd done ever since she was old enough to remember and probably long before. 'Goodnight, love.'

She thought about her father's words after he'd gone, as she chased cutlery around the sudsy sink. Thought with a pang of guilt about how long it had been since she'd seen her mother. Thought about how maybe her father might be right.

Because even though they'd never seen eye to eye, even though they never seemed to be on the same wavelength, maybe she couldn't walk away from her mother.

And neither did she have to run from Luca Barbarigo.

She had been running. She'd run halfway around the world to forget the biggest mistake of her life. She'd run halfway around the world to escape.

But some mistakes you couldn't escape.

Some mistakes followed you and caught up with you when you least expected it.

And some mistakes came with a sting in the tail that made you feel guilty for wishing things had been different. They were the worst mistakes of all, the ones that kept on hurting you long, long after the event.

She pulled the plug and stood there, watching the suds gurgle down the sink, suds the very colour of the delicate iron lace-work that framed a tiny grave in a cemetery in far distant Sydney.

Tears splashed in the sink, mixing with the suds, turning lacy bubbles pearlescent as they spun under the thin kitchen light. She brushed the moisture from her cheeks, refusing to feel sorry for herself, feeling a steely resolve infuse her spine.

Why should she be so afraid of meeting Luca again? He was nothing to her really, nothing more than a one-night stand that had ended in the very worst kind of way. And if Luca Barbarigo was threatening her mother, maybe Lily was right; maybe she was the best person to stand up to him. It wasn't as if there was a friendship in the balance. And it certainly wasn't as if she was going to be charmed by him.

Not a second time.

She wasn't that stupid!

CHAPTER TWO

SHE was coming.

Just as her mother had said she would.

Luca stood at the darkened balcony overlooking the Grand Canal, his senses buzzing with the knowledge, while even the gentle slap of waters against the pilings seemed to hum with anticipation.

Valentina was coming to save her mother. Expecting to rescue her from the clutches of the evil banker.

Just as he'd intended.

A smile tugged at his lips.

How fortuitous that her mother was a spendthrift with a desperate need for cash. So desperate that she was not bothered to read the terms of any loan agreement too closely. How naive of her to assume that marrying his uncle somehow made her eligible for special treatment.

Special treatment indeed.

And now the noose he'd tied was so tight around the neck of the former beauty that she was about to lose her precious palazzo from beneath her once well-heeled feet.

A water taxi prowled by, all sleek lines and polished timbers, the white shirt of the driver standing out in the dark night, before both taxi and driver disappeared down one of the side canals. He watched the wake fan out across the dark canal and felt the rhythm of water resonate in the beat of his blood; heard it tell him that the daughter was drawing ever closer.

He searched the night sky, counting down the hours, imagining her in the air, imagining her not sleeping because she knew he would be here in Venice, waiting for her to arrive.

Waiting.

He smiled, relishing a sense of anticipation that was almost delicious.

It was delicious.

He was no gambler. Luck was for suckers. Instead he thrived on certainty and detail and left nothing to chance. His version of luck happened when excellent preparation met with sublime opportunity.

The seeds for both had been sown, and now it was time to reap the harvest.

The palazzo had been his uncle's once, before that woman had stuck her steely claws into him and hung on tight, and now it was as good as back in the family fold again. But the satisfaction of returning the palazzo to the family fold was not what drove him now. Because Lily Beauchamp had something far more valuable that he wanted.

Her precious daughter.

She'd walked out on him once. Left the mark of her hand bright on his jaw and walked away, as if she'd been the one on high moral ground. At the time he'd let her go. Waved good riddance. The sex had been good but no woman was worth the angst of chasing her, no matter how good she was in bed.

He'd put her from his mind.

But then her mother had called him, asking for help with the mire of her finances, and he'd remembered the daughter and a night of sex with her that had ended way too prematurely. He'd been only too happy to help then. It was the least he could do for his uncle's widow, he'd told her, realising there might be a way to redress the balance.

So now fate was offering him the chance to right two wrongs. To get even.

Not just with the spendthrift mother.

But with the woman who thought she was different. Who thought herself somehow better.

He'd show her she was not so different to her mother after all. He'd show her he was nobody to walk away from.

And then he'd publicly and unceremoniously dump her.

CHAPTER THREE

ARRIVING in Venice, Tina thought, was like leaving real life and entering a fairy tale. The bustling Piazzale Roma where she waited for her bag to be unloaded from the airport bus was the full stop on the real world she was about to leave behind, a world where buildings were built on solid ground and transport moved on wheels; while the bridges that spanned out from the Piazzale crossing the waterways were the 'once upon a time' leading to a fairy tale world that hovered unnaturally over the inky waters of the lagoon and where boats were king.

Beautiful, it was true, but as she glanced at the rows of windows looking out over the canals, right now it almost felt brooding too, and full of mystery and secrets and dark intent…

She shivered, already nervous, feeling suddenly vulnerable. Why had she thought that?

Because he was out there, she reasoned, her eyes scanning the buildings that lined the winding canal. Luca was out there behind a window somewhere in this ancient city.

Waiting for her.

Damn. She was so tired that she was imagining things.

Except she'd felt it on the plane too, waking from a restless sleep filled with images of him. Woken up feeling almost as if he'd been watching her.

Just thinking about it made her skin crawl all over again.

She pushed her fringe back from her eyes and sucked in air too rich with the scent of diesel fumes to clear her head. God, she was tired! She grunted a weary protest as she hauled her backpack over her shoulder.

Forget about bad dreams, she told herself. Forget about fairy tales that started with once upon a time. Just think about getting on that return plane as soon as possible. That would be happy ending enough for her.

She lined up at the vaporetto station to buy a ticket for the water buses that throbbed their way along the busy canals. A three-day pass should be more than adequate to sort out whatever it was her mother couldn't handle on her own. She'd made a deal with her father that she'd only come to Venice on the basis she'd be back at the farm as soon as the crisis was over. She wasn't planning on staying any longer. It wasn't as if this was a holiday after all.

And with any luck, she'd sort out her mother's money worries and be back on a plane to Australia before Luca Barbarigo even knew she was here.

She gave a snort, the sound lost in the crush of tourists laden with cameras and luggage piling onto the rocking water bus. Yeah, well, maybe that was wishful thinking, but the less she had to do with him, the better. And no matter what her frazzled nerves conjured up in her dreams to frighten her, Luca Barbarigo probably felt the same way. She recalled the vivid slash of her palm across his jaw. They hadn't exactly parted on friendly terms after all.

Tourists jockeyed and squirmed to get on the outer edge of the vessel, cameras and videos at the ready to record this trip along the most famous of Venice's great waterways, and she let herself be jostled out of the way, unmoved by the passing vista except to be reminded she was on Luca Barbarigo's patch; happy to hide in the centre of the boat under cover where she couldn't be observed. Crazy, she knew, to feel this way, but she'd found there were times that logic didn't rule her emotions.

Like the time she'd spent the night with Luca Barbarigo.

Clearly logic had played no part in that decision.

And now once again logic seemed to have abandoned her. She'd felt so strong back home at the kitchen sink, deciding she could face Luca again. She'd felt so sure in her determination to stand up to him.

But here, in Venice, where every second man, it seemed, had dark hair or dark eyes and reminded her of him, all she wanted to do was hide.

She shivered and zipped her jacket, the combined heat from a press of bodies in the warm September air nowhere near enough to prevent the sudden chill descending her spine.

Oh God, she needed to sleep. That was all. Stopovers in Kuala Lumpur and then Amsterdam had turned a twenty-two hour journey into more like thirty-six. She would feel so much better after a shower and a decent meal. And in a few short hours she could give in to the urge to sleep and hopefully by morning she'd feel halfway to normal again.

The vaporetto pulled into a station, rocking sideways on its own wash before thumping against the floating platform and setting passengers lurching on their straps. Then the vessel was secured and the gate slid open and one mass of people departed as another lot rushed in, and air laced with the sour smell of sweat and diesel and churned canal water filled her lungs.

Three days, she told herself, as the vessel throbbed into life and set course for the centre of the canal again, missing an oncoming barge seemingly with inches to spare. She could handle seeing Luca again because soon she would be going home.

Three short days.

She could hardly wait.

The water bus heaved a left at the Canale di Cannaregio and she hoisted her pack from the pile of luggage in the corner where he'd stashed it out of the way. And this time she did crane her neck around and there it was just coming into view—her mother's home—nestled between two well-maintained buildings the colour of clotted cream.

She frowned as the vaporetto drew closer to the centuries-old palazzo. Once grand, her mother's house looked worse than she remembered, the once soft terracotta colour faded and worn, and with plaster peeling from the walls nearly up to the first floor, exposing ancient brickwork now stained yellow with grime at the water level. Pilings out the front of a water door that looked as if it had rusted shut stood at an angle and swayed as the water bus passed, and Tina winced for the once grand entrance, now looking so sad and neglected, even the flower boxes that had once looked so bright and beautiful hanging empty and forlorn from the windows.

Tourists turned their cameras away, searching for and finding more spectacular targets, an old clock tower or a passing gondola with a singing gondolier, and she almost felt ashamed that this was her mother's house, such an unworthy building for a major thoroughfare in such a beautiful city.

And she wondered what her mother could have done with the money she had borrowed. She'd said she'd needed the money to live. Clearly she hadn't spent much of it on returning the building to its former glory. She disembarked at the next stop, heading down one of the narrow *calles* leading away from the canal. The palazzo might boast its own water door but, like so many buildings fronting the canals, pedestrian access was via a rear courtyard, through an ornate iron gate in yet another steeply walled lane, squeezing past clumps of strolling tourists wearing their cruise ship T-shirts and wielding cameras and maps, or being overtaken by fast moving locals who knew exactly where they wanted to go and how to get there in the shortest possible time.

For a moment she thought she'd found the right gate, but ivy rioted over the wall, unkempt and unrestrained, the ends tangling in her hair, and she thought she must have made a mistake. Until she peered closer through the grille and realised why it looked so wrong.

She remembered the courtyard garden being so beautifully maintained, the lawns mowed, the topiary trees trimmed to perfection, but the garden looked neglected and overgrown, the plants spilling from the fifteenth century well at its centre crisp and brown, the neat hedge along the pathway straggly and looking as if it hadn't been clipped for months. Only two bright pots spilling flowers atop the lions guarding the doorway looked as if anyone had made an effort.

Oh, Lily, she thought, looking around and mourning for what a sanctuary this garden had once been. What had happened to let it go like this?

There was no lock on the gate, she realised, the gate jammed closed with rust, and she wondered about her mother living alone, or nearly alone in such a big house. But the gate scraped metal against metal and creaked loudly as she swung it open, a sound that would no doubt frighten off any would-be thief.

It wasn't enough to bring her mother running, of course—Lily was too much a lady to run—but Carmela, the housekeeper, heard. She bustled out of the house rubbing her hands on her apron. Carmela, who she'd met a mere handful of times, but greeted her now with a smile so wide she could have been her own daughter returning home.

'Valentina, *bella*! You have come.' She took her face between her hands and reached up to kiss each cheek in turn before patting her on the back. 'Now, please…' she said, wresting her backpack from her. 'I will take this. It is so good you have come.' A frown suddenly came from nowhere, turning her face serious. 'Your mother, she needs you. Come, I take you.'

And then she smiled again and led the way into the house, talking nonstop all the time, a mixture of English and Italian but the meaning perfectly clear. And Tina, who had been on edge the entire flight, could finally find it in herself to smile. Her mother would no doubt treat her daughter's attendance upon her as her God-given right; Luca Barbarigo would probably see it as a necessary evil, but at least someone seemed genuinely pleased to see her.

She followed Carmela across the threshold and, after the bright autumn sunshine, the inside of the house was dark and cool, her mother still nowhere to be seen. But, as her eyes adjusted, what little light there was seemed to bounce and reflect off a thousand surfaces.

Glass, she realised, remembering her mother's passion for the local speciality. Only there seemed to be a lot more of it than she remembered from her last visit.

Three massive chandeliers hung suspended from the ceiling of the passageway that ran the length of the building, the mosaic glass-framed mirrors along the walls making it look as if there was at least a dozen times that. Lily blinked, trying to stick to the centre of the walkway where there was no risk of upsetting one of the hall tables, also heavily laden with objets d'art, trying to remember what this hallway had looked like last time she was here. Certainly less cluttered, she was sure.

Carmela led her through a side door into her kitchen that smelt like heaven, a blissful combination of coffee and freshly baked bread and something savoury coming from the stove, and where she was relieved to see the only reflections came from the gleaming surfaces, as if the kitchen was Carmela's domain and nothing but the utilitarian and functional was welcome.

The older woman put down Tina's pack and wrapped her pinny around the handle of a pan on the stove. 'I thought you might be hungry, *bella*,' she said, placing a steaming pan of risotto on a trivet.

Tina's stomach growled in appreciation even before the housekeeper sliced two fat pieces of freshly baked bread and retrieved a salad from the refrigerator. After airline food it looked like a feast.

'It looks wonderful,' she said, pulling up a chair. 'Where's Lily?'

'She had some calls to make,' she said, disapproval heavy in her voice as she ladled out a bowl of the fragrant mushroom risotto and grated on some fresh parmigiano. 'Apparently they could not wait.'

'That's okay,' Tina said, not really surprised. Of course her mother would have no compunction keeping her waiting after demanding her immediate attendance. She'd never been the kind of mother who would actually turn up at the airport to greet her plane or make any kind of fuss. 'It's lovely sitting here in the kitchen. I needed a chance to catch my breath and I am so hungry.'

That earned her a big smile from the housekeeper. 'Then eat up, and enjoy. There is plenty more.'

The risotto was pure heaven, creamy and smooth with just the right amount of bite, and Tina took her time to savour it.

'What happened to the gardens, Carmela?' she asked

when she had satisfied her appetite and sat cradling a fragrant espresso. 'It looks so sad.'

The housekeeper nodded and slipped onto one of the stools herself, her hands cupping her own tiny cup. 'The *signora* could no longer afford to pay salaries. She had to let the gardener go, and then her secretary left. I try to keep up the herb garden and some pots, but it is not easy.'

Tina could believe it. 'But she's paying you?'

'She is, when she can. She has promised she will make up any shortfall.'

'Oh, Carmela, that's so wrong. Why have you stayed? Surely you could get a job in any house in Venice?'

'And leave your mother to her own devices?' The older woman drained the last of her coffee and patted her on the hand as she rose to collect the cups and plates. She shrugged. 'My needs are not great. I have a roof over my head and enough to get by. And one day, who knows, maybe your mother's fortunes will change.'

'How? Does it look like she'll marry again?'

Carmela simply smiled, too loyal to comment. Everyone who knew Lily knew that every one of her marriages after her first had been a calculated exercise in wealth accumulation, even if her plans had come unstuck with Eduardo. 'I meant now that you are here.'

Tina was about to reply that she doubted there was anything she could do when she heard footsteps on the tiles and her mother's voice growing louder… 'Carmela, I thought I heard voices—' She appeared at the door. 'Oh, Valentina, I see you've arrived. I was just speaking to your father. I would have told him you were here if I'd known.'

Tina slipped from her stool, feeling the warmth from the kitchen leach away in the uncomfortable assessment she gauged in her mother's eyes. 'Hello, Lily,' she said, cursing herself for the way she always felt inadequate in her mother's presence. 'Did Dad call to talk to me?'

'Not really,' she said vaguely. 'We just had some… business…to discuss. Nothing to worry about,' her mother assured her, as she air-kissed her daughter's cheeks and whirled away again with barely a touch, leaving just a waft of her own secret Chanel blend that one of her husbands had commissioned for her in her wake. Lily had always loved the classics. Labels and brand names, the more exclusive the better. And as she took in her mother's superbly fitted silk dress and Louboutin heels, clearly nothing had changed. The garden might be shabby, but there was nothing shabby about her mother's appearance. She looked as glamorous as ever.

'You look tired,' Lily said frankly, her gaze not stopping at her eyes as she took in her day-old tank top and faded jeans and clearly found them wanting as she accepted a cup of tea from Carmela. 'You might want to freshen up and find something nicer to wear before we go out.'

Tina frowned. 'Go out?' What she really wanted was a shower and twelve hours sleep. But if her mother had lined up an appointment with her bank, then maybe it was worth making a head start on her problems. 'What did you have in mind?'

'I thought we could go shopping. There's some lovely new boutiques down on the Calle Larga 22 Marzo. I thought it would be fun to take my grown-up daughter out shopping.'

'Shopping?' Tina regarded her mother with disbelief. 'You really want to go shopping?'

'Is there a problem with that?'

'What are you planning on spending? Air?'

Her mother laughed. 'Oh, don't be like that, Valentina.

Can't we celebrate you being back in Venice with a new outfit or two?'

'I'm serious, Lily. You asked me to come—no, scrub that, you *demanded* I come—because you said you are about to be thrown out of this place, and the minute I get here you expect to go shopping. I don't get it.'

'Valentina—'

'No! I left Dad up to his neck in problems so I could come and sort yours out, like you asked me to.'

Lily looked to Carmela for support but the housekeeper had found a spot on her stove top that required serious cleaning. She turned back to her daughter, her voice held together with a thin steel thread.

'Well, in that case—'

'In that case, maybe we should get started.' And then, because her mother looked stunned, and because she knew she was tired and jet-lagged and less tolerant than usual of her mother's excesses, she sighed. 'Look, Lily, maybe once we get everything sorted out—maybe then there'll be time for shopping. I tell you what, why don't you get all the paperwork ready, and I'll come and have a look as soon as I've showered and changed? Maybe it's nowhere near as bad as you think.'

An hour later, Tina buried her head in her hands and wished herself back on the family farm working sixteen-hour days. Wished herself anywhere that wasn't here, facing up to the nightmare that was her mother's accounts.

For a moment she considered going through the documents again, just one more time, just to check she wasn't wrong, that she hadn't miscalculated and overestimated the extent of her mother's debt, but she'd been through everything twice already now. Been through endless bank and credit card statements. Pored over loan document after loan document, all the time struggling with a dictionary alongside to make sense of the complex legal terms written in a language not her first.

She had made no mistake.

She rubbed the bridge of her nose and sighed. From the very start, when she'd seen the mass of paperwork her mother kept hidden away in an ancient ship's chest—almost as if she'd convinced herself that out of sight really was out of mind—the signs had been ominous, but she'd kept hope alive as she'd worked to organise and sort the mess into some kind of order—hope that somewhere amidst it all would be the key to rescuing her mother from financial ruin.

She was no accountant, it was true, but doing the farm's meagre accounts had meant she'd had to learn the hard way about balancing books, and as she'd slowly pieced the puzzle together, it was clear that there was no key, just as there would be no rescue.

Her mother's outgoings were ten times what was being earned on the small estate Eduardo had left her, and Luca Barbarigo was apparently happily funding the difference.

But where was Lily spending all the money when she was no longer paying salaries? She'd sorted through and found a handful of accounts from the local grocer, another batch from a clutch of boutiques and while her mother hadn't stinted on her own wardrobe, there was nowhere near enough to put her this deep into financial trouble. *Unless...*

She looked around the room, the space so cluttered with ornaments that they seemed to suck up the very oxygen. Next to her desk a lamp burned, but not just any lamp. This was a tree, with a gnarled twisted trunk that sprouted two dozen pink flowers and topped with a dozen curved branches fringed with green leaves that ended in more pink flowers but this time boasting light globes, and the entire thing made of glass.

It was hideous.

And that was only one of several lamps, she realised, dotted around the corners of the room and perched over chairs like triffids.

Were they new?

The chandelier she remembered because it was such a fantastical confection of yellow daffodils, pink peonies and some blue flower she had never been able to put a name to, and all set amidst a flurry of cascading ivory glass stems. There was no way she could have forgotten that, and she was sure she would have remembered the lamps if they had been here the last time she had visited.

Likewise, the fish bowls dotted around the room on every available flat surface. There was even one parked on the corner of the desk where she was working. She'd actually believed it was a fish bowl at first, complete with goldfish and bubbles and coral, rocks and weed. Until she'd looked up ten minutes into her work and realised the goldfish hadn't moved. Nothing had moved, because it was solid glass.

They were all solid glass.

Oh God. She rested her head on the heel of one hand. Surely this wasn't where her mother's funds had disappeared?

'Are you tired, Valentina?' asked Lily, edging into the room, picking up one glass ornament after another in the cluttered room, polishing away some nonexistent speck of dust before moving on. 'Should I call Carmela to bring more coffee?'

Tina shook her head as she sat back in her chair. No amount of coffee was going to fix this problem. Because it wasn't tiredness she was feeling right now. It was utter—*downright*—despair.

And a horrible sinking feeling that she knew where the money had all gone…

'What are all these amounts in the bank statements, Lily? The ones that seem to go out every month—there are no invoices that I can find to match them.'

Lily shrugged. 'Just household expenses. This and that. You know how it is.'

'No. I need you to tell me how it is. What kind of household expenses?'

'Just things for the house! I'm allowed to buy things for the house, aren't I?'

'Not if it's bankrupting you in the process! Where is the money going, Lily? Why is there no record of it?'

'Oh—' she tried to laugh, flapping her hands around as if Tina's questions were nothing but nuisance value '—I don't bother with the details. Luca keeps track of all that. His cousin owns the factory.'

'What factory? The glass factory, Lily? Is that where all your money is going as quickly as Luca Barbarigo tops you up? You're spending it all on glass?'

'It's not like that!'

'No?'

'No! Because he gives me a twenty per cent discount, so I'm not paying full price for anything. I've saved a fortune.'

Tina surveyed her mother with disbelief. So very beautiful and so very stupid. 'So every time you get a loan top-up from Luca Barbarigo, you go shopping at his cousin's factory.'

Her mother had the sheer audacity to shrug. Tina wanted to shake her. 'He sends a water taxi. It doesn't cost me a thing.'

'No, Lily,' she said, pushing back her chair to stand.

There was no point in searching for an answer any longer. Not when there wasn't one. 'It's cost you everything! I just don't believe how you could be so selfish. Carmela is working down there for a pittance you sometimes neglect to pay. You can barely afford to pay her, and yet you fill up this crumbling palazzo with so much weight of useless glass, it's a wonder it hasn't collapsed into the canal under the weight of it all!'

'Carmela gets her board!'

'While you get deeper and deeper into debt! What will happen to her, do you think, when Luca Barbarigo throws you both out on the street? Who will look after her then?'

Her mother blinked, her lips tightly pursed, and for a moment Tina thought she almost looked vulnerable.

'You won't let that happen, will you?' she said meekly. 'You'll talk to him?'

'For all the good it will do, yes, I'll talk to him. But I don't see why it will make a shred of difference. He's got you so tightly stitched up financially, why should he relax the stranglehold now?'

'Because he's Eduardo's nephew.'

'So?'

'And Eduardo loved me.'

Indulged you, more like it, Tina thought, cursing the stupid pride of the man for letting his wife think his fortune was bottomless and not bothering to curb her spending while he was alive, and not caring what might happen to his estate when he was gone.

'Besides,' her mother continued, 'you'll make him see reason. He'll listen to you.'

'I doubt it.'

'But you were friends—'

'We were never friends! And if you knew the things he said about you, you would know he was never your friend either, no matter how much money he is so happy to lend you.'

'What did he say? Tell me!'

Tina shook her head. She'd said too much. She didn't want to remember the ugly things he'd said before she'd slapped his smug face. Instead she pulled her jacket from the back of her chair. 'I'm sorry, Lily. I need to get some fresh air.'

'Valentina!'

She fled the veritable glass museum with the sound of her mother's voice still ringing in her ears, running down the marble steps and out past the five-hundred-year-old well with no idea where she was going, simply that she had to get away.

Away from the lamps that looked like trees and the goldfish frozen in glass and the tons of chandeliers that threatened to sink the building under their weight.

Ran from her mother's sheer naivety and her unbelievable inability to read the terms of an agreement and then to blithely disregard them as unimportant when she did.

Fleeing from her own fear that there was no way she could sort out her mother's problems and be home in a mere three days. Her mother was drowning in debt, just as the ancient palazzo itself was threatening to collapse into the canal and drown under the weight of tons of expensive but ultimately useless glass.

And there was not one thing she could do about it. This trip was a complete waste of time and money. It was pointless. There was nothing she could do.

She turned left out of the gate, heading back down the narrow *calle* towards the canal and a vaporetto that would take her somewhere—anywhere—her mother was not. And at the next corner she turned tight left again, too suddenly to see anyone coming, too consumed with her thoughts to remember she should be walking on the other side of the path. And much too suddenly to stop until his big hands were at her shoulders, braking her before she could collide headlong into his chest, punching the air from her lungs in the process. Air that had already conveyed the unmistakable news to her brain.

Luca.

CHAPTER FOUR

HIS eyes were shuttered behind dark glasses, and still she caught a glint of something behind the lenses as he recognised her, some flash of recognition that was mirrored in the upwards tweak of his lips, and she hated him all the more for it. Just as she hated the sizzle where his long fingers burned into her skin.

'Valentina?' he said, in a voice that must have been a gift from the gods at his birth, stroking like a pure dark velvet assault on her senses. 'Is it you?'

She tugged fruitlessly against his steel grip to be free. He was too close, so close that the air was flavoured with the very essence of him, one hundred per cent male with just a hint of Bulgari, a scent that worked to lure her closer even as she struggled to keep her distance. A scent that was like a key opening up the lid on memories she'd rather forget and sending fragments from the past hurtling through her brain, fragments that contained the memory of that scent—of taking his nipple between her teeth and breathing him in; of the rasp of his whiskered chin against her throat making her gasp; and the feel of him driving into her with the taste of his name in her mouth.

And she cursed the combination of a velvet voice and an evocative scent; cursed that she remembered in way too much detail and the fact that he still looked as good as he always had and hadn't put on twenty kilos and lost his hair since she had last seen him.

Cursed the fact that there was clearly no justice in this world.

For instead he was as beautiful as she remembered, a linen jacket over a white shirt that clung to his lean muscled chest as if it were a second skin, and camel-coloured linen trousers bound low over his hips by a wide leather belt.

He looked every bit the urbane Italian male, as polished and sleek as the streamlined water taxis that prowled the canals, the powerful aristocrats of this watery world. And she was suddenly aware of the disparity between them, with her raw-faced from her shower and dressed in faded jeans and a chain-store jade-coloured vest that was perfectly at home on the farm or even in town but here and now in his presence felt tired and cheap.

'But of course it is you. My apologies, I almost didn't recognise you with your clothes on.'

And a velvet voice turned to sandpaper, to scrape across senses already reeling from the shock of their meeting and leaving them raw and stinging.

'Luca,' she managed in an ice-laden voice designed to slice straight through his smugness, 'I'd like to say it's good to see you again, but right now I just want you to let me go.'

His smile only widened, but he did let her go then, even if his hands lingered at her shoulders just a fraction longer than necessary, the shudder as his thumbs swept an arc across her skin as they departed and left her shivery just as unwelcome. 'Where are you off to in such a hurry? I understood you had only now arrived.'

There was no point being surprised or asking how he knew. Her mother had been making calls when she'd arrived. One of them was to her father, her mother had said, but was another to Luca Barbarigo, sorting out the next instalment of her loan so she could purchase a new bargeful of glassware? She wouldn't be surprised. For all her mother's protests about the unfair actions of the man, she needed him for her supply of funds like a drug addict needed their supply of crack cocaine. She didn't waste time being polite. 'What's it to you where I am going?'

'Only that I might have missed you. I was coming to pay my respects.'

'Why? So you could gloat to my face about my mother's pathetic money management skills? Don't bother, I've known about them for ever. It's hardly news to me. I'm sorry you've wasted your time but I'll be heading back to Australia the first flight I can get. And now, if you'll excuse me…' She made to move past him but it wasn't easy. In the busy *calle* he was too tall, too broad across the shoulders. His very presence seemed to absorb what little space there was. But as soon as this next group of tourists passed…

He shifted to the right, blocking her escape. 'You're leaving Venice so soon?'

She tried to ignore what his presence was doing to her blood pressure. Tried to pretend it was anger with her mother that was setting her skin to burn and her senses to overload. 'What would be the point of staying? I'm sure you're not as naive as my mother, Signore Barbarigo. You must know there is nothing I can do to save her from financial ruin. Not after the way you've so neatly stitched her up.'

His eyes glinted in the thin light, and Tina had no doubt the heated spark came not from what was left of the sun, but from a place deep inside.

'So combatative, Valentina? Surely we can talk like reasonable people.'

'But that would require you to be a reasonable person, Signore Barbarigo and, having met you in the past, and having examined my mother's accounts, I would hazard the opinion that you have not one reasonable bone in your body.'

He laughed out loud, a sound that reverberated between the brick walls and bounced all the way up to the fading sky, grinding on her senses. 'Perhaps you are right, Valentina. But that does not stop your mother from believing that you will rescue her from the brink of ruin.'

'Then she is more of a fool than I thought. You have no intention of letting her off the hook, do you? You won't be happy until you have thrown her out of the palazzo!'

Heads turned in their direction, ears of passing tourists pricking up at her raised voice, eager to happen upon a possible conflict to add colour and local spice to their Venetian experience.

'Please, Valcntina,' he said, pushing her back towards the wall and leaning in close, as if they were having no more than a lovers' tiff. 'Do you wish to discuss your mother's financial affairs in a public street as if it is fodder for so many tourists' ears? What will they think of us Venetians? That we are not civilised enough to conduct our affairs in private?'

Once again he was too close—so close that she could feel his warm breath fanning her face—too close to be able to ignore his scent or not feel the heat emanating from his firm chest or to be able to think rationally, other than to rebut the obvious.

'I am no Venetian.'

'No. You are Australian and very forthright. I admire that in you. But now, perhaps it is time to take this conversation somewhere more private.' He indicated back in the direction she had come. 'Please. We can discuss this in your mother's house. Or, if you prefer, you can come with me to mine. I assure you, it is only a short walk.'

And meet him on his territory? No way in the world. She might have been trying to escape her mother's house, but it was still the lesser of two evils. Besides, if there were going to be some home truths flying around, maybe it was better her mother was there to hear them. 'Then the palazzo. But only because I have a few more things I want to tell you before I leave.'

'I can hardly wait,' she heard him mutter as she wheeled around and headed back in the direction she had come. So smug, she thought, wishing there was something she could do or say to wipe the expression from his face. Was he so sure of Lily's hopelessness that he had known her trip here was futile from the start? Was he laughing at her—at the pointlessness of it all?

She almost growled as she headed back down the *calle*, her senses prickling with the knowledge he was right behind her, prickling with the sensation of his eyes burning into her back. She had to fight the impulse to turn and stare him down but then he would know that she felt his heated gaze and his smugness would escalate from unbearable to insufferable, so she kept her eyes rigidly ahead and tried to pretend she didn't care.

Carmela met them at the palazzo door, smiling uncertainly as she looked from one to the other. But then Luca smiled and turned on the charm as he greeted her in their own language and even though Carmela knew that her future in this place was held by little more than a gossamer thread this man could sever at any time, Tina would swear the older woman actually blushed. She hated him all the more for it in that moment, hated him for this power to make women melt under the sheer onslaught of his smile.

'Your mother has taken to her bed,' Carmela said, apologising for her absence. 'She said she has a headache.'

Luca arched an eyebrow in Tina's direction. She ignored him as Carmela showed them upstairs to the main reception room, promising to bring coffee and refreshments. It was a massive room with high ceilings and pastel-decorated walls that should have been airy and bright but was rendered small by the countless cabinets and tables piled high with glass ornaments, figurines and crystal goblets and lamps of every shape and description, glass that now glinted ruby-red as the setting sunlight streamed in through the wide four-door windows.

It was almost pretty, she thought, a glittering world of glass and illusion, if you could forget about what it had cost.

'You've lost weight, Valentina,' came his voice behind her. 'You've been working too hard.'

And it rankled with her that all the time he'd been following her he'd been sizing her up. Comparing her to how she'd been three years ago and finding her wanting. No doubt comparing her to all his other women and finding her wanting. *Damn it, she didn't want to think about his other women! They were welcome to him.* She spun around. 'We've all changed, Luca. We're all a few years older. Hopefully a bit wiser into the deal. I know I am.'

He smiled and picked up a paperweight that glowed red from a collection from a side table, resting it in the palm of his big hand. 'Some things I see haven't changed. You are still as beautiful as ever, Valentina.' He smiled and examined the glass in his hand before replacing it with the others and moving on, finding a slow path around the cluttered room and around her, pausing to examine a tiny crystal animal here, a gilt-edged glass plate there, touching just a fingertip to it before looking up at her again. 'Perhaps, you are a little more prickly than I remember. Perhaps there is a little more spice. But then I recall you were always very...*passionate*.'

He lingered over the word as if he were donning that velvet glove to stroke her memories and warm her senses. She swallowed, fighting back the tide of the past and a surge of heat low in her belly. 'I don't want to hear it,' she said, turning on the spot as he continued to circle the room, touching a hand to the head of a glass boy holding a lantern aloft as if the golden-skinned child was real and not just another of her mother's follies. 'Instead, I want to tell you that I know what you're doing.'

He tilted his head. 'And what, exactly, am I doing?'

'I've been through Lily's accounts. You keep lending her money, advance after advance. Money that she turns straight around to purchase more of this—' she waved her hand around the room '—from your own cousin's glass factory on Murano.'

He shrugged. 'What can I say? I am a banker. Lending people money is an occupational hazard. But surely it is not my responsibility how they see fit to use those funds.'

'But you know she has no income to speak of to pay you back, and still you loan her more.'

He smiled and held up his index finger. 'Ah. But income is only one consideration a banker must take into account when evaluating a loan risk. You are forgetting that your mother has, what we call in the business, exceptional assets.'

She snorted. 'You've noticed her assets then.' The words were out before she could snatch them back, and now they hung in the space like crystal drops from a chandelier, heavy and fat and waiting to be inspected in the light.

He raised an eyebrow in question. 'I was talking about the palazzo.'

'So was I,' she said, too quickly. 'I don't know what you're thinking about.'

He laughed a little and ran the tips of his fingers across the rim of a fluted glass bowl on a mantelpiece as he passed, continuing his circuit of the room. Such long fingers, she couldn't help but notice, such a feather-light touch. A touch she remembered on her skin. A touch she had thought about so often in the dark of night when sleep had eluded her and she had felt so painfully alone.

'Your mother is a very beautiful woman, Valentina. Does it bother you that I might notice?'

She blinked, trying to get a grip back on the conversation, tilting her head higher as he came closer. 'Why should it?'

'I don't know. Unless you're worried that I have slept with Lily. That maybe I am sleeping with her?' He stopped before her and smiled. 'Does that bother you, *cara*?'

'I don't want to know! I don't care! It's no business of mine who you sleep with.'

'Of course not. And, of course, she is a very beautiful woman.'

'So you said.' The words were ground out through her teeth.

'Although nowhere—*nowhere*—near as beautiful as her daughter.'

He touched those fingers to her brow, smoothing back a wayward strand of hair. She gasped, shivering at the touch, thinking she should stop him—that she should step away—when in truth she could feel herself leaning closer.

It was Luca who stepped away, dropping his hand, and she blinked, a little stunned, feeling as if she had conceded a point to him, knowing that she had to regain the high ground.

'You told my mother we were old friends.'

He shrugged and sat down on a red velvet armchair, his long legs lazily sprawled out wide, his elbows resting on the arms. 'Aren't we?'

'We were never friends.'

'Come now, Valentina.' Something about the way he said her name seemed almost as if he were stroking her again with that velvet glove and she crossed her arms over her chest to hide an instinctive and unwanted reaction. 'Surely, given what we have shared…'

'We shared nothing! We spent one night together, one night that I have regretted ever since.' *And not only because of the things you said and the way we parted.*

'I don't remember it being quite so unpleasant.'

'Perhaps you recall another night. Another woman. I'm sure there have been so many, it must get quite confusing. But I'm not confused. You are no friend of mine. You are nothing to me. You never were, and you never will be.'

She thought he might leave then. She was hoping he might realise they had nothing more to say to each other and just go. But while he pulled his long legs in and sat up higher in the chair, he did not get up. His eyes lost all hint of laughter and took on a focus—a hard-edged gleam—that, coupled with his pose, with his legs poised like springs beneath him, felt almost predatory. If she turned and ran, she thought, even if there was a way to run in this cluttered showroom, he would be out of his chair and upon her in a heartbeat. Her own heart kicked up a notch, tripping inside her chest like a frightened gazelle.

'When your mother first came to me for a loan,' he said in a voice that dared her not to pay attention to each and every syllable, 'I was going to turn her down. I had no intention of lending her the money.'

She didn't say anything. She sensed there was no point in asking him what had changed his mind—that he intended telling her anyway—even if she didn't want to know. On some very primal level, she recognised that she did not want to know, that, whatever it was, she was not going to want to hear this.

'I should see about that coffee—' she said, making a move for the stairs.

'No,' he said, standing and barring her exit in one fluid movement, leaving her wondering how such a big man could move with such economy and grace. 'Coffee can wait until I've finished. Until you've heard this.'

She looked up at him, at the angles and planes of his face that were both so beautiful and so cruel, looked at the place where a tiny crease betrayed a rarely seen dimple in his cheek, studied the shallow cleft in his chin, and she wondered that she remembered every part of him so vividly and in such detail, that nothing of his features came as a surprise but more as a vindication of her memory.

And only then she realised he was studying her just as intently, just as studiously, and she turned her eyes away. *Because she had stared at him too long,* she told herself, *not because she was worried what he might be remembering about her.*

'I didn't have to lend that money to your mother,' he continued. 'But then I remembered one long night in a room warmed by an open fire, with sheepskin rugs on the floor and a feather quilt to warm the wide bed. And I remembered a woman with skin the colour of cream with amber eyes and golden hair and who left too angry and much too soon.'

She glared at him, clamping her fists and her thighs and

refusing to let his words bury themselves in the places they wanted to go. 'You lent my mother money to get back at me? Because I slapped you? You really are mad!'

'You're right. I can't give you all the credit. Because in lending your mother money, I saw the opportunity to take back Eduardo's home—this palazzo—before it collapsed into the canal from neglect. I owed Eduardo that, even if I wanted nothing to do with his wife. But that wasn't the only reason. I also wanted to give you a second chance.'

'To slap you again? You make it sound so tempting.' Right now her curling fist ached to lash out at something. Why not his smug face?

He laughed at that. 'Some say a banker's life must be dull: days filled with endless meetings and boring conversations about corporate finance and interest rate margins. But it doesn't have to be like that. Sometimes it can be much more rewarding.'

'By dreaming up fantasies? Look, I don't care how you while away your hours—I really don't want to know—just leave me out of them.'

'Then you are more selfish than I thought—' his voice turned serious '—your mother is in serious financial trouble. She could lose the palazzo. In fact she *will* lose the palazzo. Don't you care that your mother could be homeless?'

'That will be on your head, not on mine. I'm not the one threatening to throw her out.'

'And yet you could still save her.'

'How? I don't have access to the kind of funds my mother owes you, even if I did want to help.'

'Who said anything about wanting your money?'

There was a chilling note to his delivery, as if she should indeed know exactly what kind of currency he was considering. But no, surely he could not mean *that*?

'I have nothing that would interest any banker and convince them to forgive a debt.'

'You underestimate yourself, *cara*. You have something that might encourage this banker to forgive your mother's debt.'

She shook her head. 'I don't think so!'

'Listen to what I offer, Valentina. I am not a beast, whatever you may think. I do not want your mother to suffer the indignity of being thrown out of her home. Indeed, I have an apartment overlooking the Grand Canal ready and waiting for your mother to move into. She will own it free of any encumbrance and she will draw a monthly pension. All that stands in the way is you.' He smiled, the smile of a crocodile, the predator back in residence under his skin.

Her own skin prickled with both suspicion and fascination. He was a beautiful specimen of a man. He always had been. But she'd known the man, she'd known what he was capable of, and her self-protection senses were on high alert. 'And are you going to tell me what I have to do in order to win this happy ever after for my mother?'

'Nothing I know you will not enjoy. I simply require you to share my bed.'

She blinked, expecting to wake up at any moment. For surely she was so jet-lagged that she'd fallen asleep on her feet and was busy dreaming a fantasy. No, not a fantasy. *A nightmare.* 'As simple as that?' she echoed. 'You're saying that you will let my mother off the hook, you will gift her an apartment in which to live and pay her an allowance, and all I have to do is sleep with you?'

'I told you it was simple.'

Did he imagine she was? Did he not realise what he was asking her? To sell herself to him like some kind of whore—and all to save her mother? 'Thank you for coming, Signore Barbarigo. I'm sure you don't have to trouble Carmela to find your way out. I'm sure you can find the way.'

'Valentina, do you know what you are saying no to?'

'Some kind of paradise, apparently, the way you make it sound. Except I'm not in the market. I'm not looking for paradise. I certainly wouldn't expect to find it in your bed.'

'You might want to reconsider your options. I do not think you are giving this offer the serious consideration it deserves.'

'And I don't think you're giving me any credit for knowing when I've heard enough.'

'And your mother? You care not for what happens to her?'

'My mother is a big girl, Mr Barbarigo. She got herself into this mess, she can damned well get herself out of it.'

'And if that means she loses the palazzo and ends up homeless?'

'Then so be it. She'll just have to find somewhere else to live, like anyone else who overspends their budget.'

'I'm surprised at you. Her own daughter, and you will do nothing to help her.'

'You overplayed your hand, Luca, imagining I even cared. I will play no part in your sordid game. Throw my mother out if you must. Maybe then she might learn her lesson. But don't expect me to prostitute myself to bail her out. When I said what we had was over, I meant it.'

He nodded then, and she felt a rush of relief like she had never known before. She had just consigned her mother to her fate, it was true, but it was no worse a result than she had come here half expecting. Perhaps if her mother had been more of a mother, one who inspired loyalty and affection, she might even consider Luca's barbaric bargain. For five minutes at least. Then again, a mother like that would never put her in a position such as this. A mother like that would never have fallen victim to such an opportunistic despot.

'In that case you give me no choice. I will go. And I will call your father and let him know the bad news.'

'My father?' she asked, with an ice-cold band of fear tightening around her chest. Lily had been talking to her father on the phone when she'd arrived and she'd never got around to finding out exactly why, even though it had seemed odd. What had they cooked up between themselves? 'Why would you call him? What's Mitch got to do with this?'

'Does it matter? I thought you wanted no more part of this.'

'If it's about my father, then of course it concerns me. Why would you need to call him?'

'Because Lily spoke to him today.'

'I know that,' she snapped, impatient. 'And?'

'And he didn't want to see your trip wasted. Lily told me he would do anything for you, and apparently she was right. He offered to put up the farm as security if you could not find a way to help.'

CHAPTER FIVE

'I CAN'T believe you dragged my father into this!' Tina burst into her mother's room, livid. There was no risk of waking her, she'd just ordered Carmela to bring her brandy. 'What the hell were you thinking?'

Luca had departed, taking his smug expression with him but leaving a poisoned atmosphere in his wake and now Lily wasn't the only one with a headache. Tina's temples pounded with a message of war.

'What are you doing in here? What's all this screaming?'

Tina swiped open the curtains in the dark room, letting in what little light remained of the day. Too little light. She snapped on a switch and was rewarded by a veritable vineyard lighting up above her mother's bed head, clusters of grapes in autumn colours, russets and pinks and golds, dangling from the ceiling amid wafer-thin 'leaves' of green and pink. For a moment she was too blindsided to speak.

'What the hell is that?' she demanded when at last she'd found her tongue.

'You don't like it?' her mother said, sitting up, looking up at the lights, sounding surprised.

'It's hideous. Just like everything else in this glass mausoleum.'

'Valentina, do you have to be so rude? I'll have you know I don't buy things to please you.'

'Clearly. But right now I'm more concerned about whatever it was you got Dad to agree to. Luca said he'd put the farm on the line. For you. To bail you out. If I couldn't find a way.'

'You saw Luca?' Lily scambled from the bed, pulled on a rose-pink silk robe that wafted around her slim body as it settled. 'When? Is he still here?'

'He's gone and good riddance to him. But not before he put his seedy deal on the table. Were you in on it, mother dearest? Was it you who came up with the idea of swapping your daughter for your debt?'

Lily blinked up at her. 'He said that?' And her mother looked so stunned Tina knew there was no way she could have been in on it. 'That does explain a few things, I suppose. Well, aren't you the lucky one. And I thought he wasn't interested in sex.'

'You didn't! Oh, please God, tell me you didn't proposition him.'

She shrugged, sitting at a table, picking up a cloth in one hand, a glass dolphin in the other, absently rubbing its head. 'Turning fifty is no joy, Valentina, you mark my words. Nobody wants you. Nobody sees you. You might just as well be invisible when it comes to men.'

'There's nothing flattering about being asked to be someone's mistress, Lily!'

'But of course there is. He's a very good-looking man.' And then she stopped rubbing and stared into the middle distance as if she was building an entire story around the possibilities. 'Just think, if you play your cards right, he might even marry you…'

'I told him I wouldn't do it.'

Her mother looked at her, and Tina saw an entire fantasy crashing down in her eyes. 'Oh.'

'And that's when he told me about Dad, and agreeing to put up the farm. Is that why you were on the phone to him, Lily? Looking for a Plan B in case I couldn't save you? Begging for favours from a man you abandoned with a baby more than twenty-five years ago? A man who by rights should hate your guts.'

'He doesn't, though. I think Mitchell was the only man who ever really loved me.'

'Well, you sure made a mess of that.'

'I still don't understand what your problem is. People would kill to sleep with Luca Barbarigo.'

And the desire to shock her mother just for once, instead of being the one who was always shocked, was too great. 'That's just it. I *have* slept with him.'

'You sly girl,' she said, swapping the dolphin for another, this one with a baby swimming alongside. 'And you never let on? So why make such a big deal out of it now?'

And that simple question told her more about her mother than she ever wanted to know. 'It ended badly.'

'Because he didn't express his undying love for you? Oh God, Valentina, you're so naive sometimes.'

Her mother's words stung, deep inside where she'd promised she'd never hurt again. And maybe that was why she said it. Because she didn't want to be the only one hurting here. 'He said I was a chip off the old block. That, like you, I did my best work on my back!'

Her mother paused, forgetting momentarily about the delicate glass dolphin in her lap that she'd been lovingly dusting till then. And then she laughed, absolutely delighted. 'He said that? And you didn't take it as a compliment?' She took one look at her daughter's stricken face. 'You didn't, did you?' She shrugged and started polishing again, before she gave it a final check in the light and replaced it with another ornament. Rub rub rub. Polish polish polish. And the more she polished, the more Tina's nerves screamed.

'Would you please stop doing that?'

'Doing what?'

'Dusting those wretched ornaments of yours.'

'Valentina,' her mother said, incensed, rubbing on, 'they're Murano glass, they deserve to be shown to best advantage. Of course I have to dust them.'

'I was pregnant, you know!'

Lily looked up at her, and this time she put the ornament right back on the side table where it had come from. Finally, Tina thought. Finally she managed to look aghast. 'You were pregnant? To Luca Barbarigo?'

Tina nodded, a sudden tightness in her throat, a sudden and unbidden urge to cry stinging her eyes as she released a secret she had been holding inside for too long. Finally her mother might understand.

Finally.

Lily just sat there and shook her head. 'So why didn't you make him marry you?'

'What?'

'Don't you know how rich he is? His family were once Doges of Venice. He's Venetian nobility and you didn't marry him?'

'Lily, we had a one-night stand. One night. A baby wasn't part of the deal. Anyway, I lost the baby. And thank you so much for asking about the fate of your grandchild!'

'But if you'd married him,' her mother continued, unabashed, 'then we wouldn't be in this mess now.'

Tina's world reeled and spun. 'Didn't you hear me? I lost the baby. At twenty weeks. Do you have any idea what that's like, giving birth to a child that is destined to die?'

Lily flicked away the argument as if it were no more than a speck of dust on one of her ornaments. 'You didn't really want a child, did you? Besides, you could have been married by then. You would have been, if you'd told me at the time. I would have arranged your marriage within a week.'

'And what if I didn't want to get married?'

'That's hardly the point. You should have made him do the honourable thing.'

Tina doubted she had ever hated her mother quite so much. 'Like you made Mitch do when you got pregnant? Tell me, Lily, were you hoping for a miscarriage once you had that ring on your finger? Were you hoping to escape the birth once you had the husband, given you never really wanted a child?'

'That's not fair!'

'Isn't it? Sorry I didn't oblige. Lucky, though, in a way, given the mess you're in now.'

She turned to leave. 'Goodbye, Lily. I don't expect to see you again while I'm here.'

'Where are you going?'

And she looked back over her shoulder. 'To hell. But don't go thinking it's on your account.'

The taxi dropped him back at the water door of his own palazzo overlooking the Grand Canal. Aldo came down to meet him, swinging open the iron gate as he alighted from the vessel. 'And the company you were expecting?'

'A change of plan, Aldo. I will be dining alone tonight. I will eat in the study.'

Luca crossed the tiled floor and took the marble steps up into the house three at a time. A temporary change of plan, he had no doubt. Once Valentina slept on the choices she had, she would see she had no choice at all. She would soon come crawling, begging for him to rescue her family from the nightmare of her mother's making.

He entered the study, but eschewed the wide desk where his computer and work waited patiently and went straight to the windows instead, opening a window door leading to a balcony and gazing out over the canal at night, the vaporettos lit up with the flash of a hundred cameras, the heavy barges that performed the grunt work in place of trucks. Never did he tire of the endless tapestry of life in Venice, the slap of water against the pilings, the rich tenor strains of a gondolier as he massaged his gondola's way along the canals. But then his family had been here for centuries after all. No wonder he sometimes felt his veins ran not with blood but with water from these very canals.

It spoke to him now. Told him to be patient. That he was closer than he thought.

He saw the colour of her eyes in the golden light from a window across the canal. Amber eyes and hair shot with golden lights—she might have lost weight, she might have been travelling for more than a day and the skin under her eyes tired, but the intervening years had been good to her. She was more beautiful than he remembered.

And he hungered for her.

But she would soon come crawling.

And he would have her.

She got the address from Carmela, who hugged her tight to her chest before putting her at arm's length and kissing her solemnly on both cheeks. 'You come back if you need anything, anything at all. You come back and see Carmela. I will help you, *bella*.'

She hugged the older woman back, clutching the piece of paper with the address and the rough map Carmela had drawn for her. Luca had said it wasn't far. It didn't help that evening had closed in and that the canals were inky-black ribbons running between islands of jam-packed buildings, it didn't help that she knew she had been awake for a dozen hours too many to feel alive, but she was running on anger now, her veins infused with one hundred per cent fury, and there was no way she was staying in her mother's house a moment longer and no way she could have slept if she tried.

She made a mistake with the vaporetto, boarding the wrong one in her rush to get away and she had to get off at the next stop and backtrack to find another. She found herself lost in the dark *calles* three times, stumbling onwards as if she were blind until she found a sign on a wall with a name she recognised, telling her she was on the right track.

But all of these inconveniences just gave her the time to think. To reconsider why she was so prepared to jump into the lion's den—a place she had promised herself never to go again.

It wasn't for her mother, she knew. She'd been prepared to turn her back and walk away and leave her mother to her own devices.

It wasn't for herself. Oh God, no. She hated him after what he'd said, and what he'd done. Hated him for not caring when he could have. Hated him for the unsettling, unwanted effect he had on her, even in the midst of hating him. She wanted nothing more to do with the man.

No, this was for her father, who somehow thought that if he helped Lily in this current crisis, he was making it easier on his daughter. What had Lily told him of her plight? What dramas had she woven around the thin ribbons that still bonded them together, even after a divorce of more than twenty years?

But their property was operating on a shoestring, already mortgaged heavily to the banks. Another mortgage, another bad season would see her father's dream ruined.

She could not let him do that, for whatever misguided sense of loyalty he still had.

She could not let it happen.

She made another wrong turn and swore under her breath as she retraced her steps again. But all of the inconveniences of her journey, all these frustrations fed into her anger. So by the time she reached the sign on the locked gate that announced she was at the right number of the right street, she felt ready to tear the gate apart with her bare hands. Instead she pressed a buzzer, waited impatiently the few seconds for a response and asked to see Luca Barbarigo.

When she met with hesitation, she countered it with, 'Tell him it is Tina Henderson…*Valentina* Henderson. He will see me.'

A few moments later the gate clicked open and a stony-faced valet met her at the door, giving her a once-over that told her that in faded jeans and a cheap zip-up jacket she was seriously underdressed for a meeting with his boss. But that was okay because she had plans for her wardrobe.

'Signore Barbarigo will receive you in the study,' he said, before gesturing for her backpack. 'If you would care to leave your bag?'

'I'm good with it,' she said, her hand on the shoulder strap, 'if it's all the same to you.' Luca would be under no misapprehension why she was there if she had anything to do with it. He would know she meant business if she turned up with her pack. Besides, if she was going to be sharing the master's bedchamber, it was going to have to be carried upstairs at some stage.

The valet nodded, his disapproval clear on his set features, and led the way up the wide flight of stairs leading to the noble floor. A stunning palazzo, she registered as they climbed, with terrazzo floors and stuccoed walls and heavy beamed ceilings so high they were in no way oppressive.

Or were they?

Only one flight of steps, but suddenly she needed oxygen, as if the air was thinner the higher they climbed. But it wasn't the air, she knew. It was being here, in the lion's den, about to take on the lion at his own game.

It was anticipation, both terrifying and delicious, for what would come next.

And what could have been a spike of fear and the chance for cowardice to surface and set her fleeing down the stairs turned into a surge of strength. Did he really think she could be forced into something, to tumble meekly into his bed? Damn the man but she would not crawl to him like some simpering virgin begging for favours.

The stairs opened to a sitting room so elegant it could feature in a magazine—maybe the sofas and dark timber leant towards the masculine—but the overall effect was of light and space.

How her mother's house was meant to look, it occurred to her. Probably had looked, before Eduardo had taken her for his wife and she'd become addicted to the factory shops of Murano and let her passion for glass suck up every last euro and every available inch of space.

Through a set of timber doors, the valet led her, and yet another reception room until finally they were at another set of sculpted timber doors where he knocked and showed her in, pulling the door closed behind him as he left.

Her heart kicked up a beat when she saw him.

The lion was in.

He sprawled arrogantly in a chair behind an acre of desk across a room that went on for ever and then some. And still he owned the room. It was an extension of him, paying tribute to his inexorable power. She wrenched her eyes from his and studied the desk before him. Antique if she wasn't mistaken, but masculine and strong and with legs that were solid and built to last whatever the ages would throw at it.

It would do nicely.

'Valentina,' he said, without standing, his voice measured, his dark eyes waiting for answers. 'This is a surprise.'

'Is it?' She looked around at the door. 'Does that lock from the inside?'

He cocked his head, the shadow of a frown pulling his brows closer together. 'Why do you ask?'

She shrugged the straps of her backpack from her shoulders, hoping no hired help was about to rush in—not with what she had planned—before letting the weight drag it to the ground at her feet, making no move to stop it hitting the floor. She summoned up confidence along with a smile she didn't feel. 'It would be a shame to be interrupted.'

'Would it?' he asked, as if he didn't care one way or the other, and she almost panicked and fled while she could. It was so long since she'd last made love. Years since that last unforgettable night with Luca. Was she kidding herself that she could pull this off? She was so unpractised in the arts of the seductress, so unskilled.

And she almost did flee.

Except she noticed the way he'd already eased his body a fraction higher in his seat, his limbs a little less casually positioned.

And so she licked her lips in preparation for the show. Oh God, she was such an amateur! Such a fake! But still she touched a finger to the zip of her jacket and toyed with it a while, teasing it lower—she was way out of her depth and it had to show!—until she was certain he was watching. 'It's warm in here. Don't you think it's warm in here?'

'I can open a window,' he said guardedly, his eyes not leaving her fingers, no part of him looking like it was willing to move far enough to open a window any time soon.

'It's fine,' she said, feeling suddenly empowered, sliding the zip all the slow way down, peeling it from her shoulders lovingly, like a lover would do from behind, sighing a kiss against one bare shoulder. 'It's probably just me.'

'Why are you here?' The words were short, but his trademark velvet voice was thick and already curdling at the edges from heat.

She smiled and flicked off her sandals, cursing when one needed another kick, feeling clumsy. Inadequate for the task. But he wasn't looking at her feet and so she pressed on. 'You offered me a position,' she said, letting him wait for the rest. She tugged the hem of her singlet free from her belted jeans, waited just a moment to ensure she had his full, undivided attention, before pulling it over her head, letting her hair tumble free over her bare shoulders. She put her hands to the belt at her belly, letting her arms frame her breasts, clad in their white T-shirt bra. It was probably the plainest, dullest bra he had ever seen, but right now it was all she had and it was too late to worry about her underwear. Besides, from the glint in Luca's eyes, he probably hadn't even noticed that she was wearing one. That glint gave her the courage she needed if she was going to do this, courage to bare a body nobody had seen for three long years. A body that had been shut away from the world lest it betray her again. Was she asking too much of it now?

She held her breath as she slid the leather of her belt through the buckle and popped the button on her jeans. 'I'm accepting it.'

She slid the zip down, gave a wiggle of her hips to help push them down and hesitated, leaning forward just enough to turn cotton-clad breasts into a cleavage. He wasn't looking relaxed any more, she noticed. He was sitting up. Paying attention. 'Oh. I thought of something,' she said.

'What?' he croaked, his eyes not shifting.

'Conditions.'

Was that a groan she heard or a growl? It didn't matter. Either worked for her. 'Tell me,' he said.

'How long am I supposed to be your mistress? Only you didn't say.'

'I hadn't thought about it. However long it takes.'

'I thought a month.'

'A month?'

'A month would be more than adequate. I mean, I don't know what the going rate for mistresses is, but I'm thinking high end, late model, low mileage—well, that has to be worth more. Right?'

'If you say so.'

'Only I have work to do back home. And I'm sure you have something to be going on with. And it's not like we want this thing messing with our lives, right?'

'Right.'

Her hands lingered at her hips. She looked at him, watching her, feeling the power of his need feeding the anger that had been building ever since that phone call from Lily, the anger that had worked itself into a volcano set to erupt today, and smiled knowingly. *You utter bastard*, she thought with satisfaction. *And you thought you were going to have this all your own way.*

It was almost too good to be true. *Almost.*

'And you will never contact or threaten my father with anything financial or otherwise. Never again.'

'Never.'

It wasn't just too good to be true. It was perfect.

'You have such a lovely big desk, Luca.' She edged her jeans a fraction lower, spun around to give him a view from the back as she eased the soft denim lower, making sure her underwear went with it, and looked at him over her shoulder. 'It would be such a shame to waste all that glorious space on work, don't you think?'

'I think,' he said, standing awkwardly, kicking off his loafers while he attacked the buttons of his own shirt, shrugging it off to expose a chest made in heaven and stolen from the gods. 'I think you need help getting those jeans off.'

CHAPTER SIX

CONTROL. It was one of the things Luca prided himself on. He had patience. He had nerve. He had control of his life and his world. It was the way he liked things to be. It was the way things had to be.

But watching a flaxen haired, amber-eyed minx from Australia strip down to her underwear in his study was threatening to bring him undone.

If only she could get those damned jeans off.

She laughed when he picked her up, the sound half-hysterical, half-intoxicated, wild and free, and he was intoxicated as he spun her around and headed for the desk, sweeping it clear with one arm, sending papers and pencils and phones scattering in all directions before he planted her hard upon the desk and ripped off her jeans, tearing the bra from her breasts with a snap in the next testosterone-fuelled action.

That gave him pause. Naked on his desk, her legs parted by his, she was almost too much to take in with his eyes, too much for one hand to drink in as it swept over creamy skin from knee to thigh to belly to cup one perfect breast.

She stopped laughing then, her breath coming fast and furious, her eyes wide as he pulled his belt free, tugged his zip down and kicked off his pants, her eyes so suddenly cold as he freed his aching erection that she looked almost…*angry.*

'I hate you,' she said, confirming it, her lips tight around the words, baring her sharp white teeth, and that was fine. That was good, because for a moment she'd blindsided him with that impromptu striptease and he'd felt a glimmer of…*something*…that had hovered and curled around uncomfortably in his gut. But hatred he could work with.

Hatred would make her submission all the more satisfying.

And then he would dump her and she could hate him even more.

'Excellent,' he said, slamming open a drawer and rummaging through the contents until he found what he was looking for, shaking a packet free one-handed from the box. He tore it open with his teeth and had it on in record time, spreading her thighs wider to find her centre.

Slick and hot. Oh God.

He calmed himself long enough to stay poised at her entrance, his thumb working at that sensitive nub, watching the hatred in her amber eyes muddy with need, sensing the panting desperation of her breathing. *Oh yes, she hated him all right.*

'I'm so glad we understand each other,' he said, and he drove into her in one long exquisite thrust.

She cried out, her back arching on the desk like a bow, her hair rioting around her head, her eyes stuttering closed.

Hate was definitely underrated, he thought, as he braced her hips and drew slowly back, feeling involuntary muscles protest around him, try to keep him, seeing her eyes flicker open, confused and bereft and wanting more.

He gave her more. The second lunge took him deeper. She cried out again and this time when she bowed her back, he scooped her up from the desk so that she was sitting astride him, her breasts pressed against his chest, her legs curled around him and as he lifted her hips and let her fall, it was his turn to groan.

She needed no help to find the rhythm. She damn near set about setting it. She might have looked stunned before, but now she squirmed her bottom in his hands and braced herself on his shoulders, levering herself higher, letting herself take him in, increasing the speed, driving it, while her mouth worked at his throat, sharp teeth finding his flesh, every nip and bite timed to perfection, agony melding with ecstasy.

She was like a wildcat in his arms, untamed and unleashed, and it was all he could do to hang onto her while she used her body against him—all he could do to hang on, full stop.

Until she pumped him one too many times and any vestige of control vanished as he exploded inside her, the fireworks of her own orgasm ricocheting, magnified, through his.

Gasping and sweat-slicked, he hung on, her limbs heavy now, her head low on his chest, carrying her through an adjoining door to his suite. Awkwardly he pulled back the covers and then eased her onto the bed, where she closed her eyes and sighed into the mattress.

No tears, he thought, no recriminations? Half expecting both. That was a bonus. Though there probably wasn't a whole lot more to say after *I hate you.*

Unless it was *I still hate you.* He smiled as he headed for the bathroom, already contemplating round two. He could think of worse ways to spend the night. That first coupling had been so fast and furious, already he was contemplating the pleasures to be had in other, slower, methods. Next time he would take his time. Explore her body in more delicious detail. Next time he would be the one to set the pace.

He caught a glimpse of his neck and shoulder in the mirror, shocked at first at the marks of her teeth standing out bright and red. He smiled as he fingered them, the skin tender where she had left her brand. He remembered her biting him, but nowhere near this many times. Foremost in his mind had been the ecstasy. She was a tigress all right. Wild and untamed, and as unexpected as her surprise arrival tonight.

But then not entirely a surprise. Clearly he'd hit on the one thing that she held dear.

She'd surprised him with her vehemence. She'd been so prepared to walk away from her mother—to let her face the consequences of her overspending and be thrown out onto the streets if it came to that. He'd misjudged the relationship between mother and daughter badly. But then he'd only really had Lily's side of it to go by and in Lily's world, it was all about Lily.

But suggesting Lily ask her first husband to help, that had been a stroke of genius. Finally he'd found the one person Valentina did care about—the one she would do anything to rescue—even if it meant sacrificing herself to his bed.

Everyone had their price, it was said. He had just found Valentina's.

He padded back from the bathroom to find her curled kitten-like into a ball in the centre of his bed, her breathing even and deep and fast, fast asleep.

So much for round two.

Bemused, he climbed in alongside. She stirred and murmured something in her sleep and he wasn't planning on holding her but she curled herself against him and settled back into her dreams on a sigh.

It wasn't what he'd been expecting. He wasn't used to holding anyone when he slept. He wasn't used to anyone sleeping on him. Certainly not a woman he wasn't done with yet. He willed away an erection that was more wishful thinking than opportunity and tried to relax. She was warm and languid and, for all her muscled leanness, she was soft too, and in all the right places.

Relax? Fat chance.

But at least he could think about what might happen when she woke up.

One month she'd agreed to stay.

It had seemed more than ample when she'd suggested it. He'd only ever planned to keep her long enough that she thought she was safe, that maybe he might provide the answer to all her needs. Long enough to feel secure and so comfortable in her position as Venice's first lady that she wouldn't see it coming. Her public humiliation.

And then he remembered what had happened in his study and how she had turned the tables on him and milked him for all he was worth. And the thought of thirty nights of Valentina hating him and proving it every night in his bed—or on his desk for that matter—seemed nowhere near long enough.

She came to gently, slowly, with the strange feeling she was still moving, and for some vague period of half-sleep, she believed herself back on the plane.

Until logic interceded and she realised that last-minute bargain economy seats on passenger planes did not come complete with sublime mattresses and pillows big enough to land that plane on.

Venice.

She sat up in bed, realising she was hearing the chug of a passing vaporetto rather than the constant hum of jet engines, and she remembered the argument with her mother, and an explosive session on Luca's desk. And then—*nothing.*

She dropped her head into her hands.

What had she done?

She lifted the covers. Of course she would be naked. And of course it had been no dream. She'd performed some kind of amateur striptease in front of him. She'd offered herself as a conscientious objector instead of him taking her as an unwilling sacrifice. And she remembered a desk and the feel of him inside her.

How could she ever forget the feel of him inside her, the sense of fullness and completion and the exquisite side effects of friction?

In three years she hadn't forgotten and nothing, it seemed, had changed. Her memories were true.

But she couldn't for the life of her remember a bed. Luca's bed, she recognised, not only by his lingering scent and the presence of a jet-black hair on the pillow, but the sheer masculinity of the room, as if he'd stamped his personality on it by the sheer force of it. She'd slept in his bed and he'd slept alongside her and, surprisingly, that act seemed even more intimate than the one they'd shared on the desk.

But where was he now?

A robe lay on the coverlet. Silky and jade-coloured. She snatched it up and wrapped it around her in case he suddenly appeared. Strange, to feel shy after what she'd done last night, but she wasn't practised in negotiating a deal while taking off her clothes. She'd never expected to seal one in such a way. But last night fury had given her courage to do what she had done; rage had given her purpose. This morning she was still angry with both her mother and with Luca, but now there was wonderment too at her brazen behaviour. Not to mention a little fear, for what she might have let herself in for.

One month of sleeping with Luca Barbarigo. Thirty nights of sex with a man who knew how to blow every fuse in her body and then some. Thirty whole nights after three years of abstinence—she shivered—it was almost too much to think about. It was almost, so very almost, *delicious*.

The silken robe whispered against her breasts. Her nipples tightened into buds. She could not let him see her like this. He'd think she was primed and ready for a second course. He might even be right to think that.

But Luca didn't arrive and the only sounds she heard were the sounds of Venice coming from outside the windows. The only movement she felt seemed to come from the very foundations, the gentle sway of time and tide.

And only then did she notice the clock on a mantelpiece. *Three o'clock?*

She'd slept the entire day?

She padded from the bed and located the bathroom, and then found the study through another door with no sign of her pack and no trace of anything that had happened last night, the floor cleared of abandoned clothing, the desk restacked with pens and phones and files and so neat that she wondered for a moment if she'd dreamed it all. But no, there was no dreaming the tenderness of muscles rarely used. No dreaming the sense of utter disbelief—wonderment—at what had occurred.

For her hastily concocted plan—a plan made in fury and rage—a plan that in the cold light of day seemed impossible and unimaginable—had come off.

She'd come to Luca Barbarigo not as his victim, but as his seducer. Laying before him her own terms, not being forced blindly to accept his. And she seemed to recall it working. Or so she'd thought before sleep had claimed her. Some seductress she'd turned out to be.

She was still searching when there was a knock on the door, and Luca's manservant swept in a few seconds later, bearing a steaming tray laden with both coffee and tea, together with an assortment of rolls and pastries. If he was unfamiliar with finding women in his master's bedroom, it didn't show.

She clutched the sides of her robe more tightly around her. She needn't have bothered. His eyes avoided landing anywhere near her. She shoved aside the niggling thought that this wasn't the first time, but there was no point dwelling on it. Her deal was for one month. She didn't care who filled his bed all the other nights of the year.

'Would the *signorina* like anything else?' he asked, putting down the tray and moving towards the window. 'Signore Barbarigo said you would be hungry.'

It's so long since I've eaten, she wanted to add. 'That looks perfect,' she said, because the contents of the tray looked more than adequate, but also because clearly somewhere along the line she'd been promoted to something a little higher than something that the cat had dragged in.

'Where is the *signore*—Luca, I mean?' as the man swept rich vermillion curtain after rich vermillion curtain open, splashing light into the room with every broad sweep of his hands.

'Signore Barbarigo is of course, at his offices at the Banca d'Barbarigo.'

'Of course,' she said, but the sound came out wrong. She hadn't meant to sound disappointed. She'd meant to sound relieved. Hadn't she? It wasn't as if she expected him to hang around and wait until she woke up. After all, he'd got what he wanted, hadn't he? And he knew she wasn't going anywhere for at least a month. He knew where to find her when he wanted her.

The thought rankled, even though she'd known what she was letting herself in for.

'If there is nothing else?'

The valet was standing at the door, ready to take his leave. 'Actually there is.' She felt herself colour when she remembered where she'd left them. 'I can't seem to find my clothes.'

'The clothes you were wearing last night?'

And left scattered indecorously across the study floor? He didn't have to finish the sentence so she chose to answer it with another question. 'And my bag. I couldn't find it.'

He showed her into an adjoining dressing room and pushed against a panel in a stuccoed wall that she'd assumed was just a wall, revealing a closet secreted behind. And there, tucked away, was her pack, with yesterday's clothes folded neatly on a shelf. 'Your clothes have been laundered and pressed. Unfortunately the brassiere could not be saved.'

'Never mind,' she said too brightly, secretly mortified as she remembered the snap and tear when Luca had all but wrenched it from her, while Luca's valet seemed not to blink an eyelid at the carnage.

'The rest of your wardrobe should be here shortly.'

She frowned, searching for meaning. 'But I left nothing at my mother's.'

'The *signore* has organised a delivery for you. I am expecting it at any time.'

A delivery? To replace one plain old bra that had seen better days? He needn't have bothered, she thought, rummaging in her pack after the valet had departed. It wasn't as if she travelled without a spare.

Half an hour later she emerged from the bathroom wearing a floral miniskirt that she loved for the way it flirted around her legs and a cool knitted top and found the delivery man had been. Or men, plural, because it must have taken an entire team to cart the lot filling the dressing room wardrobe.

A veritable boutique was waiting for her, dresses of all descriptions, from day dresses to cocktail dresses to ball gowns. She flicked through the rack, many of the items still in transparent protective sleeves, along with racks of shoes—one pair for every outfit, by the look of it—and the drawers filled with lingerie of every imaginable colour.

And not a T-shirt bra in sight.

So much for imagining Luca wanted to replace her bra. He wanted to replace her entire wardrobe. She almost laughed. Almost. Because it was ridiculous.

Not to mention unnecessary.

More than that. It was downright insulting.

She pulled open the bedroom door and called for the valet. Who the hell did Luca Barbarigo think he was?

She was writing an email to her father on her clunky old laptop, pounding at the space bar that only worked when it wanted to, when the double doors to the living room opened. She didn't have to turn her head to know it was Luca. The way her heart jumped and her skin prickled was enough to tell her that. And the way heated memories of last night and a certain desk jumped to centre stage in her mind, she was grateful to have something to focus on so she didn't have to look at him until she'd wiped all trace of those pictures from her eyes. She banged her thumb once again on the space bar, trying to appear unmoved, while feeling the weight of his gaze on her back.

'What are you wearing?'

'I'm trying to get this space bar to work. It sticks all the time.' She pounded on the key again, hoping it covered the thump of her heart and this time it worked and she managed to rattle off another few words before she noticed her fingers were on the wrong keys and she'd written nonsense.

'No. Not, what are you doing. What are you *wearing*?'

The correction took her by surprise. She forgot the email and looked down at her simple outfit and then around at him. She almost wished she hadn't. The dark business suit and snowy white shirt made him look powerful. The five o'clock shadow darkening his olive skin turned that power into danger. Or was that just the way his eyes narrowed as they assessed her? She might just as well be a butterfly pinned in a display cabinet, being examined for the colour of its wings. Being found wanting.

'Just a skirt and top.' And she half wondered whether he was still seeing her in those jeans, as she edged them down over her hips. Had he been expecting to find her wearing them again? Had he been hoping for a repeat performance? She shivered in anticipation—suddenly half hoping… 'Why do you ask?'

'What happened to the clothes I ordered? Did they not arrive?'

Oh. She'd forgotten the clothes. She swivelled out of her chair and stood, keeping hold of the desk behind her, solid and strong. Sitting down he loomed too tall and imposing, but standing up wasn't as easy as it looked. Not when it looked as if the Furies were about to descend upon her. 'They came.'

'Then why aren't you wearing something from that collection?'

She hitched up her chin. 'How do you know I'm not?'

He snorted. 'Believe me, Valentina, it shows.'

'So what's wrong with what I'm wearing, anyway?'

'Nothing, if you want to look like a backpacker. Go and get changed.'

'Excuse me? Since when did you tell me what to wear?'

'Ever since you agreed to this deal.'

'I never—'

'You made your conditions known last night, if I recall rightly. I remember nothing about choosing what you wear being one of them. In which case…'

'You can't make me—'

'Can't I? I have a dinner reservation in one hour. At one of the most exclusive restaurants in Venice. Do you expect to accompany me wearing those rags?'

'How dare you?' They weren't rags to her. Maybe nothing in her wardrobe cost more than fifty dollars, maybe they weren't weighed down in designer labels, but they were hardly rags. She bundled up her outrage and fired it straight back. 'Anyway, those clothes you had delivered…'

'What about them?'

She allowed herself a smile. 'I sent them back.'

'You *what*?'

'You heard me. I sent them back. I didn't ask for them, I didn't want them, so I told Aldo to send them back.'

Luca stormed to the door. 'Aldo!' he yelled, his booming voice echoing around the palazzo, before turning around and striding across the room, eating up the length of it in long powerful strides, wheeling around when he reached the end. 'I can't believe you would do such a stupid thing.'

'And I can't believe you would order clothes for me like I was some kind of doll you want to dress up and play with!'

He stopped right in front of her. 'You will be seen on my arm. You will look the part.'

'As your strumpet, you mean. As your whore!'

'I didn't see you complaining last night when you

agreed to this deal. You seemed quite willing to spread your legs for me then.'

The crack of her palm against his cheek filled the room, the resultant sting on her hand a mere shadow of what he must be feeling.

He rubbed his face, his cheek blooming dark beneath his hand. 'You seem to have an unfortunate habit of slapping me, Valentina.'

'What a coincidence. You seem to have an unfortunate habit of provoking me.'

'By calling a spade a spade? Or by buying you clothes and insisting you wear them? Most women would not object. Most women would be delighted.'

'I'm not most women and I am not your whore. And I agreed to share your bed, yes. But that doesn't mean I'm happy to be paraded on your arm like some kind of possession.'

'Did you expect to stay one month chained to my bed? While I must admit the idea appeals on some primitive level, given I have your agreement to this arrangement, it seems such drastic measures will not be necessary.'

'What a shame,' she snapped. 'I imagine someone like you would get a real kick out of that.'

'I don't know,' he countered. 'Why would I restrict you to my bed when you have already shown such willingness for spontaneity?'

Aldo coughed at the door, signalling his presence, and two heads swivelled simultaneously. Tina wanted to curl up and die while Luca might just as well have been talking about the weather for all the embarrassment he showed. *'Prego,'* said Luca. 'I'm looking for the clothes that were sent, Aldo. The ones Valentina says she had sent back.'

'They are downstairs in the studio. I thought, under the circumstances, it might be wise to wait.'

Tina forgot her embarrassment. 'What? I told you to send them back. You told me you'd take care of it.'

He bowed his head. '*Scusi.* If that is all?'

'No,' Tina said, 'that's not all—'

'What Aldo is saying—' Luca interrupted '—is that I am master of this house. You are a guest and an honoured one, but you would do well to understand that I make the decisions here. Not you.'

He turned to his valet. '*Grazie*, Aldo. Perhaps you might be so good as to select a few outfits for our guest to choose from. It seems designer fashion is not one of her strong points. She may need your assistance.'

'I don't want to go out.'

'Find her something sexy, Aldo,' he said, as if she hadn't spoken. 'Cocktail length would be perfect. High heels. Choose something that shows off her figure. I want every man in that restaurant to be salivating for her and every woman to be hating them for it.'

Aldo bowed and turned, a man on a mission, clearly unsurprised by his master's bizarre request and equally clearly expecting her to follow meekly along now that they had both been given their orders.

She stood her ground. 'And meanwhile,' she said, 'while all these people are busy either drooling or planning to murder their partners, what will you be doing?'

His smile returned, and a flare of something hot and dangerous in his dark eyes sent a bolt of heated anticipation coursing straight through her. 'I'll be imagining bringing you back here and tearing whatever it is you're wearing right off you until you are lying naked and spreadeagle on my bed.'

She shivered at his words, even as his smile widened dangerously. 'And now,' he said, his white teeth almost glinting, 'so will you.'

CHAPTER SEVEN

How was a girl supposed to think of anything after that?

Numbly Tina followed Aldo down the marble staircase, wishing she had a way to prove Luca wrong and wipe that knowing smile from his face, but there was no denying the delicious thrill of anticipation that had accompanied Luca's dark promise. And it was a promise, for it could hardly be called a threat. Not when her blood fizzed at the knowledge that in a few short hours he wanted her back in his bed.

Was it wrong to look forward to sex with a man that you hated, who held you hostage to a debt you hadn't yourself incurred? But maybe that was the wrong question to ask, for that question led to more questions, and all kinds of answers she didn't want to think too much about.

Maybe it was simply better to ask if it was wrong to look forward to an act that you knew would blow your mind and your world apart—an act that your body hungered for on a scale you had never known—an act you had already agreed to undertake for one entire month and so what was the point of asking anyway?

Surely that was the better question.

It felt better, from where she was standing.

'This one,' said Aldo, intruding into her thoughts as he handed her a dress, feverishly intent on his task and already searching for the right accessories as she took the hanger. He soon found what he was looking for and before she knew it she was back in her dressing room and wearing a dress that fitted as if it had been made for her.

And in spite of her protests that she didn't want any of Luca's clothes and her order to send everything back, she adored the dress the moment she slipped it over her head. It felt delicious and sinful and decadent all in one go.

Cocktail length, the cobalt satin dress skimmed her shape without a ridge or seam in evidence beneath—perhaps because she was wearing gossamer-thin silk underwear instead of her usual plain, cotton bras—or perhaps because it was so superbly right for her, the dress nipping in at the waist to make the most of her curves, hugging her shape like a caress.

Aldo had somehow even managed to conjure up earrings to match, sapphires set with diamonds that sparkled when they caught the light, the blue stones echoing the rich colour of her dress. A touch of make-up and a simple uptwist of her hair were all she needed to do herself, and even she was astounded by the results. The rich colour of the dress did something to her eyes, turning amber into gold, although maybe it was the thoughts of what would happen later that seemed to turn them molten.

'You look amazing,' Luca said when she emerged, his rich deep voice working its way down to her bones, and he made her believe it. When she looked into his dark eyes, she felt his desire. When he took her hand to step down into the water taxi, she felt the spark of his need ignite her own.

Mad, she thought, as he finally let her hand go so she could precede him into the interior; she must be mad to feel this schoolgirl breathlessness, this overwhelming sense of anticipation. It was not as if she was going on a date with a man she wanted to be with. It was not as if they hadn't already made love. In fact he was really nothing to her but an obligation—thirty days and nights to spend in his bed—a deal made with the devil.

But knowing that was somehow still not enough to stop the racing of her pulse as he ducked his head and curled his long body onto the leather divan alongside her. Knowing that was no protection against the lure of his signature scent or the sheer magnetism of his body heat. In fact, logic seemed pathetically irrelevant when the devil looked like Luca Barbarigo.

The water taxi cruised slowly down the Grand Canal, past yet more examples of Venice's architectural treasures, and out past the crowded St Mark's Square with its magnificent Doge's Palace and towering Campanile. Across the basin, the church of San Giorgio Maggiore and its bell-tower stood majestically on their own island.

She'd come here not as a tourist. She'd come to Venice with no thought of sightseeing, but it was impossible not to drink in the sights and be awed by the spectacle.

How could anyone remain unmoved, when the shifting view revealed such a feast for the eyes with every turn? And then Luca turned his head and she caught his profile and the feasting continued.

Such sculpted perfection, she thought, such classical chiselled features. He belonged here in Venice, amongst the beautiful and the magnificent. He was a part of it. And as she drank his dark beauty in, she wondered…

Would their son have grown up to look like him?

Pain, sharp and swift, lanced her heart and so suddenly that she gasped with the intensity of it. A single tear squeezed from each eye and she had to cover her mouth with her hand to prevent her grief escaping via that route.

'What's wrong?' he asked, but all she could do was shake her head as she remembered.

Their tiny son.

Born too early to save. Born too late not to love. A child lost.

A child his father knew nothing about.

'It's nothing,' she lied, knowing that the only good thing she had taken from their baby's premature death was the relief that she would never have to tell him—that it didn't matter because she would never see him again.

But where was that relief now that she was here in Venice, forced to share a month with the father of that child? Where was the certainty now, that what she had decided back then was right?

She'd been a fool to ever believe it would be that easy. For the relief had turned to guilt, certainty had turned to fear, as the secret she had tried to lock away now hung over her like the sword of Damocles.

How could she begin to tell him the truth about their child now? Where would she start?

'It's the wake from the vaporetto,' he said alongside her, misinterpreting her distress. 'We're over it now.'

She nodded and smiled thinly, and wondered if she ever would be.

The water taxi berthed a few minutes later down a side canal at a plushly canopied hotel landing.

'Feeling better?' he asked, as he handed her out of the taxi.

'Yes.' And she was, if only because she was surprised by his concern. It wasn't one of the things she associated with the man. Arrogance was a given. Lust she expected. But concern hadn't figured on her list of Luca's character traits. Then again, maybe he was just worried that his playmate might be too ill to play games tonight. And that sounded so fitting that she even managed to dredge up a smile. 'Much better, thank you.'

Through an elegant arched doorway and the hotel lobby opened up like an Aladdin's Cave. Ceilings soared, magnificently decorated with gold leaf, while pink marble columns stretched high to reach them and a wide red carpeted staircase wound around the walls on its way heavenwards.

'It's stunning,' she said.

'You are.' And when she turned to look at him, he simply gestured around. 'Every head is turned your way. Hadn't you noticed?'

No. 'If they are, it's because I'm with you.'

'They're all wondering who you are, it's true,' he told her as he led her towards the magnificent staircase, 'but every woman in this hotel wishes she looked like you.'

'It's the dress,' she countered, needing to change the subject, before she started believing him. 'However did you know what size to have delivered?'

'Wouldn't you expect a man like me to know what size his lover wears?'

She shivered. His lover? That seemed too personal. Too intimate. Theirs was a business arrangement. A deal. So she schooled her features, aiming for cool and unaffected and definitely uncaring. 'Clearly you've had plenty of practice to be so good at it.'

'Clearly.' His smile widened. 'Does that bother you?'

'Why should it? I don't care who you sleep with. I don't want to know.'

'Of course,' he said. 'Although perhaps I am not so expert as you would like to believe. Aldo found your clothes. The tags were still readable apparently. But only just.'

Another reminder of her wanton behaviour. Yet another reminder of the age of her clothes. And she had no comeback either, other than to blush. So she concentrated on the stairs beneath her feet and just hoped her face didn't clash with her dress.

The restaurant ran the length of the building, half enclosed, half terrace, all understated elegance with red upholstery and cream linen tablecloths, with touches of gilt for highlights around artfully placed mirrors. Heads turned as they passed, men greeted Luca like an old friend, women preened for him and stared openly and questioningly at her. He swept through the room like a rolling wave, refusing to be distracted for longer than a second, even when it was clear that he was being welcomed to share someone's table for the evening.

Clearly Luca had other plans.

Through wide glass doors they were led onto the broad terrace, where Luca's table stood waiting for them at the far corner, boasting uninterrupted views over the San Marco Basin and the Gulf of Venice. Below them tourists paraded along the Riva degli Shiavoni enjoying the balmy September evening while water craft darted across the basin lit up like fireflies.

Luca sat back in his seat and smiled. The views from the terrace were sublime, it was true, but then his view was even better. He hadn't lied. She looked amazing tonight. There was something about the colour of her cat-like eyes. And there was something about the colour of that dress, the way the shadows danced across it in the light whenever she moved. His fingers envied those shifting shadows and itched to dance their own way across her skin. 'Are you hungry?' he asked as they were handed their menus. He was, but what he wanted to feast upon had nothing to do with his stomach.

She'd left him hungering for more last night. He'd imagined a second course before leaving for work, but she'd been so deeply asleep this morning that letting her sleep had seemed the far wiser action. He wanted her wide awake when he made love to her again. And this time he wanted her to last all night.

This night.

The thought was as delicious as anything offered on the menu, which suddenly seemed too long and filled with far too many courses. He lost interest in the choices, returned to watch her instead, enjoying the tilt of her head and the curl of slim fingers angled around her menu.

'A little,' she said, her eyes drifting upwards, widening when they caught him watching her. She swallowed and he watched the slight kick of her chin and the movement down her throat. 'Is there something special you can recommend?'

Plenty. But if she was talking food—he skipped straight to the main courses, already impatient to be home. Surprised a little by how much. 'The monkfish is excellent here, or there is always the rabbit.'

Something flared in her eyes, something challenging, as if she could read his thoughts. 'I think the beef,' she said, and he smiled.

'Excellent choice,' he said, thinking she would need it and ordered for them both.

Sparkling prosecco arrived, poured into glasses spun with gold. 'A toast,' he said, lifting his glass to her. 'To…' She arched one eyebrow, waiting. He smiled, a long, purposeful smile. '…anticipation.'

Her expression gave nothing away. Only her eyes betrayed the fact she felt it too, this thread between them, as fine as that trace of gold spun in their glasses, pulling inexorably tighter. 'To anticipation,' she echoed, a husky quality infusing her voice as she lightly touched her flute to his.

Giddy.

She hadn't even had one sip of the wine and she already felt giddy. But how could she not? The setting was sublime, the view magical and the man opposite was looking at her as if she was more tasty than anything on the menu.

And no matter what she thought of him, she could not help but like the way he looked at her and what it did to her body. She liked this delicious heat simmering under her skin and the way his eyes warmed her from the inside out. She liked the way he seemed impatient to have this meal over with when he had been the one who had insisted on coming out. There was something empowering about his need, something that meant he didn't hold all the cards.

Yes, she had agreed to his deal. She was his for the month, it was true, but did he not realise that by dressing her up and turning her into something worthy of his attention he was handing her a decent measure of his power?

All she had to do was play her part. It wasn't hard. Whatever she thought of Luca Barbarigo and his ruthless determination to get his own way, there was no hardship in anticipating the pleasures of the night to come. Just as there was no hardship in anticipating the pleasures of walking away one short month from now.

Oh yes, she'd drink to anticipation.

'So this is where we make small talk,' Luca said, breaking into her thoughts. 'Where we sit and converse like two civilised people when there is somewhere we would both rather be and something we would both much prefer to be doing.'

There was no need to ask what he would rather be doing, not when his dark eyes were thick with desire. But if he wanted small talk… 'Maybe we could talk about the weather,' she suggested. 'It's a beautiful night.'

'The weather does not interest me.'

'No? Then we could talk about the view. You could point out the places of interest. There seems to be no shortage of those.'

He shook his head. 'I could do that. But that would be dull. We would just be marking time. I would rather talk about you. How long is it since that night? Two years? More?'

That night. What an appropriate way to put it. 'Three years come January.'

'So many.' He took a sip of his wine and sat back, his dark eyes searching hers. 'Which begs the question: what have you been doing all that time?'

Well, now there was a simple question. How to find a simple answer for all she had been doing?

Nursing a bruised ego.

Discovering that she was pregnant.

Grieving the loss of that child.

Hating...

She picked up her water glass, a tumbler that bore the swirling logo of the restaurant, clearly made locally in Murano, and she wondered that, for all her vast collection, her mother had never managed to find anything near as simple or as beautiful. She studied the piece so that she didn't have to look at the man sitting opposite. She stared at it so he wouldn't know how much his questions unsettled her. 'Working on my father's property, mostly.' The mostly was important. She wasn't about to confess that for the first few months she'd been holed up in a friend's one-bedroom flat in Sydney while her life lurched from one turmoil to the next.

'What kind of property? Lily said something about wool?'

She buried the spike of resentment that rose at the mention of Lily and the farm in the same sentence. 'Yes. Sheep and some cropping. Lucerne mainly.' She looked around at their watery world, lined with buildings that went back at least five centuries. Some years the farm didn't see rain, the dams dried up and the sheep turned red with dust. The last drought had lasted so long, some local kids had grown up thinking sheep were supposed to be red. 'It's different from here,' she said, making a massive understatement, 'that's for sure.'

'So you're close to him, then. Your father.'

She shrugged. 'Of course. He was the one who brought me up after Lily walked out.' Whereas Lily, she thought, had been a some time holiday destination—her visit usually coinciding with a wedding. There'd been two more of those before her marriage to Eduardo. One to a Swiss ski school owner. Another to an Argentinian polo player. Neither of them had lasted either.

Funny, she thought, how life ran in circles sometimes.

She'd met Luca at her mother's wedding to Eduardo. By then, aged seventeen, she'd well and truly realised that her mother's life was as empty and pointless as they came. And by then she was hardly going to fall into bed with someone who happened to be Eduardo's nephew, even if he was the most perfect male specimen she had ever laid eyes upon and even if he made no bones about his attraction to her…

Luca snapped a breadstick, jolting her back to the present. 'I have trouble picturing Lily on a farm.'

'They should never have married. I'm sure she imagined she was going to end up some rich farmer's wife and play tennis and drink tea all day.'

'But it didn't turn out that way?'

She shook her head. 'She hated it, apparently—the flies, the heat—she left when I was six months old. Just packed up and left Mitch with a baby and a hole where his heart had been.'

'It seems—' he hesitated a moment, as if searching for the words '—an *unlikely* match. Someone like Lily with someone who works on the land.'

'I think their differences were what attracted them to each other. She was the original English flower, on holidays to visit an old maiden aunt. He was the rugged Australian right down to his leather workman boots and as exotic to her as she was to him. When they met at some charity event in Sydney, it was lust at first sight.' She sighed. 'In normal circumstances it would have run its course and they would have both gone back to their separate worlds but Lily ended up pregnant with me and before you know it they were married. Pointlessly as it turned out.'

'You don't approve?'

'I don't think an unplanned pregnancy is any reason for a marriage! Do you?'

Maybe she'd sounded too strident. Maybe her question had sounded too much like a demand because she needed him to agree with her. But across the table from her, Luca merely shrugged instead of agreeing. 'I am Italian. Family is important to us. Who's to say if it's the right or wrong thing to do?'

'Mc,' she said, knowing that if he knew—*if hc had only known*—he would think differently. 'I've lived my life knowing their marriage was futile, a disaster from start to finish. I would never do that to a child of mine. I might be Lily's daughter, but I am not Lily!'

'And yet here you are, still picking up after her.'

'I'm not doing this for Lily,' she hissed, with rods of steel underpinning her words, 'but you threatened to bring my father into this and there is no way on this earth I am going to let you suck him into Lily's nightmare. He's worked hard for every cent he has and I won't let him lose any of it on her account!'

She was breathless after her outburst. Breathless and breathing fire, but she was glad too, that he had reminded her of all the reasons she hated him, that he thought he could manufacture the result he wanted by manipulating people and using them for his own ends.

'Do you realise,' Luca asked, leaning forward and cradling his wine glass in his hands, 'how your eyes glow when you are angry? Did you know they burned like flames in a fire?'

She sucked in air, blindsided by the change in topic, but more so because she had expected anger back in return. She had been prepared for Luca to fight, expecting him to fight, if only to defend his low actions. Whereas his calm deliberations and an analysis of her eye colour had knocked the wind from her sails.

'I was angry,' she said, uncomfortable and unnerved that he could find things about her that nobody else had ever told her. Things that she herself didn't know. 'I still am.'

'It's not just when you're angry though,' he continued as their meals arrived, the waiter placing their plates with a flourish before disappearing on a bow. 'They glowed like that last night when you came. I look forward to seeing them burn that way for me again tonight.'

She wasn't sure which way was up after that. The meal passed in a blur, she ate and the beef melted in her mouth, but five minutes after her plate was whisked efficiently away, she couldn't have described how it tasted. Five minutes after he said something, she couldn't have remembered his words. Not when her whole being seemed focused not on the meal, but on the senses he stirred and by the knowledge of what would come afterwards.

Every word he spoke stroked her senses. Every heated look stoked the fire burning deep inside her belly. Every single smile had the ability to worm its way under her skin.

God, but he looked so good when he smiled. Generous lips swept open to reveal white teeth. Not perfect teeth, she noted with some satisfaction, for one eye tooth angled and hugged too close to one of his front teeth to be absolutely perfect. And yet somehow that made him more real than make believe. Somehow that only worked to make him more perfect. And still he looked so good that logic got spun on its head and she might even imagine for one infinitesimal moment that…

But no.

She brought herself up with a thump. Took a drink of *frizzante* water to cool her heated senses. There could be no imagining. Not where Luca Barbarigo was concerned.

But there could be tonight.

An entire month of tonights.

Her body hummed as dessert was short-circuited for coffee.

Anticipation built to fever pitch in her veins, as lingering to enjoy the view was short-circuited for the promise of pleasure.

The boats were still darting across the basin like fireflies; most of the tables around them were still full, when Luca had clearly had enough. 'It's time,' he said throatily, and there seemed nothing left to say when the hunger in his eyes told her all she needed to hear.

He guided her through the restaurant, the touch of his hand at her lower back no more than the graze of his fingertips, and yet every part of her body seemed focused on that spot, as if he'd tied a ribbon between them that kept her close.

And this time Luca all but ignored the greetings that were called out to him. He ignored the eye contact that would ensure recognition and guarantee acknowledgement. He stopped not once in his quest to get her out of the restaurant and down the stairs and into the waiting water taxi.

For me, she told herself. He is avoiding them for me, and that knowledge was as empowering as it was intoxicating.

All the more empowering given he had forgiven a debt—a massive debt—for the pleasure of her company.

And a question that had been niggling away at her wanted answering.

What was this all about?

Why her? Sure, her mother owed him a fortune, but surely there were plenty of women who would be prepared to grace Luca's arm and his bed for however long it took without sacrificing a cent of her mother's debt. Why did he want her? What was his game?

On the taxi he suggested they stand outside and watch the moving light show along the canal, and he took her hand and led her through to the rear deck. 'You're frowning,' he noticed, wrapping his arms around her as she held onto the rail as the taxi moved away from the dock.

She stiffened a little. 'Maybe because I don't understand you.'

She felt him shrug against her back. 'What's so hard to understand?'

'Why you want me.'

'I'm a man who likes women,' he said, peeling her away to spin her around to face him. 'And you are—' his eyes lowered, raking over her, and they might just as well have been raking hot coals over her skin '—unmistakably all woman. Why wouldn't I want you?' He leant down closer, his lips drawing closer, and fear the size of a football kicked off in her gut. She turned her head away.

'Don't do that. Don't kiss me.' People who liked each other kissed. People who were in love.

'Why not?'

Because kisses were dangerous. You could lose yourself in a kiss, and she didn't want to be lost with Luca Barbarigo.

'Because I hate you and I don't think you particularly like me that much. It just seems false.'

'And sex doesn't?'

'Not when it's just sex.'

'Just sex. Is that what you thought we were having last night—just sex?'

'What would you call it?'

'Mind-blowing. Earth-shattering. Maybe even some of the best I've ever had.'

She gasped, her eyes searching his face for laughter, finding no trace. It had been like that for her…but for him? And whether it was the sudden acceleration of the taxi as it joined the main canal, or because she didn't want to prevent it, but this time when his mouth came closer—so close that his lips brushed hers—all the air disappeared from her lungs in a rush of heat, leaving a vacuum that could be filled only by him.

He filled that vacuum with the more solid press of his lips upon hers. He filled it with the taste of him in her mouth.

Coffee and wine and heat combined in a knee-trembling cocktail that threatened to bring her undone, and only his arms around her kept her standing. And as his lips made magic against her mouth, it occurred to her that she'd been right to worry, because a girl could not only get lost, but drown in a kiss like that.

She was already drowning—in sensation. There was nothing between them but silk and cloth and the knowledge that when they came together it would be explosive.

His hands moved over her like both a caress and a demand. His kiss promised her his soul while it wrenched free her own.

She could not afford to let go of her soul.

She turned her head away and pushed against his chest, determined to show him she was unmoved while she still could, before she got lost for ever in his kiss. Before she believed its promise.

He let her go and she spun away, grabbing hold of the railing like a lifeline. 'I wish you hadn't done that,' she hissed.

'Do you?'

'Yes! Because this whole thing still makes no sense, when you could have your pick of any woman in Venice. Any woman anywhere for that matter and without having to blackmail them into the deal.'

'But I didn't want any other woman,' he said, peeling her away from the railing and back in his arms. 'I wanted you and you alone.'

'Lucky me.'

He laughed. 'And would you have come to me if I hadn't blackmailed you into my bed?'

'No,' she said breathlessly, still trying to grapple with the sense of it all. 'I wouldn't have come to you if you were the last man left on earth.'

'Then there you have it,' he said with another of those deadly smiles, his lips pressing to her forehead. 'You gave me no choice. Your not wanting it makes having you all the more satisfying.'

CHAPTER EIGHT

ANGER was good. Anger she could harness and mould and shape into something to sling right back at him. And it would not be simpering submission, but forged in hatred, and it would be slung back at him on her terms.

Anger coloured desire and turned it into a weapon. Anger shaped passion and turned it into something much more dangerous, much more lethal.

So that by the time the water taxi arrived back at the palazzo she didn't feel fearful or afraid or vulnerable.

Instead she felt stronger than she had ever done. She had survived his kiss, she had suffered his taunts, and if he thought he was going to take and take freely of her, he was very much mistaken.

Because she'd make damn sure she would take more than she would give. No, there was nothing to fear from Luca Barbarigo.

Aldo greeted them discreetly at the water door, just as discreetly evaporating as Luca ushered her upstairs, every slight caress of the hand at her back a siren's call to her senses while ratcheting up her simmering resentment; every silken whisper of his presence both a caress and a curse.

And it didn't matter any more that she didn't understand

whatever game Luca was playing. Because she knew what was expected of her as they climbed the stairs.

And what was expected of her was the easy bit.

It was just sex, after all, whatever he wanted her to believe. It wasn't as if she needed to put on a special performance. All she had to do was take off her clothes and get into bed with him. Nothing to it.

Dinner had been interminable. He'd wanted to be seen. He'd planned to give time for his dinner companion to have been photographed and image searched and found to be someone with links to him. But still it had taken too long—far too long when what he most wanted was to have her in his bed. But it had been necessary.

It shouldn't take anyone curious too long to work out.

His uncle's widowed wife's daughter.

She wouldn't be hard to trace, not with today's search technology. Soon there would be articles in newspapers and magazines. Soon the world would know she was living in his palazzo and that they were an item.

A few more outings and the papers would blow it out of all proportion and wedding bells would be predicted and gambled upon.

And she would start believing it herself.

That was when she would be the most vulnerable.

That was when she would be starting to believe the fairy tale. And she would. Even now, for all her protests of hating him, she melted in his arms like wax.

She was his.

She'd made that plain last night with her impromptu striptease, when she'd offered herself to him on his desk. She'd made that plain the way she'd stunned herself with the force of her orgasm.

Soon she would forget all about hating him and start believing in dreams.

And that was when he would unceremoniously dump her.

But that was later.

First there were more carnal pleasures to be enjoyed.

Starting now.

The bedroom lighting was low, the air body temperature, the wide bed turned down on both sides. He smiled as he closed the door to the suite behind him, watching the seductive sway of her hips as she headed across the room, liking the way the dress clung to her curves. He liked her in that dress. It would be such a shame to tear it off.

Then again…

'Where are you going?'

She stopped, looked over her shoulder at him. 'My dressing room. I'm guessing you expect me naked for tonight's performance.'

'What? No impromptu striptease tonight?' he asked, flicking open the top button of his shirt, tugging at his tie. 'No office antics?'

She blinked, golden eyes glinting and hard, watching him remove the cufflinks from his shirtsleeves. She made a move to walk away.

'Come here.'

'I don't take orders from you.'

'Come here,' he repeated, his voice velvet over steel.

'Why? So you can rip this dress off like you would… like the caveman you like to keep dressed up under those fancy Italian suits of yours? Nobody's fooled, Luca, least of all me.'

'Maybe you should come here and find out.'

Fire flared in her eyes, shooting flames straight to his groin.

'I like this dress, I don't want it ruined.'

'I like it too, as it happens. Maybe I just want the pleasure of peeling it from your body.'

'Fine,' she snapped, 'have it your way.' But there was a husky edge to her grudging agreement that signalled she wasn't as in control as she made out, even as she crossed the room and spun around in front of him, presenting her back.

Not so fast, he thought. Instead of reaching for the zip, he put his hands on her shoulders and dipped his mouth to the place where her throat met her shoulder. Her gasp was his reward, her tremor was his vindication.

'You see,' he murmured against her throat, 'even the caveman can play nice.' And she trembled again.

He ran his hands down her arms, taking his time to drink in the feel of her smooth, toned limbs, curling his fingers possessively around hers before starting the long road up. There was plenty to enjoy. There was plenty of time. Last night's lovemaking had been so rushed, he'd missed a lot.

And there was so much more to explore. His fingers found the catch of her zip and he slid it slowly down, letting just one fingertip trail a line down the skin beneath. Another involuntary gasp from his reluctant playmate and the temptation to slide his hands underneath the fabric and ease it over her shoulders and be done with it was almost too much.

Almost.

Instead he spun her around and cradled her jaw in his hands, lifting her face towards his. Her lips were parted, her breathing shallow and fast and her amber eyes swirled with confusion. There was resentment there and heated anger, but there was a flicker of vulnerability too in those amber depths, a flicker that was almost endearing.

'Where is your caveman now, Valentina?' he asked, searching her face, watching her mouth and those lips, parted and panting and just begging to be kissed. He wasn't about to disappoint them. He dipped his head and brushed her lips with his and sighed with the simple, exquisite pleasure.

Just sex, she told herself. It was just sex. His kisses meant nothing, the tenderness meant nothing.

It was just sex.

It meant nothing.

So why did it feel so very good?

His lips moved over hers like a piece of music, a symphony that built and grew and slowed to tender lows and soared to great heights and everywhere in between.

His hands traced a path down her throat. She felt the brush of silken straps over her shoulders and the slip of her dress as it fell to the floor. She felt air that cooled and caressed her naked breasts and turned her nipples even harder.

She felt his hands slide down her bare back and pull her against him.

She felt him, long and hard against her belly. Felt the aching need for him between her thighs and her hand moved of its own volition, unable to resist the temptation to curl her fingers over that rigid column.

Breath hissed through his teeth. He lifted her from the circle of her dress and into his arms, took three long strides and tossed her into the centre of the waiting bed. Chest heaving as if he'd run a marathon, he looked down at her on the bed, eyes raking down over a body clad in nothing but gossamer-thin shreds of silken underwear, a pair of killer heels and a pair of earrings, while his hands were busy pulling off his shirt, his shoes, his trousers.

She could not take her eyes from him, from the lean and

sculpted perfection of his body, from the heart-stopping size of his erection as it sprang free. Looking at him made her blood fizz and her flesh ache.

And then he kneeled alongside her on the bed and slipped off first one shoe and then the other, kissing the soles of her feet, sliding his hands up her legs to catch the scrap of silk that was her underwear, sliding it down and tossing it over his shoulder.

'Did anyone ever tell you,' he said, his voice thick with need as he gazed down upon her naked form, 'that you look amazing in sapphires?'

She was sure she would have remembered if someone had, but right now there was no space for raking up memories, no room for anything that might have happened in the past. This moment was all about what was happening now.

He lowered his head and put his mouth to her breast, drawing it in, rolling his tongue around her nipple while one hand swept down her body from neck to breast to thigh to knee, his long fingers spread wide, missing nothing, leaving no part of her untouched, leaving no part of her to his imagination. Through his scorching touch, he drank her in until she felt more liquid than solid, her senses flowing, eddying.

She shuddered under the heated assault, her senses alive, her need building like a whirlpool; spinning as he rained hot kisses down her belly; spinning as he spread her legs wide and dipped his head between her aching thighs.

The first touch of his tongue was electric, sending her arching against the mattress. She cried out, something incomprehensible—meaningless—other than as a reflection of the exquisite agony of his hot tongue circling her pulsing core, and his clever lips toying with that screamingly tight bud of nerve endings. And all the while the whirlpool built inside her, sucking her deeper, rendering her senseless, her world ever shrinking, until it consisted of nothing more than a spinning sea of sensation.

She was lost in that sea. Cast adrift. And still it wasn't enough. Still she needed more.

'Tell me that you want me,' he murmured, sensing her distress, and she felt his words on her secret flesh.

Her head thrashed on the pillow. 'I hate you.'

He caught her between his lips, suckled harder.

'Tell me that you want me.'

'I want you,' she half cried, half sobbed, the confession wrenched bodily from her as he continued to work magic with his mouth, as the circling storm inside her wound tighter and inexorably tighter like a coiled spring until she would die with it.

'I want you now!'

And his mouth was gone and she had one moment of relief, one moment of loss, before she felt him nudge at her core and drive himself home.

It was the trigger she needed, the trigger that released that achingly tight coiling spring and sent her soaring. She exploded around him as he held her and filled her and completed her.

'You should hate me more often,' he joked as she came down from the high, her body slick and hot and humming in secret places.

'I do,' she said, panting, hating him right now for his ability to do that to her, to turn her incendiary with his clever hands and clever mouth.

'Good,' he said, moving inside her, making her gasp as she realised he was still hard. 'Keep on hating me.'

She could do that. But there was no time to tell him, no time to get her breath back. He leaned back, lifted a lifeless leg and flipped her neatly onto her front before she knew what was happening, all the time still buried deep inside her.

Shock rendered her speechless, not only at his sudden manoeuvre, but at the tightening and dance of muscles she'd thought wasted, muscles that welcomed another chance to play.

Large hands anchored her hips as he drew back and she hated his leaving almost as much as she hated him.

Maybe more.

He took his own sweet time coming back, inch by excruciating inch until she thought she would go mad with want, until he was seated deep inside her, his thighs pressed hard against hers.

She sighed with the exquisite fullness of it. Oh God, he felt so good this way, so deep.

And when he moved it was even better. He started slowly, inviting her into the rhythm of his dance, taking her with him. His hands grew hungrier, sliding down her spine, curling around a breast, slipping around a thigh to stroke her sensitive nub. He was everywhere around her. He was inside her. He possessed her.

The rhythm built, the pace increased, the slide of flesh against flesh set to the sound of the slap of skin against skin and the feverish need for air as he wound her need around him, tighter and tighter than it had been before and left her teetering on the edge of a precipice.

He paused, leaving her on the brink. She heard a sound like a whimper, needy and desperate, before she realised it had come from her own throat.

And then it was his turn to cry out—a cry of triumph borne of pain—as he thrust one last desperate time and sent her to that place where hate and want coalesced in a fireball that consumed her.

He followed her over the edge, pumping his release and catching her to ride the wave together.

I hate you, she thought, as he collapsed alongside and gathered her close.

I hate you, she thought, as a single tear rolled down her cheek. *I need to be able to hate you.*

But after what they had just shared, the sentiment rang hollow and empty.

CHAPTER NINE

LUCA couldn't remember the last time he'd slept late. Not that he hadn't woken earlier. But this morning she'd stirred too and she'd been warm and malleable in his arms and it had been inevitable that they'd made love again.

But then instead of rising like he'd planned, he'd fallen back to sleep. If Aldo hadn't woken him with a subtle knock at the door, he'd still be sleeping.

'What time is it?' he asked as Aldo placed a tray of coffee and rolls on a table. Beside him Valentina stirred, still sprawled on her stomach, her hair in disarray around her head, testament to the riotous night they'd spent rediscovering each other's bodies. How many times had they made love? Was it four? Or five? He'd lost count along with his sleep.

'Ten o'clock,' the valet said in response to a question Luca had forgotten he'd asked. 'I wouldn't have disturbed you but Signore Cressini called and said he needed to talk to you.'

'Matteo called?' he asked, lashing a gown around himself while Aldo opened the curtains.

Aldo nodded. 'He said it was important.'

He left the room as Valentina lifted her head from the pillow and sniffed. 'Mmm, coffee,' she muttered before dropping her head back on the pillow and Luca smiled and reached for the pot, filling them both a cup while he wondered what Matteo wanted.

Mind you, he owed his cousin a call—he had, after all, put paid to the spending habits of his best customer. Matteo, no doubt, wanted an update.

He reached for his phone and immediately thought better of it. He was already late for the office and it wasn't as if there was anything pressing or that there weren't any number of bright young things who wouldn't be happy to cover for him for the day. Besides, right now bright autumn sunshine was flooding the room with light. Late September and the weather was still holding. Any time now the storm clouds of a European winter would come sweeping down from the north, and the heavens would turn grey and dark and open up and turn Venice from a watery wonderland into a rain-lashed water world.

Maybe he should to take a little time out while his guest was here before that happened. A run out to the island of Murano wouldn't take that long. It would make for more photo opportunities of them together for a start. And then afterwards there'd be time for a late lunch and a long afternoon siesta. He might not be Spanish, but there were plenty of reasons to like the practice. Making love in the middle of the day was one of them. Thirty nights could stretch a little that way.

But not if she was going to spend it all sleeping. He pulled off the covers and slapped her bare rump, almost tempted to linger at the sight of her creamy flesh. 'Wake up, Sleeping Beauty. I've got plans for you.'

She didn't exactly jump at his suggestion of visiting Murano and his cousin's glass factory. The glass that formed her mother's addiction was not something that held her fascination—she'd seen enough of it at Lily's palazzo to last a lifetime. And it wasn't as if she needed a reminder of how her mother had been manoeuvred into debt—yes, because she was feeding a compulsion of her own making—but also by probably two of the best in the business.

After all, who else to feed a glass-infatuated woman's habit but a financier who wanted to steal her house out from under her and his cousin, the man who owned the factory and who supplied her fix?

What worried her more, she reflected as she tied back her hair and swiped gloss over her lips, was spending time with Luca—time when they were not making love. It was one thing to share his bed and his nights—that had been the deal she'd made. She just wasn't sure she wanted to share his days. Because she needed time alone. Time to think. Time to regroup.

Time to put into perspective their love-making, to bundle it up in a box marked *meaningless* and shove it under the bed until the next night.

It was harder to do than she'd thought. Harder to separate the passionate Luca from the hated. Harder to hold herself together, even when she was coming apart.

No, she didn't need to be reminded in the daylight hours of the tender caress as he'd stroked her skin or the way he'd turned her molten with one flick of his clever tongue. She needed the lid put on that box and put on firmly and for it to be all tied up tight.

But he'd insisted. Why? To rub her nose deeper in her mother's mess by taking her to the scene of the crime? Surely he knew better now than to think that she cared enough about Lily's foolishness for that.

So he'd insisted and she'd relented. Besides, the weather was sunny, the skies clear blue, and she'd found a gorgeous floral print sundress that was just begging to be worn. Why shouldn't she see something of Venice while she was here?

And if Luca could put up with her daylight company for a few hours, she could hardly confess that she was afraid to do the same. She would just have to work harder to keep a lid on that box.

And when all was said and done, what was she afraid of, anyway? Actually liking the man? There was no chance of that, not after all the things he'd done.

Luca was in his study making calls when she emerged, so she pulled out her laptop and curled into a chair to try to finish the email to her father. He would be wondering what was happening over here and when she was planning on coming home. She was wondering how best to tell him without having him launch himself halfway around the world brandishing a shotgun to save his daughter from the clutches of the evil Luca.

She smiled at the thought as she pounded on the space bar, trying to imagine him in Venice, surrounded by water, practically living on top of the water. He'd taken her to the beach for a holiday once, when she was ten. A wide, sandy beach framed by rocky cliffs and wild waves and an endless, endless sea. He hadn't stopped staring at the sea for days, and when she asked what he was looking for, he'd just shaken his head and muttered, 'All that water.'

A bubble of sadness rose up unbidden to sully the memory and she felt a familiar pang of loss. And then the space bar stuck again and she wrote a line of jibberish and she cursed, distracted. The damn key was getting worse. No question about it.

'You look good enough to eat.'

Her mouth went dry. She swallowed, suddenly reminded of another time, another feast, the lid well and truly ripped from the box.

Was he thinking about last night too?

She took her time closing her laptop, wishing away the burning in her cheeks. She didn't dare meet his eyes. 'I didn't hear you come in.'

'I'm not surprised. Is that a computer or a brick you're banging away on?'

'It's all right,' she said, putting it down, happy to talk about anything other than the reason for her blushing. 'It does the job. Most of the time. It's just seen better days, that's all.'

He came closer, picked it up and tested its weight with one hand before discovering he needed two. 'It's seen better centuries.'

'It's fine,' she said, even though it weighed a ton and was so slow it was good for little more than the occasional email.

He grunted and put it down. 'The driver's here, if you're ready.'

Beyond the crowded canals of Venice, the driver opened up the engines. The sleek timber craft's nose leapt clear of the water, the boat skipping over the surface of the lagoon in a rush of power.

Luca asked her if she wanted to go inside, but it was exhilarating standing at the back of the vessel, the wind tugging at her hair, and she shook her head. Besides, the view outside was just too good. There was something about seeing Venice from the water, buildings standing where by rights there should be none, rising vertically from the lagoon like a mirage.

But the city was real. Just as the man standing at her side was real. Heart-stoppingly, devastatingly real, when she thought about their love-making last night; ruthlessly, unscrupulously real when she remembered why she was here, and if there was a mirage anywhere, it was this game they were playing, pretending to be lovers.

He'd told her last night he wanted her so badly that he would use her mother's debts to blackmail her into his bed. Then, with the wick of anticipation already lit and burning down towards their inevitable coupling, it had almost seemed reasonable. Today logic demanded a better explanation. Because she wasn't that special. What was really going on?

He put a lazy arm around her shoulders and she looked up at him. 'Why am I here?' she asked, her words tugged away by the wind. 'The real reason this time.'

His eyes were masked by dark glasses. 'Don't you want to see Murano?'

'No,' she said, not knowing if he had deliberately chosen to misunderstand her question, 'I don't mean that.' But, before she could clarify, he squeezed her shoulders and pointed ahead. 'Look, we're almost there.'

They slowed and landed at a small dock where a man stood waiting for them. He waved as they pulled alongside and she had no doubt who he was. Cousins could be brothers, both lean and long-limbed and good-looking enough for a dozen men. 'Matteo,' called Luca as he bounded onto the dock. The pair embraced before he turned to offer Tina his hand.

'And this,' he said as she joined him on the deck, 'is Valentina Henderson, Lily's daughter.'

Matteo smiled and greeted her like a traditional Italian, a kiss to each cheek before standing back, a wide smile on his handsome face. 'Lily's daughter, yes, I see it, but much more beautiful too. Do you share your mother's passion for our local glass, Valentina?'

'No,' she said, ignoring the compliment and hoping to knock on the head any hope he might hold that he had gained himself a new client. 'It holds no interest for me at all.'

'Valentina has—' Luca looked at her and smiled '—other passions, don't you, Valentina?'

One day she would grow out of blushing, she swore, as she tried to look anywhere but at the two men standing opposite. Maybe just not today.

'Come,' said Matteo, clearly enjoying the joke as he clapped his cousin on the shoulder, 'let's see if we can change that.'

She wasn't about to have her mind changed. Not when she was led into the large warehouse room, warm from the heat of at least four fiery kilns. Men worked there, doing whatever it was they did, but it was the chandeliers she noticed hanging from the warehouse ceiling, magnificently ornate and totally incongruous examples of the glassmakers' craft in the yawning airspace above her, that made up her mind.

So this was where her mother had found her inspiration for her disparate collection.

'If you would excuse me,' Luca said, 'I have to talk with my cousin. Would you mind waiting here for a few minutes? The glassmakers are about to put on a show. You might enjoy it.'

She raised her eyebrows. They did a show? Bring it on, she thought cynically, but still she welcomed this brief respite from Luca's presence. She welcomed the chance to breathe in air not tainted by the scent of him in space he didn't own. So she let herself be led to a small stand of tiered seating where a couple of other family groups were already seated, ready and waiting. There was space in the front row still, and she sat down and almost immediately wished she hadn't.

A toddler was sitting on the floor to her side, his mother

nursing an infant behind him, his father on the other side. The child looked up at Tina as she sat down, all huge eyed, mouth gaping, clearly wondering who she was to be invading their space.

He would be about the right age, she reasoned with a sizzle of recognition, feeling her stomach churn. *Their son would have been about the same age as this child.*

She looked away, thought about leaving, her palms suddenly damp with sweat before his big dark eyes drew her back like a magnet.

Dark eyes. Long lashes.

She had seen her baby's eyes open, and they had been dark too, like this child's. Like his father's.

The boy looked up at his mother, who was still busy tending the baby, before he looked back at her, blinking.

She smiled thinly, trying to will away the churning feeling in her gut, trying not to hurt herself more by thinking about their son growing up. But it was impossible.

She'd read the books, even before he was born. He would be two now. Full of life. Inquisitive. Driven to explore his new world. Sometimes challenging.

This child was no doubt all of those things and more. He was beautiful as he looked at her, his expression filled with question marks, and so distracted that the toy bear in his hands slipped from his grasp to the floor.

Without thinking, she reached down and scooped it up and for a moment, when he realised, he was all at war, mouth open with brimming outrage, little arms pumping fisted hands.

Until she handed back the toy and he looked almost shocked, before his face lit up with a smile as he clutched the teddy to his chest and squeezed it for all it was worth.

And that smile almost broke her heart.

Somehow she managed a tentative smile back, before

she had to wrench her eyes away from the child who reminded her of too much, from the child who was not hers.

From the ache in her womb that would never let her forget.

Tears pricked her eyes as she looked plaintively up at the high ceiling, to where the gaudily coloured chandeliers hung bold and totally shameless, mocking her, and she wished to hell she'd never come.

A collective gasp from the crowd and she turned to see one of the workmen wielding a rod tipped with molten glass dancing at its end. White-hot and fringed with red it glowed, fresh from the fire, stretching down long in its melted state before the artisan used a blunt implement and smacked it short.

The blob seemingly complied, buckling under the commands of a stronger force, melting back into itself.

From then on it was a dance of heat and fire and air, the sand turned molten glass, the rod spun and spun again over rails of steel, cooling the liquid magma until it was cool enough to be tweaked, a tweezer here and there to tug upon the glass and pull a piece outwards, a prod there to push it in, seemingly random.

She watched, but only half-heartedly, determined not to be impressed, finding a welcome distraction when she noticed the craftsman was wearing nothing on his feet. Molten glass and bare feet, she thought with horror, but happy to think of anything that would provide a distraction from the child alongside her, watching now from his father's knees in open-mouthed fascination.

She clasped her hands together tightly on her empty knees.

And then, as she watched, the bare-footed artisan's purpose became clear. A leg, she realised. Two legs, fine and slender. A roundness and then two more legs, with a twist to make a neck before the tweaking continued, the artist's movements now almost frenetic, working the glass before it cooled too much and set before he was finished.

She gasped when she realised. A prancing horse had emerged from the glass, with flowing mane and tail, and mouth open to the air, alive.

With a snap it was free, set down on a table where it stood balanced on its back legs and tail, front hooves proudly held high in the air.

She applauded louder than anyone and, when the glass had cooled, the artisan presented it to her.

'For the beautiful *signorina*,' he said with a bow, and she held the creation still warm in her hands, blinking away tears she hadn't realised she'd shed.

'It's magical,' she said, turning it in her hands, marvelling at the detail—the tiny eyes, the shaped hooves—the glass glinting in the light. 'You are a true artist.'

He bowed and moved away, back to the kiln for his next work of art.

She turned to the family alongside, who were all watching with admiration and held it out to the mother. 'You take it, please,' she said to the startled woman, pressing it into her hand. 'For your son, as a memento of this day.' *For the tiny child who could never receive her gift.*

The woman smiled and thanked her, the husband beamed and the little boy just blinked up at her with those beautiful dark eyes.

She couldn't stay. She fled. She strode away, feigning interest in a cabinet filled with numbered jars of coloured sand, with curled samples of glass hanging from a board, her back to the family, arms wound tight around her belly, trying to quell the pain. Trying not to cry.

'Did you enjoy the demonstration?' she heard Matteo ask. 'Did you like your souvenir?'

She had to take a deep breath before she could turn and face anyone, let alone them. She plastered a smile on her face that she hoped looked halfway to convincing.

'She gave it to the boy,' called the artist before she could say anything, gesturing with a grin towards the family, who were all still gathered around admiring it.

Luca laughed and slapped his cousin on the back. 'I told you she doesn't like glass.'

His cousin shrugged as a woman came running from another room, a large bunch of flowers in her arms that Matteo took from her, thanking her for remembering.

'Thank you for delivering these,' he said, handing Luca the flowers. 'Tell her I will come and see her soon.'

They left then, Matteo kissing her cheeks again as he bade them farewell, before the boat set off, the flowers lying inside on one of the long loungers.

'Who are they for?' she asked, curious, when Luca hadn't spoken for a while.

He looked straight ahead, his jaw grimly set. 'Matteo's mother. It's her birthday today but he has to take his daughter to the hospital for an appointment. He won't have time to visit her.'

'Where does she live?'

'There,' he said, pointing to a walled island she belatedly realised they were heading towards.

She shuddered. 'But surely that's…'

'Yes,' he said grimly. 'Isola di San Michele. The Isle of the Dead.'

CHAPTER TEN

THE brick walls loomed larger the closer they got, dark walls with white detail in which was set a Gothic gateway framing three iron gates.

Behind the walls the heavy green stands of cypress and pine did nothing to dispel the sense of gloom and foreboding.

She shivered.

'You must have been here before,' he said as the boat pulled alongside the landing.

She shook her head. 'No. Never.'

He frowned. 'I remember now. You didn't come to Eduardo's funeral.'

She sensed the note of accusation in his voice. 'I didn't make it in time. My flight had engine trouble and was turned back to Sydney. By the time I arrived, the funeral had already been held and Lily was barely holding herself together. There was no chance to pay my respects.'

He studied her, as if trying to assess if she was speaking the truth. Then he nodded. 'So you can pay your respects now, if you wish. Or you can stay with the boat if you prefer. Some people are not fond of cemeteries.'

'No,' she said, thinking nothing could be more forbidding than those imposing gates. Nothing could be worse than waiting to the accompaniment of the endless slap of water against the boat. 'I want to come, if you don't mind. I liked Eduardo. I'd like to pay my respects.'

Once again he paused, as if testing her words against what he knew of her. Then he gave a careless shrug. 'Your choice.'

Inside the imposing walls she was surprised to find the gloom fall away, replaced by a serenity that came with being in a well-tended garden. The sounds of motors and the chug of passing vaporettos seemed not to permeate the thick walls. Only birdsong and the crunch of gravel underfoot punctuated the silence. Here and there people tended graves, or just sat under the shade of the cypress trees in quiet reflection.

Luca led the way, past rows of neat graves adorned with marble cherubs and angels and freshly cut flowers. Everywhere she looked seemed to be bursting with the colour of fresh flowers.

He carried the bunch in his arms almost reverently. Flowers might soften a man, she thought, but not Luca. They only served to accentuate his overwhelming masculinity. Big hands, she thought, and yet so tender, the way they cradled the flowers.

Like he might cradle a child.

What would have happened had their child lived? If he had not been born too prematurely to be saved? Luca would not have welcomed the news that their one night of passion had ended with more than a face slap and that he was a father, but would he have wanted to meet his child? Would he have cradled him in those big hands as gently as he cradled those flowers and smiled down at him? Could he have loved him?

She dragged in air, shaking her head to escape the thoughts. There was no point in thinking what-ifs. Nothing to be gained but pain layered on pain.

Through different garden rooms they walked, and around them the closely packed lines of graves went on.

'It's quite beautiful,' she said softly, so as not to interrupt the pervasive sense of calm. 'So peaceful and well maintained. More like a garden than a cemetery.'

'Their families look after the graves,' he said, turning down a side path. 'They are all recently deceased. Space is limited, they can only stay here a few years before they are moved on.'

She remembered reading something of the sort. Probably around the time Eduardo had died. It seemed strange in one way, to disturb the dead and move their remains, but then again, who wouldn't want a chance to rest, at least a while, in such a beautiful setting, with the view of Venice just over the sea through the large iron gates?

'Matteo's mother died recently then?'

'Yes, two years ago, although space is not an issue for my family,' he continued, leading her towards a collection of small neoclassical buildings. 'The Barbarigo family has had a crypt here since Napoleonic times when the cemetery was created.'

Of marble the colour of pristine white sheep's wool, the crypt stood amongst others, but apart, more the size of a tiny chapel, she felt, no doubt demonstrating the power and wealth of his family through the centuries. Two praying angels, serene and unblinking, overlooked the gated entry, as if watching over those in their care, guarding who went in and who came out. Tiny pencil pines grew either side of the door, softening the look of the solid stone.

She took the flowers for him while he found the key and turned the lock. The door creaked open and cool air rushed out to meet them. He lit a candle either side of the door that flickered and spun golden light into the dark interior and took the flowers from her. And then he bowed his head for a moment before stepping inside.

She waited outside while he said some words in Italian, low and fast, she heard Matteo's name and she knew he was talking to his mother, passing on his cousin's message.

So true to his word.

So honourable.

So...*unexpected.*

She didn't want to hear any more. She breathed in deep and moved away, faintly disturbed that it should bother her.

It was peaceful and quiet in the gardens, dappled sunlight filtering through the trees, leaves whispering on the light breeze—so serene and unpopulated when compared to the crowded Centro, and she thought what an amazing place Venice was, to have so many unexpected facets, so many hidden treasures in such a tiny area.

She found another treasure amongst the trees—a gravestone she'd happened upon with a sculpture of a child climbing a stairway to heaven, fresh flowers tied onto his hand, an offering to the angel smiling down on him, waiting patiently for him at the top. She knelt down and touched the cool stone, feeling tears welling in her eyes for yet another lost child.

'Would you like to pay your respects now?'

She blinked and turned, wiping a stray tear from her cheek, avoiding the questions in his eyes. 'Of course.'

She followed him into the tiny room, the walls filled with plaques and prayers to those buried here over the years.

'So many,' she said, struck by the number of name plates. Flowers adorned a stone on one side—Matteo's mother, she reasoned.

'Eduardo is here,' he said, pointing to a stone on the other wall. 'His first wife, Agnetha, alongside.'

She moved closer in the tiny space, Luca using up so much of it, and wishing she had stopped to buy a posy of flowers to leave in the holder attached to the stone.

'I'll leave you to it,' he said, and moved to go past her. She stepped closer to the wall to let him, and it was then she noticed the names on the wall alongside. 'Your grandparents?' she asked and he stopped.

'My parents,' he said, stony-faced, pointing to a spot lower down on the wall. 'My grandparents are in the row below.'

He turned and left her standing there watching his retreating back. His parents? She looked again at the plaques, saw the dates and realised they'd died on the same day as each other nearly thirty years before.

Luca must have been no more than a few years old…

He was cold and distant when she emerged a few minutes later, his sunglasses firmly on, hiding his eyes. 'Ready to go?' he said, already shutting the door behind her, key to the lock.

'Luca,' she said, putting a hand to his arm, feeling his corded strength beneath the fine fabric of his shirt. 'I'm sorry, I had no idea that you'd lost both your parents.'

'It's not your fault,' he snapped.

'But you must have been so young. I feel your grief.'

He pulled his arm away. 'You feel my *what*? What do you know of my grief?'

The pain of loss sliced through her, sharp and deep as he walked away. 'I know loss. I know how it feels to lose someone you love.'

More than you will ever know.

'Good for you,' he said, and headed back towards the boat.

* * *

She found a box waiting for her on their return, on the table next to the bed. 'What's this?' she asked. 'I didn't order anything.'

'Open it up and find out,' he snapped, before disappearing into the bathroom, the first words he'd spoken since the cemetery. His silence hadn't bothered her during the journey home. Instead she'd welcomed it. It restored him to the role of villain. It balanced any glimpse of tenderness he might have shown—the reverent way he'd carried the flowers for his aunt—the quiet respect he'd shown when he'd entered the crypt.

It helped her forget how good he could make her feel in those moments where she could put aside thoughts that this was all a pretence, all a hoax.

And she didn't need to find things to like about him. She liked him being cold and hard and unapproachable and totally unforgivable.

It was better that way, she reasoned, as she tackled the box, looking for a way in.

Easier.

Necessary.

She found the end of one tape, ripping it from the seam of the box. Found another and swiped it off, opening a flap and then another layer of packing.

No!

Luca returned, his tie removed, his shirt half unbuttoned, exposing a glimpse of perfect chest. She tried not to look and failed miserably as he kicked off his shoes. And then she remembered the box.

'Where did this come from?'

He shrugged, and pulled his shirt off over his shoulders. 'You needed a new computer.'

'My computer is fine!'

'Your computer is a dinosaur.'

'You're a dinosaur!'

He paused, halfway to tugging off his trousers, and in spite of herself, she couldn't help but feel a primitive surge of lust sweep through her as she considered all the reasons he might be undressing, her mind lingering longingly on one particular reason… 'And there was me thinking you considered me a caveman.'

'Dinosaur. Caveman,' she said, trying not to notice the bulge in his underwear, trying to hide the faltering sound of her voice, 'It's all the same to me. All prehistoric.'

'Surely not the same,' he said with a careless shrug of his shoulders that showed off the skin over the toned muscle of his chest to perfection as he turned towards her. 'I would have thought a dinosaur would be lumbering and slow, and awkward of movement. Whereas a caveman could have more fun, don't you think, clubbing women over the head to drag them back to his cave to have his wicked way with them.'

She swallowed as he reached out a hand and stroked back the hair from her brow, winding a tendril of it around his finger. It was hard to think with a naked man standing in front of her, his proud erection almost reaching out to touch her. The caveman taunting her with his club. Making her hungry for him. 'You're right,' she said. 'You do the caveman thing particularly well.'

He smiled, and tugged on the curl of hair he had wound around his finger and drew her mouth closer to his. 'Surely not the only reason you're here, Valentina? Don't you enjoy being with me?'

'No,' she said, as he tugged on her hair and drew her still closer to his mouth. She held her breath. 'I'm counting down the days until I will be free.'

He smiled as if he didn't believe a word of it. 'In which

case,' he said, 'I'd better make the most of the days that are left.'

He pulled her face to his, his lips meshing with hers, insistent but still coaxing, inviting. And when he finally took his mouth away and she breathed in again it was to have her whole body infused with his scent and his taste.

He sighed. 'I'm sensing a problem here.'

It was impossible to make sense of his statement through the thick fog of desire clouding her brain. She licked her lips, tasting him on her tongue. 'What problem?'

He put a hand to her breast, cupped the aching weight of her through her dress. 'You're wearing far too many clothes.'

And she almost sighed with relief as she gave herself up into his kiss. Of all the problems in her life right now, an excess of clothes was one problem she could fix.

She'd imagined he wanted quick sex, fast and hot and furious. What he did was make love to her as if she were as fragile as that tiny glass horse.

His hands were slow and hot, his mouth scorchingly tender, his tongue an instrument of exquisite torture, and with all these things he spun a web of silken arousal around her, so that when she came, it wasn't wrenched from her or like being caught in the maelstrom of a storm, but almost like an admission. A confession. A giving up of herself to him.

She lay there panting, eyes open and afraid, staring at the ceiling.

Because sex was one thing. She could handle sex. Rationalise it. Treat it as a currency if she must. And she could stick it in that imaginary box under the bed in the cold light of day and shove the lid on and divorce herself from what was happening.

But giving herself up to him, losing herself in him when

she knew she was going to walk away empty-handed in a few short weeks, that scared her.

It wasn't just the sex that was making her feel this way, she knew. It was Luca himself who was changing. Showing concern when she felt shell-shocked on the boat—buying her a new computer because her old one was decrepit and inefficient. She knew he could afford it a million times over—she knew a few hundred euro would mean nothing to him—but it was the fact he'd even bothered that cut her deepest. For he didn't have to do those things. He didn't even need to find Lily an apartment when she already owed him so much.

Why did he have to appear half human when she wanted him to stay one hundred per cent monster? Why did he make it so hard to keep hating him?

She wanted to hate him.

She had to hate him.

She closed her eyes and sent up a silent entreaty to the gods. Because if she was ever to walk away from here with her head held high and her ego intact, she needed a reason to hate him.

Now, more than ever.

He should take more days off. He lay in bed listening to the rumble of his stomach—he would have to get up and have lunch soon, he supposed, before it turned on him and ate him alive—but there was something so utterly decadent about spending the middle of the day in bed. Especially when you had a good reason not to get out of it.

Like Valentina.

Idly he stroked her hair, listening to her soft breathing as she lay alongside him. He liked that she didn't feel the need to chat incessantly or ask him if it was good for him. What he liked even better was watching her eyes when she tipped over the edge. He shifted one leg, making room. God, but just thinking about it made him hard all over again.

He should do this more often.

Then again he could, at least for the next month. Or what was left of it. Plenty of time yet. Maybe even tomorrow. Thinking of which…

'I'm seeing your mother for lunch tomorrow,' he told her. 'Would you like to come with me?'

He felt her body tense. Wary. 'Why are you seeing my mother?'

'There are some papers to be signed, to finalise the transfer of the properties, the palazzo to me, the apartment to your mother.'

'And you want me there why exactly?' She sat up clutching the sheets to her chest, her golden eyes bright with argument and accusation. 'So you can gloat about how clever you are in front of us both?'

He blinked. Where had that come from? He'd thought her half asleep and she'd come out fighting.

'I thought you might like to see your mother.'

'Like hell, you did.' She clambered from the bed, dragging the bedding with her, uncaring that she was pulling the sheets from him at the same time. He grabbed hold and pulled back and the sheets snapped tight between them, caught in the crossfire, stopping her in her tracks.

She spun around, trapped in the tangle of sheets. 'You've got what you wanted. You've tricked my mother out of her house and why—' she waved her hand around the room '—when you obviously need another house like a hole in the head? You've got a playmate in your bed for a month because it's what *you* wanted and bugger what anyone else wants. What kind of sick person are you that you need to see us together like some kind of weird trophies?'

'I thought you'd like to see your mother,' he said through a jaw so stiff it could have been made with the same Istrian stone that formed the foundations of Venice itself. 'I know I'd give the world to be able to visit mine somewhere other than in a cemetery.'

She seemed to cave in before his eyes, the fight evaporating from her in a heartbeat. 'Luca,' she said softly, making a tiny move closer to the bed.

'Forget it,' he said, throwing off the sheet. 'It was a lousy idea anyway.'

He stormed off to the bathroom. *So much for enjoying a lazy day in bed.*

She didn't see Luca after that and she suspected he'd taken himself back to the office. She couldn't blame him. She'd jumped down his throat at the suggestion of visiting her mother as if it was for his spurious pleasure to have them in one room at the same time. But then, after such tender love-making, after his impromptu gift, the foundations under her seemed to be shifting and she'd needed to see him as the villain. She needed to reclaim the anger she'd felt when she'd marched into his study and practically demanded he make love to her.

Instead she almost felt sorry for the way she'd snapped at him.

She felt as if she'd let him down.

She felt as if she'd let herself down and failed some kind of test.

Crazy.

It wasn't as if she even cared what he thought of her. Her relationship with her mother was her business. He wouldn't know about the way they'd last parted, the argument that had sent her foaming mad to his door to almost dare him to take her. He wouldn't know the fractured history that lay festering like the worst of Venice's rotting piles between them.

But his gut-wrenching admission that he'd adore the opportunity to see his mother if only she were alive…

And regardless of what she thought of Luca, regardless of her justification for acting this way, it shamed her that her relationship with her own mother was so appalling.

Maybe there was just cause given the events of the last few days. But equally maybe, now that the dust had settled on the deal that had been made, perhaps while she was in Venice she should try to heal that rift, even just a little.

She heard her father's words come back to her, the rationale he'd used when she'd tried to wiggle out of coming to Venice in the first place.

'She's still your mum, love...you can't walk away from that.'

She's still your mum.

Maybe her dad was right. Maybe Luca was right. Maybe she should make an effort after all.

While she was still in Venice.

While she was lucky enough to still have a mother.

CHAPTER ELEVEN

'You're sleeping with him, then?'

Carmela had her back to Lily as she poured Tina a cup of coffee and threw her a sympathetic smile. Tina smiled back, appreciating the shared moment, regretting just a little that it had to be with the housekeeper rather than her mother, but then again, so far the visit had been surprisingly pleasant, given all the places it could have gone. They'd talked about the weather, and all about the new apartment Lily had visited just this morning. The biggest surprise had been finding the boxes and tissue paper scattered around the floor and learning that Lily was already sorting through her trinkets and thinking about which pieces to keep and which to sell through consignment with a local gallery owner. Tina's unexpected visit and coffee had come, she'd said, as a welcome respite.

So yes, it was progress of sorts, that Lily was accepting the inevitability of her move, even if there was remarkably little so far in the 'sell' box.

Of course, she was still railing on about the injustice of the whole thing and how could she possibly fit into a 'tiny' six-room apartment? But Tina was still glad she'd come, although she'd always figured she was never going to dodge the bullets for ever.

'It's true, Lily,' she admitted, wondering how many

other daughters were interrogated so openly on who they might be having sex with. But then, what was the point of avoiding the truth? It wasn't as if it was a secret. Everybody in Venice who wanted to know must know. 'I'm sleeping with Luca.'

Her mother sniffed as she sat back in her chair, and it was hard to tell whether she was pleased or disappointed. It was obvious she wasn't surprised. 'So, will it lead anywhere this time, do you think?'

That one was easier to answer. 'No.'

'You seem very sure.'

'I am sure.'

'What about Luca?'

'He's sure too. We're both sure. Can we just leave it at that?'

'Of course,' she said, putting her cup down on its saucer with barely a clink, and Tina hoped that was the full stop on that particular conversation.

But then her mother sighed. 'And yet,' she continued, 'it seems to me that for a man to come back for a second bite of the cherry, there must be something he finds… compelling about a woman. I mean, if a man comes looking for an encore, then surely he must be—'

'—looking for an easy lay. Leave it, Lily. I don't want to hear it. It's not leading anywhere. At the end of the month I walk away. Luca stays here.' She shrugged. 'End of story.'

'Well, it just seems such a waste. I don't know why you're not taking advantage of this arrangement. You could do a lot worse for a husband.'

Tina rubbed her forehead. Why did headaches so often coincide with visits to Lily? 'I'm not actually in the market for a husband.'

'But if something were to happen…'

'Like what? Like a baby, you mean? I'm hardly going

to fall pregnant. Not twice to the same man. I'm not that stupid.'

Her mother shrugged and stood, looking around the room. 'It's lovely you dropped by, but I should do some more sorting, I suppose. Luca is sending an army of men to do the chandeliers, but I don't want them touching my precious ornaments and there's such a lot to do.' She looked up at her daughter, a decided gleam in her eyes. 'I don't suppose you could help?'

Tina blinked, not really surprised that her mother would ask for help, more surprised she wanted her to help with her precious glass. 'Are you sure? I'm hardly going to be able to decide what you want to keep.'

'Oh, I'll decide what to keep,' she said, handing over a bundle of tissue. 'You can wrap.'

Tina smiled in spite of herself, liking her mother's succinct and pointed delineation of their duties.

And because it wasn't as if she didn't have time on her hands and because maybe it would offer them a chance to talk, maybe even to get to know each other a little better than they did, she agreed. 'You're on.'

Two hours later they'd barely made a dent on the collection and there was still precious little in the 'sell' box. Lily gave a sigh of contentment as if she'd just cleared an entire room when all they'd touched was a couple of side tables. 'Well, I think that's more than enough for the day.'

Tina looked around at what was left. At this rate it would take six months to clear the room, and then there was still the rest of the palazzo.

'Oh no,' her mother said, passing an ornament across. 'This one can go.'

Tina took it from her, a strange shivery sensation zipping out along her nerve endings. It was a prancing horse, just like the one the glassmaker had made at the factory. 'Luca took me to Murano this morning,' she said, holding the horse up to the light. 'They made one of these there while we watched.'

'I suspect that's probably where it came from. You might as well throw that one away. Nobody will buy it. They're a dime a dozen.'

Tina held the fragile glass horse. Thought of the boy with big brown eyes. Thought of another child who would have grown up with horses on the property, who would have ridden before he could walk, who would never get the chance to have his own horse.

Her son should have his own horse.

He deserved it.

'Can I have it?'

'Of course you can have it. But I thought you didn't like glass.'

'Not for me,' she said, already wrapping it carefully in layers of tissue. 'It's for…a friend.'

Carmela appeared, brandishing a tray with drinks for them both, and it was only then, thinking about the trip out to Murano, that she remembered what she had meant to tell her mother. And what she most wanted to ask. 'Oh, I meant to say, Luca's cousin asked him to drop off some flowers on the way home from Murano at Isola di San Michele. I took the opportunity to pay my respects to Eduardo.'

'Oh poor Eduardo,' Lily said on a sigh, looking wistfully out of the window. 'I do wish he hadn't left me like he did. None of this would be happening if he was still around.'

'Do you miss him?'

'Of course I do.' Lily sounded almost offended. 'Besides which, it's such a difficult business trying to find a new husband at my age. It's not easy when you're over fifty.'

She turned to her daughter. 'And that's why you should take your chances while you have them. You're young and pretty now, but it won't last, let me tell you.'

In spite of herself, Tina smiled. 'The World According to Lily' would make a fabulous book if her mother ever thought to write it. It wouldn't be a thick book, certainly, but part fashion advice, part self-help, with a big dollop of how to marry into money, and all put together by someone who had lived by its principles and—mostly—prospered, it would be a guaranteed bestseller.

But just right now she didn't want her mother's advice. What she wanted was her knowledge to answer a question that had been burning away in the back of her mind ever since her visit to the cemetery island.

'I visited the crypt, of course. I couldn't help but notice Luca's parents were both dead. I had no idea and he didn't seem to want to talk about it. What happened to them?' she ventured cautiously. 'Do you know?'

Lily sipped her gin, looking thoughtful. 'That was way before my time. Must be twenty years ago now. Maybe more. Somc kind of boating accident here on the lagoon if I remember rightly. It was the reason Luca came to live with him and Agnetha, of course.'

Tina's ears pricked up. 'He lived with Eduardo? Here?'

'He grew up with them. Of course he lived here, although he'd already moved on by the time we married. I'm sure Eduardo told me. Let me see…' She hesitated a while, blinking into the distance. 'From what I remember him saying, Matteo's family offered to take him in but because Eduardo and Agnetha had no children of their own, it was decided he should go to them.'

Tina drank in the details, holes in her knowledge filling with new information. Holes filling with even more questions.

So this had been his home then.

Where he had lived with his uncle and aunt before his aunt had died and before Lily had come along…

Was that why he seemed to resent Lily so much? Because by marrying Eduardo she had stolen his inheritance out from underneath him?

Was that the reason he was so desperate to get it back?

Where the hell was she?

Luca stood at the balcony overlooking the Grand Canal wondering where she'd disappeared to. Sure, they'd had an argument, but they had a deal. One month she'd agreed to and she'd been the one to set the term. He'd checked her wardrobe. The clothes seemed untouched, her pack still there stowed in one corner. So she hadn't just decided to take advantage of his absence and renege on their deal.

So where the hell was she?

Sightseeing?

Or just blowing off steam?

He looked out over the canal that was the lifeblood of Venice, feeling sick to his stomach and desperately scanning the faces on every passing vaporetto, searching for a glimpse of Australian sunshine in a size-eight package. She was out there somewhere. She had to be.

But where?

It wasn't an excuse for the way he'd behaved, Tina thought, as she hurried along the shadowed *calles*, even if it helped explain his actions. But it still didn't excuse them. To go the lengths he had gone to get back a house simply because in other circumstances it might one day have been his—it made no sense.

Lamps were coming on around her. She looked up at the darkening sky, thinking that she'd stayed much longer at her mother's than she'd intended to, so arriving back at Luca's palazzo much later than she'd expected, the tiny horse tucked safe and sound in a stiff shopping bag Carmela had found for her.

She buzzed the bell on the gate and it clicked open, and it wasn't Aldo who greeted her at the door, but Luca.

She swallowed. After the bitter way they'd parted earlier, she wasn't sure how happy he'd be to see her.

And after what she'd learned about him, she wasn't sure she knew what to say. He saved her from having to decide.

'Have you been shopping?' he asked, looking at the bag in her hand, and after the way they'd parted she couldn't help but notice a tense note in his voice; couldn't help but feel a tinge of resentment that there would be something wrong if she had gone shopping. 'Aldo said you've been gone for hours.'

'No.' She started working herself up into righteous indignation. 'As it happens, I've been helping Lily pack some things. I didn't realise I was expected to ask for permis—'

'You were at your mother's the whole time?'

She blinked up at him. 'Do I know another Lily in Venice?'

He regarded her through eyes half-shuttered, assessing. 'You surprise me, Valentina. You constantly surprise me. You seemed so vehemently opposed to meeting with your mother.'

'I don't know why you should be so surprised,' she said, hitching up her chin as she made a move to walk past him. 'We're practically strangers. You don't know the first thing about me.'

'Don't I?' he asked, lashing out a hand to encircle her wrist, blocking off her path with the subtle shift of his body, a body built for sex, the subtle movement enough to remind her of all the heated moves it was capable of. 'And yet I know how to make the lights in your eyes explode like fireworks. I know how to turn you molten with one flick of my tongue. I know what you like and I'm thinking that's probably slightly more than the first thing about you, wouldn't you agree, Valentina?'

He was so intense. Too intense, the way his words worked in concert with his eyes, getting under her skin and worming their way into her very bones. She could scarcely breathe in his presence, so focused was his gaze upon her, the fingers wrapped around her wrist so tightly clenched.

'You can call me Tina, you know,' she whispered, desperately needing a change of subject, her words almost crackling in the heated air of his proximity. 'You don't have to do the whole Valentina thing every time. Tina works for me just fine.'

He blinked. Slowly. Purposefully. 'Why would I call you something short and sharp, when your full name is so lush and sensual? When your full name holds as many seductive hills and valleys as your perfect body?'

She couldn't answer. There were no words to answer. Not when instead of counteracting his intensity, she had inadvertently ramped it up tenfold.

'No,' he stated, with an air of authority that both infuriated her and rocked her to the soles of her feet as he pulled her close for his kiss, 'Tina does not work for me at all.'

They dined in that night, but only after they'd made love late into the night. She couldn't tell whether it was anger or relief that tinged his love-making but, whatever it was, it gave yet another nuance to the act of sex. Worst of all, it gave her reason for not hating the fact she had to be here.

Later, when still she couldn't sleep worrying about it, she slipped from the bed to stand in the big *salone* and look out through the set of four windows overlooking the Grand Canal, watching the reflection of light onto water.

Watching the seemingly endless activity of a water-borne society while her mind wandered and wondered.

What was happening to her?

She'd spent one night with him three years ago and she hadn't seen him since. After what had happened, she hadn't wanted to see him again. But sex with Luca was like an addiction that had been suppressed, a drug refused, and one taste had sent her back to that feverish place where need was paramount and hunger would not be denied.

And maybe, if she was honest with herself, she hadn't lived those three years at all.

Maybe she'd only existed in the shadow of one perfect night, one perfect night that had all too rapidly turned toxic.

Maybe she'd only barely survived.

Despite her misgivings, they seemed to slip into a routine after that. Tina would go and help her mother sort her belongings in preparation for the upcoming move. Some days Lily would be more receptive to her help than others, but she felt that finally they were building some kind of fragile rapport as they worked room by room through the maze of glass.

She still couldn't forgive her mother entirely for landing her in Luca's bed, but neither could she honestly say she wasn't enjoying the experience—at least a little.

Well, maybe more than just a little.

There was something about being with Luca that made her feel alive and sexy, vibrant and feminine, and all at the same time. It was no hardship to be seen on his arm, to feel the envy from other women, envy she enjoyed all the more because she knew it would be short-lived. It was no hardship to feel his heated glances and know what was on his mind.

And the sex was good too.

Just sex, she'd remind herself, putting the lid back on that imaginary box and tucking it under the bed when Luca went to work in the mornings.

Just sex. And in a few short weeks she would return home and it would all be a distant memory. Why shouldn't she enjoy it while it lasted?

A week after she'd arrived in Venice, she turned up at her mother's house. She heard Lily the moment she entered the rapidly emptying palazzo. The echoing torrent of French coming from upstairs almost had her turning her back and fleeing, until she realised from the few impassioned words she could understand that it wasn't fury her mother was radiating, but delight.

'What's going on?' she asked Carmela, peering suspiciously up the stairs as she peeled off her jacket.

The housekeeper took it to slide over a hanger. 'She's talking to the gallery owner, the one who has agreed to take her glass on consignment. There must be good news.'

Lily came bounding down the stairs a minute later, her eyes bright, looking more like a schoolgirl than a fifty-something woman. But then she'd changed her hair too, Tina realised, so that now it framed her face more softly, stripping years from her face.

'What is it?' Tina asked.

'You'll never guess. Antonio has a contact in London. They're doing a display of Venetian glass and they want everything I can send. Antonio thinks it will make a fortune!'

'Antonio?'

Her mother actually looked coy, her hands tangling in front of her. 'Signore Brunelli, of course, from the gallery handling the sale.'

Tina glanced across at the housekeeper, who gave a

quick nod before bustling back in to pack up the last of the kitchen, and suddenly her mother's change of mood in the last few days made some kind of sense.

And even though that was what her mother did, finding her next partner with unerring precision, Tina couldn't help but smile at seeing her so happy. 'That's great, Lily.'

'That's not all,' her mother continued, her eyes sparkling. 'He wants me to come to London with him. He says I will be the bridge between the Venetian and the British, unifying the collection and giving it purpose. He's taking me to dinner tonight to talk about the details. He thinks we should be there for a month at least.'

She took a deep breath, looking around her as if trying to work out what she'd been up to before the call. 'Well, I guess we should get to work. It will be such a relief when it's all done.'

Relief? The one hundred and eighty degree change in her mother's mood from when she'd first arrived in Venice would be something worth celebrating if only Tina wasn't left with a bad taste in her mouth. Where was her relief? Where was her upside?

She'd been the one to make the sacrifice here—forced to spend a month with a man she hated while her mother not only got on with her life but prospered. Where was the justice?

'Don't you mind about the move any more? When I came here, you were so angry with Luca, with me, with your situation—with everything! How can you be so happy now?'

'Don't you want me to be happy?' There were shades of the Lily of old in her question, shades of indignation that once would have been the spark set to combust into something more.

'Of course I do, Lily. It's just that—' She threw her

hands out wide in frustration. 'It's just that I'm still stuck with Luca while you seem to be getting on with your life now as if this is nothing but a minor inconvenience.'

'Oh, Valentina.' Her mother nodded on a sigh. 'Please don't be angry with me. Sit down a moment.' She pulled her down alongside her on a sofa. 'I have something I should say to you—Carmela will tell me off if I don't.'

She frowned. The idea of Carmela reprimanding her mother was too delicious. 'What is it?'

Lily shook her head and took her daughter's hand. 'I know we haven't always been close, but I do know I treated you appallingly when you arrived. Even before you arrived. But I was so scared,' she implored, 'don't you see? I had nobody else to turn to and Luca was threatening to throw me out onto the streets and I believed him. I had no idea he would come up with the apartment—he never hinted. I believed he would do his worst.'

Tina nodded. 'I know.' And it was good to be reminded of how afraid they'd both been; of how Luca had ruthlessly manipulated them both to get what he wanted. It was such a short time ago and yet just lately it had been so much harder to remember. 'It's okay.'

'No,' she said. 'Don't say anything. This is hard for me and you have to listen. I'm sorry I haven't been a better mother to you. I'm sorry I got you involved in all my mess. But please don't begrudge me this slice of happiness. It's been so long since I felt this way about a man.'

'I'm happy for you, Lily, truly I am. But please be careful. You've only just met the man, surely?'

Her mother smiled and shrugged, looking into the middle distance as if she was seeing something that Tina couldn't. 'Sometimes that's all it takes. Little more than a heartbeat and you know that he's the one.'

'Is that how you felt with Dad, then? And Eduardo and Hans and Henri-Claude?'

Lily dropped her head and sighed. 'No. I'm ashamed to say it's not. I'm not proud of my track record, but this time it's the real thing, Valentina. I know it. And what I want for you is to know this same happiness. Is there no chance that you and Luca—'

Tina stood, unable to sit, needing to move. 'No. None.'

'Are you sure? Has he said nothing about staying?'

'Of course I'm sure, and no he hasn't. Because he won't. He's not a man to change his mind, Lily, and I don't want him to. In fact, I can't wait for this month to be over. I can't wait to get home and see Dad again.'

'Oh. I see. It's a shame, though. Especially after what you've been through, losing his baby and everything. Surely he realises he risks putting you through all that again.'

'He doesn't know!' she said, wishing to God she'd never told her mother about her baby. 'And he won't know. There's no point in him knowing. It's...history.'

'But surely it's his history too.'

'It's too late for that,' she said, running her hands through her hair and pulling her ponytail tight, pulling her fraying thoughts tight with it and plastering a smile on her face that touched nowhere near her heart. 'Now, where do we start today?'

'You didn't have to blackmail me to get my mother out of the palazzo, you know.'

Luca and Tina had made love long into the night and now they lay spooned together in that dreamy place between sex and sleep while their bodies hummed down from the heights of passion.

He pulled her closer and pressed his lips to her shoulder. 'What do you mean?'

'All you had to do was wave that gallery owner, Antonio Brunelli in front of her nose and she would have done anything you wanted in a heartbeat.'

He stilled alongside her. 'Lily and Antonio Brunelli? Is that so?'

'I suspect she already believes herself in love with him. So you see, you could have saved yourself all this trouble if you'd just introduced her to Antonio in the first place.'

He breathed out on a sigh, warm air fanning her skin. 'I never realised it would be that easy or maybe I would have.'

It irked her that she felt deflated. She shouldn't feel deflated. She hadn't wanted to be here after all. 'So maybe you should have.'

'Ah,' he said softly, cupping one breast so tenderly in his warm hand, 'but then I wouldn't have you.'

She squeezed her eyes shut, trying to sort out the tangle of her thoughts. He meant he wouldn't have her for sex, he meant. Nothing more.

It was ridiculous to imagine he meant any more than that when his intentions had always been so clear from the start.

All the same, she wished she hadn't pushed him. She wished she'd left him saying maybe he wouldn't have bothered. She wished she didn't secretly yearn for things to be different.

And she wished to hell she understood why she wanted them to be so.

CHAPTER TWELVE

TINA checked her watch and pulled her new computer onto her lap. As much as she'd protested when Luca had given it to her, she loved what it could do. Talking face to face with her father for one. It would be around eight p.m. at home now and Mitch would be finished work and hanging around the study waiting for her call. It was good to hear how everything was going on the farm. It grounded her, and made her realise how much a fantasy her life in Venice was.

They talked of the now completed shearing, which had gone better than anticipated and Tina was already calculating what the bales of wool would bring in when she heard it in the background—a female voice.

'Who's there with you, Dad? I didn't know you had company or I wouldn't have called.'

'Oh, it's just Deidre, love. By the way, when are you coming home?'

'Deidre? Deidre Turner, you mean? But surely the shearing's finished. Why's she still there?'

'She's…er…she's helping out with the cooking, just while you're away. Now, when are you coming home?'

'Oh Dad,' she said, distracted by thoughts of Deidre Turner and what might really be going on at home while she was away. Deidre was a widow, she knew, her childhood sweetheart husband of twenty years killed in a tractor accident a few years back. She'd never so much as looked at another man. Or so Tina had thought. But maybe she was looking now.

She smiled as she framed her next question. 'Are you sure you really want me home?' adding before he could answer, 'Don't worry, Dad. There's ages yet. I'll let you know when I've booked.'

'Tina, you've already been away three weeks. If you don't book a flight soon, you won't get one.'

Shock sizzled down her spine.

Three weeks?

That couldn't be right, could it? No. Surely it was more like two?

But when she looked at the calendar she saw he was right. Eight days she had left.

Eight nights.

And then she would be free to leave, her end of the bargain satisfied.

'Tina? You okay?'

She blinked and turned back to her father. 'Sorry, Dad,' she said, shaking her head. 'Of course you're right. I'll book. I'll let you know.'

She ended the call, stunned and bewildered. How could she have so lost track of time? When she'd first arrived in Venice she couldn't wait to get away. But now—when she could count the days and nights remaining on her fingers—now the thought of leaving ripped open a chasm in her gut and left her feeling empty and bereft.

One month she'd agreed to and now that month was nearly up and, as much as she looked forward to seeing her father again, the thought of leaving Venice…

Leaving Luca...

Oh God, no, she thought, don't go there. She'd always

been going to leave. She'd been the one to set that condition and Luca had agreed. He expected her to go. Clearly she was simply getting used to dressing up in beautiful clothes and living as if she belonged here. But she didn't belong here. She didn't belong with Luca. She would book her flight home and think about how good it would be to see her father again. She'd feel better once she'd booked.

She was sure she would.

'I booked my flight home today.'

Luca stilled at the cabinet where he was pouring them both a glass of sparkling prosecco. The pouring stopped. This wasn't how he'd planned tonight to go. The trinket in his pocket weighed heavy like the ball in his gut. 'So when do you go?'

'A week tomorrow. I was lucky enough to get a seat. Flights are pretty fully booked this time of year.'

Lucky.

The word stuck in his throat. Was she in such a goddamned hurry to leave? He'd thought she was enjoying their time together. She'd certainly given him that impression in bed.

And while he'd always planned to dump her, the thought that she might hang around a little longer would have meant putting off the inevitable just that bit longer too.

But now she'd booked, he'd have to bring his plans forward. A shame when she'd provided such a useful distraction from the working day.

He finished pouring his drink and turned around, handing her a glass. 'Very fortunate,' he said, raising his glass to her. 'In which case I propose a toast—to the time we have left. May we use it wisely.'

She blinked up at him as she sipped her wine, her amber eyes surprisingly flat, with less sparkle than the wine in her glass, and he wondered at that. Wondered if she'd been hoping he'd changed his mind and might ask her to stay.

He might have. But not now, not now she'd taken the initiative.

'And we might as well start tonight,' he said, putting down his glass to reach into his pocket. 'I have a surprise for you. Tonight I have tickets to the opera, and I want you to wear this...' From a black velvet box, he extracted the string of amber beads, a large amber pendant in the middle that glinted like gold as he laid it over her hand.

Her eyes grew wide. 'It's beautiful,' she said.

'The colour matches your eyes.' He turned her gently, securing the gems around her throat, turning her back around to see. He nodded. 'Perfect. As soon as I saw them, I knew they would be perfect for you. Here, there are earrings too.'

She cupped them in her hand. 'I'll take good care of them.'

He shrugged, reaching for his wine, wanting to fill this empty hole in his gut with...*something*. 'They are yours. Now, we need to leave in half an hour. It's time to get dressed.'

Luca's unexpected gift had thrown her off balance, the gems sitting fat and heavy upon her neck, weighing her down, anchoring her to a false reality.

Nothing in Venice was real, she decided, as she caught a final glimpse of herself in the floor to ceiling gilt-framed mirror. Nothing was as it seemed.

Least of all her.

In an emerald-coloured gown, the amber necklace warm and golden at her throat, she looked as if she could have stepped out of a fairy tale, a modern day princess about to be swept off to the ball with the charming prince.

As for Luca, just one glance at him in his dark Italian designer suit, all lean, powerful masculinity, waiting for her to take his arm, was enough to make her heart pound.

She'd be gone in a week.

Returned to the dusty sheep and their wide brown land.

Gone.

Why did that thought set her heart to lurch and her stomach to squeeze tight when home was where her heart was? What was happening to her?

'Ready?' he said, a kernel of concern in his dark eyes, and she smiled up at him tremulously.

'I've never been to the opera before,' she offered by way of explanation. 'Never to a live performance at a real opera house.'

'You've never seen *La Traviata* then?'

She shook her head, never more conscious of their different lives and backgrounds. 'I don't know anything about it.'

'And did you never see the film, *Moulin Rouge*?'

'I saw that, yes.'

'Then you know the story. It was based on the opera.'

'Oh,' she said, remembering, 'Then it's a sad story. It seemed so unfair that Satine should find love when it was already too late, when her time was already up.'

He shrugged, as if it was of no consequence. 'Life doesn't always come with happy endings. Come,' he said, slipping her wrap around her shoulders, 'let's go.'

The entrance to the opera house at the Scuola Grande di San Giovanni Evangelista was set inside a small square, made smaller this night by the glittering array of people who stood sipping prosecco in the evening air. Heads turned as Luca arrived, heads that took her in almost as an afterthought, heads that nodded as if to say, *She's still here then.*

Tina smiled as Luca made his way through the crowd, stopping here and there for a brief word, always accompanied by a swift and certain appraisal of the woman on his arm. It didn't bother her any more. She was getting used to the constant appraisals, the flash of cameras going off around them. She was getting used to seeing the pictures of them turning up in the newspapers attending this function or that restaurant.

What they would say when she was gone didn't matter. Except there was that tiny squeeze of her stomach again at the thought of leaving.

She would miss this fantasy lifestyle, the dressing up, being wined and dined in amazing restaurants in one of the most incredible cities in the world.

But it wasn't just that.

She would miss Luca.

Strange to think that when at first she had been desperate for the month to be over, desperate to get away. But it was true.

She would miss his dark heated gaze. She would miss the warmth of his body next to hers in bed at night, the tender way he cradled her in his arms while he slept, his breathing slow and deep.

She would miss his love-making.

For there was no point pretending it was "just sex" any longer.

No point pretending it was something she could compartmentalize and lock away in a box and shove under the bed. It was too much a part of her now. It had given her too much.

'Just sex' could never feel this good.

He led her inside the building, more than five hundred

years old and showing it, the wide marble steps to the first floor concert hall worn with the feet of the centuries, gathering in this place to listen and enjoy and celebrate music and song.

And art, she realised, looking around her.

The ceiling soared, the height of another two storeys above them, held up by massive columns of marble, the panels of the walls filled with Renaissance art featuring saints and angels and all manner of heavenly scenes, framed in gold.

Here and there the floor dipped a little, rose again as they walked; here and there a corner looked not quite square, a column not quite straight.

Unconsciously she clutched Luca's arm a little tighter as he led her to her seat, fazed by the sensation of the floor shifting beneath her feet, as if the weight of the marble was pushing the building into the marshy ground beneath.

'Is something wrong?' Luca asked beside her, picking up on her unease.

'It is safe, isn't it? The building, I mean.'

He laughed then, a low rumble of pleasure that echoed into her bones. 'The opera house has been here since the thirteenth century. I'm sure it will manage to remain standing a couple more hours.' And at the same time she realised he was laughing at her, he squeezed her hand and drew her chin to his mouth for an unexpected press of his lips. 'Do not be afraid. I assure you it is safe.'

Was it?

Breathless and giddy, she let herself be led to their seats.

Was it simply the ground shifting beneath her feet, or was it something more?

Please, God, let it be nothing more.

Heels clicked on marble floors and then stilled, the hum

of conversation dimming with the lights until finally it was time.

The music started, act one of the famous opera, and in the spacious concert hall the music soared into the heavens, giving life to the angels and the cherubs in the delicate stuccoes, taking the audience on a heavenly journey.

The singers were sublime, their voices filling the air, and it was impossible not to be carried along with the tragic story of Violetta, as she discovered the heroine was called in this original version, and her lovers, warring for the affections of the dying courtesan. And yet, through it all, she had never been more aware of Luca's heated presence at her side, at the touch of his thigh against hers, to the brush of his shoulder against hers.

She wanted to drink in that touch while she still could. She wanted to imprint it on her memory so she could take it out and remember it on the long nights ahead, when she was home and Venice and Luca was a distant memory.

The story built, the young lovers united at last, only to be forced apart by family.

She seemed more acutely aware of Luca than ever. The score was in Italian and, while she caught only a snatched phrase here and there, she understood the passion, she felt the pain and the torment.

How ironic, she thought, that he had brought her here tonight, to hear the story of a fallen woman for whom love was painful and hard won and ultimately futile.

Had he brought her here as some kind of lesson?

That life, as he had told her before they had left the palazzo, did not always have a happy ending?

The third act came to an end. Despite bursts of elation, bursts of happiness, Violetta's death had always been a tragedy waiting to happen.

She felt tears squeeze from her eyes at the finale, wondering why this story affected her so deeply. It was just a story, she told herself, just fiction. It wasn't true.

And yet she felt the tragedy of Violetta's wasted love to her core.

Why?

When in a few days, little more than a week, she would be free to return home.

Free.

There was no chance she would end up like Violetta. She wouldn't let it.

And yet, increasingly, she felt herself tipping, tripping over uneven ground, trying pointlessly to keep her balance and all the while hurtling towards that very same finale.

'What did you think?' he asked her as they rose to their feet, the audience wild, celebrating a magnificent performance. 'Did you understand it?'

And she sniffed through her tears as she nodded and clapped as hard as anyone.

More than you will ever know.

That night sleep eluded her. She lay awake listening to the sound of Luca's steady breathing, the sound of the occasional water craft passing and all overlaid by the tortured ramblings of her own mind.

In the end she gave up on sleep entirely, slipped on the jade silk gown and resumed her vigil at the windows, feeling strangely forlorn and desolate as she stared out over the wide canal, drinking in a view that would all too soon be nothing more than a fond memory.

And even though she tried to tell herself it was the opera that was to blame for her mood, she knew it was more. She knew it came from deep inside herself.

She sighed as the light curtains puffed in the breeze and floated around her. The evenings were distinctly cooler now, clouds more frequent visitors to the skies blocking the moon and sun, the wind picking up and carrying with it the scent of a summer in decline. She stood there at the open windows and drank it all in, building an album in her mind of the scents and sounds and sights that she would be able to pull out and turn the pages of when she was home.

Next week.

Anguish squeezed the air from her lungs.

Suddenly it was all too soon.

She heard a movement behind her. She heard a noise like something tearing and she made to turn her head.

'Don't turn,' he instructed.

'What are you doing?'

'What I knew I had to do when I saw you standing framed in the window,' he said, and something in his voice gave her a primitive thrill, a delicious sense of anticipation that made her turn her face back towards the darkened canal. 'Keep watching the water, and the water craft.'

'As you wish,' she said, a smile curling her lips as she felt the heat at her back as he came close and joined her on the balcony, a smile that turned distinctly to thoughts of sex when she felt him hard and ready between them. She sighed at the feel of him. God, she would miss this. She put a hand to the nearest curtain, meaning to pull it closed.

'Leave it,' he said. 'Leave the curtains. I want your hands on the balcony.'

And with a rush of sizzling realisation, his meaning became crystal clear. 'But we can't…not here…not on the balcony…with the boats.'

He dropped his mouth to the curve of her neck, kissing her skin, his teeth grazing her flesh, stoking a fire that burned much, much lower. 'Yes. Here, on the balcony. With the boats.'

She gasped. 'But—'

'Keep watching,' he said when she tried to turn, to remonstrate, but he was right behind her and she was pinned up against the cool marble balustrade, cool at her front, hot where he pressed against her back, as another craft chugged slowly by. 'They can't see us,' he said, as she felt the slide of her gown up her calves, his fingertips tickling the sensitive skin at the back of her knees, making her shiver in her secret pleasure. 'Even if anyone looks, all they will see will be shadows at a window. One shadow, where you and I join.'

The craft disappeared, the chug of its engines replaced by the slap of water against the foundations as air curled around her legs and his fingers eased the silk of her gown higher to find the cleft between her legs and slide one long finger along that sensitive seam, teasing with just a whisper of a touch, making her nerve endings scream with impatience.

'You're beautiful,' he whispered against her throat, his teeth grazing her skin, his finger delving deeper, and it was all she could do to keep her knees locked in place and not sag boneless to the balcony floor.

Unfair, she thought on a whimper as she felt herself being angled over the balustrade, felt the delicious press of his hardness at her very core, that he could do this to her, reduce her to a mass of tangled nerve endings that spoke the same message—need. Pure and simple, unadulterated need.

For she needed him inside her just as she needed the oxygen in her lungs. Needed him inside her and all around her just as she needed the sun and moon and sky.

He gave her what she needed, pressing into her in one fluid stroke that filled her in all the places that ached but one. Because there was no filling the ache in her heart.

For in a few short days she was leaving. And she couldn't bear the thought of it.

Couldn't bear the thought of leaving Luca.

God help me, she thought, as he moved inside her, taking her once again to that amazing place, a tear sliding unbidden down her cheek, but this was more than just need.

I love him.

CHAPTER THIRTEEN

HER period arrived midway through the next day and Tina couldn't suppress a bubble of disappointment. Now there was a way to celebrate their final few days together.

Not.

But there was an upside of course, she reasoned, because at least it meant that this time she wouldn't be going home with any surprises.

And why that thought didn't please her more than it did made no sense at all.

She rested her head against the bathroom mirror, feeling the familiar ache deep inside, a niggling question she'd been avoiding all the time she'd been in Venice now gnawing at her to be noticed.

Should she tell Luca about their lost baby?

It had been so easy to avoid the question at first, when she'd thought she'd never see him again. It had been easy when she'd arrived in Venice, and when mutual resentment and a deal the devil would have been proud of had been the thing that bound them together. It had been so easy to ask herself what would be the point of rehashing the past by telling him? What purpose would it serve? It wasn't as if she owed him after what he had done.

But now, after these last weeks with him, she wondered how long she could avoid telling him—that there was a headstone on a grave in Australia with his child's name on it.

How could she not tell him?

Wouldn't she want to know if their positions were reversed?

Wouldn't she have a right to know?

She peeled herself away from the bathroom mirror and drifted through the bedroom. Strange, she mused, how love could change your view on the world.

Because suddenly there were no more reasons to avoid the truth. She wanted Luca to know everything.

And even though the news would no doubt come as a shock and he would be entitled to be angry at her for not telling him earlier, she didn't want secrets between them.

Not any more.

She'd lived with this secret too long.

As for her love? Well, that would hardly be welcome news either—for had Luca once tried to talk her out of booking her flight home?

That was one secret she could keep.

Besides which, she would have more than enough trouble working out how to tell him the first.

Luca scanned the papers and swore out loud. His assistant came running. 'I thought you said you'd checked these signatures!' he yelled. 'Didn't you notice there was one missing?'

The assistant dithered and flapped and promised to fix whatever was wrong right away and Luca swept his offer aside and snatched up the papers himself. 'I'll do it!' he growled. He could do with a walk. He'd been in a hell of a mood all day and he couldn't really put his finger on why.

Yes, he could!

He didn't want her to damned well go, that was why.

She'd melted into his arms last night on the balcony as if she'd been made of honey, golden and sweet, and he'd never wanted to let her go.

But he had to. He had no choice. There was no other choice.

And in a way he was grateful for his flustered assistant for finding him something to legitimately take his anger out on, because he'd been spoiling for a fight ever since he'd left Valentina this morning.

What better reason? Because without Lily's signature in that spot on that contract, the palazzo was still legally hers, regardless of all the other papers that had been signed and countersigned. Regardless of the fact that his people had been working on the palazzo to shore it up and get it stable before the real work began. And despite the fact that she now owned the apartment lock, stock and barrel.

Maybe it was his fault for taking too much time off lately to spend with Valentina and trusting his staff to do the jobs they should, and that thought didn't make him any happier.

He needed that signature.

Carmela let him into the apartment and showed him to the *salone*, where he paced its length while he waited. He glanced at the caller ID when his cellphone rang and pressed the receive button. 'Matteo. *Sì!*'

He grunted when Matteo complimented him on the photograph of him and Valentina at the opera in the on-line papers this morning. He didn't want to be reminded of Valentina, even if his plan to have their romance followed by the papers and have them openly speculating about the possibilities of a new Barbarigo bride had worked supremely well. 'But that's not why I'm calling,' Matteo continued. 'I was wondering if you and Valentina would come to dinner on Friday evening.'

'*Sì*. I can make it, but Valentina will be gone by then.'

'Gone? Gone where?'

'Home.'

'A shame. So when is she coming back?'

'Never.'

'Why? I like her, very much. It's time you settled down, Luca. She seems perfect for you.'

Luca laughed. 'Forget it, Matteo, I'm not looking for a wife. Least of all someone like Valentina.' He tried to remember why. Tried to dredge up all the reasons why it had once seemed so true. Tried to bundle them all up into some kind of argument that might convince his cousin. Failed, and changed tack. 'This is sport, nothing more. Rest assured, she won't be in Venice come Friday. I'm making sure of it.'

He heard a polite cough behind him and turned. 'You wanted to see me?' Lily offered, one eyebrow arched, her fingers laced elegantly together in front of her.

He cut the call and slipped his phone into his pocket and pulled out an envelope from another. 'I have some paperwork for you to sign,' he said, wondering how much she'd heard. 'It seems you missed a signature before.'

'I spoke to Valentina yesterday,' she said, ignoring him as he placed the paper down on a nearby desk and held out a pen for her. 'Her flight is on Monday. What exactly is this "sport" you are planning?'

'Who says I was talking about Valentina? Now, if you would just sign here…'

'I heard what you said. What game are you playing, Luca?'

'Just sign the form, Lily.'

'Tell me. Because if you are planning on hurting my daughter…'

'You expect me to believe you, of all people, care? You,

who shipped her out here to bail you out of the mess you'd made of your own life? You, who would sell your daughter to the devil if it profited you?'

'Guilty,' she said, 'on all charges,' surprising him with her easy admission. 'But these last few weeks I've got to know my daughter properly, and I like her. I like her a lot, so much so that I will miss her terribly when she's gone. And I know I have no right to even ask, but I so wish she did not have to go.'

The world had gone mad! Nothing was as he had thought it would be. Nothing was how it should be. Valentina was going. He should feel happy. He would be happy. Just as soon as this black cloud lifted from his shoulders.

But Lily, he'd expected to be happy too—a new house, money, a new man—the Lily he knew should not need her daughter's presence a moment longer. And yet here she was practically despairing that she was leaving.

What the hell was happening?

'Promise me you won't hurt her, Luca,' Lily inserted into the weighted silence. 'Please promise me that.'

And the frustrations of the last twenty-four hours—the news that Valentina was leaving—a night at the opera with a woman who looked like a goddess followed by a night of exquisite love-making—the missed signature—all coalesced to form one molten rage. 'I'm not promising anything!'

'But she doesn't deserve to be hurt. She's done nothing—'

'You've got no idea what she did! This is no more than she deserves!'

And her mother grew claws before his eyes. 'Oh, I'd say it's clearly much less than she deserves, after the misery you put her through.'

'What are you talking about? I gave her the best night of her life!'

'You clearly gave her one hell of a lot more than that!'

The thump in his temples thundered out a warning that pieced together in ugly sequence in his brain. 'What do you mean? What are you saying?'

She shook her head, hand over her mouth. 'I'm sorry, I shouldn't have said that. If you don't know, then maybe there's a reason for that.'

A reason for not knowing?

Not knowing *what*?

What the hell had he given her?

Why wouldn't he be told?

Unless...

And as his blood surged loud in his ears, a drum call to war, a drum call to action, the thumping beat of his heart pounded out the only possible answer and he felt sick to his very core.

'Are you saying Valentina was pregnant—pregnant with my child?'

Lily stiffened where she stood, but her eyes were wide and fearful, the fingers of one hand clutching at her throat. 'I didn't tell you that.'

He turned, already on his way out. Already with one mission in mind.

'Luca—wait! Listen to me!'

But there was no waiting. No listening. Because for three weeks he had harboured this woman in his house, treated her like a princess, made love to her like she actually meant something, and all the time she had been harbouring the ugliest of secrets.

Had she been laughing all this time? At him not knowing? At him, thinking he had the upper hand when all the while she'd already exacted her revenge in the worst possible way?

Now it was time to find out the truth.

The truth about what she had done to his child!

CHAPTER FOURTEEN

HE FOUND her curled into a window seat tapping away on the laptop, her hair hanging loose, the ends flicking free around her face, and wearing *gelato*-coloured clothes, looking like innocence personified.

Innocence?

Oh no.

He felt like growling.

Once he might have been taken in. But not now.

Because now he knew better.

She looked up as he approached and an electric smile like he hadn't seen before lit up her face for just a moment, until she blinked and the smile turned to a frown. The laptop got forgotten on a cushion beside her as she sat up. 'What's wrong, Luca? Why are you home so early?'

'All this time…' He dragged in air, needing the time and the space to get the words out in the order he wanted when so many were queued up ready and willing to be fired off. 'All this time, I never imagined you were capable of such a thing.' He shook his head from side to side as he looked at her, seeing a new Valentina where once he had seen a goddess, seeing finally the spiteful, vengeful bitch that she really was. 'When were you planning on telling me? Or was it your dirty little secret?'

The blood drained from her face, guilt leaching her

face. 'Luca?' And from where he was standing the pathetic whimper of his name on her lips sounded like a confession.

He shook his head, blood pounding in his temples, pounding out a call to war, the sound stealing the volume from his voice until his words came out rasping against the air. 'You don't even try to deny it!'

Her hand plastered over her mouth. More denial. *More proof.*

'Luca,' she implored from behind her hand as the tears started to fall. He was unmoved. Of course there would be tears. He'd expected them. Because she had been found out for what she really was.

'How long,' he demanded, 'were you going to keep it a secret?'

'Who told you?' she asked. 'Was it Lily?'

And her words damned her to a hell worse than anything he could devise. He felt sickened by her confession. Sickened that the denial he hadn't realised he'd been secretly hoping for did not materialise.

Sickened that she could have done such a thing.

'Does it matter?' He strode away, unable to look at her for a moment longer, clawing fingers through his hair until his scalp burned with the pain. And still it wasn't enough. Then he spun back. 'Why didn't you tell me?'

She looked as if she'd lost her place in the world.

She looked as if she was wondering what had gone wrong.

She looked as guilty as hell.

'I was going to!'

'Like hell!'

'I was!' And then she was up from the couch, clutching at his arm. 'Luca, you have to believe me, I was going to tell you. I know I hadn't before, but I decided this morning that you should know.'

'This morning! How convenient! What a shame someone else got there first.' He brushed her hand away. 'I don't want anyone like you touching me. Not after what you've done.'

She blinked up at him, all big golden *fake* eyes. 'But you wouldn't have wanted to know, surely? You wouldn't have wanted to know I was pregnant, not after the way we'd parted.'

He looked down at her with all the hate in the world on his face. 'I might at least have wanted a say in how our baby met its end. Don't you think I was entitled to at least that much?'

Tina stopped and stared, sideswiped by the ugliness of his words. She'd been defending one charge—that she had never told him about their child, a charge she'd known would be difficult enough. But suddenly the argument, like the ground beneath her, had shifted again and Luca was accusing her of…what?

'What are you saying? What exactly are you accusing me of?'

'Don't pretend you don't know! Because you know what you did. You murdered my child!'

The clocks stopped, while the magnitude—the sheer injustice—of his allegation rolled over her like waves upon a beach, dumping her head first into the sand, only to come up barely alive, barely breathing.

'No,' she muttered, from that vague, shell-shocked place she was. 'No, that's not how it was.'

'You as much as admitted it!'

'No! Our baby died.'

'Because you made it happen!'

'No! I did nothing! I know I didn't tell you about our baby, but I did nothing—'

'I don't believe you, Valentina. I wish I did, but you

damned yourself when you pretended you were going to tell me today. You never made any effort to tell me. You were never going to tell me.'

'Luca, listen to me, you've got it all wrong.'

'Have I? I curse myself for taking a woman like you back into my bed, knowing now what you did that first time. Knowing what you might be capable of again.'

'I had a miscarriage! Our baby died and it was nothing to do with me. Why won't you listen to me?'

'A miscarriage? Is that what they call it where you come from?'

'Luca, don't be like this. Please don't be like this. I could never do such a thing!'

But dark eyes bore coldly down upon her, judge, jury and executioner in two deep fathomless holes. 'Then why did you?'

And she knew there was only one card left to play.

'I love you,' she said, hoping to reach some part of him, hoping to appeal to whatever scrap of his heart might hear her pleas. Might believe her.

She didn't know how he would respond. Disbelief. Horror. Indifference. She braced herself for the worst.

But the worst was nothing she could have imagined. He laughed. He threw back his head and laughed, and the sound rang out through the palazzo, filling the high-ceilinged room, reverberating off the walls. A mad sound. A sound that scared her.

'Perfect,' he said, when the fit had passed. 'That's just perfect.'

'Luca? I don't understand. Why is that so funny?'

'Because you were supposed to fall in love with me. Don't you see? That was all part of the plan.'

Ice ran down her spine, turning her rigid. 'Plan? What plan?'

'You still can't work it out? Why do you think I asked you here?'

'To pay off my mother's debt. On my back. In your bed.' The words came out all twisted and tight, but that was how she felt, like a mop squeezed and wrung out and left out to dry in a twisted, tangled mess.

'But it wasn't only her debt,' he said in a half snarl. 'It was your debt too. Because nobody walks out on me. Not the way you did. Not ever.'

'All of this because I slapped you and walked out?' She was incredulous. 'You went to all this trouble to settle the score?'

'Believe me, it was no trouble given Lily's predilection for spending.'

'So why,' she asked, her hands fisting, her throat thick, but damn him to hell and back, she refused to give in to the urge to cry, not before she knew all of the awful truth, 'why did you want me to fall in love with you? Why was that part of your so-called plan?'

'Oh,' he said, 'that's the best bit. 'Because once you fell in love with me, it would make dumping you so much more satisfying.'

'But why, when I was leaving anyway?'

'Do you think I was planning to wait until your flight to cut you loose? Not a chance. And now, after finding out the kind of person you really are, I'm glad to see the back of you.' He dragged in air. 'What a fool I was. To think I let you back into my life after what you'd done. What were you hoping this time? To do it all again? To go home with another child in your belly—another child on whom you could exact your own ugly revenge?'

She blinked against the wall of hatred directed her way, as his words flayed her like no whip ever could. They scored her and stung her and ripped at her psyche.

And there was nothing she could say or do, nothing but feel the weight of her futile love for this man sucking her down into the depths of one of Venice's canals. Knowing there would be no rescue.

'I'll go, Luca. You clearly want me gone and I don't want to stay so I'll pack up and leave now and consider myself duly dumped.'

She walked to the door, holding her head, if not her heart, high. And then she turned. 'There's one more thing I should have told you about our baby. Add it to my list of crimes if you must, I don't care. I named him Leo.'

He wandered the palazzo like a caged lion. He felt like a caged lion. He wandered through his bedroom, he wandered past the windows where they'd made love, he wandered out of his home and out through the *calles* of Venice, past the scaffolding around Eduardo's old palazzo, where the engineers and builders were already hard at work shoring up the foundations, and back again and still he couldn't get her out of his mind.

Still she was gone.

But he'd got what he wanted, hadn't he? He still wanted her gone, given what she had done.

He'd got what he had wanted all along. He'd got rid of her. He'd got even.

So why the hell wasn't he happy now she was gone?

Why was he so miserable now she was gone?

Damn the woman! He'd almost wanted her to stay. He'd almost figured she'd meant something to him before her betrayal. He'd almost factored in a measure of longevity before he'd learned the truth about what she really was. He didn't want to think about the kind of person she really was.

He got back to his study and looked at the file someone had placed on his desk while he'd been away. A file he'd asked for. A file that bore a name tag he wasn't sure he entirely recognised.

Leo Henderson Barbarigo.

Why did that name send shivers down his spine? And then he opened the file and read and realised why he'd felt so sick all this time.

Because it was true that mad in that night of lovemaking that he and Valentina had conceived a child.

A son.

Because it was true that the child had been lost.

Their son.

But not because Valentina had brought an end to that pregnancy, as he'd so wrongly accused her of.

Valentina had been speaking the truth.

Oh God, what had he done?

Suddenly all the injustice in the world swirled and spun like threads and blame and hope all intermingled and tangled.

And he hoped to God it was not too late to do something to make up for it.

CHAPTER FIFTEEN

LUCA had figured a chartered jet should give him a fighting chance of catching her given a commercial flight's connections along the route. A chartered jet, a fast car and a GPS set for somewhere called Junee, New South Wales—with any luck he'd be right behind her.

So when he arrived at the gate marked 'Magpie Springs' and rattled the car across the cattle grid, he thought he'd done it, that soon he would see her. That soon he would have a chance to make up for it all.

He followed the bumpy dirt track, sheep scattering in his path and increasingly wondering where the hell any house might be and if he'd taken a wrong turn, when he rounded a bend and there was the house, nestled under a stand of old shade trees.

He pulled the BMW to a stop, sending up a cloud of dust that floated on the air. He climbed from the car, never more acutely aware of the expanse of blue sky than at this far-flung end of the world, and an October that felt more like April to him, with its promise of coming heat rather than a final farewell in the sun's rays.

A screen door opened and a man emerged, letting the door slam shut behind him. Tall, rangy and sun-drenched, he stopped to assess the new arrival, his eyes missing nothing. *Her father*, he guessed, and felt himself stand taller under his scrutiny.

'*Signore*—Mr Henderson?'

'Are you that Luca fella my Tina's been talking about?'

He felt an unfamiliar stab of insecurity. *What had she told him?*

'I am he,' he said, introducing himself properly as he held out his hand.

The other man regarded it solemnly for just a moment longer than Luca would have liked, before taking it in his, a work-callused hand, the skin of his forearm darker even than Luca's, but with a distinct line where his tan ended where his shirt sleeve ended between shoulder and elbow.

'I'm here to see Valentina.'

The older man regarded him levelly, giving him the opportunity to find the resemblance, finding it in a place that made the connection unmistakable—in his amber eyes—darker than Valentina's, almost caramel, but her eyes nonetheless.

'Even if I wanted to let you see her,' he started in his lazy drawl, and Luca felt a mental, *male*!, 'she's not here. You've missed her.'

Panic squeezed Luca's lungs. He'd been so desperate to track her home to Australia, he'd never thought for a moment she'd take off for somewhere else. 'Where has she gone?'

Her father thought about that for a moment and Luca felt as if he were being slowly tortured. 'Sydney,' he finally said. 'A couple of hours ago. But she wouldn't tell me where or why. Only that it was important.'

Luca knew where and he had a pretty good idea why.

'I have to find her,' he said, already turning for the car. If she was two hours ahead he could still miss her…

'Before you go…' he heard behind him.

'Yes?'

'Tina was bloody miserable when she came home. I only let her get on that bus because she insisted.' He hesitated a moment there, letting the tension draw out. 'Just don't send her home any more miserable, all right?'

Luca nodded, understanding. There was an implicit threat in his words, a threat that told him that this time was for keeps. 'I can't guarantee anything, but I will do my best.' And then, because he owed it to the man who had been prepared to put his own property on the line to bail out a sinking Lily, even when there was no way he could, 'I love your daughter, Signore Henderson,' he said, astounding himself by the truth of it. 'I want to marry her.'

'Is that so?' her father said, scratching his whiskered chin. 'Then let's hope, if you find her, that that's what she wants too.'

The cemetery sat high on a hill leading down to a cliff top overlooking a cerulean sea that stretched from the horizon and crashed to foaming white on the cliff face below. The waves were wild today, smashing against the rocks and turning to spray that flew high on a wind that gusted and whipped at her hair and clothes.

Tina turned her face into the spray as another wave boomed onto the rocks below, and drank in the scent of air and sea and salt. She'd always loved it here, ever since her father had brought her here as a child for their seaside holiday and he'd wondered at the endless sea while they'd wandered along the cliff-top path.

They'd come across the cemetery back then, wandering its endless pathways and reading the history of the region in its gravestones. Then it had been a fascination, now it was something more than just a cemetery with a view, she thought, reminded of another time, another cemetery, that one with a stunning view of Venice through its tall iron gates.

She wandered along a pathway between old graves with stones leaning at an angle or covered in lichen towards a newer section of the cemetery, where stones were brighter, the flowers fresher.

She found it there and felt the same tug of disbelief—the same pang of pain—she felt whenever she saw it, the simple heart-shaped stone beneath which her tiny child was buried, the simple iron lace-work around the perimeter.

She knelt down to the sound of the cry of gulls and the crash of waves against the cliffs. 'Hello, Leo,' she said softly. 'It's Mummy.' Her voice cracked on the word and she had to stop and take a deep breath before she could continue. 'I've brought you a present.'

Bubble wrap gave way to tissue paper as she carefully unwrapped the tiny gift. 'It's a horse,' she said, holding the glass up to the sunlight to check it for fingerprints. 'All the way from Venice. I saw a man make one from a fistful of sand.'

She placed it softly in the lawn at the base of the simple stone. 'Oh, you should have seen it, Leo, it was magical, the way he turned the rod and shaped the glass. It was so clever, and I thought how much you would have enjoyed it. And I thought how you should have such a horse yourself.'

He watched her from a distance, wanting to call out to her with relief before she disappeared again, but he saw her kneel down and he knew why.

His son's grave.

Something yawned open inside him, a chasm so big and empty he could not contemplate how it could ever be filled.

From his vantage point, he saw her lips move, saw her work something in her hands, saw the glint of sunlight on glass and felt the hiss of his breath through his teeth—heard the crunch of gravel underfoot as his feet moved forward of their own accord.

She heard it too, ignored it for a second and then glanced his way, glanced again, her eyes widening in shock, her face bleaching white when she realised who it was.

'Hello, Valentina,' he said, his voice thick with emotion. 'I've come to meet my son.'

She didn't reply, whether from the shock of his sudden appearance or because there was nothing to say. He looked down at the stone, at its simple words.

Leo Henderson Barbarigo, it read, together with a date and, beneath it, the words: *Another angel in heaven.*

And even though he'd known, even though it had made his job easier to find the grave, it still staggered him. 'You gave him my name.'

'He's your son too.'

His son.

And he fell to his knees and felt the tears fall for all that had been lost.

She let him cry. She said nothing, did nothing, but when finally he looked up, he saw the tracks of her own tears down her cheeks.

'Why didn't you tell me?' The words were anguished, wrenched from a place deep inside him, but still loaded with accusation. 'Why didn't you tell me?'

She didn't flinch from his charges. 'I was going to,' she said, her voice tight, 'when our child was born. I was going to let you know you were a father.' Sadly she shook her head. 'Then there didn't seem any point.' She shrugged helplessly and he could see her pain in the awkward movement. And in this moment, under the weight of his guilt, he felt just as awkward.

'In Venice,' he started, 'I said some dreadful things. I accused you of dreadful deeds.'

'It was a shock. You didn't know.'

'Please, Valentina, do not feel you must make excuses for me. I didn't listen. You tried to tell me and I didn't listen. I didn't want to listen. It was unforgivable of me.' He shook his head. 'But now, knowing that he was stolen from us before his time, can you tell me the rest? Can you tell me what happened?'

She blinked and looked heavenwards, swiping at her cheek with the fingers of one hand. 'There's not a lot to tell. Everything was going to plan. Everything was as it should be. But at twenty weeks, the pains started. I thought that it must have been something I'd eaten, some kind of food poisoning, that it would go away. But it got worse and worse and then I started to bleed and I was so afraid. The doctors did everything they could, but our baby was coming and they couldn't stop it.' She squeezed her hands into balls in her lap, squeezed her eyes shut so hard he could feel her pain. 'Nothing they did could stop it.'

'Valentina...'

'And it hurt so much, so much more than it should, for the doctors and midwives there too, because everyone knew there was nothing they could do to save him. He was too early. Too tiny, even though his heart was beating and he was breathing and his eyes blinked open and looked up at me.'

She smiled up at him then, her eyes spilling over with tears. 'He was beautiful, Luca, you should have seen him. His skin was almost translucent, and his tiny hand wrapped around my little finger, trying to hold on.'

Her smile faded. 'But he couldn't hold on. Not for long. And all I could do was cuddle our baby while his breathing slowed and slowed until he took one final, brave little breath…'

Oh God, he thought. Their baby had died in her arms after he had been born.

Oh God.

'Who was with you?' he whispered, thinking it should have been him. 'Your father? Lily? A friend?'

She shook her head and whispered, 'No one.'

And through the rising bubble of injustice he felt at the thought that she had been alone, he thought of the man on the farm who had no idea why his daughter had suddenly rushed off to Sydney barely a moment after she'd arrived. 'Your father didn't know?'

'I couldn't bear to tell him. I was so ashamed when I found out I was pregnant. I couldn't bear to admit that I, the product of a one-night stand, had turned around and made the same mistake my parents had. So I went back to university and hid and pretended it wasn't happening. And afterwards…well, afterwards…I couldn't bear to think about it, let alone tell anyone else.' She looked up at him with plaintive eyes. 'Do you understand? Can you try to understand?'

'You should have told me. I should have been there. You should not have been alone.'

She gave a laugh that sounded more like a hiccup. 'Because you would have so welcomed that call, to tell you I was pregnant, that you would have rushed to be by my side.' She shook her head. 'I don't think so.'

And he hated her words but he knew what she said was true.

'No,' she continued, 'I would have told you. Once the baby was born. But my parents married because of me, and look how that turned out, and I didn't want to be forced into something I didn't want, and I didn't want you to think you were being forced into something you didn't want.'

'You said that,' he said, remembering that night in Venice when she had so vehemently stated that a baby was no reason for marriage. 'So you waited.'

She nodded and swallowed, her chin kicking high into the stiff wind. 'Well, maybe…maybe also in part because I was in no hurry to see you again anyway after the way we had parted. But I knew I would have to tell you once he was born.' She stopped and breathed deep as she looked down at the tiny grave framed in iron lace. 'But when he came too early…when Leo died…I thought that would be the end of it. That there was no point…'

She shook her head, the ends of her hair whipped like a halo around her head as she looked across at him, the pain of loss etched deep in her amber eyes. 'But it wasn't. And I'm sorry you had to find out the way you did. I'm so sorry. Everything I've done seems to have turned out badly.'

'No,' he said with a sigh, gazing down at her while another set of waves crashed into the rocks behind, almost drowning his voice in the roar. 'I believe that's my territory.'

She blinked over watery eyes, confusion warring with the pain of loss.

'Come,' he said, tugging her by her hand to her feet. 'Come and walk with me a while. I need to talk to you and I'm not sure Leo would want to hear it.'

With the merest nod of her head, she let him lead her down through the cemetery, to where the cliff walk widened into a viewing platform that clung to the edge of the world and where the teeming surf smashed against the rocks with a booming roar.

She blinked into the wind, half wondering if she was dreaming, if she'd imagined him here with the power of her grief, but no, just a glance sideways confirmed it was no dream. He stood solid alongside her, his face so stern as he gazed over the edge of the continent, it could have been carved out of the stone wall of the cliffs.

It was good to see him again.

It was good he'd come to meet his son.

It hurt that he hadn't said he'd come to see her but it was good he had come. One final chance to clear the air surrounding their baby's brief existence.

Maybe now they could both move on.

Maybe.

They stood together in a silence of their own thoughts all framed by the roar and crash of water while Luca wondered where to begin. There was so much he had to explain, so much to make up for. The spray was refreshing against his skin, salty like his tears, but cleansing too. Strange he should think that, when he couldn't remember the last time he'd cried.

And with a crunching of gears inside his boarded up heart, he did.

When the news had come of his parents' deaths that foggy night when their water taxi had crashed into a craft with a broken light.

So many years ago and yet the pain felt so raw, unleashed by whatever had unlocked his heart.

Whoever had unlocked his heart.

Valentina.

He watched the waves roll in, in endless repetition. Only to be smashed to pieces against a wall of rock so hard the sea seemed to be fighting a losing battle.

Except it wasn't. Here and there boulders had fallen free, or whole sections of cliff had collapsed into the sea, undercut, worn away and otherwise toppled by the relentless force of the water.

Today he felt like that cliff, the seemingly indestructible stone no match for the constant work of time and tide. No match for a greater force.

He turned to that greater force now, a force that had been able to come back from holding her dying child in her arms to confront that child's father and seemingly accede to his demands, all the time working away on him while he crumbled before her.

And suddenly he knew what he had to say. 'Valentina,' he said, taking her hands in his, cold hands he wanted to hold and warm for ever, 'I have wronged you in so many ways.'

She smiled and he, who deserved no smile and certainly none from this woman, thought his newly exposed heart would break. 'I'm glad you came to see Leo.' He noted that she didn't dispute the fact that he'd wronged her. But there was no disputing it. He knew that now.

'I came to see you too,' he said, and her eyes widened in response, 'to see if you might understand just a little of why I acted as I did, even if those actions are unforgivable. I know I could not hope for your forgiveness, but maybe a little understanding?' He shrugged. 'When I was a child,' he started, 'my parents were both killed in a boating accident. You saw their tombs.' She nodded. 'Eduardo and Agnethe took me in, gave me a home. I went to them with nothing. My father had just invested everything he had in a start-up company he would be a key part in. With his death, it folded and all but a pittance was lost.'

'I understand,' she said. 'Lily told me you had lived with Eduardo as a child. You must have felt that when Eduardo married Lily that you lost your inheritance a second time around. No wonder you wanted the palazzo back so desperately.'

He laughed a little at that. 'Is that what you think? I

think I was too young to worry about any lost fortune back when my parents died. But it would have been useful later. I did worry about Eduardo and the palazzo. He was one of Venice's grand old men, but no businessman, living on his family's reputation while his fortune dwindled.

'I knew as I grew older that the palazzo needed major structural work, but there was never the money and when Agnethe died Eduardo missed her dreadfully and I think he forgot to care.

'I promised him then that I would pay him and Agnethe back for taking me in, by fixing the palazzo and restoring it to its former glory. I studied and I worked day and night to make it happen.'

'And then he went and married Lily.'

He smiled thinly at that. 'You could put it that way. She refused to consider my plans to restore the palazzo, she made short work of the limited funds Eduardo had at his disposal.'

Tina nodded, the strands of her hair catching on her lashes in the wind, and he ached to brush them away, but it was too soon, he knew. It was enough that she let him hold her hands. It was enough that she did not protest at the circles his thumbs made on her skin. 'That does sound like Lily.'

'Once the property was in her name, I tried to buy it. She refused again. But she came to me when she needed more money. It seemed the only way to get her out.'

She took a deep breath. 'I can see it would have been hard to shift her otherwise. Thank you for telling me this, Luca. It does help me understand a little better.'

'It is no excuse for the way I treated you.'

'I guess you were still mad at me for slapping you and walking out.'

'A little,' he admitted, until he saw her face and he

smiled ruefully. 'Maybe more than a little. But I have a confession to make about that time.' His hands squeezed hers, his fingers interlocking with hers. 'You bothered me that night, Valentina. You got under my skin. You were too perfect and you shouldn't have been—you were Lily's daughter after all and I didn't want to like you. I wanted somebody I could walk away from and I knew I couldn't stay away from you, unless you hated me.'

She shook her head, a frown tugging her fair brows together. 'And yet you did hold it against me.' But he took heart that her words weren't angry. Instead they searched for understanding amidst the tangle of revelations, as if she was searching for the one thread that would pull the knots free. He took heart that she was still listening and tried to find her the key.

'Because it suited me to. Don't you see? By blowing it out of proportion, by making it your fault, it gave me an excuse to get you to Venice, and to legitimise it by calling it vengeance. And it was easy to be angry, because I was mad at Lily for letting the house fall into such disrepair, and I hadn't forgotten you, and that made me even madder.

'I am sorry I said what I did. It was designed to drive you away. It was hurtful, just as the words I said before you left Venice were designed to hurt. And why? Because I needed to believe the worst of you, that you had destroyed our child.' He felt her flinch, as if reliving the pain of his accusations but he just squeezed her hands and pressed on. 'I'm so sorry. Because just as it worked that night we spent together, my ugly words worked only too well, and this time drove you from Venice.' He shrugged and looked up the hill towards the grave. 'I guess it is only just that I should be the one who paid some of the cost too, by never knowing of my son's existence until now.'

A wave crashed on the rocks below, sending spray high,

droplets that sparkled like diamonds in the thin sun before spinning into nothingness.

'I can never make up to you all the wrongs I have committed,' he said. 'I'm so sorry.'

For a few moments she said nothing, and he imagined that any time now she would pull her hands from his, thank him for his explanation and justifiably remove herself from his life once again. This time for good.

But her hands somehow remained in his. And then came her tentative question. 'Why did you need to drive me away so very badly?'

He looked into her eyes, those amber pools that he had come to love, along with their owner. 'Because otherwise I would have had to admit the truth. That I love you, Valentina. And I know you will not want to hear this from me—not after all that has happened—all that I have subjected you to. But I had to come and see you. I had to ask if there was any way you could ever forgive me.'

She looked up at him incredulously. 'You love me?'

He wasn't surprised she didn't believe him. It was a miracle she hadn't slapped him again for saying it. 'I do. I'm an idiot and a fool and every type of bastard for the things I've said to you and done to you, but I love you, Valentina, and I cannot bear the thought of you not being part of my life. When you left Venice, you took my heart with you. But I know I am clutching at straws. That you are too good for someone like me. That you deserve better. Much better.'

'You might be right,' she said, fresh tears springing from her eyes, and his freshly opened heart fell to his feet. 'Maybe I do deserve better. But damn you, Luca Barbarigo, it's you who I love. It's you I want to be with.'

Could a man die of happiness? he wondered as he cradled her face in his hands, letting her words seep through his consciousness, all the way through the layers of doubts and impossibilities, all the way through to his heart. 'Valentina,' he whispered, because there was nothing better he could think of to say, not when her lips were calling.

He loved her.

Tina could see it in his eyes, could feel it in his gentle touch. Could feel it in the shimmer of sea salt air between them and in the connection of his heart to hers.

Their lips meshed, the salt of their tears blending with the salt of the sea, and she tasted their shared loss and the heated promise of life and love.

'I love you,' he said. 'Oh God, it's taken too long to realise it, but I love you, Valentina. I know I don't deserve to ask this, but will you do me the honour of becoming my wife?'

His words, his rich voice, vibrated through her senses and her bones and found a joyful answer in her heart, her tears a rapturous celebration. 'Oh, Luca, yes! Yes, I will be your wife.'

He gathered her up and held her tight, so tight as he spun her around in the boom and spray from another crashing wave, that she felt part of him. She was part of him.

And when he put her down on her feet again, it was to look seriously into her eyes. 'Perhaps, after we are married, if you like, then maybe we could try again. For another child. A brother or sister for Leo.'

She shuddered in his arms. 'But what if…' He looked down at her with such an air of hope that it magnified her fear tenfold. 'I'm afraid, Luca,' she said, looking up the hill towards the plot where their one child already lay. 'Nobody knows why it happened and I don't think I could bear it if it happened again. I don't think I could come back from that.'

'No.' He rocked her then, wanting to soothe away her fears. 'No. It won't happen again.'

'How do you know that?'

'I don't. I wish to God I could promise you that it won't happen again, but I can't. But what I can promise you is this, that if it did happen again, if life chose to be so cruel again, that this time you would not be alone, that I will be there alongside you, holding your hand. And this time your loss would be my loss. Your tears would be my tears. I will never let you go through something like that alone again.'

The sheer power of his words gave her the confidence to believe him. The emotion behind his words gave her the courage to want to try.

'Perhaps,' she said plaintively, lifting her face to his, 'when we are married…'

And he growled at the courage of this woman and he pulled her close and kissed her again and held her tight, against the wind tugging at their clothing and the spray from the crashing waves—against the worst that life could throw at them.

And knew that whatever came their way, their love would endure for ever.

EPILOGUE

THEY were married in Venice, the wedding gondola decked out in black and crimson with highlights of gold. The cushions were made of silk and satin, the upholstery plush velvet. And while the gondolier himself looked resplendent in crisp attire, propelling the vessel with an effortless looking rhythm, it was to the bride sitting beaming alongside her proud father that every eye was drawn.

It was the bride from whom Luca couldn't tear his eyes.

His bride.

Valentina.

She stepped from the vessel in a gown befitting the goddess that she was, honey gold in colour, a timeless one-shouldered design, skimming her breasts before draping softly to the ground, both classic and feminine, the necklace of amber beads Luca had given her at her throat.

They married in the Scuola Grande di San Giovanni Evangelista, the opera house where they had seen *La Traviata*, the night Tina had felt the ground move beneath her feet and realised she had fallen in love with Luca. Her father gave her away, passing her hand to Luca's with a grudging smile, before taking his place in the front and curling his fingers possessively around those of his guest, none other than Deidre Turner. Tina smiled, happy for her father, happier for herself when the service began, the ceremony that would make her Luca's bride.

And if the wedding was magnificent, the reception was a celebration, held in the refurbished palazzo where Luca had grown up. Now restored to its former glory, its piers strengthened and renewed, its façade was as richly decorated as it once had been, befitting one of the oldest families in Venice.

'It's such a beautiful wedding,' said Lily to her daughter with a wistful sigh as the pair touched up their lipstick in the powder room together. 'But then you look beautiful, Valentina. I don't think I've ever seen such a radiant bride.'

Tina hadn't been able to stop smiling all day, but now her smile widened as she turned towards her mother. 'I love him, Lily. And I'm so very happy.'

Her mother took her daughter's hands in hers. 'It shows. I'm so proud of you, Valentina. You've grown into a wonderful woman, and I'm just sorry for all the grief I've caused you along the way. But I promise I will be a better mother to you—I am the same person, but I am trying to change, I am trying to be better.'

'Oh, Lily.' Tears sprang to her eyes and she blinked them away as Lily swung into action and passed her tissues before she tested the limits of her waterproof mascara.

'And now I've made you cry! *Sacre bleu!* That will not do. So let me tell you something instead to make you smile—Antonio was so moved, he proposed to me right after the ceremony.'

Tina gasped, her tears staunched by the surprise announcement. 'And?'

'I said yes, of course! I can't hope to change everything about me at once.' And then they were both reaching for the tissues, they were laughing so hard.

'Lily's agreed to marry Antonio,' she told Luca, as he

spun her around the ballroom's centuries-old terrazzo floor.

Luca smiled down at her. 'Do you think Mitch will agree to give her away too?'

'I don't know,' she reflected, as she watched her father spin past them with Deidre, their gazes well and truly locked. 'There's a good chance he might be otherwise *engaged*.'

Luca laughed, and hugged her closer. 'You don't mind then, that you might lose your father to another woman?'

'Not a chance. I'm happy for him. Besides—' she turned her face up to his '—look at all I've won. I must be the luckiest woman in the whole world.'

'I love you,' he said, whirling her around. 'I will always love you.'

His bride beamed up at him, felt her amber eyes misting. 'I love you too,' she pledged, 'with all my heart.'

His eyes darkened, his mouth drew closer, but she stilled him with a fingertip to his lips. 'But wait! That's not all I have to tell you. There's more.'

She leaned up closer to his ear and whispered the secret she'd been longing to share ever since she'd found out, and Luca responded the way she'd hoped, by whooping with joy as he spun her around the floor in his arms until she was drunk with giddiness. And then he stopped spinning and kissed her until she was giddy all over again, but this time on the love fizzing through her veins.

And both of them knew the day could not have been more perfect, and yet still it was nothing compared to what happened seven months later.

Mitchell Eduardo Barbarigo came into the world bang on time and boasting a healthy set of lungs. True to his word, Luca was by Tina's side, clutching her hand, sponging her brow or rubbing her back or just being there, the whole time. True to his word, she was not alone.

And just as true to his word, her tears were his tears, except this time they were tears of joy. Tears of elation.

Tears of love for this brand new family.

* * * * *